W9-CBG-560

the comedy writer

ALSO BY PETER FARRELLY

Outside Providence

PETER FARRELLY

the comedy writer

a novel

MAIN STREET BOOKS / DOUBLEDAY
NEW YORK LONDON TORONTO SYDNEY AUCKLAND

A MAIN STREET BOOK
PUBLISHED BY DOUBLEDAY
a division of Bantam Doubleday Dell
Publishing Group, Inc.
1540 Broadway, New York, New York 10036

MAIN STREET BOOKS, DOUBLEDAY, and the portrayal of a
building with a tree are trademarks of Doubleday, a
division of Bantam Doubleday Dell Publishing
Group, Inc.

"It Never Rains (in Southern California),"
words and music by Albert Hammond and Michael Hazelwood
© 1972, 1973 EMI APRIL MUSIC INC.
All Rights Reserved. International Copyright Secured.
Used by Permission.

This novel is a work of fiction.
Names, characters, places, and incidents
either are the product of the author's imagination or
are used fictitiously.
Any resemblance to actual persons, living or dead,
events, or locales is entirely coincidental.

Book design by Jennifer Ann Daddio

Library of Congress Cataloging-in-Publication Data
Farrelly, Peter.
The comedy writer: a novel / Peter Farrelly.
— 1st ed.   p.   cm.
I. Title.
PS3556.A7725C66   1998
813'.54—dc21
97-40314   CIP

ISBN 0-385-49052-6

Copyright © 1998 by Peter Farrelly
All Rights Reserved

Printed in the United States of America
May 1998
First Edition
7 9 10 8 6

for my huckleberry friend melinda

acknowledgments

special thanks to those who helped, including my parents, Dock and Mariann; my brothers, Bob, John, Tom, and Zen; my sisters, Beth, Kathy, Cindy, and Nancy; George Pelecanos; Michael Corrente; Sean Gildea; Pat Healy; Mark Charpentier; Charlie Wessler; Bradley Thomas; Herb Flynn; Dick Rubin; Mark Hurst; Andrew Jarecki; Susie Gelfand; Eliza Truitt; Pat Mulcahy; Denell Downum; and especially Richard Lovett; Nick Ellison; Bruce Tracy; and Chris Spain.

It never rains in California,
but girls don't they warn you,
it pours . . . man, it pours.

—ALBERT HAMMOND

the comedy writer

one

ever since my sign from god, I've had reason to believe there's something after this, but I'm in no rush to find out what it is. I love life. Not as much as I did as a kid, of course, but how can you after Christmas and Halloween start to lose their buzz, and booze tastes a little too familiar, as does death, and sex isn't such a new experience either? You'd have to have been a pretty miserable kid to be happier as an adult, and that I wasn't. I was a carefree little shit who searched for duck nests and caught frogs and sat up in my tree house in the summer thanking God for my youth. I always appreciated youth. I remember being eighteen and driving around Rhode Island with my girlfriend Grace and a few of the guys, drinking beer and listening to the radio, and I pulled the car over and looked at everyone and I said, "Do you realize how great this is? *We're young!*" And I felt it. And I still ache from it.

So there I am fifteen years later—it's March 1990—and I'd just moved to L.A. three days earlier, and I'm driving along listening to Jonathan Richman sing about that summer feeling, and I felt happy and the happiness turned into a craving for ice cream. I pulled into a minimall that had a big yellow plastic sign advertising a locksmith and take-out Japanese food and frozen yogurt and I got out of the car. There was a white van parked in front of the entrance to the Baskin-Robbins and a midget leaning against the van. I was about twenty feet away from the midget when I noticed a big gangly guy about my age coming toward me from about twenty feet on the other side of the entrance, meaning we were about forty feet apart. He had a broad smile plastered on his face and he was looking right at me as we were converging, and it was the kind of goofy smile that I would normally avoid making eye contact with in the big city, but then I thought, Hell, he's just a big happy guy, and so I returned a big happy smile myself, and just as I was about to enter the store and the big happy guy was passing me, and in fact we were *both* a couple of big happy guys, he said to me, "Get a load of the midget," and he kept walking and I was left standing there with a big smile and an unhappy midget glaring at me, since I was obviously in cahoots with the other smiling idiot.

I got a hot flash and a stinging, itchy feeling and I tried to think of something to say, but everything sounded lame, so I just walked into the store, but I wasn't happy now and the craving was gone. I briefly considered treating the midget to something, except I knew that would be dumb, too, like "Here, little guy, have an ice cream cone," so I just bought a small cup of chocolate yogurt for myself and ducked out of the store without looking back.

I had intended to head back to my motel, but I needed to find an apartment and I was bummed out about what had just happened and scared about being in a new city and somehow inspired by this fear, so I kept driving west and as soon as I got to the ocean, I saw the crazy woman standing on the building.

many of the important things that have happened in my life have happened by accident. I was born with great parents, I grew up in a nice town, I crashed my bike in third grade and got a concussion, I have fun brothers and sisters, I saw a UFO when I was eighteen, I had a fantastic girlfriend in high school—she died young. Serendipity. Or who knows, maybe not. Maybe more like *calculated accidents*. If you open yourself up to things, things happen. Good and bad. I didn't pick my parents, nor my brothers and sisters, but I was out at 3 A.M. when I saw the spaceship. My girlfriend Grace was out at the same hour when she got killed.

It's like when I was ten years old and I was fishing for scup down the Cape with my younger sister Kara, but I caught my dog instead. Chris was standing behind me as I was casting off the Green Pond bridge and I stuck her in the hind haunch. The hook was in Chris, but it ripped my heart out and I immediately tried to reel her out some slack. She was a big hysterical German shepherd, though, and before I knew it, the pole had been pulled out of my hands and was click-clacking up the street behind a blur of yelping fur.

My parents didn't know why their son had come running into the yard sobbing, but since Kara wasn't with me, they feared the worst. I was too upset to tell them where my sister was, so my father shook me, like in the movies, but it wasn't a movie and I just cried louder. "Where the hell's Kara?!" he screamed. After I managed to squeak out, "The harbor," my mother made a pathetic lurch in the harbor's direction—pathetic because taking the car was the call, seeing as the harbor was a mile away, and also because she ran straight into a concrete block we'd been using for second base and ended up with a cracked fibula and a row of stitches.

That's why when I saw the woman jump off the building on my third day in L.A., I just climbed back into my Plymouth Arrow and drove away. It didn't pay to get hysterical about things. I stopped at a liquor store, calmly guzzled two cans of Bud, then went to my pale blue Hollywood motel room and lay on the bed.

The woman was obviously wacko. Maybe I could have done a few things differently, but it wasn't my fault that the system had broken down. Still, I couldn't shake the look on her face the moment before she went. What was it? *Embarrassment?* And the corpse—not what I expected from sixteen stories. Not as bad actually. She'd hit a tree, landed on her back on the sidewalk. No big splatter, just a trickle coming from under her. Her eyes were open, her flesh the color of Maypo, her spirit hung over the block.

After the shadows darkened on the walls of my room, I walked up the street for a cheeseburg. Several loud bars I passed—all guys, it sounded like. I remembered it was St. Paddy's Day. Back home, I would've been pounding them at the Dockside or Clark's, or maybe some dive over in Charlestown. Along the way I picked up an armful of litter, for the karma. I don't recommend it. It starts small—a gum wrapper here, a Thai food take-out menu there—before you know it, you can't pass anything without feeling guilty.

At Hamburger House I changed my mind about eating. It was suddenly too hot for food, I felt dizzy, and there was something about the people behind the counter: the way they moved, their voices, a fleeting awareness of bodies occupied by spirits.

I went back to bed but couldn't sleep. It was an unfamiliar

room, and I wasn't at ease. Maybe I could have saved the woman. I prayed for her soul, and then for mine. The place was still warm from the day's blast and the pounding in my head started again. Ever since leaving Boston, I'd been having it, always in the same spot, the back on the left, behind my ear. I kept turning my pillow over, searching for a cool spot. The sheets were too starched; the blanket was some kind of fuzzy foam the color of a lawn flamingo. Occasionally a car headlight passed across the walls. It reminded me of staying at my grandmother's as a kid. I'd hated it there. It was a city house and I was a country kid, and my parents were gone, everyone was gone except for a nervous old lady who mumbled prayers for long-dead relatives as nonchalantly as I chewed Bazooka.

Finally I slept, only to be awakened at exactly 3:33 A.M. by the couple fighting in the next room. It sounded as if they were rolling candlepins in there. The guy screamed, she cried, he apologized, she screamed, he screamed, she cried again, he got sick of apologizing. So this is what Californians sound like, I thought. I turned on the TV, found a rebroadcast of the news. The newscaster alluded to an "unspeakable crime in Bellflower," then spoke in graphic detail about a man who'd butchered his two kids, along with a niece.

I slept fitfully, got up at seven to the sound of someone rummaging through the trash outside my window. Right away I thought of the Suicide Lady, her empty body cooling in a bag somewhere, and I knew it was true: I definitely could have saved her.

the blue terrace was an art deco motel that had lost its license and been converted into apartments. It was on the Beverly Hills side of Doheny Drive—as opposed to the West Hollywood side, which people paid a hundred less a month for but was just across the street. I wasn't exactly flying high and Beverly Hills sounded good.

When old Mr. and Mrs. Beaupre showed me the place, I wasn't impressed. Despite the strong winds funneling in heat from the desert, no one was sunbathing on the faded AstroTurf patio and, from the condition of the folding chairs, I guessed no one had in a while. They took me to a small studio, or deluxe efficiency, depending on which Beaupre I listened to. It smelled as if they'd waxed the floors with anchovy paste. There was no air-conditioning, no wallpaper, it looked out over an alley, and the shower had about as much force as Old Man Beaupre's bladder, whose sputtering drip I got to hear while his wife was demonstrating the murphy bed.

"You're nuts if you don't take it," the chunky Mrs. Beaupre said.

"You're nuts if you do," her husband added, pulling up his fly.

He was a skinny fuck with cheekbones like hemorrhoids. I got the feeling he knew his time was coming and had no reason to bullshit anyone about anything.

She stabbed at him with her nose. "Flush the goddamn toilet, you slob."

"The paper says we shouldn't flush except the big stuff. There's a water shortage, case you ain't heard."

"Then don't flush your own toilet, but Henry here don't want to look at your tinkle."

"Fuck him."

"Oh, there you go," she said. "That's real nice."

"I think I'm going to check out a couple other places," I said.

"It has a closet," Mrs. Beaupre said.

"Who you kidding?" said her husband. "It *is* a closet."

"Tell you what," Mrs. Beaupre said, "I'll knock fifty bucks a month off the rent if you wallpaper the place yourself."

"That's not necessary," I said and I started to walk.

Mrs. Beaupre followed. "You're not gonna do any better around here for seven hundred bucks. Maybe you should look for a scummy place in Venice."

"I just want to see what's out there."

Two seconds later I was done looking. She was fiddling with keys at the door across the hall. Six feet tall, vanilla hair, pool-table green eyes, and a sky blue workout suit that served up a mountain range of tanned cleavage garnished with Aunt Jemima-size nipples. I knew L.A. was the boob-job capital, but I never expected anything like this. Huge tits, *huge tits,* a couple of duffel bags. I'm not afraid to admit it—I like big tits.

That night I moved my stuff in, aired the room out, hung my cruci-fix on the wall, and walked to Carl's Market for a fifth of vodka and a skinless chicken TV dinner, which I ate in about one-tenth the time it took to cook. I didn't have any cutlery, so I kept the plastic knife and fork and washed out the plastic plate, too. It was a hot night and the oven had made the room unbearable, so I cooled myself by leaning against the open refrigerator, using its light to read a book about screenwriting. I read the chapter that explained why every character must have a character flaw. Occasionally a helicop-ter spotlight would sweep across my window, and I felt vaguely uneasy. I poured a glass of Stoly and drank it outside by the black lagoon.

As the booze tucked my nerves away, I started feeling okay again. No dizziness, no tingling, even the headache had let up. I had a car, an apartment, and two hundred and thirty-one bucks left. It didn't matter that the chaise I was resting on had only a quarter of its Miami-colored rubber straps or that the moldy diving board was broken in half. The fact was, I was sprawled beside a swimming pool with a cold drink in my hand, the smell of cut grass in my head—and it was still technically winter! The wind was gusting, but the heat made it soft, soothing, not like the slapshot of air that had walloped me each time I'd left my Boston apartment. A huge orange moon floated up behind downtown. Yeah, this was more like the California I'd heard about. The day before seemed less ominous now. I remembered it like a dream, as if it had happened to someone else. How the hell had I ended up on the roof? And where were the cops?

I forced myself to stop thinking about it.

My friends and family all thought I was moving west to further my shipping career. I'd been living in Boston a few years, working for U.S. Lines, selling space on container ships—European Export Division, a particularly hard sell in Boston. Most of the other lines went from south to north and then over to Europe, but U.S. Lines went the other way. When a company put cargo on our ships in Boston, they still had to go all the way down the Eastern seaboard, stopping in New York, Baltimore, Norfolk, Charleston, Savannah, and Jacksonville before finally heading over to England. We were also the most expensive line and our ships were older, slower, more likely to bust a prop, etc., so you had to figure only an idiot would ship with us. That's why they put the Catholic college guys in Boston's European Export Division. The guys from BC and Providence College and Notre Dame and Villanova. The guys who could get cocked and still show up for work the next day. They gave us cars, big expense accounts, and livers the size of beanbag chairs. We had season tickets to the Celts, Bruins, Sox, and Patsies. They sent us to Cranford, New Jersey, for two days each year to see who could drink the most while a Fran Tarkenton look-alike tried to brainwash us with the "secret weapon." All I got out of the weekend was a hangover, which the very best salesmen managed to hide.

Order a martini at every business lunch and dinner, they taught us. (The theory being that if you drank like a frat boy, the client would, too.) Take the client to a nice restaurant, someplace big and showy—Biba's maybe, or Jasper's—then a ballgame or a play. Booze between innings, booze at intermission. Try to get the client to bring his boozy wife along and kiss their liquored asses. Then on to Yvonne's for late-night cognacs—the expensive ones. Louis the Fourteenth. The whole bottle if they wanted it. Then when the client was out of his mind, hit him with Fran's secret weapon: "We're the only U.S. flagship sailing out of Boston."

My boss Ed was a good guy, but he would repeat this mantra with an irrational bravado, and sometimes I would, too. Patriotism, that was my angle. The other shipping lines had names like Hapag-Lloyd and Maersk—fucking foreigners. "Be an American," I'd say. "Be a goddamn American!" Just five or ten percent of their business was all I was asking. Of course, when it came to money, no one gave a shit about patriotism, and that's when I was supposed to beg.

Right around Christmas 1990, my latest girlfriend, Amanda, and I went into drydock. There's something about a broken heart that makes people become writers. I'd been thinking about screenwriting for a while, during those long drives to the seafood and leather shippers in Maine and New Hampshire, when I bounced stories around in my head. I thought about it every time I saw a movie that made me feel something. Even more when I saw one that didn't. I thought about it whenever I permitted myself to dream of a better life. Writing seemed like something I could do, something I would enjoy, a job to be proud of, to impress chicks with, but I didn't have the nerve until she was gone and I'd bottomed out and I had nothing to lose.

But I wasn't ready to tell anyone yet. They'd laugh. *Henry Halloran a writer?* For God sakes, I hardly even read. The sports section, that was about it. A half dozen short famous books: *The Catcher in the Rye, Of Mice and Men,* the novelization of *Grease.* Even those took me a couple weeks. I was a business major in college. Accounting. Partying really. It was great training for a U.S. Lines salesman, but a writer?

One horrible side effect of getting dumped is the constant nagging sensation that you're never in the right place. The right place, of course, would be at Amanda's side, and since we were apart, I wasn't there. This left me feeling left out, isolated, barred from a certain part of the city, *the fun part,* as if I were missing all the action. Even though I was living in Boston, I may as well have been on the other side of the continent, and so I decided to go there, which fit into my screenwriter plans anyway. I turned in the new company car, picked up the old red hatchback at my parents'.

The day I left Boston it had snowed all morning and then began to warm up. As the flakes fattened and exploded into rain, a low fog bloomed over the Back Bay. On the Southeast Expressway, I passed the orange, yellow, and blue gas tank that disguised a Chinese man and Barney Rubble. Behind me, the downtown skyline glowed Oz-like in the gray mist, friendly and familiar, but I knew I had to go. It would have been easier to fly to California, but I don't like to fly and, besides, I didn't want to climb in a wide-body and just *be* somewhere. I needed time to think, to plan my strategy. The trip to L.A. was to be a vacation, time to myself. The farther away I got, the less I'd think about her—that was the idea.

I picked up a couple girls hitching in New York, but they hated my guts. Later it would seem like an omen. I told them I didn't normally pick up more than one hitcher, but they were girls and didn't look dangerous. *"Women,"* one of them corrected. There was a time when this would've fried my ass—I didn't need that crap when I was doing them a favor—but I was trying to be more open-minded. I analyzed the situation; it's not as if she was out to get me, so it must have genuinely bothered her. "Right," I said. I listened as the uglier but less disagreeable one educated me on the pros and cons of karma. She spoke as if it was as widely accepted as crooked politicians. "Then how come bad things sometimes happen to good people?" I asked. "They're paying for their ancestors' sins" was her reply. Which was convenient.

Everything we did was influenced by karma, she said, or rather, *influenced karma.* When I'd picked them up, that had been good for my karma; when I'd called them "girls," that had been bad for my karma; when I drove past the psychotic-looking hitchhiker on the Jersey Pike, that somehow got me more bad juju; and when I picked up a hot dog at the Vince Lombardi Rest Area, I'd entered karmic hell. A subsequent stick of Delaware beef jerky pretty much killed the conversation and I dropped them off on the Washington, D.C., Beltway, my karma shot to hell.

The beauty of long drives alone in a car is that it's the best place to think. You can't sit on your couch and figure life out, there are too many distractions—you could be doing the dishes, or returning calls, or watching the news. Sunrise in Oklahoma City became sunset in Albuquerque, and the whole time I'd be thinking. I'd spent the first half of the trip analyzing what had gone wrong with Amanda and me. That was a waste. I had a breakthrough, though; at twenty-eight hours I slipped into a kind of transcendental mode whereby I could see the future, instead of just blasts from the past. By Vegas my mission was clear. I'd quickly polish the screenplay I'd kicked out my last six weeks in Boston, and, while that was being shopped around, I'd start another. I had to work fast. I had to make something of myself. I had to do something spectacular. I knew that was the only way she would take me back.

I didn't know how long I'd been by the pool, but the moon was above me now, white and small, framed by ripples of high clouds. The breeze was gone and the palm trees had drooped off to sleep. I could hear trucks far away. It was a confusing new city; it seemed impossible that I would ever get to know it. Despite what I'd been through, I wanted to love L.A.

i didn't get too excited when my leggy neighbor answered her door in just a bra and panties. It never came that easy for me, I had to work for my breaks. I asked if I could use her phone and she swung open the door. The place was feminine in a "Southern" way—i.e., the canopied bed, pink curlers everywhere, the big flowery bonnets all over the walls—and somewhat pushing it with its hysterically juvenile motif—i.e., the teddy bears, Barney, the stuffed duck Mr. Quackee. Worse, however, was the brazen promotion of an artificial virginity—i.e., all the above and her First Communion picture on the nightstand. Her name was Tiffany Pittman and her claim to fame was that she'd been a Miss New Mexico sometime in the mid-eighties.

"I considered dropping one of the *t*'s," she said. "That way Pittman would still be pronounced the same, except there'd only be one *t.*"

"Must be tempting."

"Not really. I like the way it looks with two *t*'s. Sort of like Pittsburgh. Where you from?"

"Rhode Island."

"Oh, I love New York." (Despite the pageant victory and big fake jugs, it turned out she wasn't that bright.)

"So, what do you do?" I asked.

"I'm a mattress."

"A what?"

"Model, actress, waitress."

She quickly rattled off a list of TV shows and movies she was up for or had had bit parts in. (Sometime later I would view her "reel"—a compendium of performances ranging from the big-titted beach bunny on *Married with Children* to the big-titted beach bunny on *Charles in Charge,* along with a few big-titted beach bunny B-movie roles.)

As Tiffany lowered a silky black dress over her head, I watched the material cling to and then slip over her hips. I had never been with a hooker and, to my knowledge, she wasn't one, but all I could think was wouldn't it be nice if she were, and AIDS didn't exist, and I could afford to fuck her until my prostate cramped up?

Tiffany said I should use the phone now, so she could leave for work. I didn't really have anyone to call, so I rung up my brother Bill collect in Providence and informed him I'd arrived alive. I lied and told him I'd set up interviews with several of the big shipping companies in Long Beach. When he asked for my number, I said I was using the phone belonging to the woman across the hall. Tiffany gave me a playful slap on the arm and said, *"Girl.* Women are old."

when the phone was installed my first call was to the *Los Angeles Times*. I'd jotted down a list of writers in that morning's paper and kept dialing until I reached one. The man I got had written a story about a young girl who'd ratted her parents out for drugs and now was being shuffled through the foster care program. I told him about the woman who'd killed herself, how the cops hadn't done shit, that he should write an article. The man told me to write a letter to the editor, maybe they'd publish it. When I explained that I couldn't possibly capture the horror of the story in a letter, he suggested I write an article myself, care of the *L.A. Times Magazine*. Said it sounded like something they might use in their Private Lives section.

I was having a hard enough time writing screenplays and wasn't thrilled about spending time on a story I had a hunch would never get published, but I kept seeing her gray face, so that night I leaned against the open fridge and fought my way through a seven-page, double-spaced story in a detached style that I felt was "journalistic." By 3 A.M. I was almost done and was starting to shake a little. I was starved, but the story had me a little freaked; death was in the air, and I didn't feel like heading out into the night. I found a box of Triscuits that the previous tenant had left in the cupboard and ate them while I read over my story. I had several facts to check—names of streets, neighborhoods, trees, etc.—but otherwise it was pretty much done, and I was pleased. I'd gotten a little cute with some descriptions, but I'd refrained from pointing fingers or editorializing about the police; I told it the way it happened. For the most part. The point of the story was that the system had broken down and really had nothing to do with the crazy bullshit between me and the woman anyway. So I felt okay about it. I did keep the part about her saying it was my fault, whatever the hell that meant.

Suddenly I felt a tickle on my neck. An ant. I killed it and felt a couple more on my cheek. Then a few on my hand. Then in my nose. I looked inside the box of crackers and saw a vibrating mass of black. I jumped up, spitting and slapping at myself, ripping my clothes off as I ran into the bathroom.

After I finished flossing out ants, I worked until 4 A.M. When I was done, I was ecstatic and wanted to call someone, but I couldn't call Amanda, so I called my mother. She was just getting up back East and we talked for a few minutes. I told her I loved her, and this left her a little concerned, but I felt good and when I went to bed, I slept okay.

money was getting low, so the next day I shaved, showered, clipped my nails and nose hairs, and went looking for a job. I considered wearing a tie but thought it too "Eastern" and settled on just a sportcoat. I jerked through the unsynchronized traffic lights of Wilshire Boulevard in Beverly Hills, bumper to bumper, past the abandoned shopping carts and the tanned, thin-nosed ladies in Mercedeses and Rollses with the BORN TO SHOP stickers. I wondered what it was that these people did that everyone could have a nice car. The women drivers all seemed to be fluffing their blonde hair or checking their faces in the mirror; the men were dark, Middle Eastern probably, and clean-cut, with neat, shiny haircuts and Euro suits. I started getting a funny feeling in my throat, a narrowing sensation, and I decided to head to the beach and work my way back.

I kept the windows up and the roof flap buttoned, careful not to let my hair blow all over the place. Recently something had been going on up there. I wasn't exactly balding, but I was having a harder time getting it together every morning. Either my hairline had snuck up half an inch, or my face had dropped. The sparkle of youth was beginning to dull into middle age, and I knew I looked better in a baseball cap.

I saw all the Carole King–looking housewives on the Westside towing their kids around in four-wheel drives. I applied at a couple restaurants in Santa Monica, then filled out a few applications in Brentwood. After a quick stop in Westwood, I made a sweep of Restaurant Row on La Cienega Boulevard, then headed farther east toward the Musso and Frank Grill and a few other old-time Hollywood haunts. On Santa Monica Boulevard I drove past a theater marquee offering GIRL SCOUT SLUTS. Underneath, in smaller print, was FOR MATURE AUDIENCES ONLY. Everywhere I looked there were bus stop benches advertising mortuaries. Leaning against one was a shirtless guy carrying a backpack and wearing red biker shorts that showed off a hard-on the size of a Little League bat. I was trying to gauge if it was for real when he noticed me looking and waved.

I drove past a playground where a bunch of guys were playing hoop and I felt a pang. I loved hoop, but I couldn't play anymore. A month before I'd left Boston I'd been in a pickup game at the

Charlestown Y when my heart freaked out. I collapsed to the court and my friends rushed me to the hospital. By the time we arrived, my ticker was beating normally again and I was all tied up in knots from hyperventilating. The doctor said I was okay, just low on potassium, but I knew differently. I'd felt the thing go crazy.

Now I was starting to shake again with the blood sugar. I searched for a place to eat. Fatburger didn't sound too appetizing, and Carl's Junior grammatically disturbed me, sort of like Howard's Johnson. I stopped at a shack called Oki Dog for a dollar-and-ninety-five-cent slab of concrete. The Oki Dog was a frankfurter with pastrami, cheese, and chili, wrapped in a soft taco. It weighed about two pounds and I knew it was horrible for me, but it tasted good and would soak up the hunger for several hours.

I sat on a picnic bench and ate next to a bunch of runaways. I was struggling with a mound of french fries that were chewier than a box of Good & Plenty when a guy sat down across from me.

"People call me Forehead," he said, "on account of the fact I got a big forehead."

It wasn't that Forehead's head was any bigger than normal, it's just that his eyes were placed where most people have a nose, and everything else was squeezed under it, thus giving his cranium the Martiany appearance. He was fairly young but had an old odor about him, and he wore Hush Puppies without laces. The fuzz on the leather had worn away and congealed into a dark resin. The sole of one shoe was detached and hung sideways, a drunken tongue, revealing a long slate toenail that curled over his big toe like a pony's hoof.

"You look lost," he said.

"Hm?"

"God is your savior. He will lead you if you follow."

He had the breath of someone a day out of oral surgery.

"Yeah."

"I used to be lost," he said, "and then one day it hit me: *God is good.* And I can prove it irrefutably."

"I bet."

"Think about it. He made it so man cannot urinate when he has an erection. Because if He didn't . . . well, there's a lot of sick dudes out there."

"Erection" had been my cue to head calmly toward the car, but he trailed behind me to complete his thought and subsequently began mumbling something about mankind evolving not from apes but beans.

"Think about it," he said. "People even *look* like beans. Some people look like string beans, some people resemble coffee beans; you, for instance, you look like a lima bean." His breath was starting to sicken me, so I handed him the rest of my Oki Dog and drove off.

I spent a couple more hours browsing the classifieds and cold-calling restaurants. When it became clear that nothing good was going to happen that day, I grabbed my sticks and drove down the sun-bleached pavement of Pico Boulevard, past the fast-food joints, power lines, and kosher meat stores, to the Rancho Park driving range. It felt good to blast a couple buckets. I hadn't swung the clubs since I'd played with Amanda's father, back when there was talk of a wedding. At the time the thought of being married and playing golf every week with the in-laws made me a little sick. Now it seemed like a great life, and working on my swing felt like a positive thing to do. While I took my cuts, I started imagining what our kids would look like. My eyes were brown, but I saw the kids with big blue ones, like Amanda's. Hers were as blue as they get, her whole family was that way. Maybe they'd slant down a little like mine. They'd all have dark hair, since we both did, and big straight fillingless teeth like hers. Things like eyes and teeth would definitely carry over from her dominant genes. And they'd be athletes, too. She was a real thoroughbred, Amanda. I put down my nine-iron, picked up a three-wood. I took a baseball cut at the striped ball, slicing it into the screen that protected the golfers on the eighteenth fairway. I realized I was being a little masochistic and I started feeling dizzy again, so I stopped thinking about kids and old girl-friends and tried to concentrate on hitting the damn thing straight.

during my first two weeks at the Blue Terrace, I saw Tiffany Pittman's pussy every other day on the average. The way it would happen is I'd be coming or going and I could see her through her peephole, which really wasn't so peepy, as it was actually a two-by-three-inch door and was always left open. Still, to see anything I had to get up pretty close, and I never would have done that, except she always called out when she heard me in the hall. In the beginning I'd stood a few feet back and only caught glimpses of skin here and there as she walked around her apartment, never looking my way, as if she were on a speakerphone. After a while I caught on that it didn't matter to her where I stood, and since it did matter to me, I started moving closer and closer and we'd talk longer and longer and eventually it got to the point where I'd have a two-by-three-inch indentation on my face every time I got in my car or apartment.

I had just come home from the driving range that night and I was lugging my clubs up the stairs, trying not to think about Amanda, and Tiff's peephole was open and there she was again, so I jammed my face into the friendly rectangle.

"Hey," I said.

"Henry!"

She smiled and I took a good gander and it was always better than I'd remembered, and of course I wasn't thinking about Amanda anymore, which was nice.

"Can I come in?"

"Honey, open your eyes, I'm not wearing nothing."

"Oh yeah."

"I'm starving," she said. "You got anything chocolate?"

"Just a pan of brownies in the oven."

"No way."

"Yes way."

"Really?"

"Uh-huh."

"Can I have some?"

"Course."

"Give me a sec, I'll be right over."

"Make it fifteen minutes," I said. "They're cooling."

I threw my clubs in my room and raced to a chichi bakery on Robertson. I bought ten large brownies for seventeen dollars and fifty cents, then rushed back home and fit nine of the brownies next to each other in a pan. The extra brownie I crumbled up and spread around the rest of the pan. I put them in the oven on broil and this gave my apartment a rich chocolaty aroma.

While the brownies were getting blasted, I threw my dirty clothes in the closet and folded my murphy bed into the wall, then thought better of it and pulled it back down and I sat on the bed and then I stood up. I was manic with lust and paced around the room thinking about how it would go. It wasn't the first time I'd thought about this. There had been opportunities to make some kind of move, of course, what with her always walking around with the pussy out, but something about her casualness had thrown off my rhythm and I'd been unable to segue from nakedness to sex, as if that were some great leap. She'd even come to my door in her bra and panties at 2 A.M., asking for popcorn, and I'd stood there like a bananahead, unable to even muster enough nerve to invite her in. But now it was going to happen, it *had* to happen, and I'd be an idiot if I didn't at least broach the subject because it was suddenly occurring to me that perhaps she wanted it as much as I.

When I heard her door open out in the hall, I ran into the kitchenette. There was a knock and I called out that the door was open, and I picked up the brownie pan using a T-shirt as a pot-holder. I heard her enter and I wondered if she'd still be buck naked, and I said, "Hot out of the oven." As I came out of the kitchenette, a tall redheaded guy with an unbelievable build was standing in my apartment, nude except for a towel around his waist.

"All right," he said and he took a big sniff. "Brownskis."

"Um . . . ?"

"I'm Tiff's friend. She's in the shower, so she sent me on a mission."

The half-naked guy walked past me and I said, "Oh."

I was sort of in shock and of course winded by all this, and before I knew it, this six-foot-four-inch fuckhead was walking out of my apartment with the whole pan of brownies and my potholder T-shirt and a carton of milk under his arm, and he said his name was

Herb Silverman and he'd see me around, and after I heard Tiffany's door shut again, I sat on my bed and all I could think was: Fucking shit, those brownies were expensive.

the only thing i knew about restaurants was what I'd learned from eating in them, and kitchen work was not one of those things. It was a job, though, and I was down to forty-three dollars and a jar full of change, so I took it. When I showed up at Ernesto's Ristorante on Melrose at nine in the morning, the chef handed me a bucket filled with a brown sauce. "Get rid of this," he said. "I need the pot."

As I was dumping it out in the sink, I noticed it smelled pretty good and thought it wasteful, but I figured there was some stupid health law whereby you had to throw everything out after a couple days. It was kind of nice to know the place had lofty standards. I scrubbed the pot, making sure to leave it squeaky clean. I was a kitchen helper now, and I wanted to be a good one. The chef, Louie, gave me a few bulbs of garlic to chop and half an hour later he asked for the duck sauce. I didn't know what he was talking about. "The duck sauce," he repeated.

"Where is it?" I asked.

"How do I know? You're the one who took it."

I squinted.

"In the pot I gave you to clean out," he said.

Now, I'd been called a fucking asshole before, but never with such conviction. He had *me* convinced, especially when he got to the part about starting the sauce at home while seeing the kids off to school. I was relieved when Louie finally smoothed down his carotids, ordered me out of his sight, and gave me twenty bucks to run out for some lettuce.

At a traffic light on Santa Monica Boulevard I saw a crumpled-up fast-food bag under a bus bench. I jumped out, tossed the bag in a metal basket, and hopped back in my car. In the process I noticed a woman bawling her eyes out. She was in an old Ford station wagon with wood on the side that was stopped right beside me.

After I put my seatbelt back on, I called out, "Excuse me! Are you okay?"

At first she didn't hear me, so I said, *"Hello!"*

When she looked over, she grew embarrassed. I did, too, because she was stunning. Maybe twenty-five, earthy, straight blonde hair, a faceful of eyes.

I adjusted my hat. "You all right?"

She smiled, wiped her cheeks. "I'm listening to a book on my tape player."

I smiled back. "Must be pretty sad."

"Of Mice and Men."

"You at the end?"

"Yeah."

" 'Tell me about the rabbits, George.' "

"Exactly."

She tilted her head and looked at me. Suddenly I was in that wagon with her, pulling away from a seaside chapel, a string of cans hanging from the bumper. The light turned green. She didn't touch the pedal.

I blurted it out: "Will you have a cup of coffee with me if I promise not to give away the ending?"

I watched her think about it. A man jogged by wearing a surgical mask. A car behind us honked. Then she did what any smart, decent woman living in a dangerous big city would do. She pinched up her face and said no. I considered putting up an argument, but the bastard honked again, and anyway I knew our moment had passed. When she drove away, it wasn't cans I saw hanging from her bumper, but my heart.

back at the apartment, I found a couple copies of my script sitting under my mailbox. Rejections, numbers nine and ten. I'd sent *How I Won Her Back* to several agencies a few weeks earlier and now I had two more form letters. One of them at least said they'd read the thing. The other claimed they didn't accept unsolicited scripts unless they came through an agent, which was a head-scratcher, seeing as I'd submitted it to them seeking agency representation. I got the hat trick when I noticed a letter from the *L.A. Times Magazine.* A senior editor named Julia Frick complimented me on a "nice read" but said the suicide story was a "St. Patrick's Day piece" and they were currently looking for articles with a summer flavor. I called Julia Frick's office. She wasn't in, but I told her assistant I'd received the note and thought it sucked.

"Calm down," she said.

"No, I won't calm down! This isn't a fucking 'St. Patrick's Day *piece'!* It's a story about people and how the system can break down because nobody gives a shit anymore and something ought to be done, goddamn it!" I felt myself losing control, so I hung up and poured a glass of Stoly. I picked the phone up after ten determined rings.

"You're a tremendous asshole," Julia Frick's assistant said, "but my boss is a bigger one, so I'm going to pass your story on to another editor."

I listened to the woman catch her breath, but I was afraid to speak. The voice reminded me of my cousin Kristen, who could also be a pain in the ass.

"All right?" she barked.

"Yeah," I said. "Thanks."

I reworked my script for a couple hours, then sat on the front steps and ate a can of sardines, which I chased with a glass of instant coffee. I watched the showroom cars drive by and envied the couples running into Carl's Market for the beverages that would start their evenings. It seemed as if the whole world traveled in twos. I felt that six o'clock feeling for a moment. It was a Saturday-only feeling, there was fun in the air. But I was staying home. There was a time when I'd gone years without staying in on a Saturday night. And now three straight.

I thought about the woman in the wooden station wagon, but the stab I'd felt earlier was gone. Those were the kinds of heartaches I could take. It was part of the game. I'd chased a lot of women in my life, but I didn't consider myself a womanizer. I was just looking for the right one, what was wrong with that? Besides, the vast majority had blown me off. They'd won. I couldn't help wondering: If I hadn't thrown the litter away, maybe I would've had more time to convince the station wagon woman to meet me. What the hell kind of karma was that?

I opened my notebook and reread the story I'd sent to the *L.A. Times:*

It was a hot winter day. The Santa Ana winds had been recycling exhaust from the valleys for at least forty-eight hours—that's how long I'd been in L.A. I'd started apartment-hunting at nine and by noon my eyes were stinging from the web of filth that hung over the Westside. The neighborhoods I crisscrossed smelled like airports. I checked out a few places in Hollywood—dumps really—then decided to look closer to the beach. There were long waiting lists for rent-controlled apartments, I knew, but I was feeling lucky.

I swung onto Wilshire and headed into Westwood, passing a row of high-rise condos layered with bushy green balconies. Traffic slowed near an expanse of modern office buildings right up until I crossed under the 405 freeway. I hung a left and a right, stopped for frozen yogurt on Santa Monica Boulevard, then shot back down 26th Street to San Vicente. This was the nicest street I'd seen in L.A. There were no traffic lights over a two-mile stretch. I could finally go over thirty miles an hour. But there was no big rush now. Not with the colorful spandexed joggers making their way up the grassy divide beneath a row of coral trees. Even the drivers around here—sunglassed beauties in Range Rovers—even they had my attention. The air cooled discernibly as I approached the water and for a split second, life was good.

First I thought it was a worker, but the guy was too close to the edge and there wasn't a wall. The hell with this, I thought, and I blew right past the building. Hanging a left, I continued about a quarter mile on a cliff overlooking the Pacific; it was the first time I'd seen the Left Coast.

Nice.

Shit.

Just check it out, I thought to myself. Maybe it's nothing.

The maniac was still on top of the building. A woman. It was something, all right. She sat down, stood up, ran her fingers through her hair, paced back and forth. I was the only one around and hadn't had practice in this kind of thing. Should I call up to her, or would that be her cue to go?

For some reason, I counted the number of floors: sixteen. That'd do the trick. I looked around for help. No one.

Then, thank God, a phone booth.

"Someone's on top of a building at the end of San Vicente Boulevard," I said after dialing 911. "Looks like she might go."

"Where are you calling from?" a man asked.

"Across the street."

"Can you see her from where you are?"

"No."

"What's the address?"

"I'm not sure," I said. "It's at the corner of San Vicente and, uh, I don't know, there's only one street sign here. It's right at the ocean."

"Ocean Avenue?"

"Yeah, that sounds right. Look, you better hurry. I got a feeling she's serious."

"What side of the street is the building on?"

"It's the only high-rise here. You can't miss it."

"What side of the street?" the man repeated.

I couldn't think clearly. "I don't know," I said. "It's the only big one. The others are all low."

No response. I concentrated and got my bearings. The ocean must be west. "It's north," I said. "North side of the street."

"Northwest or northeast?"

"There is no east or west here. The buildings are all on the north or south."

"Is it east or west of Ocean?"

"East."

"What's your name?"

"Henry Halloran."

"Address?"

"I don't have one."

"Are you homeless?"

"No."

"What was your last permanent residence?"

"Boston."

"Street?"

"What, are you kidding me? There's a lady about to kill herself and you want my résumé?"

"I need—"

"Look, you better send someone in a hurry," I said and I hung up.

I ran to get a better view. Still there, looking over the edge now. I burst into the lobby and told the security guard what was going on. He calmly thanked me and said it would be taken care of.

From the street the woman appeared to be having an animated conversation with herself, more frantic now than ever. A few joggers came by with Walkmans on, but no one looked up. I couldn't bear to watch, so I climbed in my car. I kept the plastic flap of the sunroof shut so I couldn't see her. I flipped in a Kid Creole tape and prayed she wouldn't do it. Fifteen minutes later the cops still hadn't arrived. I peaked through the flap; she hadn't budged.

Back inside, I was stunned to see the security guard reading an automobile magazine. "What are you doing?" I asked with a squint.

The man raised his eyebrows.

"I told you there's a woman on the building."

"S'being taken care of," he said.

"Well, how come she's still up there?"

"Called my supervisor. He'll be here in a little while."

"Why don't you just go up and get her yourself?"

"I'm not allowed to leave the desk. I promise you, sir, everything's being taken care of."

I shook my head. "No, it's not. You could get the hell off your butt and go get her."

The guard stood. "I'm going to have to ask you to leave—"

"Will you at least call the police? They must be lost. I already called them once."

"This is a private building, sir. We supply our own security. Now you're going to have to leave."

I did, for a moment. Then I said the hell with it. The guard was on the phone when I reentered the lobby. He noticed me just as the elevator doors were closing.

The wind was gusting hard up on the pebbled roof. At first I couldn't find her and feared she'd done it. I wasn't about to look over the side, though.

I stepped behind the raised stairwell and saw her sitting

at the precipice. She turned when I called out to her. The woman looked to be in her late thirties, her hair was pulled back tightly, and her bony frame was covered by a grimy peach sweatsuit.

"Everything okay?"

"Fine," she said.

For the first time, I noticed the view. Jesus, we were high; seemed a hundred stories, not sixteen. Despite the smog, I could see the entire coast, and even a couple islands.

"Sorry to bug you," I said, "but are you sure you're okay?"

She threw me a confusing look—one I wouldn't begin to understand until later that night—then turned around.

"Huh?" I called.

"I'm just looking around."

The woman leaned forward, downward.

"It's dangerous to sit at the edge like that," I said.

"I know," she said. "It's okay, though."

"Listen, if there's something wrong, maybe we can go somewhere and have a cup of coffee or something, talk about it."

"I don't drink coffee," she said and she turned to me.

Her face looked pinched, tense, but her eyes were making contact and for a moment I thought maybe I really could help her.

"Come on, let's go downstairs."

"I can't."

I nodded at this.

"Then tell me what's wrong," I said.

She managed a vague smile. "You're what's wrong," she said.

The head tilted a bit, as if in the midst of some sudden realization.

"Sorry," I said and then I watched as she leaned forward and suddenly she wasn't there anymore. All that remained was a plume of pearl-colored exhaust that the desert breeze had pushed out over the bay.

I stayed on the steps for a long time afterward. The Santa Anas had finally quit and as night fell a surprising chill settled over the L.A. basin. Back in my room, I drank a can of beer, then sat at the table and thought about how afraid I'd been on that roof, about how confrontational she'd been, about everything I'd left out.

two

the lung cancer arrived without warning. I woke up one day and the cough was just there. This wasn't a cold, it was a cough. Everything else felt okay except for this dry hack. A smoker's hack. I didn't smoke cigarettes, but neither had Andy Kaufman and he died from lung cancer. And what about pot? I'd smoked my share of that. Bob Marley had smoked his share, too. Jesus, I was getting carried away. Nobody was dying. Weren't there usually warning signs? Then I remembered the dizzy spells. On and off for a couple weeks I'd had them, but hadn't given it much thought. Lack of sleep, I'd figured, maybe my blood sugar was off. Everything was clear. The sense of impending doom I'd been living with, the headaches, the recurring tightness in my throat when stuck in traffic. Good God, maybe throat cancer, too.

Then a break. A big break. Health insurance at work. I couldn't believe it. My little job at Ernesto's was going to save my life. I thanked God they hadn't fired me after the lettuce disaster (having returned from the market with a dozen cabbages). Actually, Chef Louie *had* fired me, but I'd immediately gone to the owner and begged for another chance. I told him I was desperate and I didn't know much about restaurant work, but I was driven and responsible and would work twice as hard as anyone else. Joe was a middle-aged Italian guy from Jersey, and I looked him in the eye when I talked and I could tell he wanted to say no, but he had a heart and finally he caved. He'd try me as a waiter, he said—lunches only—and if I fucked up one more time, that was it, I was out of there, and he wasn't going to listen to any more of my shit.

Dr. Hoffman's office was on Roxbury Drive in Beverly Hills above an old pharmacy. In the waiting room I sat with a *People* magazine on my lap, watched the bustle of nurses and assistants behind the fogged, sliding windows. Dr. Hoffman was a couple years older than me—maybe mid-thirties—and seemed genuinely pleased to have a new patient. When asked what I did for a living, I told him I was a writer. Usually I would say sales, just to avoid the next question ("Anything I would've heard of?"), but the doctor struck me as the type who'd be married to Cybill Shepherd or a Charlie's Angel, so I guess I was networking. He was good-looking and probably getting better with age. His hair was starting to gray, which highlighted his tan, and he had big bleached teeth and trendy blue glasses.

When Hoffman heard the cough, he seemed concerned. A chest X ray was ordered up. They did it right there, in his own lab. Excellent, I thought. This was the kind of efficiency that could save a lung, or at least part of one. I could live on part of a lung, I'd just

walk less. Or slower. The hell with that, I'd walk *more*. Maybe I'd
even run! I'd stretch out that carved-up organ until it was as big as a
normal lung. I'd been blessed by this early diagnosis, given a fighting chance; I was damn well going to take advantage of it.

Then a thought: Maybe she'd come back to me now. The deathbed scene, she returns, I pull through, we fuck a lot after. This
cancer thing could be the break I was looking for!

No. If I did have it, Amanda was the last person I'd tell. She
might blame herself. These things were caused by stress. She'd certainly caused me enough stress lately.

That cunt, she was killing me!

Dr. Hoffman appeared with the X rays. He dropped them into
a wall panel and backlit them. Worse than I thought. The left lung
had at least ten blotches on it, some as big as a quarter. When the
doctor looked at me, I held my breath, what was left of it.

"Negative."

"Negative what?"

Negative, I was clean.

"But the blotches?"

"Gas."

"Gas?"

"Gas."

"*Gas?*"

"Gas."

"But what about the cough? I don't have a cold. Surely—"

"An allergy, probably to smog."

"Whuh?"

Ten percent of Angelenos had it, he said. The filthy air caused
the allergy, which caused postnasal drip, which got in my throat,

which made me cough. I should clean my nostrils with warm water every morning and night, maybe use a nasal spray, the cough would go away.

Was he certain? "Couldn't it be—"

"Get out of here."

As happy as I was about keeping my lungs, I was also a little embarrassed. I'd gotten that from my father, who was a doctor and used to bitch about all the crackpots who'd call him in the middle of the night complaining about painful hiccups. I was going to live, though, and to celebrate my good fortune, I decided to stop at Johnny Rockets on the way home for a double cheeseburg and a chocolate shake. On little Santa Monica I saw an enormous woman coming out of a fitness center. She was stuffed into a shiny, metallic aerobics outfit that made her look like a fat robot. A block farther I saw a muscular man dressed ghoulishly in a black bodysuit, wearing a black bonnet, his face covered by a black scarf. He was doing pirouettes on roller skates in the middle of the intersection and he stared at me as I drove by, and he seemed like Death, and I'd just wriggled free of him, and he didn't look happy.

Something occurred to me: What if it wasn't gas in the X rays? Hoffman wasn't a radiologist. How could he be so sure? Besides, I knew, cancer didn't always show up on X rays. Only if it was in the advanced stages. Good God, what if the tumor was so big he didn't even notice it? What if he was looking for peas and staring at a melon? Then the shame again. Hoffman was a doctor, I was a fucking idiot.

I normally didn't do writerly things in public, such as taking a pad and pen to a coffeehouse, and I always felt a little embarrassed for those who did. It seemed pretentious and calculated and Hemingwayish because, really, who the hell could do good work with twenty-five other pseudo-bohemians sitting around them using words like "masturbatory" and "bourgeois"? That said, it was midafternoon and I was the only one sitting at the Johnny Rockets counter, so I thought, What the hell? I ran out to the car and got my script and I started editing while I waited for my burger.

My server was a couple years younger than me and he was dressed in a fifties-style malt shop outfit complete with a white paper hat, straight out of an *Archie* comic book. I felt sorry for him. When he saw me editing, he asked if I was a writer, which was embarrassing because of what I just mentioned, but, as I said, he was standing there in a hamburg flipper uniform, so I fessed up.

"Anything I would've heard of?"

"No."

"Kind of stuff?"

"Um . . ."

"Film, TV?"

"Film."

"Me too."

This was depressing.

"Sold anything yet?"

"Not yet."

"Me neither," he said. "But I will. And when I do, I'm gonna kick ass. Know why?"

I lifted my chin.

"I've written *three* action spec scripts, and they all have the same lead character."

"Same one."

"See, if I could just sell the first one, I've got two sequels lined up back to back."

I stared at this lunatic, my waiter.

"Could you please get me the mustard?"

He did, but hung around as I ate, telling me about his other four unsold spec scripts and asking if I knew anyone who would read them. He also rattled off some gory statistics that I'd been blissfully unaware of—like that only one of every thirty-five thousand screenplays ever got made—and he was starting to bug the hell out of me.

"I'm bugging you, aren't I?" he said.

"No, no."

"A lot of people say I bug 'em because I push my stuff too much."

He had his elbows on the counter and I caught that cologne-in-lieu-of-a-shower smell, like a prep school freshman's dorm room—sweaty, sticky, *semeny.*

I waved him off. "Eh."

"It's just that here I am in the middle of Beverly Hills and I'm serving movie people all day and, heck, if I don't push myself, no one else will do it for me, know what I mean?"

"Amen, brother."

"You should work here, man—you wouldn't believe the people you meet. And they're hiring."

"That right?"

"Uh-huh. That's how Spielberg got started, you know—blowing his own horn. He doesn't so much now, but he did then."

"Sure."

"You know that story?"

"Sure. What?"

"About Spielberg—how he got started?"

I nodded yes, but when he kept staring, I said, "What he do?"

"He snuck onto the lot at Universal one day, found an empty office, and just moved in. He brought his scripts, moved some furniture in from another office, plugged in a phone. He waved to the guards, dropped in on executives just to say hi, ate in the commissary. Basically, he acted like he belonged there, and before long everyone was treating him like he did. That's how he got his first deal."

"No shit?"

"You've got to push yourself, 'cause if you don't, no one else will."

Tiffany was getting it again. Three-thirty in the morning, she was getting it real good. From my bed clear across the hall I could hear her. *"Fuck me, fuck me, fuck me, yes, yes, yes!"* I closed my eyes, imagined her sitting on me, those monster jugs sloshing around the room.

I was finished before she was.

Still, I couldn't sleep. I'd had a fleeting opportunity after I came, but I kept dwelling on things, keeping my brain alive, I hadn't taken advantage of the burn in my eyeballs and now it was gone. I ran *How I Won Her Back* over in my head, thought of a line for the scene in which the protagonist and his girlfriend break up: "If you walk out that door, you're making the biggest mistake of my life!" Great movie line—too perfect for a book maybe—but fine for a romantic comedy. I got a notebook out of the fridge and wrote it down. Back in bed, I got to thinking about what the hamburg flipper had said. The stupid bastard was right; no one was going to push me if I didn't push myself. I was a salesman, for God sakes, I should be selling myself. Most writers didn't have the savvy I had. Most writers were geeks. I'd been in the trenches. I knew stuff. Maybe things weren't so out of my control anymore. I felt a giddy surge of adrenaline. The wait was over. Tomorrow I was going to make something happen.

A knock. "Dude, you up?"

I pulled on a pair of shorts, opened my peephole. The Herb guy who'd stolen my seventeen-dollar brownies. In boxer shorts this time, wearing my potholder T-shirt.

"Dude," he said again.

I opened my door.

"Do you remember the theme song from *Family Affair?*"

I was so exhausted I actually thought about it for a moment.

"What are you doing?" I finally said.

"Were you sleeping?"

"What do you think?"

"Sorry. Tiff wanted to know if you had any popcorn."

I stared at him.

"Wasn't my idea. Come on, let me in. I got blow."

I sighed. "Wait here."

Herb swung the door open and a fireball of hair entered my room. He walked over to a picture pinned to the closet door, a snapshot of my high school girlfriend sitting on Santa's lap. I was Santa, though no one would be able to tell.

"Who's this?"

"Santa."

"The babe."

I picked an empty plate off the floor, brought it into the kitchenette. "Old girlfriend."

"Want a bump?"

He held up a little amber vile.

"No."

It was the first coke I'd seen since Len Bias died. Suddenly I smelled something and Herb took a hit off the roach he was carrying. "You get high?"

"Not tonight, thanks," I said.

He held the joint out, though, and I took a hit and we started talking. He'd just been laid so was in no rush to get back and he ended up staying a half hour. Herb Silverman was from South Boston, and his real name was Tommy Sullivan. He'd changed it because there was another Tom Sullivan in the Screen Actors Guild, and anyway he thought Herb Silverman was pretty cool because it made people think of—what else?—a Jew, and that couldn't hurt in Hollywood.

"But you don't exactly look Jewish," I said.

"I get that a lot, and my answer to that is this: 'What, I have to have a big schnoz to look Jewish?' They usually back off after that. Besides, Mike Medavoy and Ray Stark look more Irish than me. Least I don't got the freckles."

"And you find it helps, the Jewish thing?"

"Got me my SAG card, and I'm not waiting tables anymore."

"Because of your name?"

"Hey, it worked for Whoopi and Sammy. I mean, what's the big deal? Jews are always giving themselves Waspy names: Jerry Lewis, Winona Ryder, Bob Dylan, Marvin Davis. Why can't I become a Jew? This is a tough business. Every little bit helps."

We talked about Boston a little and when he found out I grew up in Rhode Island, Herb beamed.

"I love Newport," he said. "Went to a wedding there once—girl named Josie Keenan from Jamaica Plain. Great wedding, lot of laughs. We got divorced ten months later. I could've hung in there two or three years to make it look good, but I didn't see the point. All those know-it-alls who say to stick it out, they aren't married to her."

"I guess. Never been married."

"Well, if you do, don't ever drive cross-country with her."

"No?"

"*Noooooo*. I'm telling you, that did it for me. I found out so fucking much about her in those six days, by the time we got here I didn't want to ever see her again. Split up two weeks later, scout's honor."

I nodded.

"Two weeks," Silverman repeated.

"I believe you."

He looked back at the Santa picture and said, "Why do you have her picture on the wall?"

"I don't know."

I remembered the Jiffy Pop and went into the kitchenette.

"What's her name?"

"Grace," I called.

I came back out and Herb said, "What happened?"

"Hm?"

"Why'd you break up?"

I handed him the popcorn. "I don't know. It was high school."

"Must've stung if you've still got her picture hanging around."

"Long story."

"What, she catch you fucking around?"

This sounded like an easy out, but I said no.

"You catch *her* fucking around?"

"No."

I made a move for the door, but he held his ground.

"Well, what happened?"

"I don't know. Jesus, it's four in the morning. I've got to go to sleep, man."

I opened the door. Herb walked into the kitchenette.

"You should be over it by now, bud. Grow a chin, have some pride, take the picture down. Got any beer?"

He opened the fridge, stared in confusion. "Why the hell you got notebooks in the fridge?"

"Case of fire."

"Huh?"

"That's the only copy I have of my notes, so I figure if there's a fire and the whole place burns down, the stuff might stand a chance if it's in the fridge."

He picked up one of the pads and I moved in quickly. "No, no, no, those stay where they are." I put it back and closed the door.

"You're a writer, huh?"

"Uh, yeah."

"Anything I would've heard of?"

"I'm just getting started. Come on, I'm exhausted."

I handed him the popcorn and he took a Diet Coke, and I thought he was going to leave, but he stopped at the door. "So you doin' her yet?"

"Who?"

"Tiff," he said.

"Yeah, right." I thought about this question and said, "Aren't you her boyfriend?"

This cracked him up. "Noooo. So the truth, are you doing her?"

"I hardly know her."

"So?"

I shrugged.

"How about those toddies, huh?"

"Yeah," I said.

"What do you mean, 'Yeah'?" You won't see better nuts than that anywhere in town."

"They real?"

"*Are they real?* Who gives a shit are they real? For Christ sakes, she's got a flight recorder, too, but I'm not gonna lose sleep over it. You should see when she's riding you, it is a sight to behold. She loves to squeeze those big toddies while she sways back and forth—she just squeezes and squeezes, it's beautiful. All she does is squeeze—"

"Okay, okay, she squeezes her tits. Go."

After Herb left, I got back in bed and I knew I was too stoned to sleep unless I rubbed out another one, but I was thinking of old girlfriends now, and I couldn't do that when I thought about old girlfriends.

When I couldn't sleep in L.A., I liked to imagine that I was homeless, walking the streets, cold, tired. I imagined that I'd stumbled across my bed stuck in a cranny in some hillside, maybe honeycombed into the palisades above the Pacific Coast Highway. This made me feel warm and fortunate and I would thank God for granting me this little hole and eventually I would sleep and that's what I did.

i drove east on beverly boulevard, turned left on Highland, merged onto Franklin, then hit the 101. Muscling my way across six lanes of traffic, I made it just in time for the Barham exit, then went right and down the hill to Warner Bros. Studios. I tried to drive onto the lot but was turned away, so I parked at Taco Bell and walked past the guards, waving my lunch and a script at them.

A couple people pointed me to the executives' offices and when I easily got inside the building I thought, The hell with it, I might as well go right to the top. I asked a woman at a water bubbler where the president's office was, and a minute later I was standing outside a door with a gold plaque that read: HAL MARKEY. I took a deep breath, convinced myself I was a loser if I didn't do this, then walked into the room. There were two women manning the phones and a young preppy-looking black man at work on a computer behind them. One of the women held up an index finger, continued her phone conversation. I smiled casually, jingled the change in my pockets, played with my keys. Finally she hung up and raised her eyebrows at me.

"How are you today?" I said.

She must've thought it was rhetorical because she just opened her eyes wider like, *Come on, come on.*

"I don't have an appointment, but I was hoping I might just peek in and say hi to Hal."

"I'm sorry. He's in a meeting."

"Oh . . ."

"Maybe you'd like to set up a time to come back later?"

"No, no, that's okay, it's not business and I won't be around later anyway. No big deal. I was just on the lot and I promised him I'd pop my head in if I was ever on the lot."

"I'm sorry, what's your name?"

"Just tell him Bob's son stopped by. I'll see him next time he's on the Vineyard."

I leaned toward the door, gave her a look to chew on.

"Why don't you sit down?" she said. "Maybe I can interrupt him."

She tapped something into her keyboard, a second later there was a buzz, and she picked up the phone.

"Bob's son," she said. "He just wants to say hello."

She hung up and smiled for the first time. "You can go in."

Markey met me at the door, shook my hand, said, *"Hey,* how *are* you?" He was tall, with a winter tan—tighter, shinier than a summer one.

"Good, Hal. How are you?"

"Great, great. How's your dad?"

I stepped into a room big enough to throw a touchdown bomb. There was another man sitting on the couch.

"Great," I said. "He's great."

Markey put his hand on my back, led me to the other man, said, "Adam Levine, I'd like you to meet . . ."

"Henry," I said.

As I shook Adam Levine's hand, Markey was starting to show his impatience. He said, "Henry . . . ?" and let it hang there.

"Yes." I knew my time was short, so I said, "I'm sorry to bother you like this, Hal, but I was wondering if you could just take a look at my script when you get a chance."

I held it out and Markey took the script, but from the look on his face I don't think he was aware of that fact.

"I'm sorry," he said, "your father is . . . ?"

"Bob."

"Bob who?"

"Halloran."

Markey looked at the other man, then back at me, and said, "Bob Halloran . . . ? How do I know Bob Halloran?"

"I don't think you do. He lives in Rhode Island."

"Well . . . why did you say . . . ?"

"Just a point of reference," I offered weakly.

Adam Levine coughed up a laugh and suddenly Markey got it and he wasn't coughing up anything, and if he had he probably would have let it fly in my face.

"Get the fuck out of here, you fucking idiot."

He picked up the phone and I picked up my feet. I was out the front door and walking very fast beside some shrubs when I saw the golf carts careening toward the building. A woman security guard shot me a look as I headed out the main gate, but she didn't give chase. I jumped in my car and tore back up the hill toward the highway feeling dumb and sweaty and humiliated, and much more like Rupert Pupkin than Steven Spielberg.

When I got home, I felt tremendously creepy, like a stalker or something. I lay on my bed, stared at the ceiling. I worried what everyone must be saying back in Boston. I pictured the guys at U.S. Lines picking up their bonuses and gossiping about me. Hear about Halloran? He's nuts, he's lost it, he's delusional, he thinks he's fucking *Hemingway!* They weren't supposed to know about my writing, but I feared that word had leaked. And what must my parents be thinking? I thought of Amanda, about how good she must be feeling about her decision. A couple beers later I was really wallowing in it, and to make things worse I found a good bra ad, spread it out on the floor, then hung my head off the bed and fucked my pillow missionary-style, all of which wouldn't normally bother me, except it was four in the afternoon and I was in a crummy little apartment and there were newspapers and soiled socks and underwear on the floor, and I didn't have a real job and I didn't have a girlfriend and I was thirty-three years old and I could hear the world passing me by outside and nothing in the universe seemed to be going my way.

I fell asleep and the phone woke me up. It was a man from the *Los Angeles Times* and he said they were going to publish my story.

amanda parsons loved frisbees and hackeysack and cookouts on the beach. She loved her parents and visited them each Sunday, and girls liked her as much as guys. She was a Big Sister to a fifteen-year-old autistic kid. She rode her bike everywhere in the summer and had frizzy brown hair and soft blue eyes. She was shy around strangers and hardly ever wore makeup and she had a great body, and she laughed when someone suggested she model and everyone's mother loved her. But she was no priss. She could run like a guy, drink beer like one, too. She was sweet, but wouldn't let herself be pushed around. She fucked like a porn star.

The night I met Amanda I was on mushrooms. I'd eaten them for old times' sake with my former college friends and the six of us ended up at a Boston College mixer following a football game. We were all out of our minds and stuck in the middle of a throng of people when I turned around for what seemed an instant but was probably twenty minutes and suddenly all my stoner friends were gone. I began to panic and hyperventilate, and then I saw a hippieish woman in a hippieish skirt and I grabbed her arm.

"Have you ever tripped?" I asked.

"Yeah."

"Well, I'm doing mushrooms right now and I lost my friends and I need you to get me out of here."

Amanda pulled me through the crowd and calmed my nerves outside and when my buzz had peaked and I knew I wasn't going to get any higher, I started loosening up. She was twenty-three years old and worked for Shearson/Lehman Brothers; I was a twenty-seven-year-old salesman. I knew immediately what I'd stumbled upon and wanted badly to win her over. I'd seen her before, several times, in the Back Bay, at the Dockside, bopping around Faneuil Hall, rushing along Milk Street. She stood out.

That started a five-year run, and it didn't end until the hippie Lehman Brothers girl looked like a woman and she started playing hackeysack with my heart. She kicked it around for a few months, then stuffed it in the back pocket of her jeans and sat on it for a while. She threw the jeans in the wash and tumble-dried them on high. She put a hot iron to them, then gave them away to the Salvation Army.

Despite all this, I still loved her and when I got the good news about my story being published, I felt elated, I was a real writer, and I glanced at the phone and a few seconds later I had her roommate on the line.

Maura was kind, if a tad distant, and she quickly put Amanda on. Amanda said she was eating dinner. I apologized, but didn't let her off that easy. It had taken me three months to make this call. I told her I was in L.A. now. She said she knew, asked if it was true that I was writing. I stumbled for a second, then confessed it was true, said it was a longshot, but I was going to play it out for a while. Better now than in ten years, I said. If it didn't work out, I'd come home. No big deal. The conversation started getting more strained, so I got to the point.

"Why don't you come out and visit?" I said.

"Henry . . ."

"What?"

"I don't think that's a good idea."

"Why not?"

"You know why not."

"Look, it doesn't have to be that way. I mean, nothing's going to happen. You can just come and see California."

"I don't think so."

"But you'd love it out here, it's Beach Blanket Bingo. And just because we're broken up doesn't mean we can't still be friends."

"I can't."

"Why can't you?"

"Because . . . because it wouldn't be fair to you."

"Then don't be fair to me. Come and abuse the hell out of me. You can get even."

I wanted a laugh but didn't get one.

"We'll just be buddies."

"I don't know, Henry . . . No."

We always came back to this. And then I felt the anger.

"Is that the only word in your vocabulary now? What are you, a two-year-old? I mean, you just find it so easy to say no to me."

"You made it that way."

"What the fuck are you talking about? How did I make it that way?"

"I'm going to hang up now."

"Answer my question first. What the hell did I do?"

"Henry, we've been through this a hundred times."

"And I still don't know the answer!"

"You make me say no to you because that's the only answer to the question you're asking."

I sighed and in a whiny voice said, "But why can't you just say yes sometimes?"

"Because I can't. Now this isn't going anywhere, so I'm going to hang up."

"Wait. Don't."

I wracked my brain for the sentence that would save us, but it didn't exist. I'd told her I'd change, I'd told her I'd do anything she wanted, I'd told her I loved her until the words didn't mean anything anymore. All it did was humiliate me and destroy any pleasant memories we may have had. I couldn't think of us the way we used to be, because we didn't exist that way anymore. The memories were fraudulent. If you're a Red Sox fan, you can't think about Game Six of the '86 Series and say, "Wasn't that great! The Sox led for almost the whole game!" No, the lead meant nothing. If it ends bad, it's bad, and that's all that matters.

"Why don't you think it over," I said, "and I'll call you back next week. You can bring Maura or your sister or someone, so it won't be just the two of us."

I could imagine her rolling her eyes at Maura. It didn't matter, though. My pride was gone.

"I'll call you next week," I said.

"I can't come."

I started to sweat. It was like trying to wriggle free from a hangman's noose. "Why not? You still haven't given me one good reason."

"Because it would be getting your hopes up, okay?"

A spiked wall at a hundred miles an hour. The final blow. I

hated her for doing it and I wanted to let her know. I wanted to bomb her, to attack from all sides, but it would be a suicide mission, I knew. All I could do was hang up. Extra-hard. It made a big noise in my apartment, but to her it probably sounded like a little click.

three

one of the happiest sounds in my life was the opening
jingle to ESPN's *SportsCenter.* When I heard it, I knew I had at least
a half hour of peace ahead of me. As I stared at the day's highlights
and results, everything else was forgotten. Likewise, the thing that
got me out of bed in the morning was the thought of staring at the
sports page while sipping my coffee. I loved to see how the under-
dogs had made out. Guys like Jim Eisenreich, still playing despite
being nuts; Jim Abbott, the Angels' one-armed hurler; and Dickie
Thon, the All-Star who'd been beaned in the prime of his career and
was now hanging on by a thread. Sometimes I skipped the stories,
just checked out the stats. My favorite player was Wade Boggs. He
wasn't an underdog, but he was the most reliable and he played for
the Sox. Win or lose, something about seeing that Boggsie had

banged out two or three hits made my day. It was a fact and it was right there in black and white and this was somehow comforting.

Sunday was the best day for stats, but this Sunday, it wasn't the sports section I was thinking about when I went down to the market. It was the first Sunday in May and the *L.A. Times Magazine* was publishing my story today. A desperate-sounding editor named Arnold Sternberg had been the one to call. A piece had fallen through, they needed something quick, Julia Frick's assistant had shown him mine. I had mixed feelings. It was nice to finally be a published writer, even if it wasn't exactly accurate. At least I'd gotten part of the truth out. That was good, I supposed. It would be called *The Jumper.*

Back home I put lima beans on a soft tortilla, melted cheese on it, and took it out on the front steps with the paper, a cup of coffee, and a glass of ice water. I read the sports section, the calendar section, and the front section, and then there was only one thing left. It was making me sick thinking about it. But what happened wasn't my fault, I told myself, any reasonable person would have done the same. I heard a bell and watched an ice cream truck pull up across the street. A half dozen little ones came running with their dollar bills. No adults followed, no one stood in doorways and watched. I thought how odd it was that parents would check out babysitters, investigate preschools, glare at their own neighbors, but when that ice cream man came ringing, they set the kids loose as if they were going out to meet Christ himself. Where did the ice cream man come from? Who made his slushes? What was his name, his background, his intentions? From my angle I couldn't see the man, but I caught a glimpse as he hopped back in the front seat and drove off to who knew where.

I stared at the cover of the magazine section, a big red sickle, an article about the new Russia. It seemed so prestigious, so worldly— my name in a magazine that published stories about Russia! It would have been wonderful if I hadn't recorded the last three minutes of a person's life inaccurately.

I threw the papers in the trash and headed out to the driving range. The traffic was heavy and I checked out all the good-looking drivers in their shiny vehicles. The people were definitely better-looking out here, the girls at least. They blew those Bicnags—Boston-Irish-Catholic-No-Action-Girls—out of the water.

As I took the corner onto Beverly, a cute redhead with a big smile sped around me singing to herself. A happy woman, it had been so long! What I wouldn't give to meet a happy woman. I sped up to her. Briefly I considered ramming her Jeep, taking full blame, getting her phone number. I pulled my Arrow up on her right at a stop light. When the Happy Redhead caught me looking, she didn't blanch, just started singing louder, bobbing her head more. She checked out the cellular geek in the Lexus to her left. He was talking animatedly on his car phone, wearing tennis clothes, probably making a deal on a weekend read. When she glanced back at me, I was talking animatedly into my shoe, Bond-like. The Happy Redhead laughed, so I covered the heel and called over to her, "This is a remarkable coincidence. Here I am sitting in a car, and there *you* are sitting in a car. Let's go on a date!"

She nodded her head. I couldn't tell if it was to me or the music.

"Seriously," I said. "I know this is a little bold, but how about we go get some eggs?"

Well, of course eggs should never be included in pickup lines, and that was the last I ever saw of her.

The phone was ringing when I got home. I answered and a man said, "That was really stupid, Halloran."

Immediately I felt guilty. "Who's this?"

"Levine."

"Who?"

"Adam Levine."

It rang a bell.

"I'm sorry," I said. "I, uh—"

"Aren't you Bob's son?"

"Huh?"

"Last week when you conned your way into Hal Markey's office—I was the other guy."

"Oh . . ."

A tidal wave of embarrassment.

"Nice try," he said.

"Eh."

"Very stupid, but a nice try. Do you know why it was stupid?"

"Um . . . because it didn't work?"

"Do you know why it didn't work?

"Well . . ."

"It didn't work because *I was there*. You humiliated him. The way this town works is you make people *look good,* not bad. Markey might've thought it was funny if you hadn't made him look like a fool in front of me."

"I wasn't counting on you being there."

"You should've had a backup plan."

"Yeah, I guess."

"Anyway, I read your script."

"You did?"

"It's not bad."

"Yeah?"

"Why don't we meet?" he said.

"Do you work for Warner's?"

"No, I'm an agent. Marshall and Pinson."

"Yeah?"

"I'll have my assistant call you in the morning. We're in Century City. She'll give you the details."

"Great," I said. "Great."

adam levine referred to the Marshall and Pinson group as a "boutique agency," which sounded to me like a place specializing in gay films but was really just a fluffy way of saying they were small and preferred it that way. This was bullshit, of course. No agency *wanted* to stay small, and if they did, why the hell had they called me on a Sunday? But because they *were* small, they were able to give new writers more personal attention than the CAAs and ICMs of the world—or so he claimed.

Levine, as he preferred to be called, had long frizzy hair parted on the side and a very large hooked nose on a muscly face. A cross between Kenny G, Tiny Tim, and Fred Flintstone's phonograph. He'd graduated from Cornell and he still retained a New York accent. The man looked psychotic, but he was quite sane and he knew the business as well as anyone I would meet.

"So do you think you can sell it?" I asked after we'd bullshitted for a few minutes.

"The truth?"

"Lie to me."

"Very likely," he said.

"That a lie?"

"Yes."

"How unlikely is it?"

"You've got a better chance winning a big dick competition in South Central."

Levine walked out from behind his desk.

"Hey, hey, hey, come on," he said, "I didn't call you in here just to break your balls. We're gonna be able to use this script as a writing sample."

He picked up a small basketball off the floor.

"What do you mean?"

He took aim at a minibasket in the corner of the room, then retrieved his miss.

"You know, we'll run it around town, maybe get someone to hire you on another assignment."

"If this would get me hired on another job, then why won't they buy it?"

"They just won't."

"Why not?"

"Because the studios are looking for high concept."

"What's that?"

Levine ran his fingers through his hair and I wished I'd gone to film school.

"A 'high concept' idea is one that any idiot can understand in one line. Three bachelors find a baby on their doorstep: *Three Men and a Baby*. A cop gets a new partner, and the guy turns out to be suicidal: *Lethal Weapon*. A bunch of middle-aged yuppies yearn to be cowboys: *City Slickers*. A father shrinks his kids: *Honey, I Shrunk the Kids*. Notice a trend? Each one lets you know exactly what's going to happen before you set foot inside the theater."

"And that's what they want?"

"That's what they want. Mrs. Kornbluth in Duluth doesn't want to think—that's why she voted for Bush, remember? She wants to go to a movie she can trust. There can be blood, there can be death, there can be children burning in rice paddies—as long as she knows it's coming."

"What about *sex, lies, and videotape?*"

"A fluke. And it wouldn't have stood a chance without 'sex' in the title. Even so, the studios aren't looking to make those kinds of movies. That was a smash hit for what it was, and what did it pull in: twenty, thirty mil?"

"But it cost less than a million to make. That's what I'm offering them with *How I Won Her Back*. No chase scenes, a couple small special effects—if you did it at a major studio, it might cost three million at most. And it's a love story. Everybody loves a love story."

"If it's original."

"Mine's not original?"

"You did a good job. That's why I called you in."

"But it's not original?"

"It's okay."

"What's not original? I want to know." He rolled his eyes and I said, "Seriously, I want to know."

"All right. For instance, the opening—where he wakes up in the apartment with the beer cans everywhere, pizza in the bathtub, the alarm clock going off—you got that from watching too much TV."

"He lost the love of his life. He'd been on a bender."

"Yeah, and I've seen it a million times. I'm just saying there are fresher ways of showing a guy who's down and out."

"It's not fresh?"

"Could be hipper."

"Is it bad?"

"Not bad, just a little bland."

"What do you mean, 'bland'? You mean boring?"

"I mean *bland*. Blandsville, Bland City, Blandarama, George Blanda."

"Okay, I'll rework the beginning. I like that. That was a good note. So what else is wrong?"

"It's not so much that there's anything wrong, Henry, it's just that there's not enough set pieces."

I kept a straight face and nodded, and then I thought, the hell with it and asked what a set piece was.

"A humorous situation or interesting scene, like for instance in *Lethal Weapon* when they put Mel Gibson on top of that building with the suicidal guy. That's a nice set piece."

"But this isn't *Lethal Weapon,* it's a love story."

"And that's why I can't sell it."

"Okay, I'll come up with a few more set pieces. I'll add another layer—a subplot or something."

"You're missing the point. That's not the problem."

"Well, what's the problem?"

Levine took aim at his basket again and missed.

"What's the problem?" I repeated.

"The problem is this, man: Nobody gives a big ratfuck about how you won her back."

"It's not *me.*"

Levine sat back at his desk, annoyed now. "I know that. I was just making a point. Stop being so sensitive. If you want to make it in this town, you've got to stop being sensitive. Look, Henry, if you want to try and raise your own money and do the thing yourself, you might be able to get it done. But I'm telling you as an agent who knows this business inside and out, the studios are not looking for this kind of complicated human relations bullshit—no offense—not this year anyway. Like I said, they want a movie they can understand in one line."

"But you can understand mine in one line. The guy's trying to win her back."

"That's not as clear as you think."

"No?"

"No. It takes off in a direction I didn't expect. Like that . . . that God scene. What the hell is that?"

"There's no God scene. That's not God."

"Well, who is it?"

"Does God have wings? I don't think so. Angels have wings."

"God doesn't have wings?"

"No. And you don't call God 'Bernie.' "

"So what is that? Is it supposed to be real? Is it in his head?"

"Yeah, I mean no, I mean it's whatever you want it to be, that's up to the viewer."

"You're leaving too much up for interpretation. You can't do that in a mainstream movie."

"No offense, Levine, but I don't think you're giving the public enough credit."

Levine whipped the ball against the backboard. It ricocheted around the room, knocking a pile of scripts off the windowsill.

"Goddamn it, if you want me to represent you, you've got to start paying attention! I'm not gonna argue with you, man, 'cause I *know* I'm right."

Suddenly I felt very stupid. Who did I think I was coming up here telling the man his business?

"Now I realize you probably just spent the last year of your life busting your ass on this script, and you're hoping that everyone back in Peoria will see it on the screen, because despite what you say, we both know it's half-autobiographical."

"Not really, and I'm from Rhode Island."

"Start agreeing with me."

"It's partly autobiographical, and I'm from Peoria."

I was relieved to see him smile.

"Thank you," he said.

Levine straightened the backboard, picked up the ball, left the scripts on the floor.

"You see, I'm thinking on a grander scale than you, Henry. I don't want to just get this movie made, I want to give you a *career*." His tone softened. "Let me ask you this: What are you looking for out here? What are your goals? You just want to get this movie produced and get the hell out of here?"

I hadn't thought much past getting this first movie made, but I didn't want to seem like an idiot, so I said, "My goals are fairly modest. I want to make movies. Nothing big, just a few good movies. And it would be nice if none of them ever aired on *USA Up All Night*."

"Would you like to direct someday?"

I'm a major dreamer and you can't be a major dreamer without having a healthy ego. Because if you don't sort of believe in your dreams—by that I mean *daydreams*—then what's the point in dreaming? You'd have to be a damn psycho to dream about saving a house full of sorority girls from a raging fire, or spanking a home run over the Green Monster to win Game Seven, or spending a weekend on Nantucket banging the shit out of Elle McPherson if some part of you didn't believe it was possible. To imagine those things without believing would be hellish. Well, I'd had all those thoughts and many more outlandish ones, but never in my life had I permitted myself to dream about being a movie director.

"Sure, I'd like to eventually direct my own stuff. You know, have a little more control, do it right."

"Well, that's what I want, too. And if you do what I say, you actually stand a chance. Your script made me laugh out loud a couple times. I never laugh out loud. And your stuff isn't typical, you've got your own style. Ninety percent of all comedies written in the last ten years were written with Bill Murray in mind. And they're all the same. Some are good, most suck, but it's the same smart-alecky shit that only Bill Murray can get away with. Yours is a little smart-alecky, too, but there's something about it I like. I like the way you go for it. If you can make people laugh, you can work around here, that's the good news. The bad news is . . . you're a loose cannon and it worries me."

Levine looked me in the eye. I tried to send positive vibes, but what I felt coming out was pathetic.

"Listen, Levine, I know I can be a pain in the ass and I have a lot to learn about this business, but I'm a quick study. Give me a chance, and I'll do what you say."

There was a buzz and Levine put his headphone back on. "Yeah, put him through."

While the agent talked on the phone, I looked around the room. It was a real agent's office and I was pleased to be there. Two framed movie posters hung on the wall behind Levine. One was *Lost Angels;* the other *Someone to Watch Over Me.* I hadn't seen either, but I'd heard of both and wondered what Levine had to do with them. On the desk was a picture of the agent on skis, up in the mountains with an actress. The woman wasn't particularly talented or famous, but I recognized her, and it made me feel even better about him.

Levine covered the mouthpiece, and said, "I've got to take this. Why don't you come back another day."

"That's okay," I said, "I don't mind waiting."

"Set up a time with Meegan."

"Should we make it a lunch?"

"No."

a couple nights later i dreamed I was fucking my younger sister's ugly girlfriend with the tremendous ass, which upon awakening I found upsetting. Not because I was fucking her, but because I wasn't. I looked at the clock. Four-fifteen. I was dazed and could still imagine a woman's approving moans. They became louder and more real. I climbed out of bed, opened the peephole on my door. My neighbor, Mount Tiffany, was leaning against the hallway wall, topless, her eyes closed and mouth slung open. A short middle-aged man wearing an Armani suit and an NBA coach's haircut was attempting to scale her. His teeth were clamped pitonlike to Tiffany's left nipple as if for dear life, which also accounted, I think, for her moans. When the man's pants fell to his ankles, the two of them tumbled to the carpet and struggled toward penetration. Tiffany's dress was suddenly up around her neck, right next to her ankles, and her pink fingernails were digging into the man's pale rump. I felt a little creepy intruding on the lovebirds, but it was the closest I'd been to an aroused woman in months, so I said fuck it and started stroking my tool right up until Mr. Armani got his nut off with a melodramatic grunt and some shameless professings of love.

I sat on the bed and listened to them and he sounded exhausted and soon said goodbye. When I still couldn't sleep, I got dressed and walked up to Hughes Market. It was four-thirty and there were only three other shoppers: a couple burnt-out rockers and an old woman. I was starving and could've easily filled a cart, but I was almost broke, so I grabbed a basket and shopped carefully. I bought raisin bran, one percent milk, three apples, four bananas, bread, chicken bologna, a six of Diet Cokes, instant hot chocolate, spaghetti, generic tomato sauce, generic toilet paper, and five packs of generic macaroni and cheese. I should've had the willpower to leave then, but I kept thinking of Tiffany on her shoulder blades in the hallway and I grabbed a box of instant brownies, three more Jiffy Pops, and threw in an *Enquirer* at the register. It came to just under thirty-five bucks and on the way home my shoulder was starting to ache, but I felt centered because my refrigerator would have food again, not just notebooks, and the brownies might even help get me laid. I put everything away and read for a while, then went to bed and thought about Tiffany and I began rubbing one out again. I was very horny and the thought of tasting my own semen suddenly appealed to me, but then I came and I thought, What the *hell* was I thinking?, and I wiped off my stomach and fell back asleep.

I was awakened again by someone trying to kick my door in. The landlady Mrs. Beaupre, I somehow figured, though this made no sense. When the banging persisted, I got out of bed.

"Who is it?" I called.

"Colleen" came the answer.

Colleen. I didn't know any Colleens.

Through the peephole I observed a young woman with thin lips and large almond eyes.

"What do you want?" I asked.

"Could you open the door, please?"

"Why?"

"I want to talk to you about something."

"I don't want any."

"Henry, I'm not selling anything."

She had a persistent little voice, and she'd said "Henry." "Henry," she'd said.

"Do I know you?" I asked.

"No."

I waited for an explanation.

"Well, what do you want?"

"I read your article in the paper. Please *open up.*"

This made me swoon with fear. Suddenly I felt embarrassed about still being in bed at . . . I looked at the clock: 6:13 A.M. What the . . . ?

"Just a second," I said.

I pulled on a pair of shorts and a T-shirt, threw my hand under the faucet and slurped up some water. I took a few deep breaths and opened the door.

The woman looked to be in her late twenties, but she had the shiny forehead of a teenager. Her dirty blonde hair was long and straight, with a short puff of bangs. A red-and-white checkerboard dress was what she wore, and no stockings, and if she'd told me she'd just stepped off the set of *Hee Haw,* I would've believed it. Her body was pale and unexceptional by L.A. standards, but probably okay back in Tennessee or wherever the hell she learned to dress like that.

"I lived your story," she said.

I squinted and forced a crooked smile.

"How do you mean?"

"I mean, I really loved your story. You know, in the *Los Angeles Times.*"

"Oh. Yeah. Well, thank you. That's very nice."

"Can I come in and talk to you about it?"

"How did you know where I live?"

"Called information. You're listed. Can I come in?"

I thought again about the hour, about how odd this was, about how damn pushy she was being.

"Actually, this isn't the best time."

"Why not?"

"Well . . ." I rubbed my chin. "It's a little fucking early, that's why."

She flinched.

"Can I come back later, then? We'll go somewhere for breakfast to eat."

"I already have a breakfast meeting," I lied.

"How about lunch?"

Although I was bewildered and maybe even slightly flattered by the attention, something about her struck me as being "off," and I hesitated. Whether it was the pushiness or the fact that one almond eye was slightly off-center and larger than the other, or just good, solid intuition, I don't know, but something about her definitely frightened me. It frightened me so much that I heard myself saying "Sure" out of pure intimidation.

"Great. I'll come back at noon."

"Noon it is," I said. Then: "I have a better idea. Why don't we meet at Ed's Coffee Shop—on Robertson between Beverly and Melrose."

"Okay," and she left.

I crawled back into the crib until eleven-thirty, then showered, brushed my teeth, put on a clean white shirt, and ate a small bowl of raisin bran to rid myself of morning breath. I was annoyed that the raisins came in a separate bag. The fuckers. There were already too many unnecessary decisions in the world, now I had to decide how many raisins to allot myself. I liked the pure chance of it before—let the raisin gods decide, not me.

On the way out to meet my fan, Tiffany stuck her head out her door wearing a big grin. "Hear me last night?"

"As a matter of fact . . ."

"I was doing it right in the hallway!"

"Yeah," I said, "Yeah. What happened, you lose your keys—or just couldn't wait?"

"No, it's just that he's like this forty-five-year-old lawyer and he's pretty straight, so I thought it would be exciting for him."

"Huh."

She stepped into the hall and I saw that she was in her undies, her bra barely managing to contain its heavy cargo.

"Can you give me a lift to work?" she asked. "I left my car there last night."

As we drove up Melrose, neither of us spoke much. I was bitter. All I could think of was her animal moans and her perfect, scientifically engineered body, and this flabby-assed Porsche-driving pig, who was probably married and had three kids, getting his nut off while I was free and single and pushed to the point where I was considering tasting my own load across the hall. I dropped her off at the Moustache Cafe, then headed back to Robertson Boulevard.

It was too hot for coffee when I got to Ed's, so I sat at the counter and ate a piece of watermelon. I opened the paper to the sports section, but was too anxious about meeting my new groupie to read. I kept glancing at the door when anyone entered. Finally she came in, made a quick sweep of the room, and called out, "Monkey!" I looked behind me, then squirmed as I realized I was the chimp she was referring to.

"Have you been waiting long?"

She kissed me on both cheeks, grabbed a chunk of my melon and stuffed it in her mouth.

"Uh, no," I said. "No."

I felt like running, but before I could, she'd asked a couple singles if they minded doubling up in order to open a table for us. She took my arm and suddenly I found myself at a little Formica table in the corner with her jammed in beside me screaming out her life story for all to hear.

her name was colleen driscoll, and she was from Livingston, New Jersey, not Tennessee, as the picnicky dress had indicated. She'd been in L.A. for almost two years now, having come out alone, then quickly meeting and moving in with a personal trainer from Germany named Honus. Colleen claimed to have once been "a figure-skating champion," whatever that meant, which was why she had to leave high school early, and she was an actress now, struggling to attain her SAG card but getting by with the help of her work in the Screen Extras Guild. Most big stars started as extras, she said, and for eighteen months she'd been buoyed by the hope that a sharp casting agent would pick her out of a crowd scene on the Temescal Canyon *Baywatch* beach or off the hallways of *90210* and offer her a leading role in a big movie. It happens, she said, and I said I didn't doubt it.

While she told her story, I was thinking how wacky it was that she had called a total stranger "Monkey," and that she'd kissed me, and I wondered why she'd needed to see me so badly that she'd rap on my door at dawn, and suddenly I heard her say, "I need a place to stay."

Like an angel, a young smiling Mexican man appeared. I ordered tortillas and scrambled eggs and Colleen asked for two eggs—"snotty"—and home fries. I excused myself to go to the bathroom and asked Colleen to order me a Sprite while I was gone. The bathroom was just to give me space—I didn't really have to go—so I washed my hands a couple times and hoped I was overestimating her nerve. Back at the table I changed the subject and started querying her about acting and Livingston, New Jersey—which apparently had a lot of ponds and rinks and was a figure-skating hotbed—and basically about everything I knew nothing about, and in the middle of a question about Brian Boitano, she said again, "I need a place to stay *tonight*."

I paused and said, "Why?"

"Because Honus threw me out yesterday. The big jerko said I didn't pay him the rent."

The waiter placed a cup of coffee in front of me.

"No," I said, "I ordered a Sprite."

The man looked at Colleen and she said, "They didn't have Sprite, Monkey, just ginger ale, so I ordered you a coffee, black."

"Really?" I said, but by then she was looking for a cigarette. I turned to the man and mouthed, "Ginger ale." When he left, I said, "Well, did you?"

"What?"

"Pay the rent."

"Of course I paid him, but I was stupid and paid cash money and now I got no proof. Some birthday present, huh?"

"Today's your birthday?"

"No, next week. But he promised me we were gonna go somewhere. He knows I like to go somewhere on my birthday."

I threw her a commiserative nod.

"He even kept Puffy."

"Animal?"

She smiled. "My kitty."

The waiter appeared with our meals, and when he left I asked her where she'd slept the previous night.

"I didn't. Hung out at Ben Franks'. Drank coffee all night and read the paper—that's where I read your article, in the paper. I mean it just blew me away, like you have no idea."

"Well, thanks."

"I mean it, seriously, you have *no idea.* Just the fact that I'd be at an all-time low point in my life, and to find that article . . . The chances are just . . . Anyway, when the sun was coming up, I caught a lift over here from some guy who'd been trying to fuck me all night."

I looked up. "Fuck" struck me as a bit harsh for someone who called people "jerko."

"Oh."

"I would've slept in my car, except I don't have it anymore. I kind of had an accident."

"Yeah?"

"The car was hardly scratched, but they took my license away, so I got rid of it."

I rolled the eggs into a tortilla and asked Colleen to pass me the ketchup from the table behind her.

"Yes, Master."

"Why'd they take your license away?" I asked.

"Well . . . they said it was my fault."

"Was it?"

"It's really debatable. I mean as I recall, no, but, to tell you the truth, I can't recall. You see, I passed out for a couple seconds 'cause of my low blood pressure and now I don't remember much. Bottom line is, I hit a lady in my car."

"You rear-end her?"

"No, I hit her in the side—she was walking."

When I flinched, she quickly added, "She was okay, though."

"But they found you at fault?"

"*Exactly,*" Colleen said with a confusing conspiratorial nod, as if this somehow exonerated her. "I looked right, then I looked left to see if there were any cars coming, and there weren't any, so I started to go, and she came out of nowhere from the right, and I ran into her."

"But she was okay?"

"She was fine, the big whiner. I was only going like two miles an hour." Colleen sipped her coffee. "The baby was okay, too."

I stopped chewing.

"The carriage got knocked over and the baby was crying and everything, but he was just in shock."

"You ran over a baby."

"Then this cop comes over and I'm allergic to smog, so I ended up going to jail, you know."

"You ran over a baby?"

"And the judge was a real asshole."

"A *baby* you ran over?"

"I didn't run him *over*. I hardly tapped him, and it wasn't my fault."

"Baby was okay?"

"Yeah, I told you, he needed like *one* stitch."

"And where does the smog come into this?"

"That's why I went to jail."

"Because of smog?"

"Yeah, 'cause when the cop looked at me, he saw that my eyes were all diluted and red as a bunny's, like Michelle Pfeiffer or something, and he figured I was on drugs, which was just the smog I'm allergic to, so he sent me downtown for three days 'cause it was a weekend and court was closed. But, like I said, first I passed out and by the time the ambulance got there, the baby had already stopped crying, but the judge was an asshole and he took away my license, so I got rid of my car. Now, what do you say? Can I live with you?"

"*Live* with me?"

"I mean stay. Just for tonight. My girlfriend from San Diego's sending me money, but it won't be here until tomorrow."

"Colleen, you saw my place—it's really small."

"You won't even notice me, I'm tiny, and I'm real quiet."

"Yeah, I know, but I also have a girlfriend back home. This would not . . . she would . . . it wouldn't be good."

"Oh, come on, she won't know."

"Ah . . . I don't even know you."

"Listen, Henry, I'm begging you. Just tonight. I'll be gone to-morrow and you won't never hear from me again . . . never."

"Um . . . no. I'm sorry."

Colleen shot me a look as if I was throwing her out on the street along with our five kids.

"Thanks a lot!"

She smashed out the cigarette, grabbed her bag, and rushed from the room.

I shrugged at the couple whom she'd just almost bowled over, then I grabbed the newspaper off the counter. While finishing breakfast, I checked out how the playoffs were shaping up for the Celts and Bruins, then stared at the top ten batting list for a few minutes. Boggsie had gone one for three.

Colleen was leaning against a pay phone when I came out. I tried to slink by her.

"You know, Henry Halloran, you're a real hypocrite! You write about trying to be a hero, but when it comes right down to it, when it comes down to really helping a human being who will accept it, you say, 'Fuck off!' "

I opened my car door. "I didn't say, 'Fuck off,' I just don't have a real big place—it's a studio—and I don't know you from a hole in the wall."

"Did you know her?"

"No, but I didn't ask her to move in with me, either."

"Why am I different than Bonnie? Aren't I good enough to help?"

"Don't you have any other friends? What do you mean, 'Bon-nie'? Who's Bonnie?"

"All my friends abandoned me when Honus and me broke up."

"Again, who's Bonnie?"

She swung her head side to side. "Do you think this is easy for me, man? I been living here two years and I got no friends. You think I feel good about that?"

"I don't understand. Who the hell's—?"

"Bonnie was my fucking sister!"

I stared at her.

"Bonnie . . ." she said, and her voice trailed off. "You tried to save her . . . my sister . . ."

We dragged her bags out of some bushes in a small park off Robertson, along with a foot-high pile of *Psychology Today*s. There was an uncomfortable silence on the drive back to my apartment, and then she said, "I wonder why they're so red."

"What's red?"

"Michelle Pfeiffer's eyes."

"I don't know. Maybe she swims a lot."

This cracked Colleen up and she hit my arm and said, "Maybe she swims a lot."

I glanced at her and shrugged.

"Where you from?" she asked.

"Originally Rhode Island."

"Why is it that everyone from Rhode Island is so funny?"

"Who? Who's from Rhode Island?"

"I don't know. Everyone."

On the corner of Santa Monica and Doheny, a fucking lunatic with a shaved head and a blue ponytail pulled up beside us in a truck and asked if we wanted to buy a joint for five bucks.

"Sure," she said.

He tossed the joint into her window and Colleen looked to me.

"*I'm* not paying him," I said.

"I don't have any money."

"Then give it back."

She searched the floor for the joint as honks came from behind me.

"Come on, buddy!" the truck guy yelled, and I heard someone behind me yell, too.

"What are you doing?" I said as I felt around in my pocket. All I could find was a crumpled-up tenner, so I threw it to the truck and asked for change, but he shot me a look like, "Yeah right, pal," and then he said exactly that and sped away.

colleen sat on her knees on the bare floor in front of the black-and-white Motorola for two and a half hours, never budging, turning her attention only to reach for a pack of cigarettes. I was at the table trying to work, listening in succession to *Gilligan's Island, The Jeffersons,* a couple game shows, and *Entertainment Tonight.* Earlier I'd brought up the subject of her sister, I had a million questions, but she said she was too tired to get into it and in a way I was relieved. She had, however, provided me with a snapshot— unsolicited—of her and Bonnie and the similarities were unmistakable. This was definitely the dead woman's sister. I glanced at Colleen occasionally, but she didn't notice. She was hypnotized by stale one-liners, celebrity innuendo, and trivia. I thought about what had happened on that roof and couldn't help but feel a little responsible for this poor woman who apparently had no one and nothing.

Colleen finally landed on *Tom and Jerry* and almost immediately started coughing up approval, a one-person laugh track. I tried to concentrate, but the room was full of whistles and zipping sounds with Colleen's guffaws keeping the beat.

"That's what I wanted to be before I became an actress."

"What's that?" I asked.

"In cartoons."

"Cartoons?"

"Yeah, you know, like Schulz. Know how much money that guy makes off Charlie Brown alone?"

I gestured that it was a lot.

"Only thing is," she said, "I can't draw to save my rear."

"Too bad."

"I still want to do children's stories, though."

"Great."

I looked back in my notebook and tried to focus. Colleen grabbed the three-wood out of my golf bag and took a practice swing that came inches away from my only reading lamp.

"Whoa," I said. "Put that away, you're going to break something."

"Yes, Master."

She dropped the club and started jumping on the bed.

"What are you doing? Stop that."

"Why?"

"You're going to break the thing."

"You saying I'm fat?"

"I'm saying it's a cheap piece of shit. Now get off it."

She sat on the floor, crossed her legs.

"I have an unbelievable idea for a children's story. Wanna hear it?"

"Little later," I said. "I'd like to finish up here first, okay?"

"Sure, okay. It's about this kitty that gets depressed and tries to commit suicide."

Her hook was too good.

"This a children's story?"

"Uh-huh. Most people don't know this, but animals get depressed, too. So I figured I'd teach kids to be nicer to their pets, so they wouldn't get depressed—the pets."

"That's a darn nice message."

I surrendered to the fact that I wasn't going to write anything worthwhile with the constant interruptions, so I flipped back a few pages and started editing.

"The kitty in my story gets so bummed out that she jumps out of a big building."

My head stayed down, but the eyes swung toward her.

"Happens all the time, you know," she said, "cats jumping out of big buildings. I even heard about a pig who bit into an electric wire and got electrocuted."

"Suicide?"

"Well, pigs ain't stupid, you know. They're smarter than dogs."

Without uncrossing her legs, Colleen hopped on her hands over to me. I smiled at her uncomfortably and returned to my task.

"Thanks for letting me stay here, Henry."

"Eh. No big deal."

She unwrapped three sticks of gum, stuffed them in her mouth. When she lit a cigarette, her eyes lit up, too.

"Hey, isn't that funny," she said. "You wrote a story about suicide, and I was gonna."

"Huh."

"I don't know, guess some things are just meant to be."

I forced my cheeks up in a vague smile.

Colleen stayed on the floor, cracking her gum, blowing smoke rings around my head. I pushed on, though, cutting and adding, trying to focus. When she stood behind me and read over my shoulder, I had to stop. A bubble the size of a soccer ball hung from her mouth.

"Isn't there anything on the tube?" I asked.

"*Beverly Hillbillies,* but I already seen all them twenty times already."

I closed my notebook, pulled on a sweatshirt.

"You done?" she asked.

"Uh-uh."

"Oh, come on, you been working all day."

"Sorry, but I've got to finish this. I'm going to the library for a couple hours."

"Why?"

"I need quiet."

"What do you mean? I been quiet."

On my walk to the Beverly Hills Public Library, I picked up a few scraps of paper and a couple soda cans and I felt good about that. Of course it had occurred to me that I really didn't know Colleen Driscoll, and she could be cleaning me out, but I had my notebooks and money on me and there wasn't much else of value.

A couple hours later, I walked home the long way, down Wilshire. At the Security Pacific Bank a nauseatingly gorgeous woman with short blonde hair pulled up in a red Mercedes. She swung out a pair of shiny brown legs and hurried to the cash machine. I couldn't help but stop and stare at the way she pushed her hair back while waiting for the fresh dough to roll out, and the black dress that clung to muscular dancer's thighs and the perfect, propped-up be-hind. She threw me a smile as she drove away, and as she turned the corner, I stared at the spot where I'd last seen her. I reminded myself that it was an illusion, she couldn't possibly be that fantastic, but still it killed me that she existed and I would never know her.

I stopped at Kate Mantilini and ate a fourteen-dollar plate of meat loaf at the bar. It was an indulgence, but I was craving meat and I chased it with a Sprite. Afterward I was still in no rush to go home, so I ordered a Heineken and struck up a conversation with the guy next to me. Almost immediately he started telling me about the woman who was suing him for palimony, even though they'd only lived together for three months and she made more than he did. I thought about telling him about my breakup, compare notes, but it was my experience that when people told each other similar sob stories, neither paid attention, they just thought about their own situation, so I decided to keep my mouth shut and maybe learn something from his breakup, rather than tell mine to a blank stare.

Colleen was back in front of the tube when I returned. She glanced up as I entered, but didn't speak until a commercial released the box's clutch on her.

"I want to go to sleep when this is over, okay?"

"Sure," I said, though I was wide awake now.

I considered going out for another beer, but I figured the sooner this day ended, the better. Tomorrow she'd be gone and my life would be returned to me. Maybe someday I'd have my own little Mercedes-driving, sweet little dancer butt staying here. Wouldn't that be nice?

When *Matlock* ended, Colleen flipped off the television, ate a sandwich, made a racket in the bathroom for twenty minutes. She came out wearing one of my T-shirts and my boxer shorts, smelling like soap and toothpaste. I brushed my teeth, and for the first time put on the pajamas Amanda had bought me two years earlier for Christmas. When I came out of the bathroom, Colleen was leaning against the radiator with her legs crossed, smoking a cigarette.

"So is this furniture all yours?"

"It was here when I moved in."

"No offense, but it's kind of cheesy. You should go to the Rose Bowl flea market and get some decent stuff in here."

I sat on the murphy bed.

"So where do I sleep?" she asked.

"You've got the right side, I'll take the left."

She looked as if she'd sooner cuddle up to a piece of fiberglass insulation. "I don't think I know you well enough," she said. "You might rape me."

A double take on that one. "Huh?"

"I said I don't know you well enough and you might rape me."

I scratched my chin, Colleen flipped the butt out the window. She sat in a chair and stared at her feet as I climbed under the covers.

"Can't you sleep someplace else?"

I was astonished by this request. "Where?"

"The couch?"

"That's not a couch, it's a half-couch."

"Curl up."

"I don't think so."

She whispered, "How about on the floor?"

I couldn't help but smile at this—at the sheer *balls*. "I'm sorry," I said, "but I'm prone to bad backs. Trust me, I'm not going to touch you, I'm just going right to sleep."

"You say that, but how do I know you're not going to rape me?"

"Enough with the rape thing, huh? For Christ sakes."

"Well, how do I know?"

"If you're so concerned, then *you* can sleep on the floor, and I'll see you in the morning, okay?"

"Fine."

I always thought about Amanda just before I fell asleep. I couldn't help it, I had to mention her in my prayers and then there she was. Usually the same image, a positive one. We're driving to a Patriot game in September, it's sunny, we're on a back road in Wrentham with a lush canopy of leaves above us—green mostly, a blotch of red here and there—shadows are flying across her tanned face, Amanda is smiling at me, in love . . .

Suddenly I heard Colleen shuffling about in the dark. Next thing I knew, the light was on and she was standing over me with her arms folded. "I'm mad at you," she said.

"For what?"

"For being a shit. Just because I don't want to do it with you, you make me sleep on the floor, and I think that's pretty crappy."

I sat up. "Colleen, I never said you had to sleep on the floor, I said you could use the bed."

"Yeah, if I slept with you."

"That's right, *slept* with me, not anything else. I just want to go to sleep."

"Oh, yeah, and I was born like yesterday, right?"

I was suddenly itchy. "Look, I'm trying to be a nice guy letting you stay here, but if you'd prefer, you can go to the motel up the street and there'll be no hard feelings, okay?"

"Well, maybe I will!," and she started packing like she was on one of her game shows where she got to keep everything she could stuff in her bag in thirty seconds.

I was going to let the melodrama pass without saying anything, but then she started crying. I didn't want a crying woman storming out of my apartment. Besides, I knew she didn't have any dough. "Calm down," I said, and I closed her suitcase. She continued throwing bras and panties and little white cosmetic cases at the bag, and when I sat on it, she threw stuff at me, too. "Just take it easy," I said. When Colleen had finally exhausted herself to the point of blowing a white bubble of snot onto her upper lip, she charged into the bathroom and slammed the door.

I poured us each a vodka and sat on the bed. After a few minutes, I said, "Come on out, I made you a drink."

She didn't open the door, and I could hear her in there, still on the crying jag, as if someone had died, and I kept thinking, Man, what a nut, and then I remembered, well, someone *had* died, and it was only for one night, she'd be gone tomorrow, and at least I'd have done the decent thing.

"You can have the bed," I said, but still she didn't respond.

After I finished both drinks, I walked out back in the sweet air and relieved myself under a sycamore. It was a cloudless night, but there were no stars visible and the moon was a mushy blur. I thought about that: stars everywhere, except in the sky, and I pictured Amanda again, but this time it was winter and her tan had faded and so had everything else.

when i came to at ten-thirty, Colleen had already packed up and left. On the bathroom mirror I found a surprisingly sweet note written on a napkin, which was doubly nice, seeing as I was out of toilet paper. In my mailbox, along with some junk mail, I discovered a sample packet of Kellogg's Mueslix. This was going to be a good day. After eating the powdery oats and raisins mixed with tap water, I worked for a few hours, then decided to drive downtown to the *L.A. Times* offices and pick up my check. I was down to thirty-seven bucks and a quarter tank of gas, so I couldn't wait for them to mail it to me.

As I was getting into my car, I heard someone yell, "Hey, fucky!" and spotted Herb Silverman laying in a chaise across the street, his oiled body glowing like a mirror while he swigged a beer. The actor waved me over and I considered ignoring this, but I didn't.

"I been thinking about what you told me," he said. "You should've lied, you know."

"When?"

"When your old girlfriend caught you doing whatever she caught you doing, you should've just lied."

I heard a distant bell ringing and kids started appearing out of nowhere. I felt a burst of dizziness and my neck tightened; I wondered if there was a connection between the two. Maybe I'd dislodged a vertebrae and it was pressing against the part of the spinal cord that controlled the inner ear and equilibrium. Last night on the floor had probably made it worse.

"Give me one of those," I said.

Silverman pulled a can of Bud out of a little red-and-white cooler and tossed it to me.

"When a girl's in love, she'll believe anything," Silverman said. "It's like that Richard Pryor joke where the chick catches him fucking around, and he goes, 'Who you gonna believe, me or your lying eyes?' " Herb rubbed more baby oil onto his stomach and said, "So what's the scoop? You jammed Tiff yet?"

"No."

The ice cream man pulled up and the little tykes were sitting ducks with their paper money and innocent expectations.

"What is wrong with you? Start paying her a visit every night before bed. Believe me, you'll forget all about old what's-her-name."

"I have forgotten about what's-her-name."

"Then what's she doing on your wall?"

"Look, I've got too much work to do to be visiting Tiffany every night."

"Right. Presidents of the United States are fucking starlets during missile crises, but Mr. Waiter-Slash-Unemployed-Writer can't find time to walk across the hall to get his dick sucked. Jesus, it's not like you gotta romance her. You know the ten minutes every night you spend jerking off? Well, instead, open your door, knock on hers, glue her eyes shut, then go home. First night I met her that's what I did."

"First night?"

"Maybe fifteen minutes and she was rocking on top of me, playing with those big toddies."

After the last child had been served her ice cream, I made a head count and, satisfied, hit the road.

At Times Mirror Square I was told that my editor was in a meeting, but that the assistant I'd dealt with—she of the cousin Kristen bitchiness—would be right out to see me. Even though she'd played a major role in getting the story published, I wasn't crazy about the prospect of meeting her, so I told the receptionist I'd come back in an hour.

I was still at the elevator when a young woman came searching for me. She was dressed in a nice suit and was a nick heavy, or maybe just big-boned, with what I imagined "proud breasts" to look like, and she had an odd, attractive face. Her manner hinted at an education—someplace like Wellesley—and she was holding an envelope.

The receptionist told her that I'd left, but as she turned away, I called out, "Um, hello."

She looked at me, emotionless really, but at the time it felt like annoyance.

"I'm Henry Halloran. I was going to come back later when I might get a chance to meet Arnold."

"Fine."

She started back toward her office.

"But on the other hand, I might as well take the check now, just in case."

She pivoted on her heel. "Just in case what?"

"Well, you know, just in case I can't get back . . . today."

A nod, and she handed me the envelope. Then she walked away.

I left the building with a thousand-dollar check in my pocket and an empty feeling in my gut. I popped into the minimart next door for a pack of Tums, briefly considered purchasing a three-pack of back-issue porno mags with the titles torn off, but was too depressed and decided against it. When I got to my car, the proud-bosomed assistant was striding out of the *Times* building lugging a wooden chair over her shoulder.

"Excuse me," I called, and I caught up to her. "Are you aware that you have a chair hanging from your back?"

She glanced at the chair, then straight-faced said, "Oh, man."

"Must've gotten snagged when you left the office," I said.

The woman permitted herself a smile.

"I liked your story," she said.

"Thanks. Look, I'm sorry about our run-in on the phone. I was kind of frustrated."

"I've gotten over it."

"Prove it by having dinner with me tonight."

The young woman flinched. "I don't think so."

"Come on, I'll cook."

"I don't even know you."

"Sure you do. At least as well as you can know anybody in this town."

"Oh, Jesus. Was that supposed to be deep?"

"I don't know what it was supposed to be. I couldn't think of anything else."

She glanced around, searching for someone to bail her out.

"Please," I said. "I don't know anybody in this town, and I'm sick of eating alone."

"Don't I feel special."

"I said I'd cook you dinner. That's special, isn't it?"

"Or cheap. Depending on how you look at it."

That kind of stuff I liked.

"Hey, Henry, get real here. You don't even know my name and the only thing I know about you is that you have extraordinarily bad luck with women."

"It's just dinner. I'm not asking you to go up the coast with me."

She didn't say no.

"For all you know, I could have a boyfriend."

"Bring him."

When she still didn't cave, I said, "Okay, let me put it another way. Do you realize that if you go out with me tonight, and we hit it off, and then if you go out with me again, and we start having a real good time, and then if maybe in a few weeks we do take a trip up the coast or to the mountains or someplace, and somehow, incredibly, we fall in love—" She started to interrupt, but I held up my hand. "And then if somewhere down the line we actually got married and ended up having kids and grandchildren and a wonderful life together, do you realize that right now will have been one of the greatest moments of our lives?"

"Sounds as if somebody's been doing a little writing."

"That was spontaneous, I swear."

Then she tilted her head, and I could see she was considering it. "What do you say?"

She waved at someone in a car, then she looked me in the eyes and I knew I had her.

on my way home, I thought about the fact that I'd passed on the porno mags and ended up with a hot date. Maybe that brief stretch of high road had earned me some karmic mileage. Maybe it was true. If I'd chosen to buy the porn, I probably would have been back at the cash register or staring down at some stranger's air-brushed beaver when the *L.A. Times* girl walked out of the building. Jesus, I'd forgotten to ask her name.

I cashed the check at a check-cashing store downtown, then hurried back to a supermarket in the Swish Alps section of West Hollywood and spent twenty-eight dollars on shells, broccoli, margarine, kielbasa, and two bottles of wine. The place was raging with clean-cut, preppy-looking guys. A muscleman with bleached-blond hair, shredded jeans, no shirt, and a white silk scarf was talking to any fey prepster who would listen while carrying around a bleached-blond poodle wearing a matching scarf.

Back at the Blue Terrace, I made my bed, showered, scraped the stubble from my face. From Mount Tiffany I borrowed a couple pots, silverware, a screwdriver in lieu of a corkscrew. I was setting the table when I noticed the light on my phone machine blinking. Two messages. My heart sank. She was canceling. I pushed the button and held my breath. A man's voice I didn't recognize. He sounded unsure of himself.

"Um, I hope I have the right number. If this is the Henry Halloran who wrote the story in the *Los Angeles Times Magazine,* I'd appreciate it very much if you would call me. My name is Gus Anders . . . I thought it was very well written . . . Um . . . anyway . . . please call me . . ."

He went on to leave his phone number twice because he was afraid he'd said it wrong the first time, which he hadn't. I had mixed feelings about this message—another psycho calling?—but at least it wasn't my date canceling. The next message was from Levine's assistant Meegan. He was pushing up tomorrow's meeting. Instead of four o'clock, we'd do lunch. I was on a roll!

There was still an hour before my young Lois Lane was due to arrive, so I decided to flip on the clock radio, mix a stiff one, get in the mood. Unfortunately, there was only a centimeter of vodka left in the freezer. I had the wine, but I didn't really like wine. That was for her. I thought about running out for a fifth, but decided against it. It was Monday night, I just wouldn't drink, that's what people did on Monday night. There was a knock at the door.

Colleen Driscoll was standing in the hallway, a suitcase in each hand, her face bloated and covered with zigzags of barely clotted cuts.

"Jesus," I said.

She burst into tears, dropped her bags, and rushed into my arms, except my arms weren't open, so she just knocked me back a couple feet.

"Puffy's dead," she sobbed.

"Who?"

"My kitty. He killed her."

"Who did?"

"Caesar, that bastard. We were moving out and he attacked her."

"Who's Caesar?"

"The stupid dog!"

I put my arm on hers and she began hiccuping as she sobbed.

"He's a pit bull . . . She was just a kitty . . . Didn't stand . . . chance."

I wanted to help, but all I could manage right then was "Oh" with a downward lilt. She came in and sat on my bed, but I kept her bags out in the hall. Colleen racked her head back and forth in abject mourning, as if it wasn't a pet she'd lost but a child.

"What happened to your face?" I asked and handed her a clean undershirt to press against the scratches.

"Puffy," she said. "Honus just stood there, so I tried to break it up and Puffy freaked out." Colleen let out another gut-wrenching wail. "She was all I had . . ."

This sounds melodramatic now, but it got to me then, and I felt a tinge of guilt because what I was really thinking was that I had my sassy journalist on the way and how the hell long would this scratched-up lunatic be here? Didn't she have a train or plane to catch?

Then the kicker: The money hadn't arrived. She'd called her friend, who'd confirmed sending it, but the money wasn't there when Colleen got to the post office. "It doesn't make sense," she said. "How long could it take to get one thin letter from Japan?"

"You said she was sending it from San Diego."

"No, I didn't."

"Yes, you did."

"No, I said she's *from* San Diego. She's modeling in Japan now."

This took the wind out of my sails.

"Can I stay here one more night? Please, that's all I need. Please, please, *please* . . ."

She looked up at me with those pathetic crossed eyes, her chin dimpled and quivering.

"Ah, fuck. You can stay here until you get your shit together."

I was as stunned as she to hear this.

"I can?"

"Just take it easy. I'm sure the money will be here in a day or two, right?"

"Definitely. And if it's not here by Monday, I'm just gonna hitchhike or something. I'm definitely, definitely, *definitely* outta here by Monday."

"Fine. You'll get your money and go back home. I'm not going to throw you out on the street."

I wasn't exactly sure why this was sliding off my tongue, but it cheered her up and suddenly I could more easily envision my newspaper friend servicing me with a karmic boffing. Colleen's money would be here tomorrow anyway, I figured, and only an ogre could say no to the poor kid, sitting there all scratched up like one of the frozen ponds of Livingston, New Jersey. Besides, I needed something to cushion the impact of my next line, which was "But you can't be here right now."

"What do you mean?"

"I'm expecting a guest, and it's business, so I really shouldn't have anyone hanging around."

She rubbed her nose with the back of her wrist.

"That's cool," she said. "I'll just go out somewhere."

"Yeah."

"Where?"

"I don't know. Wherever."

"But I don't really know where to go."

I was going to suggest she visit a friend, but I remembered she didn't have any or she wouldn't be laying all this shit on me.

"The Hard Rock," I said.

It was nearby, the crowd was tame, what the hell, I'd even lay ten of my new dollars on her. She could get a burger, a couple Cokes—anything to get her out of my hair fast. And just to make sure she didn't dilly-dally, I'd drive her there and pick her up later—much later—after my "meeting."

As we pulled away from the Blue Terrace, I unfastened the roof flap.

"What's with the glasses?" she asked.

"I wear them when I drive."

"What for?"

I looked at her. "So I can see."

"Well, you look better without them."

"That's why I wear them. Otherwise I'd have women all over me. It'd be bang-a-lang-a-ding-dong all day long."

"Not *that* much better."

Colleen smiled, and there was something about the smile and her battered face and her needing me so much that got to me. As we drove, I handed her a twenty and told her to go crazy.

"You know something, Henry? I knew you were a good guy when I read about you trying to save my sister. You are. You go the extra mile for people."

"Eh," I said.

She pulled out the joint that she'd bought in traffic the day before.

"I bet you get along with everyone."

"Not everyone," I said.

"Do you get along with your father?"

"Sure."

"Do you love him?"

This seemed an odd question.

"Yeah, I do."

"How about your mom? You love her, too?"

"Yup. Love my mom."

"That's unusual."

"Not where I come from."

A woman started to pull out in front of me, then hit her brakes at the same time I did.

Colleen said, "Sounds like all-right parents. I like that. Good people make good people. *Go, you cunt!*"

The woman pulled away and I continued on.

"They're pretty cool," I said.

I watched her light up. She took a hit and held it.

"Ever do drugs with them?" she asked.

"Not that cool."

She held out the bone.

"No thanks."

"Come on, it'll loosen you up."

I wondered if it was noticeable.

"Do I seem stiff?"

She rolled her eyes. "Just a bit."

"Yeah?"

"Come on."

She put it in front of my face.

"Yeah?"

"You're getting all worked up about your meeting. This'll relax you."

"You think?"

"Sure."

I stared at the joint. Maybe she was right, I was too stiff. Maybe one little hit would be good. Maybe it would bring the soul to the surface, help us connect, me and the *L.A. Times* woman. I leaned toward her fingers and inhaled.

i remember the first time I ever heard of the Hard Rock Cafe. My friend Willy Bodalay had visited the original in London. At the time (early eighties) I pictured it as raucous, decadent, cutting edge. Maybe it was, back then, but no more. The place I stood in was a teenybopper fern bar full of Pepsi signs, Woodstock posters, gold records, and electric guitars on the wall. But no Janis Joplin types. This crowd was mostly tourists with Hollywood signs and Marilyn on their T-shirts, and local girls in the thirteen-to-sixteen-year-old range carrying designer shopping bags and bitching about their mothers.

After the joint, I'd needed a drink, so I'd come inside for a quickie. Colleen had run to the bathroom as soon as we entered, so I placed her vodka collins on an antique Coke machine, which I leaned against as I gulped down a Rolling Rock. Right away I knew this was a mistake. The lights, crowd, and energy were getting to me and I started feeling dizzy. I wanted Colleen back, so I could give her her drink and go. I finished my beer, started on Colleen's highball. Five minutes later I was standing there with two empties. I wanted to reload but flinched when I saw the crowd around the bar. A fake blonde with a fake tan in a fake French high school jacket walked by and I grabbed her arm.

"Excuse me, would you be kind enough to get me a beer, please?"

"I don't work here," she said.

"I know."

She threw me a look and joined a big good-looking kid at the bar. A smirky whisper, he glanced my way, I was overcome by a wave of paranoia. The crowd around the T-shirt stand was backing up all around me. My fingers started to vibrate; the pot, I assumed. When ten more minutes passed with no Colleen, I courageously wedged myself into the bar and ordered another vodka collins and a Rock. Those went down faster than the first two.

Twenty minutes later I was starting to freak out. I was supposed to be having a date soon. Where the hell was Colleen, and what was in that weed? This wasn't normal. I felt as if I was tripping. After four pops, my nerves shouldn't feel like this. I was conscious of my breathing, of the beating of my heart. This was a mistake. I was way too stoned to be in this crowd. I calculated how far I was from Cedars Sinai. Close, but was it close enough? I should go to the emergency room, I thought, and wait this thing out. I started dancing in place, which diverted my attention from how stoned I was to how ludicrous I felt.

A pale well-fed woman tentatively approached. "You Henry?"

"Why?"

"Your date's in the bathroom."

I nodded yes. And . . . ?

"She can't stand up."

Ten baby blondes were waiting for three stalls, eight of them chattering at the same time, fussing with their hair in the mirror. They hooted when I entered. I wasn't happy about being on their turf, but I knew I had to do something fast. My fingers were still buzzing and swollen from adrenaline. There were drugs involved here, and I didn't like it that my "date" was apparently OD'ing. What if she died? I was the one who'd paid for the weed, I could be charged with something.

Colleen was sitting on the toilet with her pants up and her head between her legs.

"I can't get up," she said.

"Yes, you can. Just take a deep breath and we'll get out of here."

"I can't. I have low blood pressure. Every time I stand, I feel like I'm gonna faint."

The woman who'd tracked me down asked if she should call an ambulance.

"No!" I snapped. "She'll be okay."

I turned back to Colleen. She was pale but calm.

"Has this ever happened before?" I asked.

"Oh, yeah. When I had my car accident, remember?"

I was going to have to carry her right through the restaurant. It would be a scene. I was too stoned to handle a scene.

I found a fire exit next to the restroom, but it had an alarm handle, so I tracked down the manager, a guy about my age with thick George Burns-style glasses and a ponytail. I explained the situation: My date was in the throes of food poisoning. "Throw out your goddamn potato salad and open the back door!" I screamed.

I carried Colleen over my shoulder, past the jeering blondes, past the panicky manager. He shut the fire exit door with a sheepish wave and I laid Colleen down on the sidewalk. Again she put her head between her legs. I tried to get my bearings, but the Beverly Center is a big mall and I had no idea where we were in relation to where we had parked.

When Colleen assured me she was stabilized, I sprinted about a quarter mile around the side of the building, looking for an entrance to the parking garage. I finally found a brightly lit escalator, but it wasn't the one I'd ridden down before. I ran up it anyway, then tried to remember if I'd parked on the second or third levels. Or was it the fourth? I tried the fourth first, figuring I'd work my way down, but nothing up there looked vaguely familiar, so I went down to the third, which looked even less familiar and brought me to the second, which I knew for a fact I had never before laid eyes on. All three levels were packed with cars yet strangely void of people and, being as stoned as I was, I felt as if I was losing my mind and was overcome with an irrational, ineffable fear. I was thirsty and my heart shook against my ribs, and I was sweating and out of breath and my fingertips were numb. I thought of my dinner guest arriving with no one there and Colleen down on the street with no blood pressure and suddenly I had to take a shit and my tongue got drier and drier and I stopped running because my throat was making a clicking sound every time I tried to swallow and the stomach cramps got worse and for the first time I realized this wasn't about finding a car, it was about *survival,* because if I didn't get something to drink soon, I would surely choke to death. I'd been fighting an adrenaline rush for about forty-five minutes now, and for the first time, I felt I was losing. My esophagus was starting to spasm and I was afraid it was going to close entirely and that's when I saw the Coke can sitting on the pavement next to a concrete pillar. I picked the can up; it was warm and sticky. A half inch of spew swished at the bottom. I looked around. No witnesses. I made one last effort to work up some spit, to coat my throat, to save myself from doing this.

colleen's butt was slumped over my shoulder as I read the note pinned to my door. Four words: HENRY. CAME. WENT. JENNA. Heartsick, I flopped Colleen onto the bed, then walked down the street for a six-pack of Mountain Dew and a bottle of Listerine. Colleen guzzled three sodas in front of me before I went out front in my boxers and sipped half the Listerine. I tried to look on the bright side—I finally knew her name. And she seemed levelheaded. She hadn't threatened me or made any snide remarks. She was smart, secure. Why not, though? For all she knew, I could've had a terrible accident.

When Colleen joined me outside, I was sitting on the steps, knees plugged into armpits, my head gazing thoughtfully at my own crotch, coincidental but ironic, seeing as I blamed that part of me for the night's failure. Things had started to go south as soon as I thought about putting the plank to Jenna. Originally my intentions had been pure; I'd just wanted company. But by thinking about what the good karma of helping Colleen would bring me, I'd brought on bad karma.

I couldn't hold Colleen responsible for what happened at the Beverly Center. I was the idiot who'd smoked the joint. I was the one to blame, not her. Over and over I reminded myself of this. This is not to say that I wouldn't have loved to see her come down with a Third World–style bladder infection.

"You feeling okay?"

I groaned yes and said, "You?"

"Oh, I'm fine. My blood pressure's normal again. I can feel it."

The crickety whir of a coasting ten-speed rose and faded into the night.

"So the businessperson you were supposed to meet with left, huh?"

"Yeah."

She laid on an exaggerated guilty look and said, "Gulp."

The lacerations on her face had dried and blackened, her chin was a blur of scabs. I took my tenth swig of mouthwash, swallowed a little, spit the rest into the bushes.

"Henry's my favorite name, you know."

"Huh."

"Yeah, in fact, I was gonna name my son Henry. I mean, you know, when I have one."

"Don't worry, I didn't think you had a kid somewhere without a name."

She pushed me. "You Rhode Islanders." Then: "Hey, do you know Anna Gaye?"

"Who?"

"Anna Gaye. Marvin Gaye's wife."

"How the hell would I know Anna Gaye?"

"I don't know. She used to come into this store I worked at. She's really nice."

"Well, that's great to know. And so pertinent."

"So *what?*"

"Never mind."

"What was that, some kind of insult?"

Suddenly she was all paranoia, leaning back, taking no shit, *feinting*.

"It was nothing," I said.

"Bullshit it was nothing. It meant something. What, do you think I'm stupid?"

"It meant nothing. It meant work on your segues."

"My what?"

"Forget it."

"Fine then."

I looked back at my crotch and thought about what I was going to tell the *L.A. Times* girl, Jenna. I knew one thing: It wouldn't be the truth.

"You want to go to sleep now?" Colleen chirped.

Her rage had passed like the hiccups and she liked me again.

"Little while," I said.

"Don't worry. Everything's gonna be okay. You could just reschedule your meeting."

She put her arm around me and together we looked back down and stared, and after about twenty more minutes of crotch-watching, we went inside and Colleen jumped in bed and turned on the radio and she was fast asleep before my head hit the floor.

At five in the morning I was jolted awake, as if someone had stuck chocolate smelling salts under my nose. A small light was coming from the kitchenette and I heard the clanking of tin against Formica. I pulled myself up, shuffled toward the light. Colleen was crouched over the counter, her face inches from a fresh pan of brownies, the icing melting, steam still billowing from the pan, half of them already devoured. She looked up, startled, her cheeks smeared like a chocolate clown.

There was a beat, I didn't know what to say. Finally she blurted out, "I have an eating disorder."

"Cool," I said. "Whatever."

She looked embarrassed and her chin started to quiver. "I miss her sometimes . . . okay?"

I nodded and went back to my spot and listened to the whine of the refrigerator through the floorboards.

friday lunch at the palm was jammed. I showed up at five to one, and while waiting at the bar I saw Tom Hanks and Teri Garr enter, not together. I ordered a Stoly soda, checked out the caricatures of famous people on the walls, then called the *Times*. Jenna wasn't in. Levine arrived fifteen minutes later looking sharp in a European suit, trailed by a group of similarly attired agents and studio execs. They joked around as they entered and dispersed to their own tables before I was able to gain any introductions. Levine wasn't a very good-looking guy, but he was certainly striking in that suit with the sunglasses and long hair and everything, and on the way to our table I noticed the actress Nicolette Sheridan check him out.

After we ordered, Levine said to me, "I've decided to send you around town to meet people. I'm going to represent you."

"Aw, man, great!"

I held out my hand and we shook.

"I reread your script last night. It's funny. I can definitely sell you as a comedy writer."

"Comedy writer? Wait, can't you just tell them I'm a regular *writer* writer?"

"Why?"

"Well . . . they're going to be disappointed. I'm not that funny in person."

"Comedy writers aren't supposed to be funny."

"Huh?"

"If you were funny in person, you'd be a comic or an actor. Even the best comedy writers in town aren't that funny."

"No?"

"Nah, they're just like you."

"Oh. I can do that."

"Yeah, you just have to be funny when you write."

"Uh-huh, okay."

"Now today I'm going to school you in the art of getting a job. To get a writing job, you have to know how to pitch, and to pitch you gotta know how to bullshit. Do you know how to bullshit, Henry?"

"I guess."

"No, Henry, you *definitely* know how to bullshit. Remember Hal Markey? Trust me, you're a bullshitter. I wouldn't be working with you if you weren't."

"All right."

"And remember you told me how a major studio could make *How I Won Her Back* for around three million dollars?"

"Yeah."

"That was bullshit. There's no way they could make that thing for under eight mil. They wouldn't even want to."

"Well, I was thinking if they did it without big-name stars and—"

"Henry, stop it. You sound stupid. Seven to ten mil is rock bottom for a major. You don't know what you're talking about. For Christ sakes, you've got him playing poker with God."

"An angel," I said and I chewed on a slice of bread.

"Now as much as we both like this script, I'm sure you have a lot of other ideas, right?"

"Sure."

"Like what?"

I shifted in my seat. "I don't know, tons of them. I write down new ideas every day."

"See, you *do* bullshit, Henry, and you do it fairly well. You're quick on your feet, that's why you've got a chance to make it. You and I know that you don't write down ideas every day, but those idiots out there don't. Now you're only gonna get one chance to make a first impression, so you better make the best of it. Even if you have to lie. Because whether you realize it or not, that's the business we're in: lying. Picasso said that art is a lie that tells the truth. For the sake of argument, we'll pretend that movies are art, too, and when you think about it, what are they? Just big lies. They're never real, they're made up, like a lie. Even the ones based on true stories have little lies in them. Most movies are *total* lies."

"Uh-huh."

"And everyone in this business lies, too. Every single one of them, they all lie. That's the first thing I learned when I got out here: Don't be afraid to lie. It's not like the rest of the world. Lying is accepted here. It's as much a part of the game as bluffing is to poker. If you don't like it, you don't have to play. Go play the slot machines, be an accountant. Moreover, lying is presumed here. If you don't lie when expected, it fucks people up. People lie so much in Hollywood that when they want to tell the truth they preface it with 'True story . . .' And usually they're *still* lying. Now of course there's bullshit, and there's bullshit. To do it right, you've got to believe it yourself."

"Like daydreaming," I said.

Levine blinked and said, "Whatever. Take the three-million-dollar movie. I have no doubt you actually believed that—even though you had no idea what the hell you were talking about."

"True," I said with a laugh. "I did!"

"Good, good. Now the next thing you have to remember is this, and I can't impress it on you enough: This town runs on one thing—fear. That's it. That's the whole ball of wax. If you figure that out—and I mean (A) *really believe it* and (B) understand the psychology of fear—then you're in. Any executive in this town will tell you it's a hell of a lot easier to say no all day than to say yes even once. Because when they say yes, that's when their ass is on the line. Which is why everyone decides by committee. They don't want to be the only one to say yes. They want a group yes. There's an old joke about the studio exec who reads a script and someone asks what he thought, and he says, 'I don't know. I haven't talked to anyone yet.' That's what fear does—it makes very very bright people very very stupid. Give you example: If there were a flat, two-foot wide strip of metal on the ground and I asked you to walk along it for fifty feet, you probably wouldn't have any problem, right? But if I took that same strip and put it a thousand feet in the air, it'd be another story. You probably wouldn't have the balls to try crossing it, but even if you did, if you mustered up enough guts to set foot out there, odds are you wouldn't make it. And the reason is this: *Fear impairs people's judgment.* That's your ace in the hole.

"You see, it really doesn't matter if your idea is good or bad because the powers that be are past the point of recognizing either. They're a thousand feet up, man! It could be the biggest piece of shit that ever came down the pike or the *Citizen Kane* of our time and they wouldn't know the difference. So what separates them? What gets *Wise Guys* made overnight and keeps *Big* sitting on a shelf for years? *You,* that's what. In that first pitch meeting you will insist on your own development deal and you'll get that development deal because fear is in the room and fear is your friend. They'll never have seen you before and that'll be to your advantage, because they won't have anybody to call to ask about you except me and I'll tell them you're the greatest thing since penile pumps and any idiot would know I'm hyping the hell out of them, but of course their judgment will be impaired by fear, so they'll be asking themselves, 'Is Henry Halloran a genius or just another scumbag with a powerbook crash-landing in Hollywood?' And you will look them in the eye and tell them that this is the best fucking idea they've ever heard and that they're fucking idiots if they don't go for it and I'll tell them that you're on your way to the next studio in a couple hours and so help me God you will have those skittish little worms calling up business affairs and offering you a Guild-minimum deal because forty-two-five is a pittance to pay some potential idiot when it allows them a couple months peace of mind before the finished script comes in and the entire committee decides whether to make it or not. And their decision will be easy, because despite their blank stares and their standoffishness and their fear of saying yes, they're even *more terrified* of saying no to someone who has a clear vision and defends it ruthlessly, because if that young visionary goes out and makes that movie somewhere else and it grosses a hundred mil and turns into a cottage industry, then they're even more fucked than if they said yes to three *Joe Versus the Volcano*s in a row."

On our way out of the restaurant, Levine stopped to schmooze Penny Marshall, who was digging into a plate of fruit slices and cottage cheese. I was standing there hoping for an introduction, which I didn't get, when suddenly I noticed who Penny was having lunch with. Geena Davis. I loved Geena Davis. She was beautiful, talented, she seemed like fun, and she was from Cape Cod. She glanced up, caught me staring. I nodded and she nodded back. I didn't want to bug her, but it seemed silly not to say something—Cape Cod, we were practically neighbors. Finally I rationalized it this way: If she wasn't famous and I knew she was from the Cape, I would definitely say hi. So I said hi.

"Hi," she said.

"I'm from the Cape."

Geena Davis looked at me, confused. "You're okay?"

"No, I'm from *the Cape.*"

"Oh," she said.

I could have told her I was from Cuntfartia, for all the enthusiasm this elicited. Levine glanced at me, but kept talking to Penny. I got to wondering if I'd been misinformed. Maybe Geena wasn't from the Cape after all. I said, "Aren't you from the Cape, too?"

This seemed to snap her to attention. "Oh. Oh, yeah. I'm from Cape Cod."

"I'm from Mashpee—summers. Actually grew up in Rhode Island."

She nodded. "That's great. Rhode Island."

"Biggest little state in the union," I said and boy did it sound dumb.

When she turned back to her cobb salad, I slouched toward the door.

I'd parked my car around the corner to save the three-fifty valet cost, but I stood with Levine while he waited for his.

"Thanks for lunch," I said.

"Don't ever do that again."

"Do what?"

"You know what. You acted like a fan. It was embarrassing."

"But she grew up in the town next to me."

A black 300 Mercedes pulled up. Levine handed the red-coated Mexican four dollars and climbed in.

"Oh, come on. What's the big deal?" I said. "If she wasn't famous, it would seem rude not to mention we were from the same area."

After the attendant had closed the door, Levine rolled down his window. "But she *is* famous," he said, and he drove off.

it was while taking a shower that I first felt the tumor. There'd been no pain, no heaviness there, I'd stumbled upon it. I'd come home with a resolve; I was going to straighten up my life, organize. My first move would be to get Colleen on her way. Unfortunately, she wasn't in, so I cleaned the apartment, then tried the *L.A. Times* girl at the office, but she didn't take my call. After washing my plastic plates, I decided to wash myself. I was a healthy man when I stepped into that shower, but now a lump. On my balls.

A goddamn lump on my balls!

I was sick. No, that wasn't sick, that was dying. Time to see Hoffman. No, I should see a different doctor this time, someone a little more thorough, a little older. Then I figured, what the hell, Hoffman had my chart, the insurance info was already in his computer. And he'd know what to look for, he'd already checked out my lungs.

The lungs! Of course! I'd been right after all. It probably *was* cancer I'd seen on that X ray. Cancer spreads. If it was in my balls, surely it was in my lungs, too.

Oh, boy. Why was everything coming down on me now? First the Suicide Lady, then her sister, now this. Maybe there was something to this karma thing after all. But what about Amanda? Hadn't that been the big karmic in-your-face slam dunk? I didn't deserve this. I was no saint, but I wasn't Hitler, either.

"Emergency," I said to the doctor's assistant, "I must see the doctor as soon as possible." She told me to come in in forty-five minutes. Traffic was light and I arrived early, so I sat downstairs at the pharmacy's lunch counter and had a piece of pecan pie and an orange drink. I stared at the orange and purple liquids circulating in big rectangular bowls. I wondered how long the stuff swished around in there before it all got drank. Probably filled them up every week or so when they got half-full, I figured. Maybe some of it lasted years. I still had time, so I ordered another pie, lemon meringue this time. Why not? I was a dead man. I finished my orange drink, then stained my teeth with a grape one.

I considered the possibility that the tumor was benign. Wouldn't it hurt more if it were really killing me? Maybe they wouldn't even have to take it out. Unlikely. How were they going to know it was benign if they couldn't cut into it? Maybe they could stick a needle in, take a sample. I shifted in my seat.

Still, that there was no pain had to be a promising sign. Then I remembered a story about the congresswoman from Rhode Island, Claudine Schneider; how she'd found out she had cancer. Her husband had noticed it. The woman was sitting there minding her own business, probably feeling immortal, like we all do when we're not sick, and her husband saw the lump. It was sticking out of her neck like an early pea. Cancer didn't always telegraph its arrival. Besides, I'd been dizzy lately, there were the headaches—how much notification could one expect? It was time to face facts. I was a dead man. It didn't matter that Claudine Schneider had beaten it. She didn't have it in her balls. Then a thought: What if they said I could live, providing they . . . ? Oh, good God, my cock would look ridiculous standing there all alone, ball-less.

Dr. Hoffman didn't seem alarmed when informed of my discovery. He asked if there'd been any pain while urinating. None. He told me to drop my drawers and stand in the middle of the room. I looked at the ceiling while the man rotated my nuts in his fingers.

"I don't feel anything," he said.

I gently captured the lump between my thumb and forefinger. "Right there."

The doctor started fiddling with it. Again I thrust my chin to the ceiling. I inhaled sharply as he started lobbing my other nut around.

"You have one here, too," he said.

I felt for myself. Jesus, it was true! My pathetic sack was carrying *two* tumors; my life expectancy had just been halved.

"Those are the epididymides," Dr. Hoffman said.

"Do you think they're malignant?"

The doctor smiled. "It's not cancer."

"What?"

"Everyone has them."

"Huh?"

"Well, every *man*."

"Seriously?" I started to smile now, too.

"Seriously. I'd show you mine, but you might start thinking I'm a weirdo."

Hoffman dropped his gloves in the wastebasket.

"How come I never noticed them before?" I asked.

"Maybe you don't play with yourself enough."

I was starting to feel good again. I was blessed with a funny doctor and a second chance.

"So it's normal?"

"It's normal. I can't tell you how many guys have come running in here after discovering those things, thinking they were gonna be sounding like Mike Tyson in a couple weeks."

I was giddy and laughed a little too hard at this. "Yeah, that's what I thought!"

As Dr. Hoffman started scribbling something on the chart, he said, "Go home, Henry. Your balls shall live to see another day."

on the way back to the apartment, I was happy and ashamed. I knew the doctor must think I was a big pussy. But why shouldn't I be? Who the hell has satellites around their balls? Everybody, according to him, but how would I know? I stopped and bought a bottle of vodka. To hell with the embarrassment, my nuts had been spared, it was time to celebrate. Tonight, after my shift, we'd do it up big. That's right, me and Colleen. Because she was the reason for my good fortune. I do something nice, God lets me live, karma again. Maybe that really was the way the world worked.

On second thought, perhaps booze wasn't such a good idea. What if we got smashed and something happened? That I didn't need. I was doing a good deed letting her stay there, the karmic pendulum was swinging in my favor. Getting laid might send it rocketing back the other way. Might get her hopes up, encourage her to stay in touch from New Jersey. This was one pen pal I didn't need. Then I reminded myself to think nice thoughts about her. Poor thing was to be pitied if anything. The vodka would get tucked away for a rainy day. Maybe tomorrow we'd take a drive, a tour of the city. I'd be nice to her. I'd be nice to her all weekend. But not too nice. And then Monday, one way or another, Monday she'd be gone.

Colleen was lit up by the tube when I returned, yukking it up at Wile E. Coyote's expense. When I started to speak, she said, "Shhh," and that was all right with me. I hid the vodka in a cupboard, along with the two bottles of wine, then sat at the kitchenette table and started reading *Adventures in the Screen Trade,* which was informative and depressing. When her cartoon ended, Colleen changed the channel a couple hundred times, then gave up and tried striking up a conversation, except I said, "Shhh," so she made a face and started flipping through one of her *Psychology Today*s. Of all the magazines in the world: *Psychology Today?* But there they were, fifteen or twenty of them sitting on top of her bag, all dog-eared to hell. I never actually saw her read one; she'd more or less browse through them like a ten-year-old flipping through *Ulysses.*

Soon Colleen tossed the magazine aside, pulled my driver out of my golf bag and started swinging it around.

"Not in the house."

"Yes, Master," she said, and she leaned it up against the bag.

She lit a cigarette, started reading over my shoulder. I tried to turn the page and she grabbed my hand.

"Wait," she said. Then: "Okay."

I shot her a look.

"What?"

"Do you mind reading something else?" I said. "I'd like to read at my own pace."

She rolled her eyes, picked up her magazine. "Let's go get a frozen yogurt," she said.

"Later."

"You know your phone kept ringing today."

I pushed the button on my machine. Seven hang-ups. Colleen went in the kitchenette, came out with my notebooks.

"What are you doing?"

"What?" This with a forced nonchalance.

"Put those away. You don't go near that stuff."

"I just wanted something to read."

"Okay, let's make something clear here: You put that stuff back in the fridge now and never go near it again."

"Why not?"

"Never mind why not. Those are important papers and you don't go near them."

"Okay, okay."

I was halfway down the next page when she said, "Do you like cats or dogs?"

"Dogs," I said without looking up.

"I knew it. You look like a dog guy. Why don't you like cats?"

"I don't know."

"Come on, you must know."

"I don't trust 'em."

"Why?"

"Because I had one as a kid and even after fifteen years she still always looked like she was about to take my eye out."

"What's her name?"

"Fluffy. She's dead."

"I mean your girlfriend."

"What?"

"What's your girlfriend's name?"

"Uh, Amanda."

"How come she didn't come out here with you?"

"Long story."

She wouldn't let it go.

"She just didn't," I said. "She works. Now, please, I'm trying to read here. Can we have a half hour of quiet time?"

She dragged on her cigarette as if she were throwing me the finger. "Don't treat me like a kindergartner, Henry. I'm not in kindergarten."

I didn't look up, just kept reading, and after a few herky-jerky minutes, she started reading aloud from some play. She read the woman lead as if she were playing a bad soap opera actress within a movie, and the rest of the roles sounding like Steven Wright. I bore down, got fifteen pages under my belt before she made a game-show buzzer sound.

"Half hour's up," she said. "Time for a yogie."

"Were you on Ritalin as a kid?"

"Yes!"

I'd meant it as a joke, but something about her expression cracked me up. She started laughing, too, and said, "What? *What?*"

"Nothing."

"How did you know that?"

"I didn't. I was just kidding."

She threw her script on the floor. "Are you ready for a yogie and some playtime?"

"Colleen," I said, "don't treat me like a kindergartner. I'm not in kindergarten."

She stuck out her mug. "Oh, good one."

We walked up Santa Monica Boulevard, past the gay bars and restaurants, to a place called Culture Class. We sat in the parking lot on white plastic chairs and ate frozen yogurt. Colleen was staring at me in an unsettling way; I couldn't decide if she was pretty or not. She looked as if she was going to be a beautiful baby, then her mother did a lot of acid during the third trimester. Like Christy Turlington in a carnival mirror. To the casual observer, I'm sure she was cute. She had the dainty dress and the frizzball bangs supplying lubrication to her forehead and the teenage ass, too, but something about those lopsided cat eyes made me uneasy.

"I can tell you'd probably make a good boyfriend."

"Nah."

"You're nice to me. Not like Honus. You wouldn't believe some of the mean shit he did."

"What he do?"

"Everything."

"Like what?"

"Like *everything*. He was *so mean*."

"Give me an example."

"He just . . . he just treated me like shit. But I guess I had it coming."

"No one deserves to be treated like shit."

"Well, then, why does everyone treat me that way? *Everyone*. Sometimes I think it must be me."

"Maybe it's just the people you hang out with."

"I've thought about that. But the thing is, I believe in people, and I think they're basically good, I do. And then you gotta wonder . . . I mean, they can't all be wrong . . . right?"

that night I served a three-year-old girl a Bacardi cocktail.

My boss Joe had called the day before asking me to cover a dinner shift. This was good news, as a dinner shift meant at least a hundred bucks and a few hours away from my houseguest. In retrospect, I should've examined the dinner menu, but I assumed it was the same as the lunch menu, except with higher prices and larger servings. This proved to be not the case, and the dinner patrons were also more demanding.

I never was a particularly good waiter. I came across more the friendly idiot than the culinary expert, but my tips had always been commensurate with those of the waiters who could rattle off every last herb and the brand of butter in the bouillabaisse, so I slid by contentedly. Usually I made up the answers as I went along, but suddenly I was getting questions like, "How many grams of saturated fat in the Medaglione al Cognac?" I couldn't even give them a ballpark figure, so I'd have to turn to Chef Louie, who was very stressed and always a few minutes behind and apparently pinpointed the duck sauce incident as the precise moment he'd fallen off-schedule.

My section had four four-tops and a party of seven, which was a pretty good load for a trainee, and with all the questions about dishes I couldn't pronounce and "special orders" and salad dressings on the side and nonfat decaf iced lattès, I quickly got in a hole. When I finally did get around to taking the big table's drink order, I had two other tables waving to me and I was really in the weeds, so I didn't question it when the last man ordered a Bacardi cocktail for his three-year-old daughter. There were six adults and the little girl and, sensing my anxiety, they'd thoughtfully rattled off their drinks in short order and the last man said, "I'll have a vodka martini straight up and a Bacardi cocktail for the little lush here." Everyone laughed, including me, but when they returned to their conversations without clarifying the matter, I just shrugged and assumed the Bacardi was for Dad, too, and anyway a bell was ringing in the prep room and I didn't have time to argue.

When I returned with the drinks, I laid them all out and was left with the Bacardi cocktail, a fruity concoction served in a martini glass, and the man said, "That would be little Hannah's." Naturally I thought this odd, but several tables were beckoning and a row of dishes was cooling on a stainless-steel shelf in the kitchen and Louie was hotter than ever, so I put the drink down and ran off without giving it another thought. At one point I did glance over and saw Dad pouring a sugar packet into the toddler's highball—presumably she had complained about the flavor—and this helped her get it down, and when they ordered a second round, she sucked that one down, too.

When a couple of my parties had left and I had a moment to lean against the server station, I nudged a waiter named David and said, "Strangest thing. Those people over there ordered their little girl two Bacardi cocktails."

"You're not serious."

"Uh-huh. I know they do that in Texas—the old man can order booze for the kids. Something else, huh?"

He stared at me for a long time and said, "Henry, are you sure they didn't order the *Party* Cocktail?"

He opened a menu and there it was, a kiddie drink called the Party Cocktail.

My first impulse was to rush over and confess my error. David yanked me back, however, pointing out that this would do no good, the tyke was doing fine rolling around on the floor in a pile of empty sugar packets, and surely it would mean the end of my job here. And so I dropped the check off and said goodbye and thought that was the end of it, except of course David had to share his amusement with another waiter, who shared it with the busboys, who filled in the prep crew, who told the dishwashers, who regaled the cooks, who snitched to Louie, who fired my ass—not for making an innocent mistake but for not confessing my error, which of course I'd been dissuaded from doing by the motherfucking blabbermouth David.

Colleen and I were lying in bed listening to the radio. Actually, I was lying *on* the bed, which is to say, on top of the covers, and I was very annoyed. She'd granted my request to sleep in my own bed, providing that I not get under the sheets with her. So I had a blanket under me and a beach towel on top, but it seemed okay after the hard floor. The mattress was now on the floor due to a bent murphy bed frame, which had mysteriously occurred while I was at work. *"I swear on my mother's soul I didn't jump on it."* But that's not what was bugging me; it was the radio. Colleen always needed it on to sleep. Music didn't matter—she could listen to talk shows or Spanish stations or just plain static—it was the noise that comforted her. Each night, as soon as she would doze, I'd click it off, careful not to wake her. If she did awaken, she'd put it back on. This night, though, when she kept flipping through her *Psychology Today,* I killed it anyway. Colleen stared at the box.

"Hey."

I rolled over.

"I like to keep that on while I sleep," she said.

"Yeah, well, I don't. Come on, put the magazine down and turn off the light."

Surprisingly, she did.

"Thank you."

"You're the boss."

She lit a cigarette in the dark and, as was her style, smoked it like a joint. She gulped it in and held the smoke a few seconds before exhaling.

"What's with the magazines, Colleen?"

"I like them."

"Yeah . . . ?"

"My sister used to give them to me . . . Bonnie. To read. You know . . . she's the one who killed herself."

"I remember Bonnie."

"I didn't know if you remembered her name. That's the business she was in: psychology. She was good at it too, they said. Who knows? I mean, that's what they said. I guess I gotta take their word."

"Where did she work?"

"One of the colleges."

"Which one?"

"I don't remember. It begins with a U."

"UCLA?"

"Yeah. I think. She was always moving around. I know she used to work at University of Rutgers, and then I lost track."

"Were you guys close?"

"Oh, yeah. I mean, we used to be. She was my best friend when I was growing up. But then she kind of changed. The more stuff she learned, the less interesting she was."

"That happens. Do you have any idea why she did it?"

"I think she was just really sad."

"I mean beyond that. Was there a note?"

"I don't want to talk about it, it makes me want to cry."

"I'm not a psychiatrist, Colleen, but I think it's probably good to talk about things that make you want to cry—I mean, as opposed to bottling them up."

"You're right on that one—you ain't a psychiatrist. So what kind of stuff do you write anyway?"

"Um . . . comedy. I guess I'm a comedy writer."

"You don't seem like one. Tell me a joke."

"It doesn't work that way. I'm not personally funny, I just *write* funny."

"Huh?"

"You know, like situations, character stuff—not jokes."

"Like give me a for instance."

"Um, okay. Like, uh, like this screenplay I just wrote. This guy's trying to win his girlfriend back and he . . . uh . . . he . . . he does a lot of funny stuff. You'd have to read the whole script to understand."

"Oh. That sounds good."

I listened to her finish the cigarette. When she stubbed it out, she said, "I thought of one."

"Hm?"

"I thought of one of the mean things Honus did."

"Yeah?"

"Last year on my birthday, we went up to Big Bear for the weekend and stayed with some friends of his. And I was really excited 'cause we'd never taken a trip together, but the whole time he acted like I wasn't even there. And then the last day we all went out and got shit-faced. We drove all the way around the lake and we were drinking beer and everyone had to pee, so we pulled over and the guys were all writing stuff in the snow with their pee, and Honus made a big heart and put his initials inside it, so I said, 'Hey, how come you didn't put my initials in there, too?', and he says, in front of all his friends, he says, 'I ran out. But if I had to take a dump, I woulda put your name,' and they all laughed their asses off. Now, that's not something a guy who supposedly loves you says."

I could hear someone jingling keys out in the hall.

"Is it?"

"No, it's not."

"Especially on your birthday, right?"

I touched her arm. "Go to sleep," I said, and I kept my hand there until she did.

"los angeles must be stopped!" the man cried.

It was early Saturday morning—we'd been up since six—and Colleen and I were standing among a crowd of tourists listening to a sidewalk preacher in Venice Beach. Roller skaters and bicyclists zipped around us and, behind the preacher, in a concrete park, several skateboarders did tricks on small ramps for tips.

"It's killing us *all!*" the preacher continued. "It's spread to the great rain forests and the magnificent ice caps of Antarctica, and now to the fragile coral reefs, which are dying en masse for the first time in recorded history!"

A few of the tourists walked on, but Colleen and I stayed and listened, mainly because to my left stood a barefoot and slightly dirty beach girl with a tattoo on her ankle and a healthy set rolling around in a baggy T-shirt. Then, in keeping with the whole karmic thing, the preacher picked me out of the crowd.

"Do you, sir, know the average annual temperature of the water in the Caribbean Sea?"

The preacher was a scrappy old guy and slightly intimidating. He was missing most of his teeth and, from the looks of things, could probably lose the rest by biting into a banana.

I shrugged.

"Take a guess, good sir! Take a wild stab at immortality!"

"Seventy-five degrees."

"Ah, but there was a time when this was nearly true. The average temperature during the last four decades has ranged between seventy-eight-point-eight and eighty-four-point-two degrees in the good name of Fahrenheit. Guess what it is today."

Thankfully, he pointed to a bearded man with no shirt and a filthy tan. The man's corduroy shorts were bleached white, like the coral, and his legs were covered with a layer of permanent grime.

"One hundred and eight degrees," he guessed.

The preacher jumped back, appalled. "You, sir, are an idiot. Go back to your failed commune and educate yourself." He turned to

Colleen. "The average temperature this year in the Caribbean waters is eighty-nine-point-two degrees. *Eighty-nine-point-two degrees!* The coral is dying. And do you know why the coral is dying, my precious angel? Because of Los Angeles of the Californias! Smog is spewing from cities everywhere, it is warming the planet, it is killing the fish! We're burning the rain forests, just so a few men can afford money-squandering sports franchises. The world is going to end, people, and it's because Bo Jackson makes ten million dollars a year!"

"Wow," Colleen said.

I took her arm, led her away. Of all the landmarks I'd visited in L.A., Venice Beach was the biggest disappointment. I'd had images of beautiful blonde roller skaters and a happy hippie subculture. What I got was a tawdry tourist trap with rip-off artists at every scummy turn. This wasn't a sunny place, it was a dark one. Hundreds of homeless people had set up a permanent camp, and there were fifty gangsters for every cop. The roller skaters were mostly skanky, tattooed crack addicts, and if you didn't keep your eyes to yourself, you'd have some turban-headed schizophrenic rolling along beside you singing a song that only a whale could understand and demanding money to get him to shut his blowhole.

"Can you believe that Bo Jackson?" she said as we walked along. "What an asshole."

"It's a little more complicated than that."

"Not much more, I bet."

While Colleen swam, I read the sports section and checked out the topless tattoo babes nearby. I started really enjoying myself until I got hit in the face with a mouthful of water, which was doubly annoying, seeing as I was sitting about three hundred yards back from the shoreline and after traveling that far swishing about in

Colleen's cheeks, it had the consistency of egg yolk. Colleen giggled and plopped down on the newspaper, making sure to hang over me and shake like a dog first.

"Ever notice how you never see baby seagulls?"

I didn't answer, and she said, "Did you ever notice that?"

"I guess."

"Not even any halfway-grown seagulls?"

"Mm," I said.

"I have a theory. I think that baby seagulls probably lay low until they're completely grown up."

"You're really going out on a limb, aren't you?"

I put down the sports section and rolled over, facing the six bare knockers. Colleen picked up the paper.

"Want me to quiz you?" she asked.

"On what?"

"Sports."

"Sure."

"What's NBA stand for?"

"National Basketball Association. You can get trickier than that. Ask me who the top ten hitters are."

"Don't tell me what to ask. Okay, here's one: Can you tell me who the NBA's leading scorer of all-time history is?"

"Kareem."

"Kareem *what?*"

"Abdul-Jabbar."

"Right. And who's the second all-time leading scorer?"

"Wilt." She cupped her ear until I said, "Chamberlain."

"You're good," she said. "Hold it. Who's Alex English?"

"Plays for Denver."

"I never heard of him. How come he's in the top ten?"

"He's good."

"But how come Magic Johnson and Larry Bird aren't in the top ten?"

"They haven't scored as many points."

"Bullcrap. They're better than he is, any day."

"Points, this is about points."

"So you're saying Alex English is better than them? *Right.*"

"I'm saying they haven't been in the league as long, and English has been consistent."

"Oh, I suppose Magic Johnson isn't consistent?"

"Alex English has averaged twenty-five points a game for the last ten or fifteen years. That's why he's in the top ten and they're not."

She glanced suspiciously at the stats, then threw down the paper.

"That still doesn't make it right."

After Venice we hit the Universal Studios tour, which was better than I expected, except for the attraction called *Earthquake!,* which I thought in bad taste, particularly in a region where people live in fear of quakes—sort of like opening up a *Nuked!* in Hiroshima. We took Coldwater Canyon back from the Valley and went looking for the Manson house but couldn't find it. We couldn't find the Playboy Mansion, either, but we did stumble upon Ron and Nancy's retirement home while looking for Jed Clampett's place, which was another one we failed to locate. I paid two-fifty for a map of the stars' homes, but it was more for a souvenir than anything and most of the stars they listed I hadn't heard of. Finally we stopped off in Westwood at the wall Marilyn Monroe is buried in. I thought about the

RFK affair rumors and the irony of him losing his life in this city, too. It almost seemed like karma again, except I didn't believe those rumors. I heard something behind me and there was Colleen blubbering like a Middle Eastern woman, attracting curious looks from the small group of tourists gathered around Natalie Wood's headstone a few feet away. Colleen couldn't leave without throwing herself on that grave, too, which by then I was witnessing with disgust from a distance.

A moment later she came skipping across the cemetery, calling out, "Let's get a frozen yogie, Monkey!"

As we drove home, Monday suddenly seemed light-years away.

"You know what they should invent?" she said.

"What's that?"

"Windshields with subscription lenses. That way you wouldn't have to wear your glasses when you drive, but you could still see."

I looked at her. "Am I that ugly in glasses?"

"Well . . . this would be better, 'cause this way you wouldn't have to wear glasses or even contacts. Do you think Phoebe Cates is pretty?"

"Yeah."

We passed the grim reaper roller skater again, this time on Wilshire. He had the skates off and a radio to his ear, jamming away, oblivious to the fear he projected.

"You know what?" Colleen said. "I'm gonna invent it. You wait, someday I'll be rich."

"One little problem: The passengers would be getting splitting headaches."

"Not if they had the same twenty-twenty." Colleen smiled. "If I don't get a yogie soon, I'm gonna die."

She lit a cigarette, tossed the empty pack out the window.

I started to perspire. "Brilliant."

I hit the brakes, backed down Wilshire until we were beside the crumpled red-and-white ball.

"Go get it," I said.

"Why?"

"Because it's littering."

"This is a nice neighborhood, someone'll pick it up."

"I know. *You* will."

Colleen sat there hitting her smoke.

"Get out and pick it up."

When she didn't budge, I snatched the cigarette from her lips. *"Pick it up."*

"You're crazy. You almost broke my tooth."

"Just open the door and *pick it up.*"

She squinted at me. "Why are you being such a fark?!"

"A what?"

"A fark."

"A *what?*"

"A fark, a fark—a dog dink, you idiot!"

I grabbed a hunk of my own hair. "Look, either you pick it up . . . or get the hell out of this car."

There was a brief standoff, and then Colleen climbed out and folded her arms. I waited a moment, realizing I couldn't very well abandon her with her belongings back at my apartment. And then I thought, the hell with it, I'd call her bluff, and I drove the mile home without ever glancing in my rearview mirror.

———

i went for a walk along a grassy park that ran adjacent to Santa Monica Boulevard. I passed a sign that said BEVERLY HILLS—SISTER CITY OF CANNES, FRANCE. It appeared that the whole park was covered with duck shit, but it was just plugs of dirt. I saw a pay phone and called the *L.A. Times* again looking for Jenna, but the man who answered said she didn't work on Saturdays anymore. This time I left a detailed message on her voice mail, an alibi, and after I hung up, I kept walking. I saw an old ripped, weathered magazine against a fence and felt a surge of lust. A few homeless people were settling in for the night, so I kept going without checking it out. I went past Palm Drive, then Maple, then Elm. Menendez country.

I went right at Rexford, found myself in a tree-lined residential area. The air was rich with the smell of eucalyptus and freshly cut lawns. Outside a school, a group of men were playing a pickup game of basketball. I watched from behind the chain-link fence. God, I missed the game. What used to be my obsession was now my great fear. It was almost pitch-black now, but the players didn't seem to notice. It was a loud, violent game—no pure shooters, just a bunch of musclemen shoving their way inside. No one was passing, no one was firing from more than three feet away, most of the guys were plowing their way to the hole, and those who weren't didn't score. A black man with a scraggly beard and dirty work pants grabbed a rebound, took it end to end, got rejected, and called a foul. An argument ensued. It was a good call, except that no one else had been calling fouls, and there had been plenty. As the guys wandered to the sidelines, the Dirty-Work-Pants-Foulee refused to turn the ball over to the Dodger-Jersey-Fouler. "Listen to me, you motherfucker," said Work-Pants. "I lost my home, I lost my job, I lost my fuckin' old lady and babies a long time ago, so I ain't in no big rush to go anywhere, you understand? Now you can scream all night, scream till the sun comes up, you can *scream till your fuckin' throat bleeds Dodger blue,* but I ain't gonna lose this motherfuckin' argument!"

The man in the Dodger jersey saw that he was facing an asphalt filibuster, so he backed down and the game resumed. Then first time back down the court someone turned an ankle. While they checked him out, I got a rush of fear that they were going to try to recruit me, so I hurried back toward my apartment.

Herb Silverman and Tiffany were cooking popcorn and trying to convince Colleen to change her name. "Face it, you're not a Colleen," Herb said. "You're just not."

"Why not?" she asked.

"Because Colleen sucks. It's old and it means nothing and it'll only hold you back."

My phone machine was blinking, but there were just a bunch more hang-ups.

Tiffany said, "You're an actress, right, honey? Well, start acting like one and get yourself a decent name."

Turned out Tiffany's real name was Debbie and she'd changed it for the Miss New Mexico contest, which of course had paid off in spades.

"Try to think of a successful Colleen," Herb said. "They don't exist. People aren't looking for Colleens to be in their movies today, they're looking for Winonas and Kirsties and Tiffanys. Take Henry here. He's got an old-fashioned name, so he attracts old-fashioned babes. If he called himself Trent or Hunt or Trevor, I guarantee you he'd be getting laid a lot more."

"Herb isn't such a new name," I said.

He kept addressing Colleen. "I don't have to worry about getting laid, he does. Anyway, I didn't change my name to get women, I did it because Herb's a powerful name in the industry, and it's retro."

It was only eleven-thirty when I went to bed, but I was exhausted. Colleen and I hadn't spoken since the litterbug incident, and that was okay with me. Just as I fell asleep, I felt the kick. I sprang up, looked at Colleen. She was sitting up, too.

"What the fuck?" I said.

This didn't straighten the smile on her face.

"Well?" she said.

"Well, what?"

"Well?"

"Well, what?"

"Are you going to be the first?"

"Huh?"

"Are you going to be the first?"

"The first what?"

"Are you going to be the first?"

I rolled over and closed my eyes.

"Are you going to be the first?" she repeated.

I didn't answer.

"Are you going to be the first?"

"I'm not playing this game."

"Are you going to be the first?"

Five more times she assaulted me with this question. Five times I fought back the urge to boot her out of bed. Finally I sat up and faced her. "The first *what?! Am I going to be the first what?!*"

She beamed. "The first one to wish me Happy Birthday."

I looked at the clock. It read 12:03.

"No," I said and I went back to sleep.

i don't ask for much in the way of material goods. I don't need fancy clothes or nice cars or stereos or VCRs. I don't need wide-screen TVs; I don't need a television at all. I never wanted a lot of money or nice furniture or imported carpets. Fresh drinking water delivered to my apartment would be nice, but I do without. All I require is a little food and a bed and a roof over my head, and if I'm real lucky, I get to live near a respected emergency room and a pharmacy where they know my name. What I never wanted nor asked for was this woman.

But it was Sunday, and Sunday was Colleen Driscoll's birthday, and, more importantly, it was the day before Monday, which was when she was going away. And so I sucked it up all morning while she watched cartoons, and I went for a walk in the afternoon while she took in the figure-skating championships, and I even brought her back a big wedge of chocolate cake and some birthday candles and all the time she was pouting like a teenager in a jeans commercial. Because it was clear to her that this was it. There would be no reprieve tomorrow, there would be no last-minute call from the karma governor. One way or another, she was history.

It was a tremendous feeling, a sense of impending freedom, like getting extricated from a horrible marriage without even hearing from a lawyer. Rebirth. Hope. Joy. All these things I felt, and not even her petulant puss could dampen my spirits, because I was happy, happy, happy!

And then I felt a crushing pain rip through my skull, starting at one temple and exiting the other. I found myself floating off-balance, felt my eyelid rip against the corner of the coffee table, then came the nauseating blackness. I didn't know if I'd been unconscious or just in shock, but when my head cleared, I tasted blood and Colleen was kneeling beside me tugging on my sweatshirt. Cerebral aneurysm came to mind.

"911 . . ." I groaned.

"Don't worry, you'll be okay."

"Please . . . an ambulance . . ."

"Shake it off. I didn't hit you that hard."

I noticed the two-iron in her hand.

"You hit me with a golf club?"

"Gulp," she said, and she crinkled her nose.

"You hit me with a fucking golf club?!"

"I didn't mean it."

I staggered into the bathroom, examined myself in the mirror. The slice above my eyebrow looked like a fish gill—deep and red, but no blood coming out. There was also a lump blooming in front of my ear, about a half inch below my temple.

"You hit me with a fucking golf club *in the temple*," I said.

"Double gulp."

A pair of clean underwear was taped to my eyebrow and I was laying on the bed with a T-shirt full of ice cubes pressed to the side of my head when she finally put the weapon back in the bag. She pulled out my putter and lined up the balled-up sock I'd been reaching for when struck down. "Put that away," I said sharply.

She shot me a puss, dropped the club on the floor. Then she leaned against the windowsill pretending to read one of her shrink magazines.

"Pick up the golf club and put it back where you got it."

She crossed her legs, flexed her jaw muscles. This somehow pleased me; she was giving me all the ammo I needed. As if sensing this, Colleen got up and put the club away.

"Happy, Master?" On her way back to the window, she muttered, "Dink."

"What did you say?"

"You heard me."

I started to sit up, but the pain zigzagged to my forehead. "I don't believe this shit. I get clubbed in the skull with a piece of wrought iron, and *you're* pissed at *me.*"

"I said I was sorry. What do I have to do, kill myself?"

"No, you didn't say you were sorry. You *never* said you were sorry."

"Well, I am, okay? There, I said it."

"Unbelievable."

"Hey, *you're* the one who bent his head into it like a big dumb moosey-goose!"

I pulled myself up on my elbows. "Listen, lady, I live here, this is my home. I make the house rules in my home and house rule number one is that I pick up my fucking socks whenever the hell I want. Besides, I told you a million fucking times not to swing those fucking clubs in this fucking apartment!"

"That's a lie. You just said not to swing the wooden ones. And you only said that *twice!*" She made a *t*-sound. *"A million. Right."*

My head was starting to pulsate, I was seeing flashes of white, so I caved back onto the mattress. Sensing my vulnerability, Colleen sprung on me. "You're acting like a big baby! For God sakes, grow up, it's hardly even bleeding."

I got to my feet, stumbled toward her. "Zip it up, sister! I should be in a fucking emergency room, not listening to this bull-shit!"

"Nice language. Is that the only word you know?"

"Shut the fuck up, you fucking fuckhead!"

I was hoping she'd say something—*anything*—because I was ready to plow her right out that door. She managed to shut up, though, and I lay back down, and the phone rang, and it was the *L.A. Times* girl, Jenna.

What a trooper. She wasn't mad, she was concerned. The message had just gotten to her from work. How bad was the accident? Was it a head-on, was I hit from behind?

"Sideswiped," I said. "A drunk lady from New Jersey." I scowled at Colleen. "A fucking ugly one."

Jenna hesitated. "Are you okay?"

"Just a bump on the head. I'll live."

We gabbed for a while and she said we should try it again, and she said how about dinner, and how about tonight, and suddenly the pain in my brain wasn't so great. After I hung up, I told Colleen to get lost for a few hours. I didn't care what she did or where she went, but she couldn't stay here. She took this pretty well. For about ten seconds. I was in the bathroom dressing my wounds when she appeared in the doorway.

"Why do I have to go?" she said.

"Because."

"Because what?"

"Because I have plans."

"What plans?"

"None of your business what plans."

"I know you're going out to dinner with Jenny. I'm not stupid, you know. I heard you on the phone."

I didn't respond.

"I can't believe you."

"What can't you believe, Colleen?"

"I can't believe you're gonna cheat."

I turned to her. "I beg your pardon?"

"On your girlfriend."

"Let me worry about that."

She sat on the toilet, started to pee.

"So if you're going out to dinner, why can't I stay here?"

"Because I want to have my apartment available."

"Available for what?"

I noticed specks on the bathroom mirror and took Windex to them.

"Look," I said, "you can come back anytime after one. I just want to have a place to come to if the need arises."

"You mean if you get lucky."

"I mean if the need arises. Maybe she'll want to see my place, maybe we'll come back here and play Monopoly. It's none of your business."

"So why can't I be here? What's she gonna care?"

"*I'm* gonna care."

"*Why?*"

"Take a look around. Have you noticed how tiny this place is?"

Colleen tore off some paper, wiped. "So I suppose you're just gonna drop me off at the Hard Rock again like I'm some little piece of shit you can control?"

"You supposed wrong. You're walking, honey."

"Why can't you just admit it, Henry? You just want to have the place so you can fuck her."

"What happened to the country bumpkin who showed up here a few days ago?"

"Admit it, you're gonna fuck her, aren't you?"

"That's right! I'm gonna fuck her, I'm gonna jam her till the cows come home, I'm gonna *bone her brains out,* okay?"

"Fine, Henry, just fine," and she walked out of the bathroom without flushing.

before meeting jenna at the restaurant, I stopped at "The Car Wash of the Stars" in West Hollywood. A Mexican man sold me on the twelve ninety-five special, which included Armor All, and asked if I also wanted car freshener.

"Sure," I said.

"Lemon, cherry, piña colada, new car, or mint?"

"What would you use?" I asked, which was a mistake.

While I waited for my car, I bought a tin of Altoids and an oldies tape called *Freedom Rock.* I checked out the photos of the stars who washed their cars there. It's amazing how many stars there are that you've never heard of.

Jenna Weingarten was one year out of the UCLA masters program in journalism. The *L.A. Times* job was a disappointment—she wanted to write stories, not answer phones—but at least it put her on the right track and she expected to be promoted in a year or two. She was strange-looking, almost ugly—the nose was big, the teeth slightly horsey, the lower lip droopy, the upper one too thin—but they'd all fallen together miraculously, and she was indisputably beautiful.

"Know why I decided to go out with you again?" she asked as our salads were being delivered. No alcohol was served here, so we drank water from Northern California.

"Not a clue," I said, and the waitress threw me a smirk.

"Because when I was driving home the night we were supposed to go out, I saw two streetlights blink off. I believe in signs. Streetlights don't just turn on and off by themselves. So I figured maybe someone was trying to tell me something."

"That's why you decided to give me another shot, because a couple streetlights didn't work?"

"Uh-huh."

I ate my salad and considered this.

"Do you think that's weird?" she asked.

"Yeah, kind of."

She studied the welt on my forehead. "Ooh, that looks like it hurt. You must've hit the steering wheel pretty hard."

"Yeah, well, not as bad as it looks."

"Your car seems all right."

"Wasn't my car. A friend's."

"Oh, no. Was he mad?"

"He was driving."

"Then how'd you hit your head on the steering wheel?"

I sniffed out a laugh. "Yeah. See, we got sideswiped from the left and I went flying toward him and cracked my head."

"You weren't wearing a seatbelt?"

"We'd just gotten in. I was putting it on—what are you, from the insurance company?"

"Sorry. Reporter at heart."

We talked about movies and she was riled up about Arnold Schwarzenegger claiming he wasn't responsible for the violence in his films. He said it was "Hollywood" who made the movies and he was just an actor. "Right," she said, "and Auschwitz was just a bakery." When Jenna found out I'd lived in Boston, she told me she'd been there while checking out grad schools, but the place was too racist for her—"just look at the Celtics"—and anyway New York was the only city she could see herself living in on the East Coast, with the possible exception of Washington. I knew it was hopeless trying to defend Boston to a Laker fan, but I pointed out that the Celts were the first team to hire a black head coach and let it go at that. Jenna told me about her trip to New York—how she'd discovered the best places to get bagels and pizza and Thai food and leather. I listened attentively until she mentioned the crush she had on Leonard Bernstein, at which point I changed the subject.

I spoke of the dizzy spells I'd been experiencing the last couple months, throwing in a half dozen or so of my prognoses, ranging from an inner ear problem to too much sugar to Ménière's syndrome. She suggested I visit a physician, but I waved her off bravely, saying it would probably go away on its own. What I didn't tell her was that I was certain as we spoke that I had a tumor sitting in my skull the size and consistency of the avocado she was devouring.

Jenna had just been to the doctor and he'd taken blood tests that left her arm black-and-blue like a junkie's. I didn't ask what the tests were for, but she quickly offered, "Don't worry, I don't have AIDS. They just wanted to see if I was hypoglycemic."

This AIDS remark was encouraging, the inference being that she didn't want me to count her out as a possible sexual partner. Then she took it a step further and asked if I was seeing anyone.

"I was, back in Boston, but no more."

"Why'd you break up?"

"I don't know. I live here, she lives there. Too difficult, I guess."

As we ate in silence, I thought about the best way to answer this in the future.

"I'm seeing someone," Jenna said.

I was surprised by the stab I felt. What a pussy. For God sakes, I hardly knew her.

"So you're cheating on me?"

"I was going to go out with him tonight, if we didn't go out."

"You mean you had a Plan B?"

"Actually, he was Plan A."

"Ow."

"I'm just being honest, Henry. You could never accuse me of being dishonest."

"Or tactful."

When she didn't defend herself, I said, "Let me ask you something: Why do people always say things like that to me? I mean, everyone's nice to everyone else, but when it comes to me, I don't get the gentle brush and the sugarcoating, I just get the hard ugly . . ."

"Truth?"

"Yeah."

"Probably because you can take it. That's what I like about you."

This took the wind out of my sails, and I hardly touched my meal. She was eating asparagus and mentioned how it affects one's urine odor. I sensed that she wasn't having the time of her life, so I tried to force the fun by steering the conversation, and of course nothing came of this except a kind of canned dialogue that I would wince at later.

Seeing as the night had taken an ugly turn, I suggested we move things back to my place, where I hoped a little alcohol might reunite us.

She said, "I have to get up early for work."

"I'll have you home first thing in the morning."

She wasn't amused, but I persisted and she caved.

Back at the Blue Terrace, I poured two triple vodkas, which I sweetened and colored with OJ and limes and disguised in tall glasses. It occurred to me I might never see this woman again, so I decided to get to the point.

"What's the shortest you ever knew someone before you slept with them?" I asked.

To my surprise, she didn't balk.

"Slept?"

"You know . . ."

"Gone all the way? I don't know, probably a month or so."

"Hm."

"What does 'H m m m' mean?"

"I didn't say, 'H m m m', I said, 'Hm.' "

"What does 'Hm' mean?"

"That's kind of a long time."

"A month is a long time?"

"Well, for your all-time shortest, it is."

"You said *all the way.* There *are* other avenues of expression. But the truth is I didn't lose my virginity until I was a junior in college. And that was to a guy I thought I was going to marry."

"What happened to him?"

"Nothing. We just grew apart—we're still good friends."

"And did you enjoy sex at first?"

"Loved it," she said pointedly. "I'm very sexual, Henry, don't get me wrong. I've been having orgasms since I was eleven—I just don't like to fuck for the sake of fucking."

"Why not?" When she shot me a look, I quickly said, "Where'd you have your first orgasm?"

"None of your business."

"In the bathtub?"

(Where Amanda had hers.)

"No!"

"Well, where?"

"Boy, are you nosy."

"Hey, I'm a writer, too."

Jenna resqueezed the lime, licked her fingers. "I can't believe I'm telling you this. If you must know, I was on my horse."

"You're kidding!" A bit too enthusiastically.

She blushed.

"Please tell me everything—from the beginning."

"Why are you so interested in my orgasms?"

"Well . . . come on."

She flipped off her shoes, pulled her legs up on the couch.

"It was great," she said. "I was on my horse Bakey, just riding around, and I felt pretty good down there, like I think all girls do when they ride. And as I bounced around, the feeling just got better and better, and I leaned into Bakey and it felt better and better, and I pushed down and it was even better . . . and then it happened."

I took a gulp of vodka, chewed some ice. "Jenna, was this horse by chance on its back?"

When she gave me a playful slap, her proximity permitted me to pull her close and I stabbed her ear with my tongue, then rolled her on top of me on the couch. This would allow her to feel in control, even though my hand was suddenly under her shirt stroking the smooth of her back, and my knee was working her like old Bakey.

"That feels good," she said, and I began to grind my leg into her a little harder.

"My back," she said. "Why don't you give me a massage?"

I stayed on the couch and Jenna sat on the floor in front of me. First I squeezed her neck and the muscles around it, then I worked my way down both sides of her spine, one vertebra at a time. As I did this, I softly brushed my tongue over her neck. When Jenna dropped her head and let out a low moan, I ran my fingertips lightly up the inside of her arm. She seemed to be letting go, so I gambled and slid my hand over her right breast.

"What are you doing?" she asked.

"Releasing tension."

"I'm not tense there."

"Mine."

"Henry, I should warn you right now. My goal is to be out of this room in fifteen minutes."

"Then let's get crackin'."

We began to make out and as I pulled her on top of me, she quite naturally positioned herself over my knee and we were off to the races. As I yanked her shirt over her head, she said, "You don't know anything about me."

"I know you've got great tits."

I moved my mouth to the pink and faint blue of her breast.

"You don't even know my birthday."

She started unbuttoning my shirt.

"When's your birthday?" I asked.

"July tenth."

I started unbuckling her pants while I worked her neck.

"And where do you live?"

"Hancock Park."

I slid my hand into her panties and she opened her mouth.

"Do you like it there?" I asked.

She arranged herself on my finger and slowly nodded.

The phone rang once, the answering machine clicked on, Colleen's voice: "Hi, it's me. I was just wondering if you were through *'boning your date's brains out,'* as you so nicely put it—"

I managed to punch the machine off at that point, glancing back just in time to see Jenna Weingarten getting up off the floor—where I'd thrown her in my haste—pulling on her shirt, grabbing her bag and shoes, and storming past me with a snortiness that would have cleared the streets of Pamplona.

I chased her down to the car, but there wasn't really much I could say other than "Let me explain," and of course I was glad she didn't. I ended up standing on Doheny Drive in my bare feet watching her Alfa hang a left onto Beverly Boulevard, and then I listened to it rev away toward the safety of the Hancock Park apartment I would never see.

neither of us spoke much on the way to the bus station Monday morning. I had already given Colleen the eighty-dollar fare to New York, which she'd snapped out of my hand with a grunt. She was too pouty to talk, and I was too pissed off and dizzy to force the conversation. At first she'd refused my generosity, saying she'd prefer to wait for "those idiots" at Western Union "to get their shit together." After the previous evening's horror show, there was no way in hell I was permitting her to stay another night in my apartment, but I humored her by agreeing that Western Union was indeed a fly-by-night operation—had been for over a hundred years—and insisting she take my money because the fools might never come through. When she still declined my "charity," I told her not to be silly, that I fully expected remuneration when she landed on her feet back in New Jersey, that I knew she was good for it.

I didn't anticipate ever seeing the girl or cash again. I wanted her out of town, out of my life. Nevertheless, she made a production of writing down my number, which I dictated with little enthusiasm. It was a write-off, I figured, and a damn wise one. I'd rather lose my phone, get evicted, even starve before I'd spend another night with this checkerboard-square monster.

"Why does it stink like a piña colada in here?" she asked.

"I happen to like the smell."

I double-parked in front of the bus station, carried her bags into the terminal. The bus was due in on schedule in forty-five minutes, which pleased me. Something about the cavernous room and the sad-looking people kick-started my vertigo, so our goodbye was brief.

I put her bags down in the middle of the room, shook her hand.

"Well . . . so long," she said.

"Yeah."

As I turned, she said, "By the way, I thought of another."

"What?"

"You know, another shitty thing Honus did."

"Yeah?" I said absently.

She sat on a bench beside a young black woman.

"He never thanked me for nothin'. I did a lot for that guy. I mean *everything*. He didn't know anyone when I met him. He couldn't even hardly speak English. He was all alone before he met me. All alone. One thank you, that's all I was asking for . . . but I never got it."

Her eyes started to well up, but she may as well have been picking her nose and flicking it at me, for all the sympathy I felt.

"He could've at least said *danke*."

"Yeah, well . . . I'll see you."

"Will I? See you?"

I scratched my head. "No."

"Well . . . thanks for helping my sister."

At the door I glanced back at Colleen sitting there on the bench, all *Hee Haw*ed up in another pretty country dress, her hair pulled back in a ponytail—not an L.A. ponytail with the hair on top, but hanging from the back of her head like they used to wear it— quietly reading her *Psychology Today* like a thoughtful, sedate, guile- less little angel. The image that came to mind was of those fancy deep-sea fishing lures—all frilly and happy and bright and fun-look- ing, and deadlier than a silo full of strychnine.

four

spring wasn't particularly noticeable in Los Angeles. Except for an occasional blue street, slick from the fallen petals of the jocaranda trees, and a ghostly fog that haunted each morning and was exorcised by noon, it seemed just like winter. Spring, though, had come to my heart. I'd fixed *How I Won Her Back* to my agent's specifications and had begun another spec script. I was getting used to the hamburg flipper uniform and the compassionate stares from the customers at Johnny Rockets, where I was now assistant grill man to a seventeen-year-old dad named Kelvin. Levine was doing his job, too. He had me making the rounds, getting to know execs and producers who liked *How I Won Her Back.* Strange meetings.

One was with Rodney Dangerfield. He wanted someone to re-write a script he'd written about a schmuck who becomes a great opera singer when he drinks wine. It was a comedy and it had its moments, but I told him it could be funnier and the wine thing was confusing. "I'm not clear why it makes him sing so well," I said. "Is it a particular wine, or just any wine? Is it magic wine?"

"How the hell do I know?" he said. "It's a movie, for Christ sakes! How do you shrink your fucking kids?"

Most of the studio execs I met were young educated males. There were female execs, too, but they didn't seem interested in comedies, at least not the ones I was writing. The execs paid me compliments, we talked about back East, and then I'd leave. Sometimes there were brief queries of what I was working on, or they'd mention one of their projects, usually a rewrite, but no offers. There were plenty of irons in the fire, though, and this gave me hope, which is often more inspiring than success itself.

When I found out that Letterman was looking for top ten list writers, I was quick to apply. To prove that I could be topical and, more importantly, fast, I found a news item in the morning paper, wrote a top ten list, and had Levine fax it to New York that afternoon. The article was just a blurb, really, about how some radio stations were refusing to allow the band name Butthole Surfers to be spoken on the air. I came up with *Top Ten New Names for the Butthole Surfers,* which went as follows:

10.) Megadump
9.) The Spastic Colons
8.) The Dan Quail Surfers
7.) Collonica
6.) Public Enema
5.) Stool Sample
4.) Salt and Sphincta

3.) The Turdles

2.) The Traveling Dingleberries

1.) The World's Most Dangerous Gland

Never heard from them.

Didn't matter, nothing was going to get me down. I was free of the woman. Free! I practically skipped down the street, smiling at strangers, picking up more litter than usual, giddy over my new independence. I was putting down five pages a day on the average. Writing late at night, I would sleep until noon, grab a quick workout at the Beverly Hills Health and Fitness (ninety-nine bucks a year and not even in Beverly Hills), read the paper over a sandwich, then start writing again. At five I'd take a walk in the park off Santa Monica Boulevard. The homeless would be setting up camp for the evening. Armies of Central American maids stood silently at the bus stops. A couple times I tried to speak to them, but they just smiled at my broken Spanish and said nothing. I figured they didn't like to talk, because I never saw them speak to each other, either.

At six I'd go to work at Rockets, return around eleven, shower, watch the news, write for an hour, watch Letterman, write for another few hours. When I crawled into bed, I felt at peace. It was the first time in my life I'd really gone for something, put my soul on the line. As the sky started to lighten each morning, I was full of the satisfaction that comes with courageous efforts. But just as the dark hours unleashed imagination and optimism, the noon sun greeted me like a line drive in the face. I would awaken in fear, wondering if I was just a megamaniacal fool who had nothing to say, who had no right to write. Fortunately, these doubts would fade as the day progressed, and by evening I was inspired and feeling sufficiently immodest to write again.

Discipline was key. When the urge to meet women struck, I'd drop fifty cents on a porno newspaper and put an end to that. I'd never had much guilt about masturbating, but now I actually derived a degree of pride from it. I knew it was the right thing to do and spanking it became as vital to my routine as writing and working out.

I tried calling Jenna Weingarten a few times, with no response. A couple afternoons I had the notion to drive to the *Times* building to see her in person, but I chickened out.

One day I decided that I wasn't well read, so I went to the library, found three famous relatively short books, and spent the weekend reading them. On Friday I drank several cups of coffee and stayed up all night fighting my way through *Rabbit, Run*. I kept a dictionary beside me and looked up every unknown word and wrote the definitions on a piece of paper. *Rabbit* was jammed with the densest prose I'd ever seen and I felt proud and sophisticated, not simply for reading it but for loving it. Saturday when I awakened I got in the tub and stayed there until the water was as gray and cold as a November Boston sky and I'd hit the century mark of *The Great Gatsby*. A few hours after my supper shift, I was so flushed from having read two books in two days that I dove right into *Lolita* and got about seventy-five pages under my belt before nodding out at dawn. "My mother died in a freak accident. (Picnic, lightning.)" God, I loved that. I continued reading without ever getting out of bed on Sunday and by 9 P.M. I was finished and my brain so addicted to the written word that I ran out to Book Soup to seek out one more thin celebrated novel.

Walking down Sunset, I approached a man who appeared to have his arms behind his back, but upon closer inspection had no arms at all. When I realized this, I glanced away, but it was too late, he'd nailed me—it was midgetville all over again—and I was pissed for not knowing how to act around people who were different. He was probably immune to the gawks by now, that's how I tried to rationalize it, and then I said the hell with it, I wasn't going to let this hang over me, so I spun around and caught up to him.

"Excuse me," I said. "Can I ask you a question?" He didn't answer, but stopped walking, so I said, "I just moved here and I can't find a decent fucking bookstore. How's Book Soup?"

The "fuck" was for effect; I wasn't going to treat him with kid gloves, just because he didn't have arms. Again he didn't answer and I repeated the question, this time without the "fuck," and finally he said, "Book Soup is a marvelous bookstore. It's very good."

I nodded and he moved on and it hadn't gone the way I wanted, so I gave chase. "Hey!" I said. I ran past him and he was a little nervous now (what with his limited defenses), so I quickly said, "Look, like I said, I just moved here and, uh, someone gave me a couple tickets to the Dodgers, and I don't really know anyone and, I don't know, you want to go?"

"Dodgers?"

"Yeah."

"No."

"How about the Angels? Maybe we'll catch Jim Abbott."

I honestly didn't make the connection until I got to "Jim Ab . . ." By then it was too late. I had just asked one of the two armless guys in L.A. if he wanted to watch the other one pitch. "Or, uh, or, uh, someone . . . whoever."

By then he was off again, with a brisker pace, and I knew that was that, so I just blocked the whole thing out and continued on to Book Soup.

The novel I purchased was *The End of the Road* by John Barth, which wasn't famous but was short and was recommended by the pretty cashier. I didn't put it down until I finished at 6 A.M., at which point I calculated that I'd read approximately forty percent of the books in my lifetime during that one exhilarating weekend.

after another fruitless meeting, I bought a smoked turkey and coleslaw sandwich and ate it between the baby World Trade Center towers that are the crown jewels of Century City. The concrete was loaded with suits. Lawyers, stockbrokers, and entertainment execs, I presumed. The place, this miniature metropolis, was amazingly clean—it looked more like a movie set than a city. Somebody's assistant, a fresh young beauty straight out of Central Casting, sat down beside me and started eating her lunch. Suddenly I felt good about being single and unattached, able to lust after this woman without guilt. It gave me a happy feeling to know that anything could happen, the possibilities were boundless, we could fall in love, or she could just blow me, and then I realized nothing was going to happen unless I did something fast. Surely one of her coworkers was on the way, or some scoundrel would zoom in and lay on his slimy moves. But how to break the ice? Everything seemed obvious, awkward. I saw another young man approaching, white deli bag in tow, ostensibly looking for someplace to sit, clearly up to no good.

"Excuse me," I said. "Do I have something in my eye?"

When she looked up from her salad, I was pulling on my eyelid, my left eye crossed, revealing the bulbous white of the back of my eyeball, along with the pink tint coming from the inside of my skull. When she didn't answer, I blinked a few times.

"Is there a lash or something in there?" I asked.

Finally she stood and examined me.

"No," she said, "I don't see anything in your eye . . . but there's something in your teeth."

I sent a spritz jetting through them and felt the dislodged leaf with my tongue.

"Thanks."

After a minute of uninspired small talk, I said I was late for a meeting, and then, unjustifiably buoyed by her forced smile, turned back and asked for her number. She looked as if I were asking her to join the Manson Family. I finally managed to wangle her work number out of her, but this I quickly forgot, as I knew she had no interest in ever hearing my voice again, and she wasn't so hot to begin with.

I was in an elevator going down to get my car when the man beside me spoke.

"Keds?"

When I looked over, I couldn't believe it.

"Excuse me?" I said.

"Are those Keds?"

Sometimes when you see famous people in person, they look completely different. Robert Redford didn't. He looked just like Robert Redford, and he was gesturing toward my sneakers.

"Uh, no. Cons."

He smiled at them. "When I was a kid, I used to love those."

I nodded. "Yeah."

There were a million things I wanted to say, but I reminded myself not to be a "fan" and kept my mouth shut. The elevator doors opened. Sundance and I headed into the parking lot.

"So you a writer or an actor?"

"Writer," I said.

"What's the script?"

I almost spit up a laugh. This was getting ridiculous, he was asking me about my script.

"It's called *How I Won Her Back.*"

"Good title."

Suddenly a rush of adrenaline. What an opportunity! I should ask him to read it, he'd be perfect for the lead. He was a little older than I'd envisioned, but it could be rewritten.

Then I saw what a fuckhead I was being. Every scumball who met him probably felt the exact same things. *What an opportunity! What could he do for me? How could I have a piece of him?* It was a slimy sensation. He was being a regular Joe, I shouldn't ruin it for him. If everyone he talked to hit him up for favors, he'd never talk to anyone. He'd turn into Howard Hughes or Michael Jackson. He'd be a freak.

"Will you take a look at my script?"

It was insidious, this power he possessed, the ability to green-light movies. This was the corrupting aspect of Hollywood. I was experiencing it firsthand, the chipping away of my soul.

"Please read it," I said. "It's really good."

"Why don't you submit it to Sundance?" Redford said. "We have a young writers' contest every year. If it's good, you may win."

He was adroit at deflecting assholes like me. A punch in the face wouldn't have gotten his point across better.

"If you write honestly," he said, "then you're a good writer and you'll succeed."

I thought about the *L.A. Times* magazine piece. Honest it wasn't. Honest would have complicated it. Honest would have announced to the world that I was a coward, not a hero. I asked him how the film festival had gone that year. This was obviously some-thing he liked talking about because he stopped in his tracks and told me about it for forty-five minutes. Occasionally someone would walk by and gawk, and every ten minutes I had to fight back a new urge to force my script on him. But we stood there and chatted about his film festival and institute, and when I ran out of questions, we shook hands and he wished me the best, and I drove out of there thinking I'd just met one of the greatest guys in the world.

i called the Greater Los Angeles Big Brothers Association and asked what I had to do to get involved. They sent me an application several pages long, which I fastidiously filled out and promptly re-turned. A week later I got a phone call saying I'd been approved for a preliminary interview. When I questioned the "preliminary" part, a man sternly explained that the screening process would involve several detailed interviews, as well as a psychological evaluation, and could take up to six months. This was a disappointment, as I'd envisioned myself playing catch with the little tyke out in Will Rog-ers State Park any day now, but given the state of the world and the man's tone, I couldn't argue.

On the morning of my first interview, I put on my salesman suit and left early to drive to Big Brothers. Unfortunately, the offices were downtown and what normally would be a twenty-minute drive took over an hour and I showed up fifteen minutes late. The middle-aged woman who interviewed me was very tall, with brittle yellow hair. Despite my tardiness, she was cordial, unlike the man on the phone who'd made me feel as if I were calling from NAMBLA. She inquired about my personal life, my family, the girlfriend I'd referred to in my application, but I knew I couldn't tell her the truth, that I had no one, it was pathetic, not to mention the red flag it would raise. I didn't care to talk about Amanda, though, she was still a sore subject, so I went on and on about the former figure-skating champion I was dating—living with actually. I thought it kind of ironic that psycho girl was servicing me in some way—karma strikes again—and of course this thought reversed my karma when a moment later Margo Jones was demanding a name and I saw her write down *Colleen Driscoll* and she asked when was the best time she could interview this girlfriend of mine on the phone.

So the Big Brothers were history and on the way home I started not to care. I guess I could've coached Tiffany into playing the Colleen Driscoll role for a half hour, but even then I was looking at a half year before I could hook up with my kid. The hell with the Big Brothers, I decided to take a crack at the Best Buddies program instead. They were newer, probably not as bogged down with bureaucracy.

At a red light I saw a guy about my age crossing the street with his three kids. Suddenly it occurred to me: *Why didn't I have kids?* Forget the fact that I wasn't married or attached in any way, but why hadn't I ever gotten anybody pregnant? Most of my friends growing up had, at one time or another. I'd been with enough girls in those pre-AIDS days when precautions were seldom taken. I used to think I was just lucky, but now I wondered. Could I be shooting blanks?

I stopped at a phone booth, called Dr. Hoffman, asked him to recommend a urologist.

"Why?" he asked.

"Piss-stinger."

"What?"

"It stings when I piss."

This was to get on my old Ernesto's insurance plan. Twenty minutes later I was sitting in one of Cedars Sinai's black medical towers talking to Dr. Gerald Stein. He was kind to take me without an appointment, I said, and I bullshitted him a little about the alleged painful urination before matter-of-factly inquiring, since I was there, how would I go about getting a sperm count done? Well, nothing in life is free, and even though the insurance company would indeed cover my visit, I couldn't wangle my way out of Dr. Stein's office without first having him plunge the world's huskiest finger up my keister. He massaged my startled prostate until a dewdrop of cum dripped from my screaming urethra onto a slab of glass. I did, however, leave there with a sperm count instruction sheet and a small plastic cup, as well as a tremendous piss-stinger, for real this time.

That day on my machine I had another message from the Gus guy. He "desperately" wanted me to call him back about the suicide woman, he said. He needed "information." Around seven the phone rang again and I was afraid to answer.

"Adam Levine calling for Henry Halloran," a woman said.

I picked up. "This is he."

I was put on hold for five minutes, then Levine's new assistant Sheri came back. "I'm sorry, Henry. Adam's going to have to call you back. He picked up another line."

"I'll be here."

At 7:45 she called back and a moment later connected me with Levine in his car.

"Sonya Abrams in Ted Bowman's office called. I gave her your script over the weekend and she loved it."

"Great."

"Don't get your hopes up. I'm not so sure you want to be in business with this guy."

"Why not?"

"Bad guy."

"How bad?"

"Bad."

"Asshole?"

"If you go by all your senses alone, yeah. But he does get movies made."

"How bad we talking?"

"Hitler without the conscience."

"Nice."

"The worst human being in Hollywood, hands down."

"Give me an example."

"He's been married seven times, he still does blow, he's fucked every actress who's ever worked for him, he also fucks boys; for that matter, he's fucked everybody he ever knew in one way or another, he takes months to read scripts—"

"Months?!"

Levine laughed, then he wasn't there. As I hung the phone up, it rang. "Sorry," he said, "I'm going over Coldwater. Bowman's also been known to punch out writers for turning in bad scripts or late scripts or—"

"But he gets movies made?"

"He made *Coma Cop.*"

"Set it up."

"Are you sure?"

"Levine, I haven't had a decent meeting in five weeks. Why the hell wouldn't I want you to set up a meeting with a guy who gets movies made?"

"All right, but I warned you."

"I've been warned."

Levine's voice started to break up. "I'm losing you again. I'll have Sheri call you with the details."

This Ted Bowman meeting wasn't the greatest thing that ever happened to me, but it was something to talk about, so I tried Jenna again at the *Times* and to my surprise she picked up. She was chilly and accepted my apology but wouldn't allow me to explain.

"It's not what it seems."

"Just let it go, Henry."

I was pleased to do this.

"Maybe we should go out again," I said.

"Maybe we shouldn't."

"Right, but maybe we should."

"And I say we shouldn't."

"I can give you two 'shoulds' for every one of your 'shouldn'ts.' "

"Not interested in hearing them."

"Why don't we just go to lunch this week?"

"My lunches are booked."

"Then how about—"

"Dinners, too."

"I was going to say breakfast."

"Don't eat breakfast."

"Midnight snack?"

"I'm going to hang up."

"Would you just hold on a second?"

She hung up. I waited twenty minutes to call back. It was a head fake, gave her time to cool down. She was laughing as she answered.

"Give me a chance to explain what happened."

"You don't have to. I can figure it out myself."

"Believe it or not, I have an explanation. It's not pretty, but please listen to it."

"I'm really busy."

"Wait a second. You're a journalist, aren't you? Be a little open-minded here."

"Let me put this another way: I wasn't that interested in you to begin with."

"Oh, that felt good."

"I'm just being honest, Henry. But even though I wasn't that interested, there was something about you I found entertaining. So I decided to give you a chance. I gave you *two* chances. And what happened? First you stand me up altogether—granted, that one wasn't your fault—and then you try to—"

"No, I didn't. That's what I'm trying to tell you. I just told her that to get rid of her. I didn't really expect . . ."

"Me to be such a slut?"

"Don't be sexist—I was doing it, too. Now, come on, I want to see you again, we have a lot in common."

"Yeah? What?"

"Well . . . we both aspire to write, we . . . we want to write . . . well, we probably have a lot more in common than you know about. Go ahead, ask me my opinion on anything, I'll bet we're in agreement."

"What do you think of synchronized swimming?"

"Stupidest thing I've ever seen."

"I think it's great."

"I mean stupid in the sense that it's only on during the Olympics. It should be televised weekly, like *Monday Night Football.*"

"See?"

"You can't really like that shit."

"Wrong again, Hank. I think it's beautiful. It's like ballet, except there's competition and pressure and winners and losers. I like that."

"Maybe you're right, maybe we shouldn't go out. I mean if we both don't like synchronized swimming, what kind of future would we have?"

She sniffed.

"So that's it, huh?"

"Look, I'm sure your friends think you're a great guy—"

"Stop it. I liked you better when you were tactless."

"You didn't let me finish."

She giggled, which irritated me; a mini-Amanda scene.

She said, "I knew we had nothing in common when I saw that your bed was on the floor."

"Really?"

"That says a lot about a guy."

"You know what it tells me? It tells me the guy's bed frame is fucking bent. Where do you come up with these things anyway? Remember you told me the only reason I got a second chance was because a couple streetlights blinked off on your way home? It must've meant something, huh?"

"Whatever."

"I got news for you, Jenna. It meant your headlights are pointing up. Those streetlights have sensors. They're affected by light— sunlight preferably—but crooked headlights turn them off, too. So you can get your high beams fixed and stop reading so damn much into your stupid signs."

"Are you through?"

"Yes."

"Then goodbye."

"Okay."

I hung up and looked at the phone. But of course it didn't ring.

the next morning I pumped a dollop into the cup Dr. Stein had given me and trudged out the door to stay inside the twenty-minute delivery time allotted for an accurate sperm count. Herb Silverman was out front catching rays again. He held up a beer. "Hey, fucky! Let's chase pussy tonight!" I waved my sperm and pretended not to hear.

As I was getting out of my car on Third Street, she walked past sipping a cardboard cup of coffee. Shiny brown hair, eyes like Amanda's, presumably a great body disguised in loose jeans and a Northwestern sweatshirt.

"Nice shirt," she said.

I was wearing a T-shirt that said FAILURE. (A band.) I probably could have sucked it up and gotten over her, if only she hadn't caught me glancing back and thrown me the smirk. The jiz sample was rapidly cooling, but I was sick about this girl, so I popped into a market, all the time keeping an eye on her. I grabbed a newspaper and a cellophane-sealed hunk of oat bran, held out a handful of change, which the clerk graciously counted out for me while I watched Miss Northwestern cross the street. She stopped in front of a community center. Five or six people were hanging around smoking. What the hell kind of group was this, and could I join? Then I got it. What else would a bunch of cigarette-smoking, coffee-guzzling twenty-seven-year-olds be doing at eleven o'clock on a Saturday morning in L.A.?

AA.

Perfect. I *could* join them.

A man with a red beard poked his head out, said something, and they all followed him back in. For a moment I envied them their addictions, not just because it put them in the room with Miss Northwestern. I imagined how great it would be to simplify my problems, to narrow it down to one thing, to know that if I could just knock off the booze or the drugs or the kleptomania or the food, everything would be okay.

I stood across the street, pretending to peruse the front page, trying to get up the courage to join them. This would be good for me, anything to get my mind off Amanda and Jenna. I knew it was undignified, but surely I wouldn't be the only randy sot in there trying to get pooned. Hollywood AA meetings were legendary meat markets.

A compromise: I'd check Boggsie's stats. Three or more hits and I'd go in. Less and I'd hit the road. I peeked into the sports section: three for five and Roger got the win. I placed my sperm in the car and ran across the street.

As I walked in, all heads turned my way. More heads than I'd anticipated. Fifty at least, almost all of them young and, for drunks, healthy-looking. I didn't see my girl—I didn't see anything. A burst of stage fright hit me, tunnel vision ensued. I needed to find a seat and hunker down. The stares didn't quit, but I tried to calm myself. We were all in the same boat—addicts—they'd each had to enter this room for the first time, too. I climbed over ten people to reach the lone empty folding chair. As soon as I got settled, Red Beard, standing up front, apparently the soberest of them all, spoke: "Excuse me, can I help you?"

It dawned on me that maybe these people *didn't want me here.*

Maybe they'd all started out together and felt comfortable confessing their alcohol-and-cocaine-and-crystal-meth-and-I-stole-Mom's-china stories to each other, but didn't welcome a stranger in their midst.

"Um, I just want to sit in . . . if that's okay."

Tee-hees from all sides.

Beard peered over his glasses. "Do you know what we're doing here?"

The tunnel vision narrowed. I could only see the man's eyes now; I mustered a lame shrug.

"Traffic school," he said.

My humiliation turned the room into a dungeon of laughs.

I worked my way back through the room of speeders and red light runners. At the door I glanced over my shoulder and magically locked eyes with the Northwestern one. She shook her head, amazed by my stupidity.

Outside I waited around reading the paper, insanely hoping that she'd come looking for me. After a few minutes, I knew it wasn't going to happen and realized that if I didn't hit the road, I was going to scare the shit out of her. My twenty minutes were up, the sperm was dead; I tossed the plastic cup into the backseat with all my other garbage and drove off.

I was still jacked up from my close call with the girl, so when I got home I made plans to hit the town with Silverman later on. Inside I had a few more hang-ups on my machine. Gus, I presumed. I read the paper, wrote for a few hours, put the notebooks back in the fridge, then showered and cut open my toothpaste tube to scrape out one last gob. I ate a chunk of cheese and an apple, put on pleated slacks, my FLOYD THE BARBER T-shirt, and a sport coat. I returned to Carl's Market but balked at the prices. Eight-ninety-five for deodorant? I should get my sweat glands removed for that. I ducked down in the aisle, drenched my pits with Ban Basic neutral scent. Flipping through a few magazines, I found one with an interesting cologne and folded the page around my neck. Hopeful now, I grabbed a box of Tic Tacs, dropped by the condom display. Prices had zoomed. The latex ones were in twelve-packs and went for around ten dollars. Extra-thick heavyweight lambskins were cheaper, but you might as well wear a batting doughnut. I busted open a carton of Trojans, taking out just one. I grabbed two beers, headed for the counter. A knockout at the register. Suddenly a lone rubber seemed pathetic. I considered going back for the extra-large ones, but sucked up the courage to face her. She looked at the two beers and the rubber and said, "Good for you. Everything in moderation."

We took Sixth Street, passing through Hancock Park (Jenna country), then Koreatown, then a Spanish neighborhood where crowds of people stood around, apparently doing nothing. Silverman pointed out a place called Maria's Donuts and Chinese Food, which I wanted to stop at, but we kept going until we got to an art deco diner car full of upscale, self-conscious artsy types, mostly male with stand-up-comic-style suits and greased-back ponytails. It was a "pecker party," Silverman said, so we downed our drinks and drove to a large warehouse in the skid row area for a "concert."

This was the kind of crowd where in a half hour you could round up a dozen people to go on a homicidal spree. A band called Sandy Duncan's Eye was screaming out something on a stage in the corner, but nobody was paying much attention. Everyone was dressed in black, like a convention of clergy, but these clerics wore low-cut blouses or just bras, and although they were in agreement about style, no one seemed happy about it.

"This is a pretty good concert," Herb said, "except for one thing."

"The band?"

"It's too fucking dark to see who's here."

"Let's go," I said. "I want to get something to eat."

"Eatin's cheatin'."

"But I'm starved."

"There's a pork chop in every drink."

The draft beer was served in cheap paper cups that stood up to liquid about as well as a Communion wafer. Within minutes my fingers were through and then the bottom gave out onto my shoes.

"Come on, this place sucks."

"You'll do fine here."

"I don't want to do fine here."

As if on cue, Sandra Bernhard walked by.

"Look," Silverman said.

He stretched out his neck and ran off, leaving me to stare at the beautiful girl hanging all over Sandra.

I don't know why, but the leading sundry products always work the opposite for me. When I was a teenager, I'd get a zit, put Clearasil on it, and bust out as if I'd slept on a stack of Reese's peanut butter cups. If I get a flake of dandruff and use Head & Shoulders, suddenly I have a snowdrift on my back. Visine leaves my eyes blood red. Listerine gives me bad breath. So I wasn't too surprised that the Ban Basic, though leaving me smelling pretty good, was making me sweat. I started feeling silly standing there alone, my sides soaking wet, so I made my way to the bar and did a shot of tequila.

After a reconnaissance spin around the room, I played a hunch and went after the green-lipped, big-titted girl wearing the metallic mesh cardigan over a muscle shirt that spelled out SLUT in red sequins. We chatted about the shirt (another band) and I bought her and some guy friend of hers a beer. The guy had a green brushcut that looked like a practice tee. The Slut hung around just long enough to stuff half a lime into her bottle and then disappeared into the throng. After a few more stabs at conversation, I caught on that nobody really wanted to talk, they were here for dancing. I tried this, and it worked out okay, except it wasn't getting me anywhere. We'd dance and I'd look at them and then the song would end and they'd walk away. I went back to basics and tried to spring for more drinks, but hardly anyone in the place even drank.

Finally a wide-faced Asian took me up on my cocktail offer, except it turned out she was buying shots for her friends, too, so it ended up costing me twenty-two bucks, which sucked, seeing as I was scraping toothpaste tubes and stealing whiffs of deodorant from stores. At least she hung around after, and we talked about how no one talks anymore in L.A. clubs. She was an actress who was sup-ported by her parents in Valencia. She'd just gotten her first break, though, and was about to film a Taco Bell commercial.

We did a couple more shots, then started sucking face at the bar. I didn't care that she had a ridiculously broad mug—as if her liver had gone berserk—because the rest of her body was lithe and she had major league potstickers. I assumed they were paid for, but they looked good and Silverman was right—who the hell cared? For the moment I was pleased just to be kissing her, and then I thought about it and realized I didn't even know her name, and I was a little alarmed that *she* was kissing *me* when I hadn't said anything particu-larly charming, and let's face it, it's not like I was Kevin Costner, even though my face wasn't nearly as bloated as hers. Her tongue was thick and felt like sandpaper and I thought about Epstein-Barr and abruptly asked her to dance, then I thanked her and took off.

I couldn't find Silverman, but I bumped into the metallic-sweatered Slut back at the bar, and since she wasn't with Driving Range Head, I tried to strike up a conversation. "Remember me?" I said. "I was hitting on you a little earlier?" Apparently she did because she looked past me without responding. I started feeling creepy, so I slinked away through the puddles of beer, bumping straight into Herb.

"Who were you just talking to at the bar?" he asked.

"Myself."

A bouncer came by, took the soggy cup out of my hand. "Bar's closed," the man said.

I started for the door, but Silverman grabbed me and said that the club was still open until four for dancing. He led me to a booth and introduced me as "Trevor" to two seventeen-year-old models. The one I chatted with—a Floridian named Shareeka—was just back from Milan. When I tell you she had the most beautiful face I've ever seen, it's probably an exaggeration, but you get the picture. She talked about how much she hated modeling, it was such a stupid profession, but who could pass up five hundred bucks a day, and soon she was going to get into a business where she could use her brain: acting. Ambitions aside, she was rather articulate for someone who'd left school in the ninth grade, but like most impressionable young girls sent to make their way alone in the urban centers of Europe, she was affected beyond salvation.

She explained to me why French men were better lovers than Americans ("They're more feminine") and told me the difference between French and Italian food ("Italian food you eat, French food you *savor*"). I could almost smell the nicotine and body odor on the forty-year-old Frenchman who had polluted her with this crap. Shareeka said she wanted to buy a Golden Retriever, which she planned to name Canine. She asked me if I knew what "canine" meant. I thought this a trick question and meekly offered, "Dog?" She beamed. "You speak Italiano!"

When the models went to the bathroom with their rolled-up dollar bills, Silverman asked what I thought of mine.

"Beginning to hate her guts," I said.

"Are you out of your mind? Any guy in here would kill to fuck that chick."

"I didn't say I wouldn't fuck her, I said I hated her guts."

Silverman's face dropped as a lizard approached. Red hair, blue-white skin; the woman was about my age and slightly gawky, with strange conical breasts that came to a sharp point in a snug lizard-skin bodysuit.

"Hey, Sully," she said, and she kneeled on the seat beside him. Silverman looked past her into the crowd. "Hey," he said flatly.

I said, "Hey" also, but the reptile didn't "Hey" me back.

"How you been?" she asked.

"Good," Silverman said. "I been real busy, you know."

"Yeah, I figured that when you didn't call me last week when you said you were gonna."

"I never said I was gonna call you. I said I *might* call you."

"Yeah, well, whatever. No biggie."

The lizard held her ground, but no one said anything. Silverman shook his head as if he couldn't believe his bad luck, but she couldn't take a hint, or was just past the point of caring. I felt bad and wanted to bail her out, but didn't know how.

"So you wanna do something this week?" she asked.

"Can't," Silverman said. "Got to prepare a couple scenes for class."

She nodded at this. "Well, call me sometime before class."

Silverman's eyes followed a waitress holding a tray of Death cigarettes. "Okay," he said. "I'll try."

After the poor, sad lizard disappeared into the crowd, I asked who she was.

"Someone I don't like to see."

"Well, you hid it very well."

"Really?"

"You were about as subtle as a boa constrictor on a rat. You call yourself an actor?"

"Hey, F. Scott, don't start."

"Why the big frost?"

"Because some people can't take a fucking hint," he said.

"Did you go out with her?"

"I was *married* to her."

I thought about this.

"I'm going home," I said.

"What for?"

"I hate this place."

"We'll go somewhere else."

"L.A., I mean."

"What about Shareeka?"

"She'd be great if she were about eight years older and not on drugs."

"Henry, have you ever wondered why guys in prison are getting married and you can't get a date?"

"Many times."

"I'm serious. You haven't even fucked Tiff. *Everyone's* fucked Tiff."

The girls sat back down and the young actress Drew Barrymore approached Shareeka. They kissed each other's face on both sides and said, *"Mmwaa,"* then Silverman hugged Drew and said, "Come on, like you mean it," and they hugged a little tighter. Drew had grown quite a bit since I'd last seen pictures of her. After she disappeared back into the crowd, Silverman told me he'd met her just a few months ago, at Drew's fifteenth birthday party.

I drove back down Sixth Street, swinging by Maria's Donuts and Chinese Food, but it was closed, thus denying me the peculiar joy of ordering a half dozen crullers and a pu-pu platter. The swarm of people still stood vacantly on the sidewalks and police were everywhere, like the aftermath of a tragedy, or the prelude to one. I hung a right on Vermont, went up to Santa Monica Boulevard. In West Hollywood I passed a leather bar letting out. Dozens of gay bikers hung around the sidewalk doing last-minute negotiating. There they were, a bunch of fey muscleheads with black jackets, tattoos, and overly accessorized Harleys. Their whole lives they'd been outcasts, yet somehow tonight they'd found each other.

It saddened me that I couldn't remember the thoughts that had made me feel so good earlier in the evening. I cringed at the way I'd behaved, the way I'd felt. I'd been too desperate. What did I care if some shark-net slut liked me? Why had I kissed the bloated sandpaper-tongue, why had I wasted my money on people I didn't know? Thirty-three years old and partying with teenagers. Pathetic.

I took a shower, chewed a couple aspirins, threw a pile of frozen french fries onto a pan in the oven, then started editing some pages

I'd written that day. I dipped the fries in mustard while I worked and soon the birds were waking up, so I forced myself to put the notebook back in the fridge. When I couldn't sleep, I threw Miss June on the floor and made love to Miss Pillow. I was still thinking about my script and having a hard time bringing the overglossed centerfold to life, so I rolled onto my back. With my hand and saliva and a brand-new fantasy, I was able to rub one out pretty quickly, felt an instant burn in my eyes. I wiped a dirty sock across my stomach, threw it in the corner, pulled up my underwear, and felt lower than I had in a while. I knew that I was twisted and I was bad, and that the only thing that had allowed me to spill my seed onto my boozy belly was the thought of fucking that little Drew Barrymore.

the sunrise was gray and I had only been asleep an hour when the ringing started. I closed the *Playboy* on the floor before picking up the phone. The woman on the other end was already in high gear. "That's it!" she screamed. "I've had it with you! I hope you rot in hell, you scum! I never want to see you again!"

"Who is this?" I said.

"You son of a bitch. Don't give me that innocent crap!"

I leaned on one elbow, looked at the clock. Ten past six. Colleen. I hung up.

A minute later it rang again. I unplugged the phone.

At noon I awoke, the sun burning into my skull straight from hell. Was it a dream or had she really called? I lay in my sweat, said a prayer to God not to hit Southern California with the big one today. The thought made my stomach or heart flutter, I couldn't tell which.

I sat up, took several deep breaths, fought back a wave of nausea. The previous evening had left my body perilously low on electrolytes, and I became concerned about an arrythmia, like I had on the basketball court. Most heart attacks, I knew, happened on weekends. In the first two hours after waking. Platelet activity was at its highest then, and with the depletion of liquids in my body, clumping was a possibility. My earlobes stung and I knew that if I wasn't careful, one day I was going to wake up with creases in them, and then I might as well put a gun in my mouth because that meant my arteries were all shot to shit.

I trudged into the kitchenette for hydration, scraping off a patch of dried cum on the way, as if I'd slept with a glazed doughnut on my stomach. A large glass of tap water to lubricate my cells. Three aspirins, half at a time, so I didn't choke. A refill of H_2O, this time fizzing with Alka-Seltzer Cold Plus. Back in bed, I consoled myself with the knowledge that Cedars Sinai was no more than five minutes away by ambulance. Faster in my own car. I wondered what would be better—to drive myself to the hospital in three minutes, stumble through the emergency room doors, hope they got to work on me fast; or call an ambulance, maybe arrive a tad later, but have them prepping me on the way. I tried to recall if all ambulances were required to carry defibulators. I ran my address over in my head, in case I had to call 911. Then a thought: Was the apartment number on my door? Of course it was, I was being ridiculous. Anyway, one of my neighbors would surely lead the medics to me.

Unless everyone was out to brunch.

Help could come and go while I was turning blue—my scumbucket neighbors off sipping mimosas, eating their baked eggs— after four minutes, even if I survived, it would be goo-goo-ville. I took a deep breath, dragged myself to the door—the number was there. I forced down two rotten bananas for the potassium they would provide and went back to sleep.

At three I got up again, this time for good. My nerves were calmed and after showering I felt well enough to plug the phone back in. Everything was in the sink, so I ate a bowl of Cheerios out of a Teflon pot. Five minutes later it rang. More shrieking.

I said, "What are you screaming about?"

"What am I screaming about?! I'll tell you what I'm screaming about!"

Oh, it was an ugly, ugly tale. After I'd "abandoned" her at that "slum" of a bus station, Colleen claimed to have had to wait twelve hours for the next bus because the one she was supposed to get on was overbooked, "so it was either wait or stand all the way to Chicago." She recounted how she'd found a bench to sleep on, how upon awakening she'd been surrounded by a gang of homeless men, how they'd dragged her outside to "have their way with her," how she'd "fought like the dickens and screamed bloody murder" as she was taught to do, but nobody gave a shit anymore, not even the "three goddamn cops" who drove by but were "too fucking chickenshit" to do anything. After biting one of the fuckers right on his balls—she described this with great gusto—she managed to escape with her life, but all her money was gone and—

"Stop right there," I said. I took a moment, tried to catch my breath. "Are you telling me you've been in L.A. *this whole time?*"

"Of course I have. I told you, dum-dum, all my money was tooken by the rapists."

"Well, why the hell didn't you buy your ticket when you got to the terminal, which would've precluded the robbers *tooking* it eight hours later?!"

"What?"

"Why didn't you buy your fucking ticket right away?"

"Oh, yeah, right, that's all I need. I buy my ticket in advance, then Greyhound goes belly-up and I'm out eighty bucks."

I hung up the phone and kept it unplugged for the rest of the day.

At about six I went out for the paper and a couple tacos. I read the L.A. Times at home, drank a can of Diet Coke to give me energy, then sat down and started reworking How I Won Her Back. One of my favorite scenes was when the protagonist Joe is working at a flea market and meets a guy who shows him how he can get back the woman he loved and tragically lost ten years earlier. The scene accomplished a lot. It was funny the way the guy and Joe clash at first, sad when you realize how much this woman meant to Joe, and it let the audience know exactly what the movie was about (if the title hadn't already filled them in). A common complaint, however, was that people wanted to know more of what the couple was like back when they were together. I thought this idiotic and had resisted making any changes. They'd been in love, madly in love, or obviously Joe wouldn't be going to so much trouble to get her back. What they were like, how they met; hey, this wasn't a miniseries.

Now I started seeing it differently. I thought about The Natural. Would audiences have cared as much if it started with Redford already recovering from his gunshot wound? No way. They cared because they'd seen him strike out Babe Ruth at the train depot. They cared because he could've been something great, and it was a tragedy he wasn't. Suddenly I saw how showing the good times would give the audience more to root for, and I knew a way to do it without adding thirty pages. I'd just let them meet, slip in a few happy scenes leading to their tragic demise, and cut to ten years later. Ten pages, tops.

Following the Northwestern beauty into traffic school, though embarrassing, was funny. With some fine tuning, it could be *really* funny. That's how they'd meet. Joe sees Joan at the store, they make eye contact, the big lunk is smitten and follows her into what he assumes is AA. But this is where art enhances life. When the man with the red beard asks Joe what he's doing there, Joe stands up, takes a deep breath, and says, "Hi. My name is Joe, and I'm an alcoholic." Everyone in the room laughs at him (including Joan, who's onto his game), and Red Beard says, "That's great, Joe, but this is traffic school." Better still, Red Beard could say, "Unless you were drinking and driving, Joe, we don't care," and so on. Joe then slinks out of the room and, just when he's given up all hope of meeting her, Joan comes out and says, "Hey, alky, why don't we get a drink later?" Big smile from Joe, and we cut to them dating.

There was a short knock at my door and Herb Silverman entered.

"I need the fifty bucks."

I couldn't hide my annoyance.

"Now?"

"Yeah now. And by the way, what the hell were you thinking last night?"

"I had to go home. I was tired."

"You were tired? We're sitting there with two of the hottest chotch in town, *in the world,* and you're tired?"

"Herb, when I was a senior in college, I felt a little funny going out with freshman girls. I did it, but I felt funny. Now eleven years later I'm going to go out with high school kids?"

"She's not in high school."

"I know. She dropped out in ninth grade. She'd be a junior."

"A lot of actresses leave school early."

"A lot of actresses are stupid. Besides, she's a model."

"Oh, what are you, Mr. Fucking Intellectual? You only screw Rhodes scholars now? Give me my fucking money."

His tone was really bugging me, seeing as how technically I didn't owe him anything and in fact *he* owed *me,* but he was working some kind of Ponzi scheme that I'd lamely allowed myself to be sucked into, and so I had to bite my tongue and take it. What happened was this: Herb had borrowed two hundred dollars and a couple weeks had passed without any mention of it. I needed some dough and wanted to remind him he owed me without seeming rude, so I asked if he needed to borrow *any more* money.

He said yes.

I wasn't expecting this and didn't have any money to lend him and I told him so.

"Then why the hell did you . . . ? Oh, I get it, you wanted to remind me that I owed you money."

I scoffed.

"Don't worry," he said, "I remember."

"So . . . do you have any of it now?"

"No."

"Not even half?"

"I just told you I needed to borrow some from you, remember?"

"Come on, Herb, I'm in a pinch."

"Sorry. I only have enough for my rent."

"How about fifty?"

"Uh-uh."

"Don't be a dick."

"Jesus, Halloran, I wouldn't've borrowed the damn dough if I knew you were gonna go Gotti on me."

"Just give me fifty. It won't count as payback on the money you owe me."

"You'll pay *me* back before I pay *you* back?"

"Right. Soon as I get dough. Then you'll still owe me two hundred and you can pay me whenever you get it."

He thought about this. "Okay. But don't fuck me. You're not gonna deduct it from what I owe you?"

"No."

"That would be real sleazy, Halloran."

"Give me the fifty bucks, for Christ sakes."

So here we were three days later, and he was treating me like a deadbeat, and I was annoyed as hell, but I'd agreed to the terms, so what could I do?"

ted bowman was a morose man in his late forties who rarely looked me in the eye, which was okay with me, because at eleven in the morning his eyes hung down like shucked oysters and when they did slide my way, it was in a suspicious, accusing way. His development person, Sonya Abrams, had read *How I Won Her Back* and I assumed she'd liked it, though she didn't speak much, just took notes, nodded occasionally, and twice asked me if I wanted a Pellegrino water. The second time I accepted, but it was just to get her out of the room, which is what I think she wanted, because she never returned.

"So what have you heard about me?" Bowman asked.

His voice was flemmy—a low milk-shaky rattle that came more from an aggressive laziness than an ear, nose, or throat problem.

I paused, searched for the right words. "Well . . ."

"The truth."

"I've heard that you're difficult and you're brilliant."

"Don't bullshit me."

"I've heard that you're difficult."

"You retracting the 'brilliant' part?"

"I've seen your movies. You *are* brilliant."

"You thought *Coma Cop* was brilliant?"

This was tough. It was okay. Big star, big director, great special effects, run-of-the-mill story. Brilliant, no. Definitely not brilliant. But it had made a hundred million dollars.

"With a capital B," I said.

Ted Bowman began to floss his teeth; I fought to hold my gaze.

"So do you know why you're here?"

"Well . . . Sonya read my script . . ."

"I got twenty-seven projects in development. Every one of them is an action thriller or buddy cop movie. I told Sonya to find me a comedy writer who could write a fucking funny love story. She found you."

"Great."

"Along with about thirty other morons. See, I don't want just another fucking romantic comedy. I want a love story with a twist."

"Okay . . ."

"You follow me?"

"I think so."

"A major twist. I want to blow people's minds, turn love upside down, show them what it's really like out there in the nineties—from a guy's point of view."

"Uh-huh." I scribbled into my notebook. "Love in nineties," I said as I wrote. "Guy's POV."

"Let me ask you something," he said. "Are you in love right now?"

"Um . . . yeah, I guess."

"What do you mean, 'I guess'?"

"It's a little complicated . . ."

"You in love with a dude?"

"No, no. I'm in love, but I'm not going out with her. It's . . . over."

"Then you must know better than most how fucked up it is to be in love now?"

"It's hell," I said.

"Worse."

"*Much* worse."

"Yet it's all anyone wants. Well, I want to take love and show it for what it really is."

What love really is, I wrote.

"And that is . . . it's *death.*"

"Huh," I said, and I kept scribbling, but it was just gibberish.

Ted Bowman read something that had printed out on the box on his desk. He grabbed the phone and said, "Hey, shitball, I'm busy right now. Yeah, yeah, yeah, tell him to get fucked." He managed a laugh. "It's Greek or nothing. Call you from the car."

After he hung up, he stood and looked out the window.

"Love is death," he repeated.

Love is death, I wrote.

"Are you with me?"

"Absolutely with you. I know exactly what you're talking about."

"And that is?"

"It's a nightmare out there, and they never tell it that way. They always sugarcoat it, make it the way you'd like it to be. But you want a love story that tells the truth, shows what love is really like today—from a guy's perspective."

"Exactly."

"Great."

"And I want the guy to be a serial killer."

when it rains in l.a., cars seem to come out of the pavement like worms. It was barely more than a mist, but it was unusual to get anything this time of year in Southern California, and on my way to work everyone was driving like they were in two feet of snow. I hit my horn a couple times, took a shortcut, sped around a scrum of cars. Just as I got back into the lane, my car did a three-sixty and I thought I was a dead man, but somehow I managed to miss everything and ended up going in the right direction, only now I slowed down and drove as if I were in two feet of snow.

Bowman had kept me waiting for our meeting and the rain set me back further, so I was late for my lunch shift. The other employees gave me the cold shoulder for not helping with the prep work, which I didn't blame them for. I told them my car had broken down, which was stupid, but they were mostly teenagers and this was easier for them to swallow than the truth about the loser grillman getting tied up at the studio.

That was something I was trying to cut down on, though. Lying.

Despite Levine's speech, I wasn't convinced that lying was necessary to break into the biz, and it certainly had no place in everyday life. But I had developed a bad habit of complicating my life with stupid, unnecessary lies. Nothing big, like I graduated summa cum laude from Harvard, just stupid ones, like when I told the *L.A. Times* woman that I didn't know anybody in town. Well, actually, I did know a few people: Silverman and Colleen and Tiff. It had started back in Boston, right around the time Amanda was kicking my ass, probably out of some insecurity. Maybe I'd just been a salesman too long. If I had sex three times, I'd tell my friends it was four. If I got two hits in a softball game, it became three. If I got up at ten o'clock, it'd be *a quarter to ten*. Like it mattered. Why I did it I didn't know, but I was trying to stop.

As soon as she walked in, I rushed to the counter and elbowed a zitball named Gerald out of the way. She was unbelievable. Not just beautiful and big-titted and all that. *Mature. Elegant.* Grace Kelly-esque. Way out of my league. She was with a handsome older couple who turned out to be her parents. The folks were very kind to me right off the bat, and I thought I detected a vibe from her. I cracked a joke, made eye contact, shared a generational smile. I took the order, then forced the conversation until I found something we had in common: Though the family was from Illinois, she worked in Boston as a flight attendant for American Airlines. The parents were returning from a business trip in the Far East, she had a stopover in L.A. They only had a few hours together. Anyone with a speck of sense would've let it go at that.

I told the lie because all avenues of conversation had been ex-hausted and I'd been wearing the hamburg flipper uniform just long enough that I was deluded into thinking that a good woman could see past it. I had visions of more stopovers, maybe I'd even get a few free flights out of it, not that I had any plans to fly soon. The lie was this: I said that my sister was also a flight attendant for American. What I expected to achieve by this, I have no idea. Time maybe. An in. A vague connection. Actually, there was a smidgen of truth. My sister Suzy had been trying to become a flight attendant a few years back, but at the time there'd been a hiring freeze in the Boston market. If I'd been a good liar, I would've said she worked out of Miami or Dallas, I would have said United, I would have said she was an air traffic controller, but it was impulsive and I said Boston and American, figuring there had to be a thousand flight attendants out of Beantown.

"What's her name?" she asked.

"Suzy Halloran."

"There's no Suzy Halloran flying out of Boston."

A definite shift in tone. More eye contact, not the kind I wanted. How could she be so sure? It's a big city, a big company. I stuck to my story.

"Yes, there is."

"No, there's not." Down my fucking throat.

I straightened my paper cap, she mentioned something about a Boston chapter of American flight attendants, something about her being prez.

"Maybe she goes by her married name," I said.

Quickly, she asked for it.

"Johnson."

"That's bullshit!"

Her parents grew uncomfortable. "Let it go, honey," her father said, delicately. "It's just a misunderstanding."

"Maybe she's not *technically* out of Boston," I said. "I know she does a lot of flying out of the Big Apple."

"The Big Apple."

"New York," I said.

"I know what the fucking Big Apple is."

At this point I was thinking this wasn't a woman I wanted to get involved with anyway. Nice mouth. I hemmed and hawed a little more, then finally shrugged and wandered over to the fryolater. It took a great act of courage to drop the check off twenty minutes later, which is why I had Gerald do it.

I first heard the moans when I was getting out of my car in front of the apartment, but I had other things on my mind and disregarded it. After the embarrassment at Johnny Rockets, I'd dropped by Rancho, hit two buckets of balls in the rain. Now I was taking my sticks out of the hatchback, thinking about the aggressive stewardess. When the moans became groans, they got my attention. I assumed Tiff was going at it again, and when they became more plaintive, I was certain of it. I started into the building but stopped when I heard the shriek. It occurred to me that someone could be in trouble. I dropped my golf bag on the front steps, followed the sound down an alley and around to the back of the building. It seemed to be emanating from one of the rear apartments on the upper floor. A combination yelping and crying now, then a wail again, and finally a gurgling sound. I didn't know who lived back there, but I was concerned for them, so I called out: "You okay up there?"

The noise ceased momentarily and I thought perhaps someone had indeed been getting reamed, but then it resumed—louder even—and I knew no one could be getting it *that* good. I called up again, but this time there wasn't the slightest cessation and I really became nervous. By the time I got to the upstairs apartment door with a sand wedge in my hand, I realized it wasn't coming from an apartment at all, but from the roof. I noticed a ladder heading up to an open skylight. I threw up a few Yoo-hoos with no response, then tentatively climbed the ladder and peeked up top.

Someone was sitting on the tarpaper, legs crossed Indian-style, head hung low, arms wrapped around, as if in an invisible strait-jacket. I had a fleeting hope that this was some kind of yoga pose and the tortured sounds a wacky mantra, but why out in the drizzle? I said hello, whistled and yoo-hooed again, and when I still got no response, I stood on the speckled tar and wondered what to do. The person, a woman apparently, was about three feet from the edge and obviously in some sort of state. I moved forward until she could see me in her peripheral vision, and when she glanced up, Colleen jumped back like a wet cat and I sprung back a couple feet the other way.

It looked as if she'd died, been revived, and someone had thrown clothes on her. Everything about her was different. She'd shrunk. She was slumped, thin, smaller, like a cooked shrimp. Her hair had lost its shine; it was browner, tangled. It would've been easier to pull a comb through a cone of cotton candy. Her skin was mushy and goose-pimpled, like the skin of a boiled chicken. Her eyes were redder than Michelle Pfeiffer's and her fingers looked as if they could use a vigorous scrubbing.

"What are you doing here?" I said.

She didn't answer, just bellowed louder, and I could see a couple neighbors looking up from the street.

"Okay, take it easy," I said. "Everything's cool."

Again with the lies, but this one I could live with, as she was now a foot from the edge, and although we were only two stories up,

I had visions of her going headfirst, which would do the trick. Each overture sent her wriggling ever closer to the precipice. I wondered of course if it were all a ruse, she was an actress after all. I crouched and again tried to calm Colleen's fears, but I couldn't connect, and part of me wanted to call her bluff and just leave, and that's the part that won.

I called 911 from my apartment, then went out front and looked up with the neighbors. Within two minutes three Beverly Hills police cruisers had arrived, which is why you pay the extra C-note, and they were followed by a fire truck, an ambulance, and a couple dozen of the curious. I told the cops what I knew and they retraced my steps up the ladder on the second floor and for twenty minutes we could see a couple officers crouched near Colleen and could hear her sobs, and a rumor began to circulate that she was suffering from some sort of diabetic shock. I wanted to escape to my apartment, but an officer asked me to hang around, and finally two paramedics accompanied a sheepish Colleen Driscoll out the front of the building, and they helped her into a police cruiser where she ate a banana. I could see that Colleen was suddenly lucid, so I started to leave, but an officer in his late thirties with an orange tan cut me off.

In 1990 the Beverly Hills Police force was the Chippendales of law enforcement. Every one of them looked as if he were hand-picked by Herb Ritts. They were all about six-foot-two or above, with tremendous physiques, chiseled good looks, and strong, silent-type mentalities. Most also had overly trimmed mustaches, which lent them a vaguely gay aura in a Rock Hudson kind of way, but the point is they were imposing as hell, and for that matter, even the women cops were studs.

The Orange Cop, who looked like the local Channel 2 weatherman Johnny Mountain on steroids, explained that Colleen was going to be fine, she'd simply had a world-class hypoglycemic attack. They'd given her potassium and fluids and she'd rebounded quite nicely. I told him I was happy for her, but it really didn't concern me, as I hardly knew her.

"You're not her boyfriend?"

"Nooo."

He held his gaze.

"I'm not her boyfriend. I just met her a few weeks ago."

"She says you're her boyfriend."

"Well, she must still have a touch of the hypoglycemia."

"So what do you want us to do with her?"

"I don't know. You tell me."

The Orange Cop conferred with a silver-haired one and they both approached me. "She says she wants to stay here for the night," Orange said.

"No, no. Absolutely not."

The silver-haired cop sneered. He annoyed me. His hair was too perfect, like frosting on a cake.

"I told you, I hardly know her."

The glare again from Orange guy.

"I don't get this," I said. "She's obviously got big problems. Why would you want her to stay with me?"

"There aren't many options," from Cakehead.

"She just threatened to kill herself. Aren't there procedures to follow? Shouldn't she be getting observed somewhere?"

Orange said, "As I explained, she's fine now. And she never threatened to kill herself."

"How can you say that?"

"She never threatened to kill herself."

"Excuse me, Officer, did you show up late? Because if I recall, she was up on a building wailing like a hyena."

"She never *verbally* threatened to kill herself," Cakehead piped in.

A few neighbors made their way into our huddle and this support heartened me.

"She was at the edge of the damn building. What more do you need?"

"Quite a bit more actually," Orange said.

"Well, how about this? If you do a little research, you're going to find out that her sister jumped off a building about three months ago. Notice a trend there?"

"I'd be violating her civil rights if I remanded her to a mental health institution without her permission."

"Even with what I just told you? I'm not making that up."

"I thought you didn't know her."

"I said I've known her a few weeks."

"What her sister did or didn't do has no bearing on the situation."

I rubbed the back of my neck. "Fine, then bring her to a regular hospital, take her to jail, send her back to New Jersey . . . Do *something* with her."

"I can't arrest her. She didn't break any laws."

"Isn't suicide illegal?"

"We don't know that she was attempting to kill herself," Cakehead said again.

"Oh, come on, guys. Use your better judgment on this one. She's out of her mind."

"So you're saying you won't let her stay here?" Orange asked.

"That's right, she can't stay here. You're reading me loud and clear. I don't want her here. Me stay, she go."

Orange flexed his jaw muscles and for a moment I thought he was going to smack me. There was a palpable shift in my neighbors' allegiances. All anyone saw was a distraught woman in a country western dress with nowhere to go and a piece of shit unemployed writer with no heart.

I said, "Don't turn this around on me, man. I made the 911 call, I did my duty. I barely even know this woman. She's not my responsibility."

"Right," Orange said. "She's not your responsibility."

He shot me a Joe Friday smirk, and Cakehead gave me the Joe Friday sidekick look, and they went to confer with a couple other officers. When they all looked my way and the neighbors shuffled off mumbling among themselves, I started feeling itchy, so I slinked back toward the apartment. I didn't get far, however, before Colleen saw me leaving and bolted out of the police cruiser. A woman officer managed to tackle her to the ground, thank God, and I yelled to the officers, "See?! She's tapioca!", and I skipped quickly into the building. From up in my apartment I could still hear her bellowing: "HENRY, NO!!! BABY, PLEASE!!!! PLEASE, HENRY! PLEASE, HENRY! PLEASE, PLEASE, PLEASE, HENRY! *DOOONT LEEEEEEEAVE MEEEEE ALOOOONE!!*"

five

the reason the roads are so slippery when it rains in L.A. is that during the long dry periods an unseen layer of smog settles on the pavement, and when the rain does come, that dust becomes slick as ice. This was explained to me by an officer during a lull in the Colleen saga and I was thinking about it as I lay in bed that night listening to *Freedom Rock*. I was also thinking about Colleen up there in the rain. That fucker. I supposed that my neighborhood was ruined for me. Every time I'd go down to the store for a soda or newspaper, someone would point out the guy who turned the hypoglycemic urchin away. Maybe some grandstander would try to sucker-punch me. And the worst part was: Something inside was telling me that maybe they were right.

I thought about how nice it would be to be twelve again, when these songs were new, sleeping in my old backyard, a sheet pulled over my mother's clothesline, my buddies telling Juan Corona stories, bullshitting each other about getting tit. When the tape ended, I tried to concentrate on the soft rattle of my window screen and the occasional siren that momentarily quickened the city's sleeping pulse. Colleen's dead sister Bonnie came to mind. A telephone rang in somebody's apartment, reminding me of what a ballbuster God is. That afternoon, after the commotion, I'd noticed my answering machine blinking: Margo Jones of Big Brothers looking for my "girlfriend" Colleen.

Surely she would return. They would let her go and she'd sprint right back. I started hearing odd sounds in the apartment below—a bang, a faucet, a high-pitched whir. I imagined my neighbor covering his tracks, his murdered wife in pieces in the bathtub. I got up, checked my lock. A couple moths fluttered around a light, sending bat-size shadows across my wall. I wondered how moths could fly while it was still misting out. The place suddenly seemed haunted. Maybe digestion would put me to sleep. At 4 A.M. I boiled a couple eggs for an egg salad sandwich, then realized I didn't have any mayo, so I crumbled the eggs on a piece of bread, slammed another piece on top, and ate it dry. I heard the downstairs door open, footsteps, and finally, unbelievably, a meek knock at my door. A shock of adrenaline. I threw down the sandwich, flew out of bed, landing on my toenails, practically soundless. My breath came through my nose; I could hear the blood gushing through my veins.

"Honey, are you up?"

I loved Tiffany right then and, yanking open the door, I embraced her like a soldier.

"I'm so glad you're up," she said. "I need some popcorn."

"I have missed you."

"Henry."

"Yah?"

"You're hurting me."

I released her and bolted the door.

I told Tiffany Pittman about the ordeal I had endured, and though she may not have grasped the horror of it (judging from the purple teeth and winey breath floating my way) at least she didn't interrupt. This allowed me to hear it spoken aloud, which was reassuring because I hadn't left anything out and I still sounded right and I was also starting to believe there was a God and He was a good and rational chap or why else would He have delivered this vaginafest to my door at such a dark hour? This had been a frequent concern—God's rationality, His sense of humor. I feared dying and having Him play back snippets of my life where I'd said something terrible, purely in jest, that He'd taken seriously, and I'd have to defend myself, which I knew would be difficult, humor being so subjective (why does Woody Allen only play in New York and L.A.?) and I'd say, *"Hellooo.* It was *a joke,"* but maybe jokes were just a human defense and he'd never understand—I mean, try making a sober German laugh.

Tiffany sat on my bed while I shook the Jiffy Pop and watched the tinfoil unwrinkle.

"Could this be cancer?"

When I peeked out from the kitchenette, she was holding her shirt up with her chin and pointing to a freckle on the rim of her left nipple.

"I've had it ever since I burned my boobs in Palm Springs."

I turned off the stove and calmly said, "Let's have a feel."

I reached for the freckle, but Tiffany lifted her chin and the shirt fell back over her breast.

"Cut it out," she said.

"What?"

"I don't fool around with my neighbors."

"I was checking to see if you had cancer, you goofball."

"How would you know? You're not a doctor."

"Then why'd you ask?"

Meekly, she said, "I don't know."

"And, incidentally, I *do* know a thing or two about nipple cancer. My father's a doctor."

"What kind?"

"Nipple-ologist."

"You liar. There's no such thing."

"He's a general practitioner. Come on, let me see those babies." When she still balked, I said, "Tiff, stop being a prude. I have nipples, too, you know."

Tiffany Pittman was no prude, and she loved that I would call her one. For once, a guy who thought she was a prude, instead of a pig.

She lifted her eyebrows, then she lifted her shirt.

Fucking unbelievable. Two perfectly shaped nips capping off a pair of scientifically engineered breasts. World-class. Fake, of course, but I'd been won over by fake. They were magical. They were high-tech masterpieces. They were two fat, man-made winners! And they were mine to touch.

I felt a lump of adrenaline in my chest as my hand felt the weight of one. I remembered what my father had told me about it not being the same in a clinical environment. The lying bastard.

"That's not the one," Tiffany said.

"I just want to compare."

I released one and cupped the other. What on earth had they done to these nipples? They were an inch long and as hard as my dick. Her heart was beating in my palm as I looked to the ceiling, once more the attending physician.

"Hmm," I said.

"What?"

"Shhh."

I put my ear to the breast—first one ear, then the other, letting my face brush the silky skin in the process. She smelled like a mixture of baby powder and fresh sweat. While my ear fondled one, I breathed in the other.

"What are you doing?"

"Shhh."

I lifted my head, ran my forefinger across the freckle, letting my thumb brush her tightening areola. Yes, it was bunching up, becoming even more erect. Maybe she wanted it. I looked in her eyes. Nothing. No excitement, no annoyance, nothing. I could feel my underwear stretching out. Soon would appear the telltale dot of wetness. Uh-oh, suddenly her areolas were flattening out like cookies on a baking pan.

It was now or never. I leaned forward and swept my tongue from her collarbone, past the carotid artery speed bump, all the way into her shiny ear.

"Cut it out, Henry."

She pushed me away and lowered the shirt.

"What?"

"I told you, I don't fool around with my neighbors."

"I'll move out tomorrow."

"I don't want you to move out." She kissed my forehead, headed into the kitchenette. " 'Cause you always have Jiffy Pop."

"What if I find a new apartment and send you a gross of the stuff?"

Tiffany sat on the counter, placed the charred tinfoil on her lap. I leaned against the windowsill and watched her eat.

"Tiff, you do it with fat lawyers in hallways, you do it with Herb Silverman; why won't you do it with me?"

"Because, for the tenth time, *I don't sleep with my neighbors.*"

"That's ridiculous. Silverman's your neighbor. He's right across the street."

"No, *you're* my neighbor, Henry. A neighbor is someone who lives across the hall or right next door."

"What if I moved downstairs? That way I wouldn't be your neighbor anymore, but I'd still be close in case you ever wanted to run down and help yourself to some popcorn."

"Sorry, Henry, but I have a rule: Once a neighbor, always a neighbor."

"You suck."

"Henry!"

"Since when have you had so many rules?"

"Honey, relax. If it'll make you feel any better, I think you're adorable."

"That doesn't make me feel any better. Fucking me silly would make me feel better."

"I'm not going to fuck you."

"Come on . . ." I whined. *"You fucked Herb."*

"Well, I'm not going to fuck him anymore."

I stomped my foot. "I don't care if you fuck him. I'm willing to give you as much freedom as you want. I just ask that you occasionally include me in your sleep plans. Tell you what, it'll just be this once. We'll do it now, and from here on out we'll just be good neighbors. You can go on doing it with lawyers and Silverman, and I'll be your Jiffy Pop guy. Deal?"

"I don't want to do it with Herbie anymore. He's the worst."

This perked my interest. "He is? What'd he do?"

"It's what he *didn't* do. He's a lazy bum. He just lies there like some stupid pharaoh. That guy doesn't know the first thing about pleasing a girl."

"No shit?"

"Put it this way. When we made love, *I had to squeeze my own boobs.*"

Despite the hour and the day's anxiety, I howled at this.

"What?"

"Nothing," I said.

"That's the problem with guys with big dicks. They think that's all that matters."

"I bet," I said, not so amused now.

She took another handful of popcorn. "So do you think I have cancer?"

"No. My girlfriend used to get the same spots every summer when she went topless."

"But mine won't go away."

"So what? It's just a freckle."

"I didn't know you had a girlfriend. Why would you want to sleep with me if you have a girlfriend?"

"I'll give you two hints, and one of them has a freckle."

"Henry."

"Besides, we're sort of in a fight right now."

"And she has spots on her boobs, too?"

"Tons."

Tiffany was cheered by this. Then her eyes narrowed.

"Uh-oh. What if we *both* have cancer? It's very common, you know. Everyone in Australia has it."

"Tiff, you do not have cancer. Amanda had her tits checked, and they came back normal."

I didn't feel bad telling this white lie. It was making the girl feel better. Then a thought: Jesus, what if it *was* cancer? I could be sending her off with a melanoma that could spread within weeks to her liver, kidneys, brain.

"It doesn't hurt, does it?"

"No."

"And it hasn't changed color?"

Tiffany lifted her shirt, studied the tiny smudge.

"I don't think so."

"Then you're okay. If it turns purple, or starts to hurt, or bleeds, or you notice any lumps, get it checked."

I stared at her breasts and thought what a pity I couldn't suckle them until the sun rose.

Tiffany dropped her shirt and said, "Thank you, Henry. I feel a whole lot better."

"That's my girl," I said. I lifted my own shirt. "Look, even I have freckles around my nipples."

"Hey, yeah!"

When she ran her finger across my chest, a shiver shot up my spine.

"What's this?" she said.

"What?"

"This bump."

"What bump?"

"Right here, under your nipple."

The pleasant sensation was replaced by a sick emptiness. I shoved her hand away, felt it for myself. She was wrong, it wasn't a bump. It was a *lump*. Why hadn't I noticed it before? I tried not to panic. After all, I hadn't noticed the lumps on my balls, either. When I massaged the other nipple, my heart sank. That one was fine. If this was normal, shouldn't I have lumps under both nips, like I did on my balls?

"What's the matter?" she asked.

"You and your tits go. I have to make a phone call."

"what's so funny?" I asked.

"I'm sorry," Dr. Hoffman said. "It's just that I haven't had many men ask for mammograms lately."

Until that moment, it hadn't occurred to me that he could find this humorous. In the waiting room, I'd thought of the different ways he could give me the news. He might show immediate alarm at feeling the tumor, or contain his emotions long enough to sit me down in his office, or maybe he'd send me to a specialist, have *him* break it to me. Who knows, maybe he'd call my father back in Rhode Island, let him do the dirty work. One thing was certain: This one was serious. Guys don't get lumps on their tits for nothing.

Despite the fear I was experiencing—and it was the dull, pukey kind—I also felt redeemed. Maybe if the doctor had taken my earlier complaints more seriously, I'd still be alive now. Well, I was alive, but that was just a technicality. If it was in my balls and tits, then it had probably ricocheted through my entire lymphatic system. Which meant it was most likely into my liver and lungs, too. Jesus Christ, I was riddled with cancer! Oh, no, the heart palpitations! Cancer of the heart, was that possible? I'd never heard of it, but until the night before I'd never heard of male breast cancer.

My father had confirmed it. I'd called him immediately after discovering the lump. I was embarrassed, so at first I'd kept the conversation to topics my father was interested in—how the job hunt was progressing, the Sox' chances, what the hell I was doing in California. Asking my father for medical advice was always touchy. Except for a rickety golf back, the man hadn't been sick a day in his life and he didn't expect his kids to be. I told him the search for employment was taking longer than expected because I wanted to make the right choice this time, then sucked it up and confessed to holding down a restaurant job. "Good move," he said surprisingly. "Don't let yourself get in a hole financially." Just before hanging up, I matter-of-factly popped the question: "Hey, is it possible for men to get breast cancer?" "Why?" "This guy at the restaurant, he says his brother got it. I think he's pulling my leg." "It's pretty rare, but men do get it."

What a place to die. Nobody would care about me. The city was rife with victims of violence and AIDS; I'd just be another stat. A stat without friends.

"I never said I wanted a mammogram," I told Hoffman.

"Yes, you did. You said you wanted me to test you for breast cancer—that's a mammogram."

"Well, isn't there a more, you know, manly way of testing it?" The prick was still snickering.

"Excuse me," he said. "I just don't get this all the time."

"Yeah, well, do you get many men who have lumps under their nipples?" I said this with a slightly righteous tone.

"Some."

This wasn't a response I expected. "Really?"

"Take your shirt off."

As I did so, Dr. Hoffman studied my chart. He seemed interested. This was good. Maybe he was noticing something peculiar, something that could save my life. He slapped his forehead.

"What?" I quickly said.

"Last time you were in here, I forgot to do a pap smear."

A cackle now. I forced one corner of my mouth to curl.

"I'm sorry. I'll get serious here. Henry, you recently complained about a testicular problem . . . ?"

"Yeah."

"And you also had the cough?"

"Uh-huh."

The doctor lowered the pages. "Anything else?"

"Well, actually, sometimes I feel sort of a lump in my throat, and occasionally my heart flutters or skips a beat or something, and I've been dizzy a lot, and nauseated more than normal, and sometimes I get these pains in my right side, just below the ribs, that you wouldn't believe."

The doctor felt my throat, listened to my heart, looked in my ears, hammered my knee. I thought to tell him about the headaches and blood sugar stuff, the occasional dust/hair in my vision, the incessant belching, but I didn't want to interrupt his examination. I sat extra-still while he listened to my ticker, so the crinkly paper on the examining table wouldn't throw him off. The man wore a genuinely concerned look when he wrapped up the blood pressure gauge. He asked me to take a seat in his office. I fought to maintain my composure. I wanted to be brave in front of him. The man had thought I was a wimp before; now he'd find out otherwise. I wondered how Amanda would take the news. Bad, of course, but I wouldn't allow her to be too hard on herself. Maybe I wouldn't tell her. It would be horrific if she had to watch me wasting away. I was astonished at how clearly I was thinking. I felt more together than I'd been in weeks. At least now I'd know.

"I want you to see a colleague of mine," the doctor said. He looked sad as he rubbed his upper lip.

"Okay," I said.

"He's a psychiatrist."

What was this, a shrink who specialized in treating the terminally ill?

"I think it would be beneficial for you to talk to somebody," he said.

"The lump?"

"It's nothing."

"What do you mean, 'nothing'? It's a huge lump. I never had a huge lump there before."

"Henry, it's not huge, and it's very common. It's a subareolar mass."

"A what?"

"It's what's called a breast bud."

"Breast bud?"

Slowly it started to sink in.

"I never heard of a *breast bud*," I said with an irrational bitterness.

"You didn't go to medical school."

"But how do you know just by feeling it? Shouldn't you do a biopsy?"

"Henry, *you're not dying*. You're suffering from anxiety. Believe me, you have all the symptoms, and they fall under the heading of hypochondriasis."

"I *knew* I had something."

"This isn't a joke, Henry, it's something you've got to deal with. For God sakes, you're in the tumor-of-the-week club."

This was humiliating. It was one thing to be called a baby, but a nut? I stood up.

"Look, Doc, I'm sorry I troubled you, but I really don't think I need to see a shrink."

"I think you do."

I stared at my shoes. "Wouldn't most people come in if they started feeling lumps on their body?"

"There are lumps all over your body, and I guarantee in a week you'll find another one, or your urine will be a funny color, or your gums will bleed when you floss, or a headache will become a brain tumor. And what'll happen is, if you don't trust me, you'll probably go to another doctor, and then another, until finally you find something you can feel genuinely sick about."

I looked out the window.

"Look," Dr. Hoffman said, "seeing a psychiatrist is nothing to be ashamed of. In your business it's practically a rite of passage. You're a creative guy, and you're probably under a lot of stress."

"Not really."

"Sometimes you can be under stress and not know it. Let's face it, you're in a competitive industry. There's a lot of pressure to succeed."

I nodded, but I wasn't really listening. The thought of walking past the secretaries was starting to make me sick—this time for real. I was a pussy, and they all knew it, and they were probably laughing at me right now.

"I can't afford a shrink. I'm not covered."

"He's reasonable. Can you afford seventy-five dollars a visit?"

"Not really. I mean, that's a couple lunch shifts for me."

"It's worth it, and he's a good man. I'll tell you something else. It's possible you may just have a chemical imbalance that can be treated with drugs. He may want to try you on a half-milligram of Klonopin or Inderal and see if it helps any."

"What if it doesn't?"

"Then we'll find other means to deal with it."

"What does that mean?"

"Just relax . . ."

"But what if we don't get rid of it?"

"Then you'll just go on worrying yourself to death."

"You mean literally? Like I could die from this?"

"Henry, stop it."

I came home and found two messages on my machine. One was from the Gus Anders guy, whom I'd still failed to call back; the other was from Levine. I rung Levine back and, to my surprise, he got right on. The general rule with my agent was that when he called, I immediately called back, and then he would return that call at six-thirty or seven. Unless I called him first, in which case he'd call back at 8 P.M. or 8 A.M.—correctly figuring that most writers were either out or asleep at those hours—so he could live with himself without actually having to talk.

Levine asked how my meeting with Bowman had gone. I tried to answer but produced nothing coherent.

"What's the matter?"

I wanted to tell him about Colleen Driscoll and my cancer scare and the humiliation of working at Johnny Rockets, but it all sounded crazy and unstable and, being new to the entertainment industry, I thought this might adversely affect his opinion of me.

"I have no idea what the hell he was talking about," I said.

"A disaster?"

"He didn't punch me out or anything."

"Did you pitch him?"

"He pitched me."

"Really? That's good. What'd he pitch?"

"Something about love in the nineties being death. And the guy in love is a serial killer."

"Oh, Jesus . . . He's been throwing that one around for years. It used to be 'love in the eighties.' "

"Well, tell me, what does he want?"

"He wants somebody to write a love story about a bunch of assholes. Something he can relate to. I'll call and tell him you're passing."

"No way."

"It's an insane project. It'll never get made."

"I don't care. I need a job."

"I'll set up some more meetings."

"When? In a month? Six weeks? Levine, I don't think you understand how broke I am. Maybe there's a way I can turn this into something good."

"This was a mistake. I shouldn't have sent you to that asshole in the first place. The guy's got the personality of a student loan officer. I'll tell you something else. If you pass, he'll have more respect for you."

"I don't need respect, I need money."

"Henry—"

"Wait a second. Let's just think about this, okay?"

"Henry, I got you a meeting with Larry David."

"Who?"

"The guy who runs *Seinfeld*. He's a friend."

"You're shitting me?"

I could hear Levine pouring something.

"He was down in San Diego for the weekend, so I sent him your script. He called with a little interest, so I put my ass on the line. Now I want you to go prove me right."

"Done. I'm perfect for that show."

"You don't have to convince me. Just go in there with a bunch of ideas and blow them away."

"Maybe I should write a spec *Seinfeld* script. I could kick one out in a week."

"You don't have a week. You're meeting with him and Larry Charles tomorrow. Anyway, these guys they don't buy spec scripts. It's rare that they even buy a pitch, but like I said, he's a friend and they've bought one or two in the past. What you do is you go in, you make him smile, hopefully he pays you to write an episode, and Larry and Jerry rewrite you until you hardly recognize it. Then if you're lucky, maybe when there's a staff opening, they think of you."

"Would I still get credit if they rewrote me?"

"You're getting way ahead of yourself. First you have to blow them away."

"I'll blow them away."

"Yuh," he said with a sniff, "good luck."

"What's that about?"

"I just know these guys. They're not laughers."

"I thought I didn't have to be funny—I'm just a comedy writer, remember?"

"What are you talking about?"

"Before, you said—"

"Forget what I said. Make 'em laugh and they'll hire you, that's the bottom line."

"But they're not laughers . . . ?"

"No. No, they're not."

I tried to prepare for my meeting, but for some reason I couldn't stop thinking about Colleen Driscoll. It's not that I was worried about her, but I did wonder where she was. I'd seen the runaways and crazies and alkies and just plain unlucky who had ended up homeless and I knew that, despite the Beverly Hills policemen's ostensible astonishment that I would wash my hands of this lunatic, they weren't about to get their fingernails dirty, either. This wasn't Mayberry, and no one was going to take her home to Aunt Bea and fill her with pot roast and sweet potato pie. At best they'd contact a relative back in Jersey, if that didn't violate her civil rights, but, from the little I'd gathered, help from that quarter seemed unlikely. I listened to the drizzle in the gutters. Two days in a row now, a record for June in L.A.; thirty-eight hundredths of an inch. I wondered if she would find a dry place to sleep. I thought about the nooks and crannies in the palisades off the PCH. It made me tired and I slept.

i walked out my front door and there was a magnificent snow-capped mountain range to the east. The air had been wiped clean like a windshield. L.A.'s blue-gray sky was now just blue and the gray was floating in the sewers toward the sea. Everything was damp and shiny from the rain, and the downtown skyline sparkled beneath the magical new peak.

It never occurred to me that Jerry Seinfeld would be in the meeting, but when I walked in the office, there he was, slouched on the waiting room couch, in jeans, a button-down shirt, and Mets cap, not reading, not talking, just slouching.

"Excuse me," I said. "Could you tell me how to get to the *Seinfeld* offices?"

He stared at me for a beat. "Uh, this is it."

"Just kidding. I'm supposed to be meeting with the two Larrys at eleven-thirty."

Suddenly the door swung shut, revealing a thin bald man sitting behind it. He held out his hand. "Larry David."

The two of them led me to an inner office and then Larry David went off looking for the other Larry. Jerry leaned against a desk, apparently deep in thought.

I gestured at his hat. "So . . . Mets fan, huh?"

"Yeah."

"They broke my heart. I'm a Sox fan."

He tilted his head. "Chicago?"

"Red Sox. Eighty-six Series."

"Oh, right, yeah. I was there."

"Boy, that one hurt."

"I bet."

We continued to stand there, nodding at each other, me trying to act comfortable. I pretended to check out the room.

"Billy Buckner," he said.

"Mm. Billy Buckner."

I closed my eyes and took a deep breath, as if it were still eating me up.

"We had Keith Hernandez on one of the shows," he said.

"I know. I thought that one sucked."

Jerry flinched. Then he got it. "Yeah, well, guess I don't blame you."

Larry David showed up with the other Larry—Larry Charles—a friendly face about my age who looked like a young Jerry Garcia. This was a nice surprise. I never pictured Seinfeld hanging out with hippie types.

"I've got to warn you," Larry David said, "this is a next-to-impossible task you have here."

"What's that?"

"Pitching to us. It's almost impossible to make us laugh. I just want you to know that, so you don't get disappointed."

"It's true," Larry Charles said. "We hardly ever buy pitches."

Jerry jumped on the bandwagon with a big fold of the arms.

Larry David said, "I think all last year we may have bought two."

"We're brutal," Larry Charles said, looking more like Manson than Garcia now.

"That's right," Larry D. said. "We hardly ever even *take* pitch meetings. But Levine talked us into it."

"All right, all right," Seinfeld said. "Let the man do his job."

I opened my notebook and dove in. Everyone was telling the truth. These guys weren't laughers. The first three stories didn't draw so much as a nod. I was starting to sweat. It's one thing to die in front of some development schmo you never heard of, but dying in front of your idol and two guys named Larry is traumatic. The development person I could write off as a humorless idiot, but these guys were funny. They'd proved that. If I couldn't make them laugh, I wasn't ready for the big leagues. I could see Seinfeld starting to lose interest. Larry David was alert but unenthused. Manson looked like he'd been kicked in the head by an elephant. "Give me another," Larry David kept saying. I was short of breath, felt flop sweat coming on. I wanted to run out the door and never watch the fucking show again.

"What about virgins?" I said. "They haven't done anything about virgins in a while."

Larry David sat up and a smile appeared like a rosebud on a rock.

"Virgins," he said. "Yeah, yeah, I like virgins."

"It used to be, back in the fifties and sixties, that every guy aspired to find a virgin. That was the consummate dreamgirl. Not now. Now it's a nightmare. The last thing you want today is a virgin, especially once you get into your thirties."

"That's true," Larry D. said.

"A virgin at that age only raises a red flag. I mean, why is she a virgin? There's no good excuse for it. Is it an AIDS thing? Use a rubber. Is it religious? You definitely don't want to be the first one in if that's the case—it'd be like fucking God over. Is she holding out for Mr. Right? Too much pressure—what if you do her and it doesn't work out? Maybe she's a virgin because she just doesn't care that much about sex. Well, then . . . you have nothing in common. The bottom line is: Who the fuck needs blueballs when you're in your thirties?"

"That's good," Larry D. said. "I like the virgin thing." I saw him write it down. "Yeah, virgins, I like that."

when a guy loses his pride with a girl, common sense often abandons him as well. So it was that upon returning home that day I found myself dialing Amanda's apartment before I could think it through. Her roommate Maura answered and I started yakking immediately to disguise how ridiculous it was that I was on the other end. Maura had always liked me, that much I knew.

"So how's California treating you?" she asked.

"Good. Not bad. Fine. You know, I joined a gang."

"Really?"

"Yeah. I'm a Crip."

"That's great, Henry."

"It's okay. I looked into the Bloods, read all their literature, but the Crips had a better dental plan, so I went with them."

She giggled. It reminded me of the old days. She'd played a big part in my decision to become a writer. So many nights, parties, bars, concerts, she'd followed me around sounding like a mini-laugh track. Even at the end, she was tickled by my efforts, my pathetic pleas, the clown trying to walk up a wall on roller skates. She didn't want it to be over; she was on my side, sort of. It had irritated me, at the end, her amusement, because I wasn't trying to amuse anyone. I felt like Dick Shawn, putting on a show, entertaining, anything for a laugh, then crashing to the floor and dying of a heart attack to a standing O.

"So have you seen any big stars?"

"Met with Jerry Seinfeld today," I said.

"Great."

She didn't ask any follow-up questions, which made me think she didn't believe it.

"I'm not kidding."

"I believe you, Henry. If anyone could meet him, it's you. What's he like?"

"He's okay. Kind of quiet actually."

"But he's nice, huh?"

"Well, you know, he's not exactly like you and me, but he's a star, what do you expect?"

"Huh. Yeah."

"So how've you been, Maura?"

"I've been good. You know, lot of work."

I sighed. "And how's she doing?"

"Okay, Henry. She's doing okay."

"Mm."

"But she's not here."

I could see Amanda back there, waving her hands, forcing Maura to lie.

"Okay . . . well . . . do you expect her back soon?"

"Well, no, not real soon."

"She out for the night already?"

"Actually, she's out of town."

"Work?"

"Vacay."

"Oh, I didn't know. I guess I wouldn't."

I tried to make this sound somehow humorous, which it wasn't.

"So I'll tell her you called."

"Wait a second. When's she getting back? Where is she?"

"She'll be back in about a week."

"Where'd she go?"

"Took off somewhere. She's all over the place."

More bullshit.

"Look, Maura, you're my friend. Tell me the truth. Is she standing right behind you?"

"What?"

"Is she dodging my call?"

"Jesus, Henry, no! What do you think I am? What do you think . . . ?"

"I'm sorry, it just sounds fishy."

"I *am* your friend, Henry. How long have you known me? Why would I lie to you? Jesus, I'm not like that. Give me a little credit."

"I'm sorry."

"It's just . . . This isn't a war. I don't take sides. I wish you guys had stayed together. I loved you guys together."

"I know. I'm sorry, I'm sorry."

"And I'll tell you something else. Mandy would never ask me to lie to you. *She* would never lie to you."

This was true. What was wrong with me? She'd broken my heart, but she'd done it in a very up-front way. As honest as a bullet, as cold as a refrigerator. I'd called her "Amana" at the end.

"I know, I know, I'm just . . . the whole thing . . . I'm just confused. You seemed to . . . I don't know . . ."

"She's in California."

Mixed emotions. Great! No, wait. *Horrible.* What? You mean? Why did . . . n't she . . . ?

"Since when?"

"Saturday."

Saturday? This was Wednesday, meaning four days. What? Maybe she didn't have my number, maybe it wasn't listed. Of course it was listed, a fucking figure skater from New Jersey had tracked me down, why couldn't she?

"She's in California," I repeated.

"Yeah."

Maura sounded like I felt, which was nice of her.

I sucked it up and said, "Is she in L.A.?"

"No, she hasn't been in Los Angeles, that I know." She delivered this firmly, trying to protect me or Amanda, I couldn't tell which. Then she said, "She's in Malibu."

"*What?* Where the fuck do you think Malibu is? Malibu *is* L.A."

Maura stumbled for a moment and said, "Maybe it's not Malibu. It's up the West Coast Highway somewhere."

"*Pacific* Coast Highway—that's where Malibu is!"

I don't know why I was blaming Maura and I could hear her having a hard time with all this, so I calmed myself and said, "Where is she staying? I'll see if she wants to have lunch with me at the studio."

This studio reference was shameful and we both knew it.

"There's no way to reach her. She's camping out."

"She's what?"

"Camping."

"*Camping?* What, is she having a nervous breakdown? She doesn't *camp*. And why the hell does she have to camp out in California? She couldn't camp out in fucking Florida? She couldn't go to New Hampshire and camp out? What, is she trying to make me crazy? I knew she was here. I could sense it, that must be why I called."

"She didn't want to go to California, Henry. She knew it would hurt you if you knew, but that's where . . . he wanted to go."

"*He?*"

"Yeah. Um . . . yeah."

"Oh. Oh, I see."

"She just started going out with him. They met on St. Paddy's Day."

"And already they take trips?"

"I don't know. I guess they just . . . clicked."

Ten seconds of dead air. Felt like ten minutes.

"That's funny. I met someone on St. Paddy's Day."

"Really? Well, that's good. Look, I just didn't want you to think she lied to you."

"Yeah, well . . . Is he, um . . . Does he live in Malibu?"

"No, no, he went to grad school there. He lives here."

"So I guess we won't be having lunch."

"Mm. Yeah. No."

I made a tick-tock sound with my tongue.

"Hey, do me a favor, huh?" I said. "Don't tell her I called."

Maura started to say something, but I was gone.

as a boy, I was awakened many spring and summer mornings by a neighbor's lawnmower or a barking dog or the distant echo of hammering, backhoes, and electric saws as one of our plat's new homes was being constructed plank by plank. Although it was very early and I was tired, an anxious, lonely feeling would chase me outdoors without stopping to brush my teeth, or flip on cartoons, or fill my stomach with sugary cereal. The sensation was of the world passing me by, of life and fun going on without me, and, even though I knew that my family and friends and most of the town were fast asleep, it was a feeling of being left out.

This sensation had long ago been dealt with and conquered.

Which recalls one of life's ironies. As a kid, you get up before your parents and they beg you to go back to bed, then as a teenager you want to sleep until two and you've got your old lady banging your feet with a flyswatter or vacuuming against your door. Mom and Dad, they'd be bursting with pride today. Here I was, on the brink of middle age, one eye stuffed into my pillow, the other staring at the bluish-white universe, my dick cemented to my underwear and a crisp wad of tissue on the nightstand next to a clock that read 3:20 in the afternoon. From my bed I could hear cars whizzing by, an occasional horn, a radio down the hall, somebody's voice trailing off in a passing vehicle. A lot of people had been at it for eight or nine hours. Somebody was having the best day of their life. When my father was my age, he had a wife, five kids, two homes, a successful medical practice, and a seven handicap. Where the hell did he find the time for a seven handicap?

I got up at four and, though it was twelve and a half hours since I'd gone to sleep, I was still tired. I didn't exactly want to go back to bed, but I had to sit down. This was a deep, unprecedented fatigue; a fog around my every organ. From the toilet seat I worked on my teeth, then leaned over and washed my face. I didn't shower. A half hour later—after aimlessly opening cupboards, staring at the floor, scratching different parts of myself—I started to read. At six o'clock I started writing. Somewhere in there I downed a couple bowls of Cracklin' Oat Bran. Now it was dark and I was starved. Cracklin' Oat Bran lasts about ten minutes with me: the Chinese food of breakfast cereals.

At ten o'clock I went outdoors for the first time. Carl's Market was closed and Hughes was too imposing. I wanted in-and-out, ready-to-eat food, few decisions. Everything good and cheap was closed, so I resorted to bad and overpriced. A garishly lit 7-Eleven on La Cienega. I nuked an orange hot dog, poured fake orange cheese on round orange nachos, grabbed a lukewarm soda out of the cooler, and now I waited in line beside a stack of Styrofoam ice chests, staring at the linoleum floor. I was having a hard time looking the 7-Eleven guy in the eye. He was an achiever. Suddenly Death was standing beside me. He was holding a pack of Evereadys, clicking his skates, and humming a song, or maybe singing, I wasn't sure, and in the middle of it he asked how I was doing without missing a beat. I broke out in a sweat, felt irrationally embarrassed.

"Good."

This was the first word I'd uttered in more than a day, and it sounded like it. The clerk was in slow motion. I felt like dropping everything and running. I looked down, felt the dark skater's gaze on me.

"I'm fine, too," he said.

Now he had me. I was forced to peek into the cowl, look him in the eye. His face was thin and white with a scruffy reddish beard covering a Muskovy duck complexion.

"Good," I said again, this time with a smile.

The clerk was really picking his ass now. When he finally got to me, I gave him five dollars on four ninety-one and told him to keep the change, which made me feel creepy on several levels, and I scurried outside to my car. The clerk was an insidious motherfucker and he rang up Darth Vader in about three seconds and before I could back out of the parking lot he was skating around my car, blocking me in, rejoicing in the reprimand he'd just served me. I waited it out and he eventually lost interest, allowing me to peel away.

After all the orange food, I felt a little better. It was unbelievable that she was here. Camping. I pictured her with a Mountain Dew guy in bike shorts with muscular tanned thighs and an extreme-sport attitude—a Dartmouth guy—jumping out of fucking airplanes with surfboards strapped to his feet, riding his mountain bike in the Santa Monica Mountains, bungeeing off magnificent cliffs. The California they knew was spectacular, twenty miles and a million light-years from the loveless shithole I was brooding in. Maura said they had *clicked.* What a mean thing to say. It reeked of laughter. Time would tell if they'd really clicked, I knew that. It's a lot easier to slip into oversized shoes than ones that fit just right, but let her try walking around in them for a while.

An ad on the radio: "Are you feeling strange?" a man asked somberly. "Does your heart palpitate?" I sat up. "Do your palms get inordinately sweaty? Do you sometimes feel faint or light-headed?"

It was me he was describing, it was me to the T. I turned up the volume.

"If you have two or more of these symptoms, you have . . . *Del Mar fever!* Come to the track this Saturday and watch the horses run!"

I wrote until five in the morning, then forced myself into bed. I watched the sky lighten, heard a few doors slam out in the hallway, footsteps, car engines turning over. I tried to sleep, but my whole body itched and my legs ached like a kid with growing pains. I wondered what that was all about.

do you think about death every day of your life? I do. Which puts a damper on things. The problem is, I've seen death in action, I know how it works. It's a sneaky motherfucker. It shows up at the company softball game, at the beach on a sunny day, when you're making love to your wife. My girlfriend Grace was coming home from a Christmas party in her new red dress when it came for her. This girl had more life in her than anyone I ever knew, and the driver cracked a joke, she clapped her hands and leaned back, the door swung open, and she literally died laughing.

Aside from expecting to die any minute, I'd always considered myself a pretty normal guy. I liked animals and had lots of friends growing up. I liked girls. Sports, too. High school had been fun, and I lost my virginity pleasantly, if not memorably. I'd never been a loner or a security guard. Suicide had never occurred to me. I'd never chopped up a rabbit with my babysitter or sucked off a scout leader.

But the day came when I had to admit there was something abnormal about this preoccupation with my health. I used to be the type of guy who would play with an injury. Now it was one crisis after another. My main fears had been of a heart attack, lung cancer, and brain tumor, but I'd also entertained thoughts of leukemia, M.S., stroke, and Parkinson's; cancers of the pancreas, prostate, rectum, testicles, breasts, spine, throat, toe, and lymph nodes; an inflamed gallbladder, AIDS, colitis, and ileitis; aneurysms of the brain, spleen, aorta, and liver; and Ménière's syndrome.

That's why, when the Big Brothers called about their psychological test, I decided to take it. I was a long way from being approved, Margo Jones said—she still hadn't even spoken with my "girlfriend" Colleen—but the psychological evaluation was necessary, so we might as well get it out of the way. I was going to tell her to forget it, but she said it was free and would be administered by a Wilshire Boulevard psychiatrist. I asked if I could get a copy of the report. She said yes, I had the right to request one. "Tell me where to go," I said. And so it was that I ended up in a ritzy medical building in the heart of Beverly Hills.

Dr. Lester Samuels was warm and effusive, almost gossipy. He even commented on the good looks of his previous patient. "And she puts it to good use," he added with a wink. The guy was more like a hairdresser than a shrink, and I found this comforting. He donated several hours a week to the Big Brothers, and I thought that pretty decent, too.

He had a list of questions, but I told him to put them away, he wouldn't need them. Then I spilled everything; how I'd kept track of my proximity to emergency rooms, my compulsion with litter, the strange dreams, the tingling in my face when I was in traffic, the feeling of impending doom, the overall sense of karmic guilt that had transcended every decision.

"What is it about your body that scares you?"

"*Everything,*" I said, "I'm a hypochondriac for the same reason I'm afraid to fly. When I'm on a plane, I think of the millions of little things that can go wrong. Maybe one of the flaps will get stuck, or the landing gear will jam, or the fuel line will clog, or the engine will crack, or the door will blow off, or the pilot will be drunk, or he'll have a heart attack, or the wings won't be de-iced properly, or we'll hit a wind shear, or be blown up by terrorists, or the radar will malfunction and we'll collide with another jet, or the goddamn toilet suction will yank my colon out into the clouds. There's so much that can happen—just like with my body. Billions of cells trying to mutate into cancers, and veins that a hot dog can clog or a good shit can burst, and organs that stop working for no reason other than fate; there's blood fighting off infections and viruses every day, intestines trying to make sense of man-made chemicals—Christ, there's a million ways I can die. I'm amazed that I haven't already."

"So what? If you die, you die."

I groaned.

"Is it the pain of dying you fear?" he asked.

"I don't think so. No, not really."

"Then what is it?"

"Well, for one thing, I've been killing myself writing a couple scripts and I'd like to see at least one of them reach fruition. I'd like to know I lived for a reason."

"So you're afraid you might die before your movie gets made?"

This sounded dumb.

"No."

"That's what you just said."

"Well . . . I *am* afraid I'm going to die before I ever accomplish anything in my life." I took a deep breath. "But that's not the thing I fear most."

"What is it you fear most?"

"Nothing."

The doctor tilted his head.

"You know," I said. "The thought of being nothing."

"You think when you die, you won't exist anymore?"

"That's what I fear most."

"So you fear nothingness?"

"Something like that."

"Do you believe in a God and heaven?"

"Depends."

"On?"

"The time of day. Sometimes I feel there's a God, and other times I don't."

"What do you feel right now?"

"I don't know. I think probably not."

"Then why do you continue to write?"

"What do you mean?"

"Well, you have to do it for somebody."

"It doesn't have to be for God. Maybe I'm doing it for myself."

"Then why do you care if you die before you finish it? You know how it's going to turn out anyway."

"Well . . . not yet I don't."

The doors were thin. I heard someone enter the outer office.

"I suppose I do it for other people," I admitted.

"Who?"

"Many people."

"Who?"

I didn't answer.

"Your parents?"

"I guess. I guess I do it for my girlfriend."

"You have a girlfriend?"

"Did. Not now."

"So she's your *ex*-girlfriend."

"My ex-girlfriend."

"Why'd you break up?"

"It's kind of complicated."

"I'm good with complicated."

I felt tired. "Basically . . . uh . . ."

"Did she end it?"

"More or less."

Dr. Samuels nodded. "And she's the main reason you want to finish your scripts?"

"I guess so . . . Yeah, probably."

"Well, it seems you have a God after all, Henry."

In the ten minutes we had left Dr. Samuels wanted to know about my childhood. I told him the truth, which was that it was wonderful. I had a great, big, loud family. We lived in a town called

Cumberland in northern Rhode Island. After school and in the summer, I was free to do whatever I wanted. There was some crying in my house, but a lot more laughing. The only time I heard sirens was at noon. In the winter we skated on the pond next door, caught snowflakes on our tongues. If we got cold, my mother would make us hot chocolate. We had dogs and cats and rabbits, too. We had a monkey for a while. There was lots of food in the house, and I could eat meals any time I wanted, except for dinner, which we all ate together when my father got home from the office around six. My parents played golf and bridge together. They fought sometimes—usually over bridge—but they always made up. We were expected to study on weeknights, and television was forbidden after dinner. I daydreamed a lot and didn't get good grades—which was a constant irritation to my father—but other than that, we got along pretty well. He took me and my friends to Red Sox and Patriot games, and every year on my birthday I'd get to go see the Celts. My mother was happy and beautiful. She wanted her kids to go to church with her on Sundays, but other than that, we didn't get smothered with religion. Virginity wasn't a big deal in my house. My parents knew that kids smoked pot. Summers were spent on Cape Cod. I was always proud of my parents.

When I finished telling all this, neither of us spoke. I sat there trying to figure what the hell had gone wrong. I'd been a happy kid, I was secure, I was confident. Now, as an adult, I was afraid of flying, I was afraid of crowds, I was afraid of fucking basketball. My mother once told me that as newlyweds she and my father would kneel next to their bed each night and pray. This wasn't what they'd prayed for.

Dr. Samuels's assistant notified him that the next patient was getting antsy.

"Did anything out of the ordinary happen to you recently?" the doctor asked when I was at the door.

"Not really."

"Nothing?"

"No."

"Nothing at all?"

I shrugged. "I saw a woman jump off a building."

i said a prayer. I always said my prayers, but this night I got a little more free-form than normal. Not that my regular prayer was from the Scriptures. As a kid, I'd learned the *Our Father* and *Hail Mary* and often recited them before going to sleep. At some point, I think in my late teens, I realized I had no idea what I was saying. These were just words that I'd memorized, like *The Star-Spangled Banner* or *Frère Jacques*. So I made up my own prayer. It started small and evolved over the years. Every single night, no matter how tired I was, no matter if I was stinking drunk or lying in bed with a girl whose pussy was more familiar than her name, I would repeat the following:

Name of the Father, Son, Holy Spirit. Amen.

Please, God, bless my mother, my father, my sister Bette, my brother Bill, my sister Kara, my sister Suzy, my brother-in-law Jim, my brother-in-law Eddie, my brother-in-law Thomas, my nephew Willy, my niece Karly, my nephew Tris, my nephew Andy, my nephew Fritz, my niece Wesley, and my sister-in-law Jackie. Please let us all live long, happy, Christian, and fruitful lives together. Forgive us our sins.

Guide us to be better people. Please give us strength, inspiration, wisdom, patience, confidence, and courage.

Please bless all my friends, especially my deceased friends, most of all . . . (Early on I would name all my deceased friends and relatives—starting with my dead girlfriend—but as I got older and more people died, I trimmed it down to the girlfriend, one or two close dead guys, and the recently departed.) *Please forgive them their sins, welcome them into Your kingdom, let them always be happy. Let them know how much I love and miss them all, but I have much to accomplish here and I'm not ready to join them. Please bless their families, especially Grace's, let them find strength and happiness through You.*

Please bless Amanda and all my friends, especially the ones who need You the most, most of all . . . (I would rattle off ten or fifteen friends who were going through difficult times, a constantly evolving list, with, sadly, one or two mainstays.) *Please give them the strength and energy to get through these difficult times. Let them feel Your love. Forgive them their sins and help them forgive themselves. Give them the strength to heal themselves when it's possible and the courage to accept it when it's not. Please bless their souls.*

Please take care of all the people in the world who are less fortunate than me, especially the children, sick, starving, falsely imprisoned, mentally retarded, mentally impaired, mistreated, crippled, deformed, homeless, murder and rape victims, grieving and depressed, and all the AIDS and war victims, and the drug addicts and alkies. Please take care of all those who are dying. Give them strength during their dark hours. Let them feel Your love and presence. Please forgive them their sins and welcome them into Your kingdom. Please also bless the people who are more fortunate than me. Give them the strength to be good.

Forgive me my sins, Jesus. Please give me the strength, inspiration, wisdom, patience, confidence, courage, and humility to become a better person. Thank You for everything You've given me, Jesus. I know I am very lucky. I'm sorry I
. . . (Here I would list some recent sins.) *Please come into my heart, show me the way to be a better person. Please do not let me stray. Let me feel Your presence inside me, let me spread Your love wherever I go. Please heal my body, bless me while I sleep. Let me wake up feeling refreshed and energetic. Thank You. I love You.*

Name of the Father, Son, and Holy Spirit. Amen.

It was a mouthful, but I'd been saying it for fifteen years, so I could rattle off the whole thing in about two minutes. On lazy or drunken nights I plowed through it without hearing a word. I tried to avoid this because it was only two minutes of my day and I didn't want it to become another *Our Father.*

Anyway, on this night I said my prayer and then I hung in there and really tried to connect. (I never said my prayers aloud, just in my head, because I'd read that Satan can hear your spoken words, which I doubted, but why risk it?) I asked God how He could expect me to believe in Him when the only proof I had of His existence was the Bible and that guys can't piss through a hard-on. The Bible had been written by men I didn't know and the very first lesson I'd been taught as a human being was to not trust men I didn't know. Don't take candy from strangers, don't hitchhike, don't even trust your neighbors, because if you do, they might kill you. And now I was expected to have faith in a book written by these killers.

It was the brain He'd given me that gave me doubts.

The world was a nightmare, people were starving, children were killing one another, space shuttles were exploding on national television, good men were being assassinated while bad men prospered, rain forests were being wiped out to make room for hamburger farms, *the coral was dying!* There was a new plague every fifty years, TV preachers were condemning the dying, priests were getting rounded up by the truckload for diddling altar boys. Yet, despite these and countless other atrocities that I was too numb to recall, the thing that really got people worked up these days, the incident that riled the masses, the lead story in all the newspapers and talk-radio shows, was that a television actress had sung the national anthem out of key.

So I asked for a sign.

Just one sign, I said. I want to believe You exist, but my faith is flickering. I need help, Jesus. Give me a sign and I will never question my faith again. One clear sign, that's all. Help me get behind You one hundred percent. I know it's asking a lot, but I need it. Everything I've been taught disputes Your existence. Give me a sign and I am Yours eternally. I will go beyond the call of duty. Give me a sign and I will become who You want me to be.

I don't know what time I fell asleep, but I woke up to someone knocking on my door, and when I opened it I had my sign.

it was the midget. Not *a* midget, *the* midget, the same verti-cally challenged fellow who'd been insulted outside the Baskin-Robbins when I first got to L.A. He'd been knocking at my door and now he was engaging me in conversation, but it was insane that he should be there and my foggy brain was trying to fathom it and the circuits were shorting out left and right.

"Did I wake you?" he asked.

"What?"

"Did I wake you?"

"No, no, I was awake, I was just . . . resting. What did you ask before that?"

"I asked if a Henry Halloran lives here."

I blurted out that I was Henry and, despite the fact that he was standing there in a tweed blazer, brown corduroys, Lacoste shirt, and big smile, I felt a rush of fear. The fucker had tracked me down. How could he . . . ?

"Gus Anders," he said, arm outstretched. "I've been trying to reach you."

This made even less sense. Was this the Gus on my machine, the one who'd read the article? Was that a ploy to get to me, or . . . ?

"Maybe this isn't a good time," he said when I offered a dead-fish handshake and similar gaze.

He was around thirty-five with a freshly carved goatee that gave him a vaguely hip presence.

"Wait, I'm sorry," I said. "How did you find me?"

"You're in the phone book."

"But . . . how did you know my name?"

"Um, well, it was in the magazine."

He said this in a slightly patronizing way, then seemed to catch himself.

"Oh, I should have clarified that. I read your article in the *Times* about . . . you know . . . and I have a few questions, if you don't mind. I've actually called a few times, but . . . ."

I played dumb about the phone calls—there'd been at least three—my machine was wacky, I told him, I hadn't received any. After another awkward moment, I asked him in. I didn't have any bloody mix in the apartment, which was a bummer, because I was a little too winded to be talking to a friend of the dead woman's, and that's what he was.

"That you're here blows my mind," I said.

"Why?"

His congeniality slipped, as if bracing for an oafish remark. I wondered whether this was wise, bringing the ice cream store up, but I had to, there was too great a chance he already recognized me and the tension was excruciating. Besides, the magnitude of this coincidence, *the godliness of it,* was something I had to share.

I'd been there when the big goon had insulted him, I said, and hastily explained how it had unfolded. I tried to convey my embarrassment about the whole thing without further embarrassing him, which, by the way, was tricky.

He claimed to have no recollection of it, that I must be mistaking him. I asked if he had a white van, he said no. Adamant now, I asked if he'd been to a Baskin-Robbins in the last several months. He said yes, then, ah, he recalled the van. It was a friend's he'd been using to move stuff. Now he recalled standing outside the store, too—it was definitely Gus—but the midget crack he'd missed entirely. He'd had things on his mind that day, other things, and he'd paid us no mind.

"Well, I feel a little better," I said.

"People get hung up too much on stupid stuff."

Then we talked about the Suicide Lady. Though I'd lived with her sister almost a week, I knew very little about Bonnie Driscoll until Gus showed up. They'd worked together at UCLA Medical Center; he was a psychologist, she a psychiatric nurse. It had disturbed a lot of people that one of their own could do such a thing without anyone picking up the warning signs. Gus had come to get information from me, but I was the one who got most of the info.

Bonnie Driscoll was a manic-depressive who had long periods of stability between bouts. At age nineteen she'd been hospitalized for a year, again at twenty-nine, and when she felt it coming on at age thirty-nine, she couldn't or wouldn't deal with it. That much was explained in a letter found in her car.

"But why jump off a building?" I asked. "It seems so violent, so angry. It would've been a lot cleaner and easier just to run a hose into the car, no?"

"Two schools of thought," he said. "Sometimes they do it because they're angry, and other times it's for the view."

I made a face.

"Sounds crazy, but . . ."

He went on to tell me about the two kinds of people who jump off the Golden Gate Bridge—those who jump off the side facing the city and the more determined ones who jump off the ocean side. Almost everyone who attempts to jump on the ocean side succeeds, while those on the city side are often talked down. They're the ones who haven't completely lost hope, who are literally reaching out to humanity. "Which side did Bonnie go?" he asked. "Neither the front nor the back," I said, "kind of on the side." He asked if there was anything I'd forgotten to put in the article—maybe a curious comment, something that made no sense to me—but I said there wasn't, just the thing about it being my fault. That was typical of suicides, he said, holding an individual responsible for feelings they can't comprehend. It was childish and cruel, but so was the final act itself, and I should not let it bother me. I asked him if he knew Bonnie's sister Colleen.

"Oh, yes, I know Colleen."

"Is she insane?"

"What?"

"Is she a crazy woman? Colleen—is she nuts?"

"No, she's a good kid. A little wild, I suppose, but I wouldn't call her crazy."

I told him how she'd come to my door, how she'd moved in on me, how she'd made my life hell. Gus seemed surprised by this. The Colleen he knew was a little troubled but had "a big heart." I wondered if I'd been had by a fraudulent Colleen, but it was her, all right—right down to the checkerboard dress. Because of a ten-year age difference, Colleen and Bonnie hadn't been close while growing up, he said, but Colleen had tried to change that after moving to L.A. She pushed too hard too fast, though, and the relationship never really improved.

"She has a way of doing that," I said. "Annoying people."

"It wasn't just Colleen—Bonnie had a hard time getting close to people."

"Maybe you didn't know Colleen like she did."

Gus sat on my bed. There he was, the ice cream midget—*the answer to my prayers!*—sitting on my bed.

"Look," he said, "I know Colleen's got problems, and sometimes her judgment isn't very good, but she's not a bad person. She's been through a lot, that kid. I won't even tell you the shit she endured growing up. Then when her sister died . . . it was like . . . They may not have been very close, but it was as close as Colleen was to anyone."

"What about Honus?"

"The German? Just a big asshole. That was pretty sad actually."

"So you're telling me that the woman who drove me crazy a few weeks ago is really a sweetheart?"

"What I saw of Colleen I liked. What's become of her I can't say. When her sister died . . . I don't know what was going on in her head. I know she blamed a lot of people, myself included, but that's typical. What's not typical is to cut everybody off. I don't know. I tried to talk to her at the funeral, but she didn't want any help from me or any of Bonnie's friends. It's too bad because she obviously needs it."

He asked me a few more questions about what happened on the roof, but I stuck to my story. He was just searching for something tangible, something that might help him to understand, and so I lied again and told him there wasn't much anybody could do, she definitely wanted to go, that it was quick and painless, and when I saw her on the ground, she looked at peace.

Before leaving, Gus encouraged me to get psychological counseling because traumas such as these could cause problems down the line. I said I was fine, I'd dealt with it on my own. When he thanked me for being with Bonnie Driscoll at the end of her life, I waved him off. He asked if he could take me to lunch someday, that it would mean a lot to him, and I said, "Of course, it would mean a lot to me, too," and then after he left I took his number and flushed it down the toilet and wiped my brow and took off my damp shirt and prayed for God to forgive me for making the same mistakes over and over.

When the sun had just set and it was still light, I went walking. I took a tennis ball along to keep me company. The shadows made everything outside look black and white, but I could see my neighbors eating dinner in their warm orange boxes or glowing blue in front of TVs. The air smelled of pasta boiling and chicken and pork chops baking, and it made me homesick. I thought how great it would be to go shopping with Amanda and pick up a box of fishsticks and fries and cook them in the oven, letting the house warm with their smell, and then to light candles and eat the fish and chips on our scratchy coffee table while we watched *Jeopardy*. I thought about how lucky I was to receive a sign from God. I didn't deserve it, I knew, but it had happened, there was no denying it. As the shadows bled into darkness, I prayed for a way to follow up on my end of the deal—to make myself what God wanted me to be—and right away it struck me, and it wouldn't go away, no matter how much I fought it, and the thought was so loud and insistent and contrary to every impulse in my body that it occurred to me maybe the voice in my head wasn't mine. So I decided to suck it up and listen.

THE CANCEL WRITER

six

the desk clerk at the Beverly Hills Police Department wasn't able to find any record of her. No Colleen Driscoll on his "guest list"; hadn't been for the past month at least, he said. I was surprised by the disappointment I felt. I really wanted to find her now. On my way out, I ran into Orange Cop and, after tossing a snippy remark my way, he straightened things out. Colleen wasn't Colleen anymore. She was *Doheny*. First and last. Doheny. Like the street. Not Doheny Doheny. Just Doheny. Madonna, Cher, Sting . . . *Doheny*. After a lot of haggling, someone gave me the address of a women's shelter in the mid-Wilshire district.

There was something vaguely Russian-looking about this part of town. Rows of nondescript high-rises, cement-colored, same shape; few trees or smiles. The shelter was in one of these boxes, but she wasn't there. They suggested another place east of downtown.

Several throbbing adrenaline rushes now as I drove through neighborhoods that would shake many a faith. I got lost, was grateful for my invisible little Arrow, finally found a shelter wedged into a strip mall. I parked in front of the door—illegally—and asked to see her. Doheny. While I waited, I kept glancing outside. A few women came in and out, some asking for coupons, others just staring up at the TV. A faint pharmaceutical smell and the palpable chasm between staff and resident gave me a whiff of an insane asylum. It wasn't that, though, which in a way made it worse. This wasn't a "shelter" in the sense of someone's sheltering arms; more like a lean-to in a blizzard.

When she appeared, I was surprised—she was clean and looked rested. I said, "Come on, get your stuff, let's go."

She was probably very startled, but she behaved as if she'd been expecting me and after matter-of-factly signing her new name on a few forms and grabbing her bags, she was sitting beside me in my car. She lit a butt, looked out the window, fiddled with the radio, all the while acting very blasé, as if I picked her up from incredibly depressing places every night about this time. She was clean, like I said, but there was a smell coming from her. Not terrible, not good; something like a grammar school cafeteria.

"I said I'd let you stay with me until you got your shit together, and that's what we're gonna do."

She hung her arm out the window, I tapped on the steering wheel. I think neither of us could believe the other was beside them.

"Ain't you gonna hate having a roommate?"

"I'm not having a roommate, I'm having a guest. Like I said, it's just until you get your shit together."

"What about your precious personal life?"

"I don't have a personal life."

"Fucking A."

Not a clue what she meant.

"And what about the fridge? Can I go in there now?"

"I never said you couldn't use the refrigerator. I just asked that you not touch my notebooks. It's important stuff, and it's also personal."

"Okay," she said. Then, surprisingly, "Thanks."

"Anyway," I said, "it won't be that bad with two of us. There's just a few things I'll have to give up."

"Like?"

"Well, like walking around the apartment wearing a bra with a peacock feather up my ass."

She smirked at this.

"That doesn't make me gay, you know."

"Of course not," she said. "It just means you're a cross-dresser."

"Right. And a bird lover."

I smiled at her and she blushed.

"Well, this is very noble of you, Henry. Very noble." She tossed her butt out the window. "Maybe you're not such a fark after all."

sometime in the late sixties, my eighty-year-old Irish grandfather came over for the Sunday afternoon dinner, as he always did, and he got smashed, as he often did, and when he started filling the air with Irish songs, my father said, "Get the hell out of here, Johnny, you're stinkin' drunk." This triggered a minor melee between my parents—not that my mother worried about the old guy weaving his way home. (This was another time, when dogs ran freely through neighborhoods and people burned trash in backyard barrels and kids rode bikes without helmets and no one thought twice about drinking and driving.) What pissed Ma off was that her father had been called a drunk in front of his grandchildren. Grandpa wasn't a drunk, I knew that. He was a landscaper who owned a dump truck loaded with hand mowers and grass clippings and every kind of rake and gardening tool conceivable. He was built like a man half his age and was the hardest worker I ever saw. But the fact was on Sundays he drank, and my father wasn't against tipping a few with him, right up until the jigs would start and my old man got surly and he'd tell the old guy to screw.

On this particular Sunday, my grandfather had just staggered out and my parents were quarreling and us kids were bickering about something, too, but this all stopped when we saw the dump truck blow past the backyard window and we heard the crash. When we got outside, the truck was bent around a large oak, its rear wheels chugging full-speed ahead, blowing a pile of black and orange dirt onto the yard. My sloshed and bloodied grandfather was sitting contentedly in the driver's seat, and when he looked to his left, he was dumbfounded to see the whole family peeking in the side window as he rumbled down some highway in his head.

Sometimes you can run head-on into an immovable object and not know it, and I guess that's one reason I went back to find Colleen. What was I supposed to do? I'd received a sign from God, hadn't I? How many people get that? And the thing that tore me up was that I couldn't even tell this messenger from above (Gus) the truth. To hell with the Big Brothers, I was going right to the source of my guilt: the dead woman's sister. So she was back, and it was my choice, and I was going to do everything in my power to help her get on her feet again. It wasn't a suicide mission—not consciously; I believed that, with a little organization and direction, I really *could* help her out.

That first night I felt like the guy who dumps his beautiful mistress for the hag of a wife and the bratty little shits. Noble. And depressed. Doheny's mood didn't cheer me up any as we shared a beer by the pool.

"My life sucks," she said.

"You're just in a slump."

"No, it sucks. It always has sucked."

"It'll get better. You just have to keep plugging."

"Why bother?"

"Colleen, you've got to understand something—"

"Doheny."

"Life is like a marathon race, Doheny. It's tough starting out, and then you get in a groove and things go okay for a while and you're moving along fairly effortlessly, and then you hit a wall and you feel like quitting, but that's when you've got to suck it up and plow ahead, and eventually you break through and it gets easy again."

"And then you get to the end and what?"

"They put a wreath on your head, I don't know."

"Why does it have to be so hard?"

"I don't know."

"And why is mine always the hardest?"

"It's not the hardest," I said. "It just seems that way. I promise you, when it comes to personal hardship, I can hold my own with the best of them."

"You think so, huh?"

"Trust me."

"Okay," she said, "try this on for size. When I was six, I saw my best friend get hit by a car and thrown a hundred feet into the air. She died. *After* being in a coma for eight months. From the time I was nine until I was thirteen my stepdad raped me a couple times a week. When I was ten, my only brother died in a motorcycle accident. On my birthday. After that we never celebrated my birthday no more. When my mother found out her husband was humping me, she blamed *me*. When I was fourteen—"

"All right, you win."

"You see?"

"You win, you win."

Doheny lit a cigarette. "I've had it bad."

"You've had it worse than me."

"Thank you."

I touched her shoulder. I thought she was going to cry, but she'd experienced a minor victory—her life was worse than mine— and she managed a small empty laugh. "Fuck," she said.

We walked up the street for a six-pack and she said she didn't feel that the acting thing was going to work but didn't know what else to do. I told her she should do the thing she loved the most, whatever that was, but she said she didn't love anything.

"That's not true," I said. "Think about it. If you could do anything in the world, what would it be?"

"I don't know. Party."

"Something where you could get paid. Would you like to be a chef? A costume designer? Work with old people? You like skating, maybe you could get a job back home at a rink. Whatever the answer, whatever the thing is that you'd like to do most in this world, that's what you should do."

"No matter what it is?"

"No matter what. Because if you really, *really* want something badly enough, you can't help but be good at it."

"I'd like to be a doctor."

"Think of something else."

"What's the matter with a doctor? You know, like at a hospital."

"You can't be a doctor. It's out of the question."

"Why not?"

"Well, for starters, you need to be able to read."

She slapped my arm. *"I can read."*

"You'd also need a high school diploma. Look, if you like medicine so much, why don't you get a job in a vet's office? You could start by clipping and bathing the dogs and work your way up to . . . well, clipping and bathing dogs seems like fun."

"Yeah, right. I'm going to work at a place where they put animals to sleep. No thank you. If I'm gonna go into medicine, I'm gonna help *save* lives."

"Okay, think of something else. Something within reason. Something where hard work and ambition and street smarts are enough."

And that's how Doheny decided to become a writer. Of course I tried to discourage her. I told her it was boring, solitary, odds are it wouldn't work out, and even if it did, she probably wouldn't ever make much money. I told her the act itself involved tapping into the wrong side of one's brain: the right side, the creative side, the lobe that housed depression and fear and anxiety and many other monsters. I told her if she didn't ache to do it, then don't. Leave that door shut, she'd be a happier person for it. She had very nice hair; had she considered hairdressing school? But no, writing was suddenly the only thing she ever really wanted to do—with the exception of skating, acting, and internal medicine—and, besides, it was easy to get started. She didn't need a degree, she didn't need a license, all she needed was a pen and pad. She could start the next day and officially be a writer. Just like me.

bad news from levine: *Seinfeld* had passed. It felt like: "The tumor is malignant." Crushing. I knew I'd connected with Larry David in some way, and the other Larry had come around, too. It must have been Seinfeld; I never did get a good vibe from him. Was it the Red Sox/Mets thing? Nah, they'd won, what did he care if I was still a Sox fan? A weak moment: He didn't think I could write for his show because I wasn't Jewish. I quickly dismissed this as paranoid and pathetic. The Herb Silverman syndrome. Sure, there were a lot of Jewish people working for the show, but that's because Jews are funny. Who were they going to hire, a bunch of Swedes? Still, the rejection hurt. "What about the virgin story?" I asked. I was certain they'd liked the virgin story. "Larry did like it," Levine said, "but it wasn't enough." On top of that, the only other meeting I had that week had been canceled.

All the irons were out of the fire and cooling fast. Nothing was happening behind the scenes. I felt Levine's confidence flickering. Despite his upbeat tone, he wasn't returning my calls as fast. This frightened and angered me. But the bottom line was, Levine had other clients to deal with, clients who brought in the ten percent. His sun didn't rise and set depending on whether Henry Halloran got a job.

"Would you lose respect for me if I figured out a way to work for Ted Bowman?"

"No," Levine said, "I'd gain it."

"Get me in there if you can. Tell him I've got a great idea for his psycho killer love story."

"I don't know, Henry . . ."

"Let me just play this out."

"It's your call."

"I take full responsibility. What do I have to lose?"

"You sure about this?"

"I'm sure. I have a plan."

"Let me hear it."

"Why?"

"Because I want to hear it."

"Bullshit. You've probably got three people waiting on the line right now, and if I do tell you you won't listen anyway."

"Henry . . ."

"Jesus, Levine, just set it up. If worse comes to worst, I'll pitch him one of my own ideas. Just get me the fuck in there."

Despite everything, I was convinced I'd made an impression on Larry David, and I could still see myself working over there if that prick Seinfeld could be won over. So I took a few days before working on my Bowman pitch and dashed off a *Seinfeld* spec script.

Meanwhile, Doheny was embarking on her own book, tentatively entitled *The Daughter My Mother Hated*. I had given her my Syd Field screenwriting manual, but she said she didn't want to write movies, they were for hacks, she wanted to be a real writer and write books. She also blew off *Strunk and White* and jumped right into the fire with a new Bic pen and a fresh Mead composition notebook. When a half hour passed and she was still staring at a blank page, she said, "I quit. That's it. This is worse than fucking homework."

"What about ice skating? Must be something you could still do. You could coach."

"I want to be a writer! Now help me."

I closed my own notebook. "Can you write a letter?"

"Of course I can write a letter."

"Then you can write a book. Just write a two-page letter a day, keep the subject the same, and in a week you'll have fourteen pages. In a month you'll have fifty-six pages, and by September you'll practically have a book."

"That's too short for a good book. Good books are always four hundred pages at least."

"Whatever. You'll be well on your way."

A couple days later I came home to find that my clothes had been picked up and washed, the bed changed, the floors scrubbed, carpet swept, dishes done and put away. There were little pink flowers in paper cups throughout the room and Doheny was in the process of papering one of the walls.

"Whoa," I said. "Unbelievable."

She held a roller behind her back, cocked her head.

"You've really been at it," I said.

"Uh-huh."

I checked out the wallpaper, which was a buttery yellow and okay with me.

"Where'd you find this stuff?"

"Your landlady dropped it off, so I thought I'd get you started." Colleen smiled and gestured toward the wall. "Well?"

"Nice. Very nice. You know how to do it?"

"I helped my sister when she moved into her place."

"Wow. I'm really . . . I'm stunned. The whole place . . . Very impressive."

"It's okay. I like cleaning when I get stoned—it relaxes me."

The apartment really did look good. She'd even fixed the Murphy bed and gone shopping ("I found some money in your pants") and there was a bowl of oranges in the fridge, already peeled. "This way they'll be ready," she said.

"Why not just peel them when you want to eat them?"

"I want 'em ready when I want 'em ready. I'm kind of anal like that."

"Well, why don't you chew up some apples and put them away for when you're ready to swallow?"

"Ha ha. Now I need you to do something for me." She held up her notebook. "Will you read it?"

I was on a roll with my *Seinfeld* script and didn't welcome the interruption. "Maybe I should wait until you're finished," I said. "This is supposed to be coming from your heart. Might not be wise to get an outsider's opinion at this point."

"Don't worry, I won't let you influence me."

"Well . . . okay."

"Now, don't be afraid to mark it up. If you see anything good, put a check next to it, and if something's funny, put an exclamation point. If something's really cool, mark it, and if a character is really great, make a note. Don't be afraid to make a mess of it. Anything good I want to know about."

She'd taken my advice literally—the book was a letter to her mother. Each chapter, twelve so far, recounted a childhood incident—usually set at an ice rink—where her mom had wronged her by playing favorites with one of her two sisters. Despite her breathless, wounded rantings, it didn't come across as the story of an evil, uncaring mother, but rather of a whiny little rink rat. If it worked on any level, it was that, because of the misspellings and an overdose of thesaurus-type malaprops, it could be mistaken for some kind of slacker parody.

By page three I had a headache. On page seven I had to go for a walk. I skimmed over the last three pages on the shitter.

"So what do you think?"

"Shut the goddamn door!" I said.

She did. Then: "Well?"

"It's wonderful."

"It is, isn't it?"

"Amazing. Great start. Keep at it, you're onto something."

"What about starting each chapter with 'Dear Elaine'? Did you like that?"

"It's a gimmick," I said with a big wipe of the ass, "but it works."

This may sound akin to egging Billy Bibbit into giving the Mother's Day toast, but I was pleased she was showing an interest in something that didn't come with a laugh track. I knew the writing thing wasn't going to last, the poor girl had Ritalin written over her every lurch. She'd get on to something else in a few days, so why burst her bubble?

i was getting in the car to go to my Bowman meeting when I heard the ringing a couple blocks away. I waited around and by the time the ice cream man pulled up, a few kids were already standing on the corner and others were on their way. Ten or twelve of them eventually stepped up to that window, all between five and twelve years old, not a guardian in sight as thick arms dished out slushes and Fudgsicles and drumsticks. Who was he, I wondered again. Had he been checked out by a county board of ice cream vendors? Why was everyone so comfortable with this unseen man, this Aqua-lung-park-bench-eyeing-little-girls-with-bad-intent stranger flying through their neighborhood?

I waited for the kids to be served, then stepped up and ordered a frozen lemonade from a skinhead. Holy fuck. The guy couldn't look more suspicious if he had sawed-off handcuffs on his wrist. Tattoos on both shoulders; earrings, nose rings, tongue rings, eye-brow rings—I think he sensed my disapproval because the smile he gave the last little one melted away as quickly as the soft white ice cream.

"What flavor lemonade?"

"Lemon."

He reached into the bowels of a dented stainless-steel chest, scooped out a cup. He wore a lime-colored T-shirt with the sleeves ripped off at the seams. I wanted to follow each kid home, tell their mothers and stepfathers what I'd seen, but I knew that would just make everyone fear me, not the ice cream man, and so I coughed up the buck and drove to my appointment at Paramount.

"So what do you have for me?" Ted Bowman asked.

"Well, I've thought a lot about what you said. It's a sensational idea and I've worked out a few good set pieces, but to tell you the truth, I'm about three days away from cracking the thing wide open."

"You haven't cracked it?"

"Oh, yeah, I have. It's just that I want to wait until I get it just right before I lay it on you."

His face darkened. "What the hell are we doing here then? You should've called and pushed the meeting back."

"I've got this other idea that I wanted you to hear. It's never been done before."

"I don't want to hear other ideas. I got enough other ideas."

"Just listen to me. This is my best story. You're going to like it."

His development person, Sonya, served me a Pellegrino and dashed off.

"I don't want to like it."

"Please, Ted, it's really good, and you're the first one I've pitched it to."

"You got three minutes."

"Okay. It's about a very unusual friendship between two very different men. But more than that, it's about homelessness and breaking stereotypes and forgiveness, and it's got a lot of action in it, too."

"Get to the point."

"Two guys. One black, one white. Denzel Washington and Andy Garcia. The black man, Gavin, is an attorney for White and Case, one of the biggest law firms in Manhattan. This guy was never poor. His father was a doctor and he went to Princeton. His wife is a beautiful editor at a publishing house."

"She's white?"

"No, she's black, too." I sipped my water. "They're madly in love, and they've got a great life, and they're decent people, too. Then along comes Migs."

"The white guy?"

"That's right. Migs's real name is Tony Migliacci. He's around the same age as Gavin—early thirties—except life isn't so good to him. Migs owns a pretty successful pizza parlor up in Providence, then his partner gets sucked in by some loan sharks. When they can't pay the vig, they lose the business, his partner gets his legs broken, and Migs is in danger of losing his kneecaps, so he splits to New York to hide out with his girlfriend who's going to graduate school down there."

"He slings pizzas and his girlfriend's in grad school? Come on."

"I told you, we're breaking stereotypes. Migs has been paying for her schooling and they're engaged. Anyway, on the train down to the city, Migs is paranoid. He suspects every other person of working for the mob. Then when he shows up at his girlfriend's apartment, he sees a couple suspicious-looking characters standing out front and he gets nervous. Instead of going through the front doors, he plays it safe and takes the fire escape. When he gets up there, he looks in the window and sees his fiancée in bed with another guy."

Bowman chuckled at this. "She's getting popped?"

Sonya slinked back in and sat down.

"Needless to say, Migs is devastated. He stumbles back down the fire escape in shock. The thugs out front see him and give chase. Migs gets away, but in the process he drops his bag, which has all his money."

"Where are we now?"

"New York."

"I mean, how far into the story?"

"I don't know, about a box of popcorn."

He sighed and a suddenly emboldened Sonya said, *"Which act?"*

The mosquito picking on the gnat: Hollywood in a nutshell.

"End of first, beginning of second. So now he's stuck in New York City with no money and nowhere to go. He can't go home, he's got no friends, he's got nothing. So he goes to a shelter. Unfortunately, it's the middle of winter and the shelter is full. Before you know it, he's living on the streets, broke, destitute, down-and-out . . . and then he runs into . . ."

As I was speaking, something came across the producer's message box. Bowman picked up his phone.

"Yeah," he said. "No, I'm not happy. Why? Because it sucked, that's why. Look . . . look . . . look . . . look, I'm in a meeting. Look . . . look, I'm in a meeting. Call me back. Yeah, call me back. Call me back."

Bowman slammed down the phone.

"Fucking asshole."

He picked a script off his desk and tossed it against the wall.

"There. That's what I think of your client's fucking piece of shit."

I sipped my drink, waited for him to calm down.

"Asshole's writing me a project called *Kiddie Cops*—about two kids who blackmail a crooked police chief and get to become cops for a day. Sort of a *Cop and a Half* with balls. Ever see it?"

"*Cop and a Half?* No."

"Burt Reynolds starred. Ron Howard produced, Fonzie directed. Could've been good, but they tried to make it for kids. I'm making this one for adults."

"Sounds great."

"Could be, if the fucking jerk had an inkling of what I'm talking about. I'm talking about temptation and power, you know? I mean, if you could be a cop for a day, what would you do? I know what I'd do. I'd have chicks blowing me or they'd get tickets."

What a poker face on Sonya.

"But what would a kid do?" Bowman said.

I said, "Uh-huh, right." Then: "Anyway, Migs is on the street, broke and homeless—"

"Your three minutes are up. I'm bored."

"I haven't gotten to the main part yet."

"Then get to it—in two lines or less. Come on."

"Okay, it's simple. It's about Gavin—a guy who has everything in the world and one day God says to him, 'Help this stranger, Migs, and you will continue to have everything,' but Gavin doesn't help him and that's his fatal flaw and he loses everything, and then he sets out to redeem himself by finding Migs and saving him."

"And it's a rich black guy who helps a poor white guy?"

"Yeah."

"Why?"

"No reason, except it's always the other way around and I thought this would be a nice change."

Bowman was starting to show interest.

"Yeah, right. A role reversal—sort of like *Planet of the Apes.*"

I couldn't tell if he was kidding, and then I could, and he wasn't.

"It's just a hipper way to go," I said. "The main thing is, it's a story about redemption. It's got a lot of action, and you love the guys because they're both tragic figures, but there's a few laughs and a real happy, satisfying ending. People are going to be walking out of the theater saying, 'I just saw a hundred minutes of great entertainment and it had a great fucking message!' "

Bowman thought it over. He walked to the window, stared out. A minute passed. I looked to Sonya, but she avoided my glance. Suddenly he spun and faced me. "No. No. Nope. Too thin."

"No, it's not. You told me to hurry. I skipped the best part."

"Well, that was stupid."

"See, the way Gavin loses everything is Migs is freezing one night and starts calling out for help and Gavin sees him from his Fifth Avenue town house window, but he doesn't do anything and eventually Migs breaks into the basement of that building and starts a fire to keep warm and the fire gets out of control and Gavin's wife dies—"

"I don't like it."

"Okay, I got another. How about this: *Six Brides for Seven Brothers.*"

He didn't blink.

"Think about it. I don't even have to say any more, it's all right there."

Bowman sighed. "Look, forget it. Get the fuck out of here. I'm busy."

I hesitated.

"Go!"

"Okay, I'll come back in a couple days, we'll talk about the other story."

"Oh, we will?"

"I'd like to . . . if you do. Look, I'm sorry if I wasted your time, but I'm very close now. That's a home run, the love in the nineties thing. Why don't we do it tomorrow?"

A blank stare that went straight to my stomach.

"Or whenever you're ready."

In Hollywood the good meetings are often worse than the bad ones. I'd never felt this low after a bad meeting. God, I was pissed. I'd been so close. I saw it in those horrible eyes. He'd really thought about it. I'd gotten to him for a second. I stopped at a phone booth on the way home and called Levine. His assistant Sheri said he was on a conference call, but I said I'd wait. When Levine got on, I told him how close I'd been, how I'd almost had the guy. He told me to calm down, it was okay, I shouldn't take it so seriously. "But he was *right there*. The fuck."

"They're all stupid," he said. "What do you expect in a town where the sun shines three hundred and sixty days a year and there's a tanning salon on every corner?"

when doheny finished wallpapering the apartment, I wanted to show her that good deeds are rewarded, so I told her to dress up, we were going out to dinner. "It's a date!" she said and, after a little pirouette, she disappeared into the bathroom. I waited out on the front steps and one hour later she came down wearing a peach halter top and jeans, and trailing behind her a strong odor of ozone-shrinking sprays. Her bangs were puffed up more than usual and looked as soft as barbed wire, but that I didn't notice right away. The fading sunlight was striking her perfectly, causing the top half of her shirt to be bathed in light and the underside darkened by shadow. This made her breasts look tremendous and got me thinking about things I didn't want to think about. On the drive to the restaurant, she went right to the sperm sample cup.

"What's this?"

"Nothing you want to touch."

"Huh?"

"Just put it down please."

She took a sniff, tossed it into the backseat. We passed a billboard that said HAVE HOPE, HELP, HEAL over a collage of four Absolut vodka bottles.

"So where we going?" she asked.

"It's a surprise."

The place—Dominick's—was just around the corner, it turned out. I considered driving home and walking back, sparing myself the valet charge, but then I thought, Hell, I'll splurge. I'd heard about Dominick's when I worked at Ernesto's. The kitchen was slow and the bartender fast and after two stiff ones on an empty stomach, I was feeling pretty good. There was a warm, powdery smell pulling at me from across our little red vinyl booth. I hadn't been around that in a while. Doheny would crane her neck whenever someone fancy passed, and she moaned when a heaping tray of food went by. Dominick's was a good restaurant, but not that good, so it was kind of sweet when she leaned forward and said, "I wonder what the poor people are doing tonight?" She giggled and I raised my glass, and she definitely looked cute. She had a nice body. The peach tits. What was I afraid of? I'd seen her medical sheet from the shelter: *HIV-negative. Then I recalled the six-month incubation period.* Okay, I'd wear a rubber. I was single, she was single—who was I holding out for? No, it was wrong, dead wrong. What the hell was I thinking? We shared the chicken croquette appetizer, split a chopped salad, dusted a bottle of red wine, and I excused myself to go to the bathroom.

On the way back to the table, I almost got bowled over by a couple busboys running out the door after a deadbeat check-skipper. Odd, I thought, at a place like this. By the time the main courses were served, we were both stuffed and happy.

"Can I ask you a question and I want you to answer the truth?"

"The truth?" I said.

"Yeah."

"No, I can't promise that."

"Come on, I'm serious. Do you really have a girlfriend named Amanda?"

It was as if Doheny knew that the food and booze provided a kind of satisfaction that allowed me to be straight with her.

"No."

"I knew it. *Amanda.* I never knew any *Amandas* growing up. It's like a soap opera name or something—I figured it was fake."

"No, there was an Amanda. She's just not my girlfriend anymore. We broke up."

"Really? She was really real?"

"Yeah."

"Who broke up with—?"

"She dumped me."

"Why?"

"No reason."

"Come on, Henry, the truth, remember?"

And so I gave it to her.

"This is the truth: I didn't cheat on her, I didn't treat her bad, my personality didn't change, I didn't get into drugs, she didn't have another guy, we didn't even grow apart."

"So . . . ? What? Come on, you're not telling me something."

"Yeah, I am. That's just it. She . . . you know . . ." I could feel it all there on my face. "She just stopped giving a shit."

"Huh? Giving a . . . ? She stopped *what?*"

"She didn't love me anymore."

"Oh. *Oh.* Wait a second, either something's missing or that's really pathetic."

"Now you read me."

Doheny managed to polish off her filet mignon and I found room for my sand dabs and we had another drink while I gave her a speech about novice scribes traditionally holding a second job, like my flipping burgers, and she said she was open to the idea. She told me she was starting a new book—a children's story about a bunch of cats who commit suicide. I told her it sounded interesting, but perhaps it would be better if the cats didn't actually complete the act. She said that was a cop-out, that kids should know the truth, and the truth was that suicide was real and there weren't any happy endings, just small victories leading up to the inevitable crushing defeat. She said if I wanted a happy ending, I should write my own goddamn children's story. All this she delivered in a chipper way, and she took my hand in hers, but I was saddened by her outlook. I asked for the check. Our waitress said it was already taken care of.

"What? By who?"

"A secret admirer."

I looked around the room.

"A secret admirer?"

The waitress smiled and left and I noticed Doheny beaming at me.

"You?"

She blushed.

"But . . . ?"

"Come on, let's go."

She tried to stand, but I grabbed her arm.

"Wait a second. Where'd you get the money?"

"Don't worry about it, I got it."

I blinked. " *'Don't worry about it?'* The whole reason you've been staying with me is because you're broke. Now you're telling me you're not?"

She seemed hurt. "That's the whole reason I've been staying with you, because I'm broke? What am I, a charity case?"

"Well . . . yeah. Why the fuck do you think you've been staying?"

"Don't swear. I got the money today."

"Where?"

"None of your beeswax."

"Yes, it is my beeswax! If you've got dough, I want to know about it!"

"Shhh. You're embarrassing me."

"I don't give a damn! I want to know where the money came from!"

When she didn't respond, I said, "All right, you got money? I want you out tonight."

She started filling up. "I don't have any more money, I just had money for dinner."

"Oh, that's convenient. What'd the fucking dinner fairy come along and give you just enough?"

She was meek and I was making a scene, but I didn't give a shit because I knew what she'd done and I wasn't going to let her get away with it. I called the waitress over.

"Did you ever get the people who ran out on the bill?"

"No."

"Give it to me, I'll pay."

Doheny said, "What are you doing?"

The waitress said, "That's not necessary, sir."

The manager or owner, a tall middle-aged woman, appeared. "Can I help you?"

"Yes," I said, "I want to pay for the table that ran out."

"Why?"

"Because I don't think that they did run out. I think they paid cash, and I think my date here stole it."

Doheny sprung out of the booth. "I did not!"

I pulled the tall woman aside. "Just give me the bill."

Doheny slammed her hands on the table and burst out crying. This was more of a scene than I counted on. The tall woman leaned into me and whispered, "It's okay. Please don't worry about it."

Her voice breaking, Doheny said, "Henry, stop it! I didn't steal any money!"

"Listen," I insisted, "I want to pay. At least give me *my* bill because she used the stolen money to pay for it."

"No, she didn't," said our waitress. "She paid with a credit card."

"Really?" An interesting twist. I turned to Doheny. "You have a credit card now?"

"That's right. Gus let me use his to buy you dinner because I talked to him today and I told him we were going out, so he dropped off his credit card and told me to charge it to him because he said he wanted to take you to lunch, but you wouldn't let him!"

The tall one was giving me a pretty good dressing down in the parking lot when Doheny stepped out and came to my defense. She was all out of tears by now and had just been treated to a shot by a table full of patrons. It wasn't my fault, she said, she'd given me many reasons to doubt her. The woman called me an asshole and asked Doheny if she needed a ride home, but she said it was okay, she was with me, and the tall woman walked inside, disgusted.

Back home, Doheny kept apologizing. I got her a dish of frozen yogurt, but she wouldn't touch it. She put it down and got in bed, and when I joined her, she said she was a jerk for embarrassing me in front of an entire restaurant. "Stop it," I said, "I'm the one who should be apologizing."

"No, I should've told you about Gus, but I wanted to surprise you."

"No, no, please, I'm an asshole to make such a scene, you didn't do anything wrong."

"You're not an asshole, Henry. I just never gave you any reason to trust me . . . I never gave anyone any reason to."

She rolled over and I thought she was crying again, and when I touched her back, I knew she was. "It's true about happy endings, you know," she said. I wanted her to stop crying, so I put my arm around her. She felt tiny. Nice. Smooth and clean. The thought crossed my mind and I knew it was wrong, not to mention what it would do to my karma, and then I thought, Wait a minute, maybe it would be *good* for my karma, I was just being affectionate, and I considered it some more, and the alcohol said, *Do it!*, and my gut said, You're an idiot! That's just the alcohol talking!, but I knew it was more than that, and she turned her head, our mouths meeting and my hand sliding under her panties in the back and then curling around to her pussy and as she gasped I crawled out of my underwear and slid up to her face and I wiped her tears with my cock. She licked the wet salt and placed her mouth around me and looked up. The visuals were always the best part and, visually, this was seventy millimeter. She said the words and I moved between her legs.

It felt great to slip into her warmth. She placed her hands on my butt and pulled me into her. I held myself up and she lifted her head to watch me slide in and out. I put one of her legs between mine and leaned into her on an angle that jazzed up the friction. It felt like I was wearing the bark off my cock, but it was working for her so I didn't stop and our bodies slapped together, making embarrassing sounds from each other's sweat. As she neared orgasm, she got loud and yappy (imagine a chihuahua with a mousetrap on his balls) and I heard a couple windows in the next apartment building close, or maybe open, so I stuffed my fingers in her mouth, which, not surprisingly, she really took to. When I was ready, I pulled out and stuffed it in her mouth, and even when I was tender, she continued to squeegee the last drops until I gently pushed her head away. Finally she gasped, as if so lost in the moment she'd neglected even air.

"That was a lot," she said.

"It's been a while."

"No kidding. You could've wall-papered the whole room with that one."

it is small sport shooting the bird who perches on the muzzle of your gun, but what hunter could keep from doing it?"

This I'd read in my little John Barth book and, after fucking the stuffing out of Doheny, I was that sad poacher. Happily, her three-quarters of the bed was empty when I awakened. Maybe she'd taken last night's talk to heart and gone looking for a job. Then a titter, a squeak really, and when I lifted my head I saw her sitting in a chair in the middle of the room. Staring at me. Just sitting there, buck naked, legs crossed, a shit-eating smile smeared across her happy mug, *staring at me.*

"You were so cute," she said. "You farted in your sleep."

I covered my face.

"Get up, sleepyhead, we're wasting the day."

She dove onto the bed and hugged me and I pulled the sheet tighter around my head. "Stop it."

She started massaging my back and neck. I resisted at first, then forced myself to relax.

"It's so refreshing to meet a man without muscles," she said. "Honus, that's all he cared about—working out, pumping weights, getting buff. He used to be at the gym all the time—Honus."

"What time is it?"

"Late."

"How late?"

"Almost seven-thirty."

"I can't get up now, I need sleep."

"Come on, up and at 'em, snoozie. The early bird catches the worm."

"And the early worm gets eaten."

She jumped on the bed.

"Get up, Monkey, we're gonna miss everything!"

"Stop it, please!"

I was growing more anxious by the second. What was this *we're* stuff? We weren't a *we're,* we were a *me* and a *her.* This was no honeymoon, I had things to do. Sure, we'd had sex, but I hadn't exactly taken her virginity. Virgins don't lick where she'd licked. They spit where she'd swallowed. They "ow'd" where she'd "oh'd." And there was something else bothering me.

Doheny had the biggest bush on the planet.

It's funny what bugs you in the morning light, but it was true, her bush was gigantic. Think home plate. Which was odd because she was otherwise fair. From the waist up, she was smooth—no fuzz on the arms, no hairy nipples, not a hint of a mustache. Below the belly button, she was Larry Csonka.

A Turkish mermaid.

Watching her prance around the apartment now was difficult. Her mound looked like ten thousand Slinkys growing out of her abdomen—she could've been hiding a set of balls in there. I had banged her, though, and I owed her whatever it is that decent guys owe the women they bang. I would live up to that debt—be it in the way of hugs, breakfast, forced banter in the Bagel Nosh line. But that would come later; right now I owed myself rest.

I stayed in bed another two hours, despondent. I slept all knotted up, in and out of nightmares, awakening every ten minutes to see her sitting in that chair, or leaning against the windowsill, always with the stare, always the grin. The last time I awoke, it was to a stale, sickening odor. She was back in bed now, sitting up under the covers. I lifted the sheets, saw the cause of my nausea dangling from her mouth.

"You have to do that in bed?"

"Sorry. I was trying to keep it from going in your face."

"Put it out."

She said, "Yes, Master," and dropped the cigarette into the empty Coke can she was holding.

"Are you wearing a fat outfit in this picture?"

"What?"

She was studying a snapshot of me and Amanda at my sister Bette's wedding.

"Where'd you get that?"

"In the drawer. Are you wearing a fat outfit?"

"It's a tuxedo."

"Oh."

I rolled over and she said, "You look like you're wearing a fat outfit. You're not wearing a fat outfit here?"

"No. *No.* I'm not wearing a fat outfit. What the hell's a fat outfit?"

"You know, something that makes you look fat."

I twisted the covers in my fist. When I pretended to sleep, Doheny grabbed my ear through the sheets; not the soft, pliable lobe of the ear, but the top part, the cartilage, the part that hurt when she bent it. She whispered with her smoky breath, "I have a prediction."

"That's nice."

"I-have-a-pre-dic-tion," she singsonged.

I floated again past the bait. "Mm," I said.

Then she said something that made my toes cramp; something so heinous, so unconscionable, that I really had to snap my butt shut to keep from crapping. "I predict that one year from today we'll be married."

Despite the authority complex, the suicide threats, the mommy thing and everything else, it was this moment that finally convinced me that the char-breathed insomniac trying to yank my ear from my skull was truly disturbed. And it scared the hell out of me. Because a thought occurred: If Doheny could believe this, and little doubt she did, then she could believe anything. *Anything.* She could believe I was the devil, or that she was an alien, or that she should cut my throat while I slept.

"Doheny," I said with appropriate meekness, "I think you're great and all, and last night was really phenomenal, but I don't think we're going to be hearing wedding bells soon."

"Of course you don't! Don't you see? You were hurt by Amanda Parsons, and now you're afraid to admit you're falling in love with me, because you think you'll lose me as soon as you do!"

Having this lunatic mention Amanda's full name out loud was

painful enough without listening to this other nonsense. I hadn't forgotten that the first two hours after waking is heart attack country. I hadn't slept much, there'd been drinks, we'd had stressful sex.

"Can we talk later?" I said.

" 'Can we talk later?' " she mimicked. "He always wants to talk later. Henry, you're a textbook case of denial, and denial is caused by fear. But there's nothing to fear, Monkey, because I love you, too!" She started sprinkling my back with tiny kisses. "Do you hear me? I love you, Henry Halloran, I love you I love you I love you, and nothing's going to change that! Nothing! Not ever!"

seven

i knew my day wasn't going to get any better when I got a bone in my hamburg. We'd driven up the highway to a strip of sand called Malibu. Besides Venice, this was L.A.'s biggest myth. Scarborough Beach back in Rhode Island had better waves, water, and sand. After staring for a couple hours at the shiny, tanned blondes in their fluorescent green and pink bathing suits, we darted across four lanes to a surfer hangout, which is where I got the bone. It wasn't just a speck of white like you sometimes find, but a legitimate bone the size and approximate color of a wisdom tooth. I'm not the litigious type, so I just threw it in the trash with the rest of my burger and my beach fries. Just one of those days, I figured, no one's fault. I wouldn't even ask for my two-fifty back. So what if the place advertised "the best burgers in the 'Bu"? Hey, south California advertised the best women in the world, and look who was sitting across the table nailing me dead-on with a double exhale.

"What, do you have a fun phobia today?"

She wanted me to do a shot with her, but I'd refused.

"I have work to do later."

"What work?"

"Work. I'm up for a project. I've got to get my pitch ready."

"Let me read your notes. Maybe I can help."

"No."

"Why not?"

"I'm not done. It's just notes. I'll send you a copy of the next screenplay I finish."

This was dangerous territory, the implication that she would be departing soon, so I quickly added, "I'm having a hard time coming up with a good ending. It's a tough nut to crack."

Doheny burst out laughing. " 'A tough nut to crack,' " she repeated.

"It's an idiom."

This kind of shit had been going on all day. On the beach, Doheny had asked me why I never jogged. When I replied, "Because I don't like breathing exhaust," she'd buckled over in hysterics and cried out, "Smoke coming out your mouth. You're too funny!" "I didn't say that, you did" was my response, and she'd even laughed at that.

"You know, it's really true," she said.

"What's true?"

"It ain't the meat, it's the motion."

She winked and I gave her a little wave.

"I'll tell you, my mother's gonna love you. I can't wait until you two meet—she loves serious people."

"I thought you hated your mother."

"Well, I used to like her when I was little, but then her hormones changed and now we don't get along so good. But she used to be nice. Like one time when I was in fifth grade, right after they got divorced, my mother made me a papier-mâché Halloween outfit and that was pretty nice. She made a green mask with fangs and a long tail all the way down my back. Then I went to school in it and this kid, Michael Smits, he goes, 'What are you, a crocodile?' I go, 'No! I'm a fucking dragon, you asshole,' and the teacher, Mrs. Pickle, she sends me to the principal's office and I spent the whole day sitting there in my dragon outfit, just praying fat Smits would come by, so I could claw the shit out of him."

Then a horrible thought—one I surely would have struck upon earlier if not so harried by the simple fact of being near her. *What if she was pregnant?* With my luck, she was probably as fertile as the grass under a cow's ass. And even if she wasn't, she could easily run out and get knocked up by someone else. Who would she point to then? Oh, how she'd love that, going home with my kid, thinking that that alone would unite us forever. Unite her and Mom! *Against me!* There were blood tests, but how accurate were those?

Doheny had already eaten fried cheese and fried calamari, so I suggested fried ice cream for dessert.

"No thanks," she said. "I don't want to blimp out on you."

I winced but pushed on. "Come on, skinny, we'll split it."

This she loved. We were joking around like a happy couple. It was a necessary evil. I didn't want to give her any reason or need to blackmail me. Go with the game, make her think I was hers—kids or not. There'd be no bitter pills to swallow; we'd just drop it in water, let it dissolve.

I sipped my Sprite and said, "When did you have your last

period?" It came out less matter-of-fact and more gargly than I'd intended.

"None of your beeswax. That's personal."

"Doheny, you had your finger up my ass this morning. How can this be personal?"

"That was between the two of us. A woman's period is her own business. Period." She lit a cigarette. "Besides, I never keep track. I figure if I'm gonna get preggie, I'm gonna get preggie. It's like last time—I was pregnant for two months and then I had a miscarriage—so I guess it wasn't meant to be."

Two bleached-blond surfer dudes walked in, surfboards at their sides, dried salt on their brown hides. Doheny whistled and called out, "Nice buns!"

"No," I groaned.

"What?"

"Don't ever do that around me."

"Just 'cause I'm on a diet don't mean I can't look at the menu."

The waitress dropped off the fried Chunky Monkey, but my appetite was gone. As Doheny brought a forkful of ice cream to her mouth, a plume of cigarette smoke spilled slowly from her nose.

Doheny kept her hand on my shoulder as we drove back down the PCH. The writing was on the wall now, it was no big deal to her if she got "preggie" and destroyed my life. She didn't keep track of things like that.

"Must've been pretty rough," I said. "Having a miscarriage."

"Not really. I just had bad cramps one day, then I started bleeding." She whistled and took a hit off her smoke. "Bye-bye, Junior."

I managed to seem unfazed. "Well, at least you know you can have children. Sure wish I could."

A huge fast exhale. "What? You can't have no kids?"

"Nope. I'm sterile."

"You're shooting blanks?"

"Yup."

"Oh, that sucks, Hen."

She placed a hand on mine.

"It's not so bad," I said. "Guess I could always adopt."

"Yeah, I wouldn't mind that. Maybe I could even quit smoking."

I smiled, thoroughly baffled.

"How'd you find out?" she asked.

"That I'm sterile?"

"Mm."

"Had tests done."

"Why? You weren't ever married, were you?"

"Nope. Went in on my own." I reached in the backseat, held up the sperm cup. "The bad-news beaker."

"Wow. Must feel weird to know you can't ever knock no one up."

"Sucks. But you learn to live with it."

Doheny lit a fresh cigarette with her old one.

"So is it a hereditary thing?"

"Huh?"

"Being sterile," she said. "Was your father sterile, too?"

The twitchiest of twitches from me.

"Uh-uh. Skips every other generation."

As I pulled up at a red light, she glanced at my feet and exclaimed, "I didn't know you tied double knots!"

I managed something like, "Ehh." A second later there was a bang, a crash, the tinkling of glass. We found ourselves five feet into the intersection.

I wasn't in a very good mood before I'd been rear-ended, but five seconds ago seemed like the good ol' days. My door was jammed shut from the impact, but what really angered me as I climbed out the window was that there hadn't been a screech or anything to warn us to brace ourselves. Somebody had creamed us dead-on, he'd been daydreaming, and I discovered that whiplash wasn't just lawyer bullshit. The ass of my poor Arrow would never be the same. The bumper was off, the lights were broken, the wheel wells were wrinkled, and the four gang members who'd clobbered me were swearing about their souped-up El Camino's broken head-light while passing around a blunt.

"No harm here," I said and after climbing back in the window, I limped home with a roaring muffler, stiff neck, and a little dragon girl with tequila breath.

levine loved the spec script I'd written for *Seinfeld* and he said Larry David liked it, too, but ultimately the decision came down to Seinfeld himself and once again he passed. I was starting not to like Jerry Seinfeld. This was the perfect script for him, it made no sense that he would pass. Half a dozen people in Levine's office had called to compliment me. I even heard from an ICM agent, stroking me a little, feeling me out. The good news from Levine was that Ted Bowman agreed to see me again. He was no Seinfeld, but at least he was giving me a fair shot and I was grateful for that.

For five days I'd managed to avoid a reprise of our tryst by whining about my stiff neck each time Doheny smiled my way. This excuse was growing thin and my neck was really starting to feel funny for holding it so stiffly, and Doheny was antsy as hell. She'd become very possessive and, each time I left the premises, begged to come along. She said she'd learn the writing business better if she could sit in on a couple meetings, but there was no way. Business was business, it wasn't philanthropy, which was the heading she fell under. However, on the day of my twelve-thirty Bowman meeting, I was starved, so I made an exception and brought her along, so she could pick up food while I met with him.

On the way there, we passed a fat man on a bicycle and Doheny called out, "Nice butt, pork boy!"

I shot her a look and she giggled.

"Did you ever think that we could be soul mates?"

"Nope," I said.

"I think we are. I think this is all meant to be. I think we really are soul mates."

She sat up and hooted at two bikers parked on Melrose.

I said, "That's really, really annoying."

"Oh, Monkey, lighten up. Just because I'm on a diet—"

"You're not on a diet. You can eat whatever the hell you want."

She took my hand.

"Would you relax? I wish you could hear yourself sometimes, you sound like a guinea, getting all worked up. I don't even like bikers."

I gave her twenty bucks, dropped her off at Astro Burger. I asked her to order me a veggie burger, a large Sprite, rice pudding, and whatever she wanted for herself. She was then to walk a block to the studio and wait for me at my car. She asked why she couldn't just keep the car and pick me up and I kind of chuckled and she got out.

"So what have you got for me? You crack this thing?"

I'd just been served my Pellegrino and Sonya was heading out of the room.

"You stay!" Bowman snapped and she slid onto the fat arm of a leather chair without missing a beat.

"Oh, yeah," I said, "but first I'm going to run something else by you."

"Another story? I don't want to hear another story. That *Planet of the Apes* thing you told me shit the house."

I laughed good-naturedly. "This one's better. In fact, there's already a couple places that want to do it, but I want to do it with you."

"Not interested. Give me your take on my story."

"Think of all the movies they've done about Vietnam: *Platoon; Full Metal Jacket; Born on the Fourth of July; Good Morning, Vietnam;* on and on, and practically every one a success. But what about the guys who didn't go to 'Nam? What about the guys who went to Canada?"

"I don't want to do a war movie. I'm more Middle America than that."

"A lot of Middle Americans went to Canada, Ted. Kent State was in Middle America."

He rolled his eyes.

"Anyway, this isn't a war movie, it's an *Ottawa* movie. It's about the guys who *ran* from the war."

"No."

"Some of them had legitimate reasons for running, some not—either way they ended up in a country that looked down on them as cowards and losers."

"No."

"It's a comedy about stoners and hippies and conscientious objectors who clash with a bunch of straight-ass, hockey-playin', lumberjackin' moose hunters."

"*No.*"

"They're in their own little war up there. They get to the point where they're like, 'Throw me in a rice paddy, this is hell.' And what happens, of course, is that something happens and these guys end up bonding with the Canadians and fighting a battle *up there*. I don't know, maybe it's a battle with a lumber company or the acid rain people—whatever it is, it's a battle they believe in—"

"Look, forget it. I'm not interested in a war comedy. Let the other studios buy it. Make a fool out of me."

"Don't forget, M*A*S*H was a war comedy—"

"*NO!* Now tell me the truth, have you figured out who my serial killer is or not?"

Suddenly my back started itching. He was pissed and I had nothing. I was facing Roger Clemens with a Wiffle ball bat and no helmet.

"What do you mean, who he is?" I said. "You mean, what actor?"

"I mean, *who is he?* What the hell is he like? How would a serial killer act on a first date?"

"Right," Sonya said.

"What do you mean, 'Right'? I'm not looking for 'right.' I'm looking for the answer." He glared at her and in a high voice mimicked, " *'Right.'* "

I scratched my face, prayed for inspiration.

"How would this man behave?" he said. "Would he be shy? Aggressive? Would he be outgoing or uptight? Would he take her to a play or a strip club? Would he bang her in his car or leave her at her front door with a handshake?"

I took a deep breath and said, "Well, it matters who he is. Not all serial killers are the same. Look at Charlie Manson and Jeffrey Dahmer—same profession, complete opposites."

"But a serial killer who could fall in love—what would *he* be like?"

More face-scratching. "Let me write you a treatment on the Ottawa movie. It's called *Canada Goose,* because the whole experience kind of gooses these guys into—"

"Get the fuck out of here!"

Bowman stood and pointed at the door like we were in a *Lucy* episode and he was Mr. Mooney.

"All right, all right, forget it."

"I've had it with you. You're wasting my time. You're a fucking bullshitter, you know that? I don't know what I'm doing here with you."

"Okay, okay, all right. I gather you're just interested in the serial killer story."

"A piercing analysis of the obvious."

"Okay. It's not all worked out, but I'll tell you what I got."

"Right now. No more horseshit. *Now.* You got thirty seconds."

"Your serial killer . . ." I said, and right then it popped into my head ". . . is an ice cream man."

Ted Bowman didn't move a muscle, but I could see the wheels turning.

"You see, ice cream men are lovable and trusted by all and that's how he can kill so easily yet get some girl to fall in love with him."

The producer sat down, then started up again, but he got only halfway and froze in an awkward crouch. I almost had him again, I knew, he was right there, I just had to nudge him over the edge.

"We'll call it *Ice Cream Man*," I said, "and the tag line is . . . 'No More Mr. Softee.' "

on my way out of the office, while Sonya was calling business affairs, I stopped to thank each of Bowman's employees for their invaluable assistance. The glass of water, the parking pass at the gate, the nod toward the waiting room sofa; each had played a small part in my triumph. I shook their hands, asked their names, then remembered them a minute later when I departed a room full of bemused faces. Out in the hall, I wanted to scream out my happiness, but that would be too theatrical, relegating my life to a beer commercial, so I just walked at a jaunty clip, emitting a giggly hum and throwing each soul I passed an exuberant "Hello!", along with a glimpse of my wisdom teeth. I was beaming, ecstatic, walking on air, any happy cliché you can think of. I felt the presence of God, a goodness in the world, a confirmation that hard work and dedication eventually pays off.

With tears in my eyes and a crack in my voice, I phoned home. It was the first time I'd told my father I'd become a writer, but of course he knew, which was funny and embarrassing, and he repeated everything I told him verbatim to my mother. They were thrilled and wanted to know who would be in this ice cream movie. It was too early for that, way too early, which confused them and tempered their joy.

Levine was next and was reluctant to get too excited, but I could hear the pride in his voice, like a dad watching his kid nail a two-wheeler for the first time. I was happy to live up to his faith in me, and I felt love for Levine, my lone supporter, and I vowed right then to never ankle his little agency, no matter how big and famous I became. Furthermore, when I started my own production company, he would run it!

Doheny was waiting in the parking lot with a Big Mac and three McCookies ("Astro Burger was all black people, so I got scared and left") but even she couldn't bring me down. I saw her suddenly as my godsend, my little distraction, the good karma girl. I smiled and calmly told her what had happened and as I walked around the car she blindsided me and the momentum sent me spinning with her on my back and the two of us were suddenly laughing and anyone watching would've thought we were young newlyweds and I'd just gotten the big break that would afford us to start working on the small fries we so wanted.

I wasn't ready to leave the studio lot just yet; this was *my* lot now, I wanted to get aquainted, to be part of it, to feel the magic. As we strolled past an enormous matte of blue sky in the parking lot, Doheny took my hand, which I shook off once and then surrendered to. I wondered what great movies this heavenly board had shined down upon. Farther on, we discovered a playground tucked inside a row of hedges and a giant soundstage with flashing red lights outside. We passed the *Entertainment Tonight* offices and *The Arsenio Hall Show* and *Wings*. A female page in a blue NBC blazer led a small group of starry-eyed tourists past us. I gave them another grand "Hello!" and they watched us walk away, probably wondering who we were to be so comfortable in such a setting.

We came around a corner and Raquel Welch was doing a scene. Wow, I thought, a big movie star, though for the life of me I couldn't remember one film she'd been in. We watched her do her stuff, and after each take a team of makeup people would descend upon her like a pit crew at Indy. A Porsche drove past with Henry Winkler at the wheel and I gave him a big Fonzee "Yo!" with the thumbs up and then some punk kid carrying a walkie-talkie asked us to move away from Raquel's set.

A ways down we entered a vacant soundstage and walked among the lumber, marveling at the tons of lighting equipment high on the ceiling. I felt nervous about being there and then I remembered I was an employee of Paramount Pictures. No more parking at Taco Bells, no slinking past security guards. They would come to know my name, these security people. I'd learn their names, too, treat them as friends, give them a bottle each holiday season. Maybe I'd even ask a couple of them up to the golf course. Bel Air—that would be my club. And if the stuffed shirts who run that hallowed track gave me any guff about bringing these blue-collar cronies who wore shorts, sneakers, and shirts without collars, well, I'd quit the damn place and go over to the Riv.

I rounded a corner and—what was this?—half the *Cheers* cast shooting hoops in an alley. I stood for a moment and savored it. What a sight: Woody, Norm, and Cliff, three icons from the premiere American sitcom of the eighties, playing a pickup game like a bunch of normal Joes, and me privy to it. George Wendt put his hands on his knees, glanced my way. We'd been nabbed, we had to go, he looked pissed, he said, "You wanna be our fourth?" A flash of terror—my heart, I could die out there, Pete Maravich city, on

THE COMEDY WRITER 275

the day of my big break. The hell with it, I thought, I couldn't pass this up. I threw down my pad and got in the game. It was only half-court, I reasoned, and even if I did expire, what a story it would make for my friends and family. What a wake!

We played for about twenty minutes while Doheny rooted us on, and my defense was pathetic—my back, I told them—but I was dogging it to save my life. I nailed a couple twenty-five-footers, however, and George Wendt and I were high-fiving. And there was George spinning to the hoop (he was very smooth for a guy so big) and Woody and John Ratzenberger talking trash. We beat them best of three and as these famous men headed back to work, they all nodded at me and I was certain my life had changed forever because now I was a real Hollywood screenwriter. I had a development deal at a major studio! I was *in!*

At the entrance to Paramount Pictures there is a gate and beyond that a traffic light. I was waiting behind a couple cars, just inside the gate, about to go home, daydreaming about my good fortune, almost oblivious to the new song every five seconds as Doheny held her finger on the scan button. Gradually I became aware of an insistent horn a few vehicles back. A Rolls-Royce. The impatient honker expected the lead car to go right on red, but I could see that our leader had his left blinker on. Suddenly the Rolls sped by on the left and hung a right around the front car without ever hitting his brakes and there was a tremendous crash as a Dodge Dart spanked into the left side of his trunk.

It was obvious who the asshole was and I'd seen the whole thing, so I climbed out my car window to serve as a witness for the Dodge Dart. As I ran to the accident scene, the other vehicles drove off with little more than a rubber neck and so I was left standing there by myself, the lone witness, as an irate Ted Bowman climbed out of the brown British sedan swearing to himself. He stormed past me to the driver's side of the Dart and said, "You fuck! Do you have any idea what you just did?!"

The driver and his four startled passengers were Hispanic, and they sat there looking dazed and guilty and thoroughly intimidated by this maniac, my savior. Bowman didn't acknowledge me, so I tried to slink off, but he called my name.

"Did you see that? Did you see what happened?"

"Well, I was in line . . ."

"So you're my witness, right?"

"The thing is, when you passed me, everything was so fast . . ."

"Good. I'm counting on you, man. We got this fucker dead to rights. We got him dead to rights!"

doheny wanted to celebrate, but I wasn't in the mood. "Let's go back to 'our place,' " she said—meaning Dominick's—but I said no. She couldn't understand how I could get the biggest break of my life and not want to get hammered. I explained to her that my big break was in jeopardy, it wasn't a done deal yet. I hated myself. If only I'd bolted the studio after my meeting, I wouldn't be in this mess. I had to be the bigshot, had to phone everyone from the studio, couldn't leave the fucking *Cheers* guys alone. For Christ sakes, that show hadn't had a decent episode in two years!

I called Levine's agency, but he'd gone home. I tried to find him in the directory, to no avail. I attempted to read *The Princess Bride,* but couldn't get past the preface. Doheny stripped down to her bra and panties, sat next to me on the bed. She put her hand on my thigh and I felt sick. She tried to snuggle; I went into the kitchenette. When I came out, she was sprawled on her back, naked. It looked like a raccoon was on her lap.

"Come here, Monkey," she said.

"No."

"What's the matter?"

"Nothing."

I poured an eight-count of Stoly and went out to the pool, stunned and dizzy. The afternoon was Everest, this was Death Valley. Why couldn't I for once get something good without something bad having to balance it out.

Doheny came out wearing one of my T-shirts. She lit a butt, chewed the polish off her nails, asked if I wanted to play a game.

"No."

"It'll take your mind off things."

"That's what you said about the joint on the way to the Hard Rock."

"Let's not talk about bad things. This is a good day."

"It's not a good day, it's a horrible day. I'm fucked."

"Just tell him you didn't see nothing."

Tempting.

"Maybe the problem will just go away," she said.

This sounded even better. Who knew, maybe it would.

"We're gonna play a game called 'confession.' You have to confess something about yourself that you never told anyone else."

"No."

"Come on, it'll help us bond."

"We've bonded enough."

"No, we haven't. You've been really distant lately. Please, don't be a poop. Let's tell each other something we did that was really stupid that nobody knows about."

She put her hand on my package. I lifted it off.

"You go first," she said.

"*You* go first."

"No, *you* go first. I called it."

She explained the rules again and I finished my drink, then I went in and poured another six-count and while I was there I took a hit off a roach. It took me a while to think of something dumb that no one knew, and then I felt the roach and remembered.

"I got one," I said, "but it's probably not what you're looking for."

"So what? So what? Go ahead."

"I had a girlfriend when I was eighteen and I loved her a lot, but I had this stupid thing in my head that I'd only tell one girl in my life that I loved her, because I thought that was the way it was going to be. And even though I loved this girl, I didn't tell her because I wasn't sure she'd be the only one." I rolled my ice around. "Since then, I've told a few of them that I love them. But I think maybe she's the one that I loved the most. And I think she loved me the most, too."

"That's pathetic, Henry."

Her light touch made me smile. "Yeah."

"What happened to her?"

"She's gone."

"Where'd she go?"

I took a big gulp.

"Away."

"Okay, you told me a story. Now I'll tell you something personal."

"You don't have to."

"I want to. Are you sure you want to hear it?"

"Just tell it."

"Okay."

She bit her thumb and kind of smiled and I kind of smiled back and I thought it was going to be a fun one, and she said, "I blew a dog once."

Back inside my phone machine was blinking. I hit the button: "Henry. Ted Bowman. Kudos on the pitch today. You're a stud. I'm looking forward to working with you, dude. Listen, lunch tomorrow, one o'clock, Ivy on Robertson. Oh, um . . . ah . . . I also need you to call my lawyer, tell him what you saw. Um . . . ah . . . well, we'll talk about it tomorrow. Ciao."

When Doheny came in, I took my pad back outside and started writing *Ice Cream Man.* I was determined to make this something more than run-of-the-mill slasher shit. I wanted to elevate the genre, the way *Psycho* did, and *The Fly;* I wanted to give it depth, make it fun. Make it so good that they couldn't say no.

Sometimes writing is hard and sometimes it's easy and often there's no accounting for either. You can be happy as a clam and all blocked up or feeling like shit and watching it flow. This much I know about creative endeavors: They're out of your control. You have to be disciplined enough to sit down and give an effort, but what comes forth is not up to you. Inspiration is not earned, it is a gift. It's why Van Gogh spit out most of his great stuff in eighteen months in Arles. It's why someone can write two great novels in a row and never write another decent chapter; why songwriters can have ten hits in five years and not be heard from again. What happened to Papa John Phillips, and the guy who wrote all the Rascals' hits, and Christopher Cross and Bobby Boyce and Tommy Hart and Brian Wilson and Carlos Santana and Peter Townshend and Nils Lofgren and George Harrison and the Jefferson Airplane? It's not that the music changed so much, it's that the spark isn't there for them anymore. It's not their fault. They were lucky to have once been blessed, but the gift was not theirs to own, only to borrow, and it moved on as good fortune inevitably does.

When I sat down to write *Ice Cream Man,* I had the flow working for me. The entire first act spilled out of my head in seven hours. I didn't think, just scribbled fast, tried not to get in the way. Twenty-four pages. I was so pleased that I celebrated by sparking a roach and jotting down fifteen more pages of notes. By sunrise I had the whole thing figured out. And what I had was good. I was proud for having dragged myself out of the gutter. I'd been inspired by my setback, taken advantage of my despair, and that, I think, is the key to success for a writer.

at 11 a.m. i drove to century city. I told Levine's assistant it was an emergency and five minutes later I was in. It was just as I'd feared. Bowman had told business affairs not to negotiate until after we talked. Levine was confused; it should've been a simple deal, Guild minimum, forty-two-five. As I started explaining,

Levine took off his telephone, mesmerized. He called in a couple other agents and I repeated the story.

"He wants you to lie for him?" a man named Adam Pollard asked.

"Yes. Well, I mean, it's not a lie to him. He really thinks he's right."

"He doesn't think shit," Levine said. "Guys like him don't think. He's a fucking sociopath—right and wrong don't matter, as long as he wins."

"Maybe he doesn't have insurance," the other guy, Flynn, said.

"He has insurance," Levine said.

"Then what's the big deal?" asked Flynn. "Why does he even care?"

"Because he's a fucking maniac."

"He must not have insurance," I repeated.

Pollard snapped, "Of course he has insurance, he has insurance up the kazoo. Listen to me, Henry, I know Ted Bowman. I once worked for a Ted Bowman. I understand the Ted Bowmans of the world. *They're fucking insane.* Give you an example: One day this asshole—name's Joe Baer, used to be an agent at ICM—anyway, he has a fender-bender. Not even a fender-bender really, more like a fender tap. Not the slightest dent in the car, just a little chip on the paint right above the headlight. So he gives me the keys and tells me to get the whole thing painted. We're talking five grand. I look at the car and look at him and I say, 'But you can't even see it. Why do you want to get the whole thing painted?' He says, 'Because it's not perfect.'"

Levine glanced at his e-mail. "There's no talking to these guys."

"Well," Flynn said, "if you want my opinion, just tell him what he wants to hear. He'll probably never need you to testify anyway."

"What if he does?"

"Let me tell you something," Pollard said. "In Bowman's mind it's immoral that you would forsake him. He's handing you forty-some-odd thousand dollars, and now you're going to pork him, that's what he sees."

Flynn said, "This isn't some movie where the good guy knows he's good and the bad guy knows he's bad. In the real world, most bad people don't know they're bad."

I put my head in my hands and growled.

"You're making way too much out of this," Levine said. "It'll probably just go away."

"It's not going to go away," I said. "I have a lunch with him today. He wants me to talk to his lawyer!"

"Okay, I have to ask this," said Pollard. "Was it even close? I mean, is it possible you saw it wrong?"

"He ran a fucking red light," Levine said.

"Well, if you want to be a boy scout about it, you could just say you didn't see anything," Flynn said. "I mean, that's a way out."

"And what about Pedro and his wife and kids?! They can't afford to fix a Rolls-Royce! They'd be better off jumping back over the fence and drinking diarrhea water down in Guadalajara!"

I didn't actually say this, which would've limited my options, but I thought it.

"Look," I said, "he said I have a deal. Doesn't that mean I have a deal?"

"Henry, I haven't received a deal memo yet," Levine said. "You don't have shit."

"You mean he can definitely back out . . . ?"

"Of course. Nobody's signed any paper."

"Then give me something to sign."

Pollard and Flynn could see I was getting irrational and bowed out of the room.

"That takes time. For Christ sakes, you probably won't see an actual contract until you're done with the first draft."

"So how do I protect myself? What can I do? Am I just fucked?"

"Don't work with guys like Ted Bowman, that's how you protect yourself. Work with Ron Howard or the Zucker brothers, not Ted Bowman."

"How stupid of me!" I yelled. "I should've taken their fucking calls instead of jerking off on that 976 line!"

"I'm just saying I warned you."

"How is this guy even allowed to operate?"

"He's able to operate because this is Hollywood." He stared at me. "So what's it going to be?"

I was stumbling. "I'll go to lunch. Of course. I'm not going to be rude, he just offered me my first deal, I think I owe him a lunch."

"And what'll you tell him when he asks you to back him up?"

"I don't know. What would you do?"

"It doesn't matter what I'd do."

Levine looked out the window at the sprawling L.A. Country Club below.

"If I've learned one thing out here, Henry, it's that there are a lot of sociopaths in this world, and they're not all killers."

the ivy was two minutes from my apartment in a nondescript building behind a distressed picket fence. You'd never suspect it was one of the fanciest restaurants in L.A., if not for the line of late-model foreign cars being valeted out front. The waiters and hostesses were all clean-cut, good-looking actors. They seemed unfazed by the celebrities and celebrity wives filling the place and were anything but impressed by my appearance at the hostess stand in shorts and a T-shirt. Ted Bowman's name perked them up, and a man in a suit—the manager, I presumed—took the menus from the unbelievably gorgeous hostess and led me to a corner table.

Bowman showed up a half hour late and immediately started reciting a kind of company riot act to me.

"If you want to work for me, the first thing you gotta do is get rid of any literary aspirations. You don't have any literary aspirations, do you?"

"No way."

When Bowman gazed at me cockeyed, I raised my right hand. "I swear on the soul of Jackie Collins."

"I didn't think so. I read a little of *How to Get Her Back* last night."

"*How I Won Her Back.*"

"Mixed reviews. When you're good, you're great, but when you're bad, you're grating."

"That's a first draft. I'm rewriting it."

"Point is, this ain't the fucking great American novel, it's just plain ol' movies and nothing else—that's rule number one. The second thing you gotta do is get rid of every selfish bone in your body. You're not gonna get your way around here, and the sooner you realize that, the better."

Bowman picked his nose while he said this, but I didn't look away.

"Nothing makes sense in Hollywood," he said, "so if you're right, you're wrong, and if you try to win, you lose, and if you've got talent, you better hope I don't notice." Someone caught Bowman's eye and he waved the booger at him. "Because I'm not looking for talent, I'm looking for *craft*—there's a big difference. Just do what I say, give me what I want, and you'll be okay."

"Talent's not going to be a problem," I said, but he didn't smile.

"Let me tell you something. Guys without an ounce of talent can work for thirty years in this town, while the talented ones who want to do their own thing never find a job. It's true. Look it up."

"I believe you. Hemingway and Faulkner, right?"

Bowman had a perpetual stuffed-up nose, so he chewed with his mouth open—it sounded as if he was chomping on shaved ice. I wondered if this was part of his act, this piggish fuck-you-I'll-pick-my-nose-and-eat-like-Belushi-anytime-I-want stuff. Maybe the clogged schnoz was from too much blow. Maybe he didn't even know he was doing it. Maybe he knew but was ingenuously carefree about it—it was just him, he was a nose picker, maybe his ancestors were nose pickers.

We talked about *Ice Cream Man* some, and I told him how inspired I was and it was going way better than I could've imagined, and could he possibly lean on the business affairs people so I might get paid soon.

"You strapped for cash?"

"No, I'm fine. Just . . . if you could hurry them along."

"If you're in trouble, tell me. I'll have them cut you an advance today."

"No, it's nothing like that, but thank you, that's very nice."

"By the way, they were trying to pork you, but I took care of it."

"Thanks." Then: "Hm?"

"Business affairs—they were going to stick it to you."

"How? How so?"

"The little pricks were talking WGA minimum, but I got you a C-note."

I tilted my head imperceptibly.

"Hundred grand," he said.

I was floundering in a crosscurrent of emotions when Bowman said, "You know, I've got to fight this fucker who clobbered me the other day."

"You . . . you got me a hun . . . ? Thank you, sir. Thank you."

"Yeah, yeah. You see, the guy's fucking lying and I need you to back me up."

"Ah, the whole thing was stupid," I said. "But what can you do?"

"Yeah," he said. "Fucking idiot."

I gestured obliquely.

"So you're gonna help me out, right? Tell my guys what you saw?"

"Tell who?"

"My lawyers. Tell them what happened."

I positioned myself for an end around.

"You know how many accidents I've had in my life?" I said. "I can't count them all."

The man who had arranged for a low-life hamburg flipper to receive a tenth of a million dollars for two months' work looked at me with his drippy, been-there-and-back eyes and I so wanted to please him.

"I wouldn't worry about it," I said. "It's no big deal."

"It *is* a big deal—but luckily I have you."

"What's the guy gonna do? He's probably not even legal."

"He *is* fucking legal, and the lying fuck says it was my fault, and he had five fucking witnesses in the car with him, and I ain't fucking paying."

This profusion of "fucks" threw me and, being a weakling around aggression, I wanted to placate him. I started calculating how much the repairs would cost, plus the personal damages, and I considered having him deduct it from my check, but of course I wasn't considering it too seriously.

"Well, you shouldn't have to pay," I said. "That's why you have an insurance company."

"You're not reading me. I'm not letting this go on my record, especially since I have you as my witness."

"I don't think it'll affect your insurance or your record either way. They let you have an accident now and then."

His eyes told me to shut up.

"You might lose the deductible," I conceded.

"Henry, I'm a millionaire many times over. This isn't about money, it's about right and wrong. I'm right, and you're going to help me prove it."

When I didn't respond in a gung-ho manner, he said, "Right?"

"Sure, whatever."

"What the hell does that mean? *'Sure, whatever.'* You sound like a *90210* pansy. Come on, you're with me or you're not. Which one is it?"

"I'm with you, I'm with you."

"Good."

"But, uh, to be honest, Ted, I'm not exactly sure what I saw."

Bowman raised his chin as if recognizing something unpleasant in my character.

"There were cars in front of me and I had the radio on and then I heard a crash and . . . I got out of my car to make sure everyone was okay."

"So you're *not* with me."

"No, no. I'm just saying . . ."

"What? You're saying what?"

"Well, you know, the whole thing was so fast . . ."

"You mean you didn't see nothing?"

"Not really."

He poured a glass of mineral water, drank it slowly.

"Why did you tell me you were going to be my witness?"

"Uh, I think I said—"

"Don't tell me what you said. Right after the accident, you came running over and you said, and I quote, 'I saw everything, Ted, I'll be your fucking witness,' and now you're screwing me. What is wrong with you? Are you a fucking stoner or something?"

"I mean, I saw you pass—I didn't know it was you, of course— and I saw that you were hanging a right and then . . ."

"And then . . . ?"

"And then I heard the accident."

"And then he hit me from behind."

I shrugged.

"And then he hit me from behind."

I nodded.

"And then he hit me from behind. I want to hear you say it."

"Then he hit you from behind."

"So what didn't you see?"

"No . . . I guess, you know . . ."

"Good. Now come to my office Monday at ten and tell my lawyer that exact story."

"Ten o'clock."

"And I'll make sure they have your check waiting, too."

a loud clang in the kitchenette when I walked into the apartment. A moment later Doheny marched out and said, "I'm sorry, Monkey. I'm sorry I made fun of your little story last night."

"Forget about it."

"No, I shouldn't have made fun. No matter what I felt, it was important to you—not telling the girl that you liked her—and I should've respected that."

"It's okay."

I threw my hat on the table, saw the two empty wine bottles.

She hooked her finger in her mouth. "You're not mad?"

"No. No big deal."

"Good."

"I see you found my little stash."

"Yeah."

"Dusted 'em both?"

Doheny approached me smiling, *leering* actually.

"Mm-mm."

I shot past her into the kitchenette. I opened the fridge and then she was behind me—right behind me.

"Henry . . ."

I wanted space between us, but she had me blocked in.

"Yeah?"

"Let's fuck."

"Oh, I don't think now . . . I have work . . . and everything. How about later? Yeah."

She put her arms around my neck, rested her forehead on my chin; her hair smelled like hair, not shampoo. I was frozen for a moment and then she looked at me with those big, brown, lopsided doe eyes, her breath reeking like a bar towel on St. Paddy's Day, and she said, "I'll suck you off if you want."

"You don't have to."

"Yes, I do," and she went for the zipper.

I slithered away.

"What?" she whined.

"What what?"

"S'matter?"

"Nothing's the matter. What's the matter with you?"

I picked up a few newspapers, stretched out some dirty socks, anything to keep from looking her way.

"I want to blow you."

Never could I imagine those five words upsetting me so.

"Nah, uh-uh, my neck."

"Oh, but you could play b-ball with *Cheers."*

"I also have a bladder infection."

"What?"

"It hurts when I piss."

"Henry, the infection you have is called fear of being close to someone."

She tried to kiss me; again I moved away. My stomach was suddenly churning, so I sat on the toilet for an hour, editing. I was done dumping in five minutes, but I was comfortable and cherished the isolation and when I finally stood up, both my feet were asleep. I took a shower, shaved, flossed, brushed my teeth, clipped my nails and nose hairs, plunged out my ears. When I finally returned, she was waiting for me in her panties, and that's all.

"S'matter?" she whined with her little Bardot finger hooked in her soup coolers.

"I'm sorry," I said, "but I have to work."

I sat at my desk, opened a notebook. Doheny came up behind me, licked my neck.

"Come on," I said.

"Where we going?"

"Good one."

I brushed her away.

"S'matter?"

"I can't work when I'm being touched."

She flopped back on the bed, making as much commotion as possible, as if she were covered with bugs. She rambled on in a stream of unconciousness, but I kept editing, refusing to listen. She opened a bag of potato chips, pulled a chair up beside me.

"Are you gay, Henry?"

"Yes, I'm gay."

"Yeah, right. That's why you got all the pictures of your so-called girlfriend."

"She was a guy."

When Doheny started to speak again, I cut her off. "Look, I'm not into volleying with you today. Now, it has nothing to do with you, Colleen—*Doheny*—but I just don't want to fool around right now, okay? It'll put me to sleep and I won't work."

She sneered. "Not too cocky, are we?"

She stuck her index finger between her cheek and gums and carved out a wedge of potato chip gunk.

"But you'd like to fuck me, other than that?"

"Other than what?"

"Other than you just wanting to write and all that hullabaloo?"

I poured a glass of tap water out of the bathroom faucet; it tasted like a pencil.

"Yes," I said. "Sure. I guess. And the bladder infection."

"Can I at least tell you what we'd do if we did have sex?"

"That's okay. I have a pretty good idea."

"No, it'd be different this time. You know what I want?"

"No," I said and I sat back down.

"I want you to fuck me in the ass."

"Oh, no, I don't think so."

"Don't be a priss."

"Uh-uh. I'm not . . . that's not . . . I have to be . . ."

"Come on, Henry, I love it up the ass, it turns me on. I've always been really anal, remember?"

"Why don't you just scrub the kitchen floors a couple times and fold all our underwear."

"I know you want it, Catholic boy. I know you want to fuck me up the pooper. You'd probably like to do it with that crucifix, wouldn't you?"

I prayed to God to forgive her for saying it and forgive me for imagining it.

"You'd like to do that, wouldn't you?" she said.

"Cut it out. I don't want to hear this shit."

"When I first met Honus, he used to stick pepperonis in condoms and jam 'em up my ass."

"What a delightful courtship."

"I'm a dirty girl, aren't I?"

"Yes, you are. Excuse me."

I walked across the street to Silverman's place. He was lifting weights in his living room. I filled him in on the last two days. The deal, the accident, Woody and Cliff and Norm, the threats, my nympho roommate with the big muff.

"She wanted you to plant one in her can?"

"Uh-huh."

"What are you, a fag? *Do it.*"

"Let's take a road trip."

"I don't get you sometimes."

"I'm disgusted by her."

"It can't be that bad. You fucked her before, didn't you?"

"She's got pussy hair on her back."

"That's called *back hair.*"

"Not with her, it ain't. It's all pussy."

"I'd like to see that."

"You would, huh? A treasure trail that goes above her belly button?"

"You never heard of a razor?"

"You don't clear the rain forest with a Weedwacker. Come on, what are you doing this weekend?"

"No plans."

And we were on our way.

it took two and a half hours to drive to Palm Springs. I told Silverman I'd pay for the gas and hotel room; we'd call our debt even. The first sixty miles was knotted with overpasses and commerce: Dennys, Carl Jr.s, 7-Eleven, In-and-Out Burger, a long stretch of auto dealers in "The Car Buying Town of West Covina."

Finally we came over a long hill and the smog stopped and I opened the can of Coors I'd brought for the ride.

"Give me half of that."

Silverman took the beer and was about to pour it into my sperm sample container.

"Nah, nah, nah, don't do that."

"Why not?"

"It's dirty."

"I don't mind."

I grabbed his hand. "You'd mind."

"What?"

"You don't want to know."

"What, is it your spittoon?"

"If it was just spit, I'd let you drink out of it."

"Piss?"

"Keep going."

"Huh?"

I made a jerk-off motion. He yelped and flung the container into the back.

"What is wrong with you?" he said.

We stopped and picked up a six-pack and as Silverman popped open his first can, he said, "We are officially in retox." Entering the desert, we saw thousands of giant windmills, their monstrous blades perpetually slicing at whomever passed, beauty and corruption aligned together, spectacular, terrifying; a fitting moat to the kingdom called Hollywood. Then came the plaster of paris dinosaurs and date shake stands. The temperature quickly climbed to over one hundred degrees, but snow somehow sparkled on the brown mountaintops. Then an oasis of green, green, green.

There's something about deserts that seems to cause time

warps. I'd only been to two and both felt like the 1960s. I'm not talking Woodstock, I'm talking about the way the sixties were for my parents. Frank Sinatra. Herb Alpert. Hi-fis. Highballs. Brazil '66. Debbie Reynolds. Joey Bishop. *These Boots Are Made for Walkin'*. Palm Springs was a lounge town. A pickup town. The birthplace and retirement home of leisure suits. It was a town undiscovered by the National Organization of Women. A gold lamé town. A Sonny Bono town. A tough-talking-big-titted-waitress-with-a-heart-of-gold town. Dean Martin and Bob Hope and Frank Sinatra each had streets named after them, and everywhere you turned was a golf course with loud golfers in double-knit slacks and shirts with big collars. It was the town that elected Richard Nixon and Ronald Reagan. The women were bathed in bright colors and even the young ones had hairdos that would be the envy of Donna Reed. The bars had never stopped having "happy hours" and the drinks were still served stiff in small glasses. There was an underlying mob mentality, similar to Vegas. Everyone claimed to be connected to a wiseguy or two, with the biggest connection being Frank himself.

The next morning we drove out to the Desert Marriott golf course, a magnificent track peppered with bouquets of palm trees, unblemished fairways, and baby powder sandtraps. We played eighteen, then threw on our shorts and laid out by our hotel pool, which was pretty much girl-free. After all that sun, I took a thirty-minute nap, then went to the spa and splurged on a massage and steam. I was starting to feel pretty healthy, so I did twenty-five push-ups and a hundred sit-ups in my room. I showered, shaved, put on pressed slacks, a fresh golf shirt, and met Silverman down in the lounge for a cocktail around seven.

We sucked down Stoly martinis while two women played backgammon in the corner. Herb noticed that their margaritas were getting low, so he sent over two fresh ones. They acknowledged this with a wave, but didn't touch the drinks, and after a while we figured out that the first margaritas weren't theirs to begin with.

After the martinis, we each drank a Dos Equis, then moved to another room and studied the dinner menu. An elegant-looking man wearing a white blazer with frilly gold epaulets on the shoulders—"the rear admiral" Herb called him—was playing show tunes on a white piano in the middle of the room. He was surrounded by six or seven younger men who listened attentively and then clapped and hooted and called for more.

"This place is a gerbil's worse nightmare," said Silverman.

I nodded, but it was all right with me because I was fried and all I wanted to do was listen to Captain Stubing play the piano and have enough drinks to numb my sunburn, and before I knew it, I was calling out for *Moon River* and Herb was shaking his head.

"You ever hear that story about what's-his-name—you know, the actor—getting a gerbil stuck up his ass?" Herb asked.

"Yeah, I heard it."

"You believe it?"

"No."

"Why not?"

"Because it makes no sense."

"It's true. These gay guys stick gerbils up their asses—they like the feeling of the thing running around up there."

"Uh-huh."

"You doubt that?"

"I doubt the movie star story."

"Why?"

"Because he's a big star and a multimillionaire," I said. "If he had a gerbil stuck up his ass, believe me, he wouldn't be running down to Cedars Sinai so everybody's best friend's sister could be checking him into the emergency room."

"Well, what's he supposed to do?"

"He's supposed to call a gay doctor, offer him a thousand dollars to make a housecall and another thou to shut up about it, and he's supposed to tell the guy to bring along a pair of forceps and some cheese."

There was applause as a good-looking Brit in his mid-forties slid in beside the pianist. The Brit had long blond hair and an above-average voice and he sang two Andrew Lloyd Weber songs for the adoring gentlemen.

"Who do you think's gayer?" Herb said. "The guy who thinks about dudes when he's fucking chicks, or the guy who thinks about chicks when he's fucking dudes?"

"Hey, let's go to a movie after dinner."

"I don't go to movies."

"Why not?"

"I just don't."

After another beer, we ordered dinner, each of us starting with a shrimp cocktail and asparagus salad.

Herb said, "You know, this stuff makes your piss smell funny."

"What is it about asparagus that compels people to talk about their urine at the dinner table? I don't get it, since when has asparagus and piss gone hand in hand? When you have chili, do you tell everyone how your shit's going to stink the next day?"

"Classic. You got a load in your car, but I can't talk about my piss at the dinner table?"

Our waitress was a little speedbag with big tits, so after the main course—he had a pepper steak and I ordered herb-encrusted salmon—Herb asked her where the best place to get laid was. In so many words. She sent us to a seventies-style disco, up on a hill, called Atlantis.

This was the kind of place that would make Telly Savalas misty. The interior was black, metallic, very shiny—rather cutting edge for Palm Springs. I'd had a pretty good time in the seventies, but going back now, in this state of mind, surrounded by loud divorcées, was sad, and I wanted to leave as soon as I paid the fifteen-dollar cover. Silverman was right at home, however, and before I knew it, I was holding a drink that looked like the blue stuff they soak combs in in barber shops.

"There's a couple flight recorders for you," he said, nodding at two women sitting at the bar. "What do you think would happen if we walked up and said, 'Hey, you two are far and away the best things in here—let's go somewhere and fuck.' Do you think that: (A) They'd try to kick us in the balls, or (B) They'd be so impressed with our honesty and forthrightness that they'd say, 'Let's go'?"

"A."

Silverman nodded. "Well, let's say hi anyway. I'll take the one on the right."

She was about forty with Dow Corning breasts and a face the color and texture of luggage. The one with the bad nose job was mine. She probably wasn't yet thirty-two, but she looked forty-five, a torn sneaker if ever I'd seen one.

"I don't think so."

"Come on, man, this is a team sport. You've got to play your role."

As Herb headed toward the women, he laid out a big smile like a line of coke and when Luggage-Face looked his way, she couldn't help but snort it up.

"You know something?" he said. "When you smile, you look just like my wife."

"That's a conversation stopper," she said.

"Oh, I'm not married. I just meant if I were, she'd probably look like you."

"What, are you trying out lines on us?"

"Actually, yes. Hunt here's a writer."

"Oh, wow, how unprecedented—a writer, in Southern California."

This came from my girl, though she never took her eyes off Silverman. I sprung for a round, which seemed to be the extent of my rap lately, and then Silverman's girl said to him, "I saw you when you came in and I said, 'That guy's pretty cute.'"

"Really?" Herb said in that lilty way that really means "interesting." "I was telling Hunt the exact same thing."

They smiled, and I said, "It's true. He was just saying, 'You know, I'm pretty cute.'"

Silverman wedged himself between the women, forcing Nose Job to turn her attention to me. We quickly checked each other out. Now I could see that it wasn't a bad nose job after all—just a few too many good ones. She had some kind of Samsonite deal working with her skin, too, as if she'd spent the last fifteen years boozing and smoking Kools under a sunlamp. Her teeth looked as if they were capped by Calloway—about a half size too big—and her hunched, indifferent posture suggested she'd just been put through the ringer. Her name was Cindy Green.

"As in mucus, money, and envy."

"Huh," I said.

She blew a megaphone-sized cone of smoke over her shoulder. When I found out she was newly divorced, I felt bad and made a bet with her that she wouldn't be single long. I said a couple other things, too, trying to build up her ego, straighten her backbone. This softened her up, and it turned out she wasn't so tough after all, just lonely, and she really wanted someone to hold, to love for a night, in return for which she would allow me or someone else to slip a cock into her body. For a minute I considered it, but I didn't want her waking up in my room, and doing it in the parking lot would just make her feel crummy, and there was no way in hell I was going to her sad, divorced apartment with the divorced furniture and the divorced kids and the divorced cat because that would make me feel pretty crummy, too.

Cindy Green told me a long story about the great deal she'd gotten on an armoire at Shabby Chic in Beverly Hills, but it hadn't been delivered on time and so on and so on, and I became self-conscious about staring at the picket fence in her mouth and developed a bad case of lockjaw. After a few more minutes waiting for Silverman to close his deal, I excused myself.

An elderly black attendant sat smoking a cigarette in the black-tiled bathroom. The place smelled strangely of Kool-Aid. I didn't have to go to the toilet, so I threw water on my face to look busy. Three guys with short hair up front and long hair in the back stood in an open stall doing blow. One man would carry on breathlessly, and when he made the mistake of trailing off, the others would yell, as if yelling were the high itself, and the loudest yeller would hold the floor for another long-winded tale of bravado. I wondered how they could do the shit after Len Bias and all the famous ruined lives.

I left the attendant a buck for my paper towel and returned to the room, but hung out on the other side. I tried to appear content, even though I'd always despised being alone in a bar. Finally I saw something of interest. Little sundress, perky butt, rich tan, amazing face. Beautiful Waspy hair. *Portnoy's Complaint* hair. Cybill Shepherd in *The Heartbreak Kid* hair. On the way over, I thought of a dozen things I could say, but they all sounded like pickup lines. I didn't want to pick her up. I wanted to know her, to make her laugh, to take her to lunch tomorrow, write her long love letters and talk on the phone for hours, to marry her in a couple years, have kids, watch them grow, have grandkids, retire down the Cape, die with her at my side.

"Hi," I said.

"Fuck you."

"What?"

"*Fuck you.* Get the hell away from me, you slimy little Dorito breath."

I winced. "What the hell's that all about? Did you just break up with someone who looks like me?"

Before she could answer, a six-foot-five-inch giant charged across the room, straight-armed me into a wall, and I was still in the running for the "die with her at my side" part.

"Hey, hey, hey," I said. "What'd I do?"

The guy stuck his mustache up to my neck (actually, he was only about five-five, but he was some kind of steroid freak and may as well have been a foot taller).

"Get the fuck away from her, she don't want to get bothered."

"Okay, okay, I'm history. Relax."

He released my arms and I said, "Jeez, if she doesn't want to be around people, she shouldn't hang out in nightclubs."

Now the little bulldozer's nose was nudging against my chin

and I could smell his breath coming through it, something like salami.

"What, you got a problem? You can't take a hint?"

"No, I don't have a problem. You made your point. I'm out of here."

"What's going on?"

Herb was holding another one of the blue drinks as well as a beer. When the bodybuilder turned toward him, I ducked out of the corner and slid behind my well-built redheaded friend. I was hoping the pit bull would calm down, but he was wearing stonewashed jeans with pockets on the side of the knees, so reasoning with him was unlikely.

"You with him?" he asked Herb.

"Yeah."

Herb handed me my blue drink.

"Get him the fuck out of here before he gets his head split open."

"Look," Silverman said, "I know this guy. If he did something wrong, it was out of stupidity. I mean, who in his right mind would want to fuck with a guy like you? Come on."

The "I know you" smile again.

"Just get him out of my face."

"Okay, take it easy, friend, we're all Americans here. Can I buy you a beer?"

Silverman put his left hand on the guy's shoulder and when the pit bull relaxed his neck muscles, the base of Herb's beer bottle slammed into his forehead. There was a fantastic popping sound over the music. The bully grabbed the wall with one hand, his forehead with the other, then recovered enough to throw a half-hearted punch at Silverman, as if he were swinging underwater, before awkwardly sinking to the floor. Despite the tremendous impact, the bottle didn't crack, and it took Herb two more whacks on the floor before it did break and the never-more-fraudulent Jew was suddenly holding the jagged glass against the dazed man's cheek.

"You're a tough guy, huh?! Real tough guy! Now, tell my friend you're sorry!"

Pit Bull paused just long enough for Herb to punch him in the face. His head snapped back against the floor, which sounded as if it hurt more than the punch.

"I said, 'Tell him you're sorry!' "

"I'm sorry, man. I didn't mean nothing."

Another punch, a little blood from the mouth.

I said, "It's okay, Herb. He's sorry."

But Silverman wasn't finished.

"You know, I think I remember you," Herb said. "Yeah, that's right, your mother sucked my dick one night when you were sleeping in the other room. Yeah, it was definitely you. I'm surprised you didn't wake up when that big black guy fucked her ass."

Another punch, a gusher of red now, a frightening twinkle in Herb's eyes.

"You uncoordinated piece of fuck! Tell him you're sorry *and mean it!"*

"I'm sorry, man, I'm sorry!" This in a pathetic cracking voice. "I don't want no fucking trouble. I'm sorry . . . I'm sorry . . ."

The whole thing lasted maybe forty-five seconds and as Herb stood back up, a slew of bouncers came running over, but they were reluctant to take on this smiling, loudmouthed redhead with the broken bottle in his hand. They made a semicircle around him and one of them said, "Okay, take it easy, dude."

My dreamgirl was suddenly back, pointing at me and screeching, "He started it! That guy started it!"

The guy on the floor sat up, teeth coated red with mucus, and said, "He's crazy, man. He hit me with a fucking beer bottle." He was rubbing his forehead, but he didn't dare stand and I actually felt bad for him because he had tears in his eyes.

The bouncers walked us to the door, but they were wary of Herb's volatility and quite nice once they saw that he wasn't going to punch any of them out. I was a little shaken by the suddenness of it all and wanted to get in the car and disappear, but the parking valet seemed to take forever. Even though the bully was down, I wasn't convinced he wouldn't regroup and come after us again, maybe with a gun. I figured he had to. Everything he stood for was at stake. He'd been beaten, he'd been humiliated on his home court, *he'd cried in front of the blonde babe.* The guy was on steroids, he'd ruined his liver and joints, taken years off his life—for *this?* He would forever be a muscly, arthritic joke to these people.

Silverman had been through this kind of thing before and couldn't have looked less threatened if they'd taken the guy away in a body bag. He was pumped up and talked with a couple girls at the door, never showing any indication of what had just happened, and I was impressed with Silverman's poise, his resiliency, and suddenly I suspected he was going to make it big in Hollywood after all.

It was after 1 A.M. and Silverman wanted to go to another club ("It ain't over till the fat lady says no"), but I was shot, so we compromised and went back to our hotel lounge, which was dead. We sat at the big stained mahogany bar and drank brandys. The only people left were the middle-aged Brit with the long blond hair and his companion, a slight woman with big droopy tits and a short dark coif. The Brit had an amiable way about him, but his friend looked miserable. I can't say she wasn't pretty, but there was something dark and unhappy about her.

Over a brandy, Herb tried to solve my problems.

"Just throw her out."

"It's not that easy."

"Why not? Is she stable now?"

"Very *un*."

"All the more reason to kick her ass out. And if she comes back again, you should push her off the goddamn roof yourself."

"Ah."

"Just do it, get her out, boot her, it's your place."

"You don't understand. I feel bad for her. Her sister . . . you know, I can't just . . . I've got to wait for the right time."

"*What right time?* She's driving you crazy, what is there to feel bad about? You tried to save her sister and she jumped—end of story. What the fuck could you do?"

"Well . . ."

"You're a fucking idiot, you know that? You deserve anything you get."

"I'll get her out."

"Want me to do it? I'll drag her out by that mop of a cunt. She won't be back either."

"I'll get her out, don't worry. You're right, I've just got to be firm."

"Be a man. Walk in there and say, 'Party's over, Superbush.' As for the producer, just cut the bullshit and give the guy what he wants."

"Really?"

"Sometimes you gotta make sacrifices to get what you want in life."

"Herb, giving him what he wants wouldn't be the sacrifice."

"Exactly. So just do it. You got off easy—you've just gotta lie to a couple lawyers—count your blessings."

When the bartender Bill brought another round, he leaned in and informed us that the Brit was a famous director. I'd never heard his name before, but I knew the movies, and Herb quickly sent them a couple drinks, which I paid for. The Brit was most grateful and struck up a conversation with Herb. As I listened, I wondered if maybe he was an Aussie or South African, or just from a dumb-sounding part of England. The somber woman never looked my way, so I started chatting up the bartender. Bill was a third-generation Californian, and we got in a light-hearted debate over which coast was superior. Bill said, "How can you defend a place that has freezing temperatures and snow half the year?"

"Sunshine is like anything else. When you don't have it all the time, it's better. Like, if you get in the car and drive up the coast and sleep at a little place on the beach and drink martinis while watching the sun go down, it'd be nice, right? But if you did it again tomorrow, it probably wouldn't be quite as nice, and if you did it every day this month, you'd undoubtedly get sick of the whole thing, and if you had to do it every day for a year, the whole trip would probably lose its beauty. See, the very thing that makes Southern California so desirable is the thing that ruins it. It's sunny and warm, and that's great, but it's exactly the same every day, more or less. Yeah, winter back East sucks. It's a tremendous letdown, a cooling off period, a drying out time. Actually, in the beginning it's okay, right up to Christmas—"

"It blows," Herb piped in.

"I second that," from the skinny sourpuss.

I looked at them, then continued to Bill. "But that's why spring is so great. You've suffered, paid your dues, frozen your ass off for five months, so that first day of spring, not March 21, but the day it really hits—is more special than you can imagine."

"I've zeen that in N'York," the Brit said. "It is truly plum."

"And back there you savor every nice day," I said. "The nice days are nicer than here—spring, summer, fall—because you know they won't last. It'll get bad again, that's a fact. Here nothing changes, and that's the problem."

"It's like pussy," Herb said. "I don't care how great the pussy is, it can be the greatest pussy in the world, but if you get the same pussy every day, you get sick of it."

"Oh, really?" from grumpy girl, looking very slutty now.

"That's right."

The director let out a huge guffaw, which made me laugh.

"What would *you* know about pussy?" Herb said, looking my way.

"Ah, Christ," I said, "here it comes. He's drunk, and he just saved my life, so he thinks he can be an asshole."

The director nodded vigorously at me with a rousing smile, then said, "Ya gonna take that, 'erb?"

"Seriously," Herb said, "when was the last time you had any real good stuff? And don't mention Sybil back in your apartment."

"I'm too tired for this. I'm going to bed."

I threw some money on the bar and started to leave.

Herb said, "Hey, hey, give me some dough, fucky. You're supposed to be covering me, remember?"

The director said, "That's 'kay, 'erb. I gotcha, mate."

I watched a rebroadcast of the eleven o'clock news, then clicked off the tube and lay in bed pondering how to make it work with Bowman. I knew there was an easy solution. There always is. An hour passed in a few minutes and suddenly it was 3:15 and I was more alert than ever. I pulled on my shorts and went for a walk on the hotel's golf course in my bare feet. The night air was still thick and warm and the grass was thick and cool. I lay down on the second green and searched for shooting stars to wish upon. The more I thought about it, the sillier the whole Bowman thing seemed. Herb was right, I was making a mountain out of a molehill. So he ran a red light and lied about it—that didn't make Bowman a bad guy. He was just vain. And it wasn't as if the Mexican was going to pay. His insurance would pick it up, and if he wasn't covered, then Bowman's would get it. It was very simple: Bowman didn't mind paying, he just wanted to be right. For a hundred grand I probably owed the man that much.

There are few places more peaceful than a desert golf course at night, until you remember that it *is* a desert and deserts have poisonous things. So I decided to head back to my room.

As I approached the hotel, I stumbled upon Herb getting a blowjob in the jacuzzi. His legs were dangling in the water and he lay back on the deck with his hands behind his head, staring up at the stars. Tiffany Pittman was right about a couple things: Herb was as well-endowed as he was lazy.

The Brit's miserable girlfriend was kneeling in the tub up to her shoulders, doing all the work. Her hair was wet and, even from thirty feet in the dim light, I couldn't miss the freakish hunk of cock in her grip. I decided to stay on the grass, take the long way around the pool, and not interrupt them.

I'd only gotten a few steps when I heard the clinking of ice cubes. Sitting on a chaise to my left, finally smiling, was the woman whom I'd just presumed to be gobbling cock. I jerked my head back toward the jacuzzi. "Don't worry," she said. "Your friend's just drunk, and mine's terribly persuasive."

Her voice triggered a splashy commotion at the tub; I heard the Brit's startled voice. The woman took a hit on her cigarette and, as I hurried away, I smashed my shin on a glass table. I kept going, though, and I three-at-a-time'd it up the stairs, and it felt as if someone was on my heels, chasing me, but no one was.

eight

my radiator hose blew open about ten miles outside Palm Springs. I got a close-up of the desert while we waited for help. It wasn't like the deserts I'd seen in movies, with the Saguaro cactus and boulders. This looked like a huge empty lot, as if there'd been something there before that had been demolished. Scraps of paper and plastic and rubber and metal and boards and beer cans were scattered everywhere. About a mile away, I could make out trailer homes and, beyond that, an extremely tall Exxon sign. I'd been avoiding Herb's gaze all morning and trying to steer what little conversation there was. Then, without taking his head out from under the hood, Herb said, "I'm not queer, you know."

I didn't respond and he said, "Do you hear me?"

"Whatever, man. Don't worry about it."

"Oh, I see." This with an attitude.

"What? Look, Herb, you do what you . . . you know, choose to do. Everyone does. It's not for me to . . . whatever."

Herb came around the car and got in my face. "Do you have any idea how hard it is to be a fucking actor?" He hadn't slept much and looked anxious, and I felt sick to my stomach for him. "No. You don't fucking know shit. It's not like being a writer, man. It's nothing like it. I have *absolutely no control.* Do you understand that? You can go home tonight and write. You can write every fucking day of the year. And each time you write, you get a little better. How the fuck can I get better, huh? Tell me. What am I gonna do—go home, stay up all night and *act?* Uh-uh. I can't act until they tell me I can act. I gotta wait for those motherfuckers to tell me I can act."

"Well . . . there's acting class."

"Yeah, and for three hundred bucks you get to stand up once or twice a month in front of a bunch of schmucks who are more interested in kissing the teacher's ass than learning how to be real. And the teachers—all they want to do is hear themselves talk, and what the hell could they possibly teach me anyway? Lecturing about acting is like lecturing about baseball. You've got to *do it* to get good at it . . . but they won't fucking let me. Why do you think I don't go to movies? Because *I can't.* Because it makes me sick to see guys up there who don't have a fucking clue . . . Because I can't get a break . . . Not a goddamn . . . fucking break."

A few vehicles whizzed by. Then: "So when an opportunity comes, well . . . yeah . . . they can suck my dick." He turned away and leaned against the car. "But I'm not . . . what you think."

I saw the wrecker approaching with his blinker on, and I said, "Herb, you're missing the point. I never thought you were gay." I picked up a rock, fired it at a paper bag. "I wouldn't be so bothered if you were."

when los angeles was founded, there were no palm trees. It was and is a desert, but white men stuck full-grown palms in the sand like flags declaring that this was their country, a place of limitless hope, a land without winter, and it was these palm trees, this promise of warmth and fun and sex, that had swayed in my and millions of other minds as we trekked happily westward toward our ruination. I passed a lot of palms on the drive from Palm Springs to Paramount, but they were listless, shark-colored nothings with razor-sharp mop-tops sagging down like a row of dead Beatles. The infatuation was over; reality had set in like a 7 A.M. pussy fart. I knew the truth now: Rats lived in the palm trees.

"Ted, with all due respect, I'm not a good witness for your insurance thing."

It was quarter of ten. I'd showed up early, before the lawyers.

"Why not?"

"Because . . . well, honestly, I saw it a little different than you."

"How so?"

"I thought I saw you run the red light."

"Yeah?"

"Well . . . that wouldn't be a good thing for me to tell them."

"I went right on red, that's legal. If the fuck hadn't been speeding, he wouldn't have clipped me."

I wanted to believe this, it was an out.

"Halloran, Jesus, you're a writer, come on. It's just about putting the right spin on what happened. You saw me go right on red, no?"

"Uh, yeah."

"Then that's what you say. I do the rest. Man, you gotta know how to shine a positive light on yourself sometimes."

I sipped my water, fought the urge to agree.

"Give you an example," he said. "I was married for a while to my college sweetheart, then we went in turnaround. So a couple years ago I go to my twenty-year reunion. Everyone wants to know where Myrna is, they want to know what the hell went wrong. Know what I told 'em? I told 'em that *Annie* lasted seven years on Broadway. See what I'm saying? I'm saying that even good things have to come to an end. It's not that it was a bad marriage, it's just that its run was over. Hey, it swept the Tonys, it brought joy to millions, it got made into a bad movie. But then it's over." He glanced out the window. "You make things palatable. You get by. Life is only as good as the spin you put on it."

"But when you go right on red, you're supposed to stop first."

"I did stop."

"I don't think you did."

"You say you don't *think* I did, but I *know* I did. So obviously you're wrong."

"Well, no. Actually, I *know* you didn't stop."

"So you're calling me a liar?"

"I think you probably think you stopped, I mean everything was happening so fast, but I watched the whole thing and I think, well, I *know,* that you didn't stop. In fact, you were the one who was speeding, not the other guy."

Bowman turned his eyes to me and it was very imposing, that stare. Luckily, I'd been a U.S. Lines salesman and knew what it was like to have to keep eye contact with a guy when I was dead wrong, and here I was dead right.

Finally Bowman nodded and said, "It's okay, I have other eyewitnesses. You weren't the only one."

"Well . . . great."

"Yeah."

I didn't say anything, just held my breath.

"Now go."

It's not that I hadn't considered this outcome—odds were a hundred to one in favor of it—but I'm an optimist, which is one reason I started writing, to improve on reality, and the right side of my brain had humored me all day with the prospect of a life-affirming, feel-good finale.

"What about *Ice Cream Man?*"

"I'll have someone else write it."

"But it's my story."

"Fuck you. I've been working on that thing for years and everyone in town knows it. Just ask your agent."

"Look, you're going to set yourself back six months, at least. I've already started this thing, I know it better than anyone, I could write this story in my sleep."

He didn't blink.

"Ted, come on, I came up with the ice cream man part. That's mine."

"You take the time to copyright it?"

"Of course. I wasn't about to pitch something without a copyright."

"You're a liar."

"I am not," I lied again. "I copyrighted it months ago."

"Then you'll have to sue me."

I started to say something but managed only a few facial tics.

"Halloran, the idea of doing a serial killer love story was mine. You may have come up with the title, but you can't copyright a title. That means *Ice Cream Man* belongs to whoever comes out with it first. As for the story—if you recall, you never really told me one."

"Exactly. And I happen to have a very good one. You should see my notes, you're not going to believe it."

"I don't want to see your notes."

"Come on, this is stupid. You're letting personal issues get in the way of good business."

"You did this to yourself, man."

I saw that wet smile again and I sweated and finally I managed to stand.

"Well, I guess you really are what you eat. Because you're a big dick."

I didn't actually say this; I thought of it on the way home. I considered calling him back and saying it, but what would that do? He'd probably just use it in a script.

kevin costner in a casket is what I felt like. He'd thought he'd had his big break once. *The Big Chill.* They'd made the movie, he was one of the stars, it centered around his character's death, there'd been tons of flashbacks of him. But they'd cut him out. All that remained was Kevin Costner in a casket. That was me. Dead. Robbed. Screwed. Then I said fuck that. Costner had gotten another chance, and I would, too. I'd write *Ice Cream Man* on my own. It was a slam dunk spec script, especially since I wouldn't have to tailor it to the lunatic's liking. He could go ahead and do his own thing, maybe he'd even get the title, but he couldn't steal what was inside my head, he couldn't steal my inspiration.

"Look, Doheny, I don't know how else to put this, but . . . we've got to break up."

I could hardly believe the madness that was spilling off my tongue, but by giving in to her delusion that we were in fact "going out," I hoped "breaking up" would allow us to complete the cycle, just like a real couple.

I was surprised by her reaction. Doheny looked genuinely hurt. This was good, she was taking me seriously.

"What are you saying?"

I avoided her shattered gaze. "I think we need time apart, you know, to sort things out."

"No . . . no, we don't need time apart."

"I've booked you a ticket. You're on a nonstopper into Newark—it leaves in two hours."

She moved toward me, a layer of tears reflecting the television screen.

"You poor baby. You don't even know, do you?"

"I'm walking you to the gate. There's no more excuses, it's really over, Colleen. I want to end this on a good note, so please get your stuff together so we can go."

I held my lips above her reach.

"Don't you see why you're doing this?"

"Well, yeah, actually, I do."

"You're trying to break up with me before I break up with you."

Maybe it was an out. "Were you going to break up with me?"

"Of course not."

"That's not why I was doing it."

"Yes, it is, Hen. Don't you get it? You got fucked over by that bitch and you don't want to get hurt again, so now you're subconsciously sabotaging *our* relationship." She waved a *Psychology Today* at me. "It's all in here, man. It's textbook."

"I'm very conscious of my motivation here, Doheny. I'm sick of living in a fucking nuthouse."

"I'm not going to leave you, Hen. You help me. I help you. We help each other."

"That's bullshit. We don't help each other."

"Oh, it's bull, is it?" She smiled. "Why don't you get your big producer on the phone, ask him if it's bull."

"What?"

"The producer, Mr. Bowmark, he'll tell you."

"What are you talking about?"

"I helped you. He called on the phone and your machine answered—Saturday, in the morning—so I dug you out of your little mess is what I did."

"You talked—you picked up the phone?"

She nodded.

"Colleen, what did you say?"

"Doheny."

"Colleen, what the fuck did you say?"

"Don't get your pants on fire. I told him that you felt bad 'cause you weren't really paying attention in the car, but that *I* saw what happened."

"And what was that?"

"I don't know, you know, whatever."

"Tell me!"

"I said I saw the Cholo speeding along and then he slammed into him. I mean, it's true—that's what I heard anyway. So now he doesn't need you as a witness—you're off the hook!"

"Get the fuck out."

"Henry . . ." In two octaves. "Henry, stop it. You don't mean that. I'm your soul mate."

"What?" With a staccatolike giggle.

"I'm your soul mate."

"Open your magazine and look up the word 'delusional.' "

"You don't know what you're doing! You don't know what the fuck you're doing!"

"Look," I said on my way to the door, "I'm going across the street for a beer. Now, when I get back in ten minutes, I want you to have all your shit together because you really are going this time."

"No!"

"Yes."

"No!"

"Oh, yeah."

" 'If you walk out that door, you're making the biggest mistake of my life!' "

I took my hand off the knob.

"What? What did you just say?"

She stepped back, thrust her chin at me.

"What did you just say?" I repeated.

"You heard me."

A ringing in my right ear, some internal teapot reaching a boil.

"Where did you . . . ?"

"Look, Henry, why don't you just go."

I moved toward her. She looked nervous, aggressive.

"I did you a favor. I told Mr. Bowmark about all the great stuff you had."

"Does he know . . . did you . . . about the notes?"

"Henry, would you relax? I helped you out. I mean, you should've heard him, he was laughing like a bastard. He didn't even know about half the stuff. I saved your white ass, Monkey!"

"You've been . . . in the fridge . . ."

"Yes, I've been in the fridge."

"You gave him my—"

"What, now I can't go in the fridge again?!"

"But you gave him my—"

"You sound just like my goddamn mother. 'Stay out of the fridge, you're fat.' Yeah, well maybe that's why I got a fucking eating disorder now, because of assholes like you!"

That's when I slapped her.

"He's crazy! Help! He's crazy!"

I sat on the bed, horrified at what I'd just done.

She kept screaming. "Help me! Somebody help me!"

"Stop it," I said.

"Please, somebody help me! He's crazy!"

"I hardly touched you."

"For the sake of Pete, somebody!"

"Shut up!"

"No, I won't shut up. *Please! Somebody!*"

I made a move toward her; she picked up a plastic knife off the table.

"Oh, Jesus," I said. "Knock off the histrionics."

"You get out of here, you!"

"You get out of here, you. I live here."

"Help! He's trying to kill me!"

"You are a fucking nightmare."

Somebody started banging on the door. When I glanced away, she stabbed me in the cheek. Luckily, the white plastic bent, but the blade's serration left me with a four-inch flesh wound, which didn't look so good when the cops arrived a hundred and fifty seconds later. We were outside by then. She'd run into the front yard to attract more attention and I'd followed to defend my name. All anyone saw, of course, was a screaming woman being followed by a bloody, guilty-looking man, and when the first frosting-headed cop arrived, I was actually glad to see him as it enabled me to step out of the prickly bird-of-paradise that two bat-wielding "heroes" had backed me into.

The officer was already talking to Doheny when I approached. She was shivering on the front steps with her arms crossed over her chest, the standard beaten-wife stance she'd picked up watching *Cops*. Two fat hippie ladies whom I'd never seen before were comforting her, and she was milking it like a newborn calf. When she saw me, Doheny jumped behind one of the women with a look of abject terror. Both women yelled profanities at me, and the officer said, "Get back where you were, sir!"

I threw my hands up and backed off. Doheny took advantage of her momentum.

"I'm sick of being codependent!" she yelled.

I turned. "What the hell is she talking about?"

"It's not 'she,' Henry. It's me, *Doheny*. I'm a real person, with real feelings and real emotions, not just some 'she' you can chew up and spit out."

"Shut up."

The officer stepped forward. "No more abusive language, sir."

Doheny was right behind him. "This is a dysenfunctional relationship and I've allowed you to push me around for long enough, but I won't do it anymore!"

"Are you insane?" I said. *"I've 'pushed you around'?* You've beaten me to a fucking pulp."

"Sir!" From the officer.

"See?" she said. "That's your view of it because you're codependent on me. You need me around to pick on, so you can feel superior. That's why you keep me hanging around but won't commit. It makes you feel good to know you're better than some-one, doesn't it?! Isn't that right? Well, I got news for you, buster, you're not and you're outta here!"

"Go, girl!" from one of the earth mothers, followed by a smat-tering of applause.

"Look, sir, why don't you just step back and cool off?"

"Because I live here. She's the one who's going somewhere, not me."

Of course I was walking away from the building when I said this. I waited on the sidewalk a few minutes. Finally Cakehead the Cop approached and said, "The young woman says she won't press charges if you just leave."

"But I live here, not her."

"She says she lives here."

"She's a liar. Ask anybody, it's my apartment."

"That's not what her friends say."

"Her friends? They're not her *friends.* She doesn't have friends."

"They say they've seen her around."

"I've seen the mailman around. That doesn't mean he lives here."

"It's not true that she's been living with you?"

"No, she hasn't been *living with me*."

"Then what was she doing on the roof a few weeks ago?"

"Playing me like a fiddle, that's what."

"You hadn't seen her before that?"

"She stayed with me a couple days, that's all. I was trying to help her out."

"So she *has* been living with you." Cakehead looked as if he'd just tricked me into a full murder confession.

"I didn't say that, I said she's been *staying here*."

Splitting hairs now was his look.

"She claims she lives here."

"And I'm telling you that's bullshit. Call my landlady, she'll tell you, I pay the rent."

"Who pays the rent is irrelevant."

"What?! Well, what the hell is relevant?"

"I'm going to ask you now to control your language, Mr. Halloran."

"I just don't see what the hell you're talking—"

"I said, 'Control your language.' Now, if you can't do this, we're going to continue the conversation down at the station."

"All right, all right. It's just that this is . . . baloney."

The officer went back to the gaggle of hags and bat-wielders on my front steps while I waited on the sidewalk catching dirty looks from all sides and then Herb Silverman came by and I was happy to see him because he was immediately on my side. I told him to tell the cops what the truth was, and he approached them, and then a few minutes later two cops and he returned, and they said I either had to go with Herb or else.

"Or else what?"

"You can either go with your friend, Mr. Halloran, or we're going to have a problem."

"What is that, some kind of veiled threat?"

"It's not veiled. If you don't leave, I'll place you under arrest."

"Then arrest me, because I'm not going to be kicked out of my own home and let this con woman take over my residence."

The officer rolled his eyes, unfastened a pair of handcuffs from his belt.

Silverman pulled on my arm. "Come on, Henry, let's go over to my place. We'll deal with it later."

I pulled away. "No! If they think I'm not staying in my own home, then they better fucking arrest me!"

My arms were grabbed from behind and I was shoved against a police cruiser and in a flash I felt cuffs snap around my wrists and I started to struggle with three cops and a quarter ton of weight on my back.

Now in retrospect the Beverly Hills cops were probably being pretty gentle with me. They held me against the cruiser and bent my arms a little awkwardly and one of them had a club or an elbow pressed against the back of my head, but it was approximately the right amount of force necessary to keep me down. At the time, however, I felt they were being assholes and I let them know this, and then I found out what a real asshole could be like when the Orange Cop showed up and spun me around, ran me into the side of a palm tree, and slammed me down on the sidewalk. I tasted something hot and salty, which turned out to be just what you'd think, and it felt like I'd chipped a tooth, but I hadn't, I'd just filed one down a little. The blood went down my throat and back into my system like a triple dose of common sense, and I immediately shut up, which calmed the Orange Cop, too, and he let me just lie there handcuffed for a few minutes while the other officers talked to my neighbors and took down phone numbers and statements and found out everything but the truth.

nine

it was a beautiful day, but there may as well have been nuclear fireballs landing around me. The world had lost its beauty. Los Angeles was a thief, under its nylon mask of smog, aiming five million exhaust pipes at its citizens' heads, robbing the young of their breath and the elderly of their lives. The palm trees were dead, soulless. The awnings were filthy, the colors muted. Flowers were frauds.

I'd once read an article in which somebody called writing "the response of a disturbed soul." It wasn't therapeutic, they claimed, it only made the agony worse. I didn't believe this when I read it, but now I wasn't sure. Peace of mind seemed a lifetime away. It was hard to imagine a time when I drove around feeling happy, hopeful, safe. I'd smile at people back then, knowing I was paying my dues, confident that someday I would feel the exhilaration of success.

Spring was over and so was hope. My toes were tingling, my legs growing weak. The nauseating terror started to build within. I would not submit to it today.

The first night I'd slept at Silverman's, then two nights at a motel on Robertson near the 10. I was lucky the cops hadn't arrested me, I reminded myself, but a manic itch continued to rattle inside my marrow. Five hours of shut-eye in three days. I tossed and turned, feet twitching, and even when I did find sleep, it was a struggle to maintain it. One afternoon I snuck into my apartment, grabbed my notebooks and a couple pictures of my dead girlfriend Grace, and bolted out the back door. I called in sick all week and they didn't question it. I prayed for my mind to stop—just four consecutive hours of rest—but my mind was my enemy and wanted me to suffer.

Now it was Thursday afternoon. I'd decided to go to the UCLA library and work on *How I Won Her Back.* What I needed was a firm chair, silence, a desk, and a world-renowned medical center nearby. When I got to the library, it happened again. The arms started to go numb, the toes tingled, I became aware of my breathing, then a whiff of nausea. Oh, God, would I be able to get the next breath? My heart fluttered. Or was it my stomach? Please, make it my stomach. But it couldn't be, I hadn't eaten for three hours. Things should be settled in there, and I couldn't be hungry already.

A bathroom! I had to find a bathroom to look at myself, assure myself I wasn't dying. I looked at my hands; good color. I squeezed my fingers together, watched the blood rush to and from the tips. This was probably a good sign.

I walked slowly, a human bomb that any movement might set off. I passed a redheaded man with a beard. I knew that he could be the last person I saw alive. Then a woman. She looked familiar. The angel of death?

My fingers were no longer numb. I was safe again. For a while. Like a woman in labor between contractions, except I was giving birth to death. I felt the fear build and subside and then build again, over and over, never quite reaching a peak, or reaching one and seeing a bigger, scarier one in the distance. In the bathroom, I looked in the mirror. I was there. I touched my cheek; a white blotch appeared. This was good, there was blood in my face.

On the way out of the library, it struck again. My chest muscle tightened, my breath shortened. That's it, it was on to the health center to get my blood pressure taken. Suddenly a burst of fear. I was admitting it, giving in to it, accepting the fact that I was dying. I ducked into a building marked WOMEN'S CLINIC. The young black woman at the front desk gasped. I imagined how bad I must look.

"I didn't hear you come in," she said.

"I know I'm a guy, but could you get someone to take my blood pressure?"

"Sorry, women only, hon."

"Please. I think something's wrong with me. I've been sweating and out of breath all day."

The woman looked at me with concern. "Wait here."

She left the room and presently a rich-looking woman in her late thirties came out to see me.

"If you have a problem, go to the medical center."

"Could you just take my blood pressure? I feel very tense."

"I'm sorry, but you're in the wrong place."

"But doesn't it just take a minute? I'm really—"

"Read my lips. You're in the wrong place."

I drove around the corner to the hospital. Four or five people were standing outside the emergency room smoking cigarettes. The inside was packed. Most of the people were minorities. Their looks told me I had a long wait. I wondered if there'd been a fire or some other catastrophe.

I walked across the street to a drugstore to get something to drink. It was a small place and as I entered I tried to remember if drugstores sold drinks. This one did. I got a ginger ale because it was free of caffeine. As I was paying, it occurred to me that this might not be a good idea. Didn't they say not to eat or drink if you're having a heart attack? I remembered my father telling me that that was the worst part of giving mouth-to-mouth: when the victim throws up.

I couldn't believe what I was seeing in the corner of the store: a blood pressure machine.

"Could you get up?" I asked the old black woman who was sitting in it sideways, waiting for a prescription.

After she did, I felt bad. Maybe she didn't realize it was a blood pressure tester and thought I just wanted her seat. Maybe she thought I was a racist. I sat and read the directions. Where was the red dot? I couldn't find a red dot, but I put my arm in the loop anyway. I plugged in my two quarters, hesitated before pushing the start button. What if I went into arrest as the thing was clamping onto my arm? I could be stuck there for thirty seconds. The black woman would surely summon help, wouldn't she? Yes, the woman I'd just insulted would save my life.

I pressed the button, but nothing happened. The coin return didn't work, either. I pressed the start again. Still nothing. I got up but didn't ask for my money back. As I walked slowly back to my car, I couldn't get a deep breath. There was no chest pain, just the sense that my lungs had shrunk, or my stomach was pushing into it, or my . . . or my heart . . . or my heart . . .

Or my heart had finally broken in half.

I sat in the middle of the sidewalk, held my hand against my chest. People passed without glancing down. I felt embarrassed for them, embarrassed for all of us. Suddenly I couldn't hear anything. I saw people and cars but couldn't hear them. I slid up against a building, put my finger against my carotid artery.

"Henry . . . ?"

I looked up and it was Gus Anders with another man.

"Are you okay?"

"Hey," I said.

"What are you doing there?"

"Waiting for someone," I said. "Gonna catch a movie."

The other man smiled at me, but it was a sad smile and he seemed to get it and started drifting down the sidewalk. It was a little early for a movie and I was spewing all kinds of weak vibes and Gus said, "What's going on?"

He shuffled about, put a hand on his knee, knelt beside me.

"I don't feel so good, Gus. My heart or something, maybe my thyroid . . . everything's falling apart."

Gus took my pulse. He started to fade out. I felt it coming on, it was within my control to halt it, but I didn't this time, I didn't run from the wave, I ran toward it and dove in headfirst.

breakdowns aren't what they used to be—at least how they used to be portrayed in the movies. I thought when you had a breakdown, they put you in a hospital, or your family came and got you. But this was the nineties, and breakdowns were now common-place and vastly underrated. The doctor gave me a prescription of Xanax and a few Klonopins and told me to go back to my room. He hadn't even termed it a breakdown but a "lapse of sanity." Even I started seeing it differently. It was just like getting a bug, or having too much sugar, or maybe a caffeine overdose. I was fine now, it *was* just a lapse. I wasn't crazy, just tired.

Gus said I could crash at his place, and he was sort of a doctor, so I didn't argue. I don't remember much about my stay. I was numb, drugged, traumatized. The blood in my veins seemed to have a vague sting to it, maybe from hyperventilating all day. Some of Gus's furniture was small, but not all of it. I recall that he was kind, feeding me a steak and baked potato with ketchup and butter and Worcestershire sauce all puddled on top. We watched a documen-tary on Louis B. Mayer and his protégé, Irving Thalberg, the two most powerful moviemakers of the first half of the century. Thalberg was to die young; Louis B. lived to be old and made many movies and apparently had his way with most of the starlets of the day, and on his deathbed his final words were: "Nothing means anything." After the show, I felt exhausted and slept on the couch with a hot, sick, drippy feeling in the left hemisphere of my gut.

I fell asleep around nine and got up the next day at noon. I could have gone even later, but Gus came back from work and put on shorts and a Woody Allen hat.

"Get dressed," he said. "I'm taking you to the beach."

I tried to beg off, claiming I had too much work to do, but he wouldn't hear it.

"You need a break," he said. "You're in L.A., for crying out loud, get a tan."

I was too weak to argue and I figured I could sleep at the beach, so I gave in.

Gus drove to a juice bar on the Santa Monica promenade and bought me a shake made with apples, bananas, mangos, and ground sunflower seeds. We picked up a couple smoked turkey subs at Bay Cities deli and drove down the hill to the beach. We parked next to the pier and walked north. Signs warned of a recent sewage spill in the bay and advised against swimming. To do so could cause nausea and/or vomiting. This hadn't kept the sunbathers away, though most refrained from taking a dip. It was primarily young Mexicans and blacks here. There was a man playing a flute.

I told Gus to keep moving. Crowds I didn't need. Kids screaming, Frisbee throwers, possible gang activity, obnoxious disc jockeys, Spanish music—my nerves couldn't take it. Flutes depressed me. I just wanted to lay out my towel and sleep.

We walked for a half mile, the click-clack of sedatives in my pocket keeping the beat like comforting maracas. The crowd thinned and, finally, perfection: an orange pup tent and two pretty girls—a blonde and a redhead—lying in front of it. We spread our stuff thirty feet from them. The girls smiled. This could be just the thing for me, I thought.

A child appeared from out of the tent, but I was too depressed to get up and move.

As I ate my sandwich, I saw the kid crawl down to the water. He did a little tumble facefirst into the surf, came up snorting. The girls didn't notice.

"Look at this," I said. "They let that little kid go down to the water alone."

"He's not in the water," Gus said. "He's in the sand."

"Just takes one big wave."

Gus finished his sandwich and lay down.

"He's only two or three," I said.

"Relax, Henry."

I watched the waves licking the boy's legs. The girls stood and approached the child. I was relieved, now I could sleep. Just as I put my head down, I saw them heading away toward the pier without the boy.

"What the hell . . ." I hit Gus's leg. "Check it out."

He raised up on his elbows.

"Do you believe those idiots?" I said. "They're leaving the kid all by himself."

Gus shrugged and lay back down. I got up, looked in the tent. Empty. The kid was all alone. They'd left a two-year-old all by himself on a beach.

"Why don't they just give him a goddamn loaded gun?"

"Mm," said Gus.

"I can't believe this. They took off. I can't even see them anymore."

Gus rolled onto his side. "Maybe someone's watching from the tent."

"I checked."

When I tried to approach the boy, he stopped digging and screamed until I moved away. I returned to my towel but didn't sit down. The kid resumed digging. I could see the suicide building on the bluff behind us.

"Goddamn it, that pisses me off," I said. "I feel like taking him to the police station, just to teach those two morons a lesson. Get their fucking names in the paper. The press would love it: 'Home Alone on the Beach.' "

I kicked at the sand. Some of it went in Gus's face.

"Sorry," I said.

He sat up, brushed himself off.

"I didn't do that on purpose."

"I know," he said.

"There ought to be a law against people like that. They have no sense of responsibility. It's a clinic on tragedy-making. He could drown, he could crawl out on the PCH, someone could steal him, he could be molested . . ."

"Take it easy, Henry."

"I'm just sick of it. I'd like to sleep sometime too, you know. But the world's full of morons. Nobody cares. What if we weren't here?"

I put Gus's hat on and kept an eye on the kid. The boy didn't budge. After about forty-five minutes, the girls returned.

"Excuse me!" I called out. "Do either of you belong to this child?"

The Blonde smiled. "I do."

"You do?" I said, approaching them. "He's yours?"

"Uh-huh."

"Where have you been?"

"We went to get cigs," the Redhead said.

She held up a pack of Camels.

"Well, I'd like you to know that while you were off *'getting cigs,'* your little boy here crawled into the water and almost drowned." It was a lie but she deserved it.

The Blonde turned red. She got a running start, cocked her arm, and slapped her son on the back. The child's lungs made a beeping sound as the air blew out of him. "I told you not to move while I was gone!" she screamed.

The boy's mouth and eyes opened wide searching for air, a white handprint showed off the sunburn on the rest of his body, and he stared up in shock at his mother's finger. The wind was knocked out of me, too.

"What are you doing?" I said.

The Blonde said, "Mind your own business."

"It's your fault," I said softly. "Not the kid's."

"Shut up," she said.

The boy found air and used it loudly.

"You shouldn't be a mother," I said. "You shouldn't be a mother!"

"Leave her alone!" said the Redhead.

I was suddenly aware of Gus pulling on my arm.

"You should be locked up!" I yelled.

The Redhead laughed. "Look who's talking!"

"Come on, Henry," said Gus.

As he led me away, the girls threw us the finger. Gus started gathering up our towels.

"Well, you certainly taught them a lesson," he said.

"Gus, I could've saved her."

"What?"

"Bonnie. It was my fault."

"That's not true. You did everything you could."

"No, I didn't. You don't know . . ."

Gus looked at me.

"She was sitting at the edge and everything happened just like I wrote . . . but then . . ."

"Yes . . . ?"

"She asked me to hold her hand . . . but I didn't."

"What do you mean?"

"She said, 'Come close to me.' I said, 'No, it's too high. You come over here.' I was about fifteen feet away. She said, 'Please, I'm begging you, just hold my hand for a minute and I'll leave with you.' "

"So . . . why . . . ?"

"We were sixteen floors up, she was at the edge, I didn't know her, she seemed crazy, I thought she might pull us both over. I started toward her, but then I stopped a few feet short and said, 'Okay, that's halfway. Now you come halfway and we'll talk.' But she didn't come. She said, 'Sorry. Halfway's not good enough any-more' . . . and then she was gone."

It seemed as if ten minutes passed before Gus moved a muscle. He picked up the rest of our stuff and started walking.

"I was afraid, Gus. I didn't know what she'd do."

"She wouldn't have hurt you."

"I didn't know that, though."

"Yeah, well . . . now you do."

We got the car, picked up a couple decafs, parked on Ocean Avenue, and sat on a park bench high over the Pacific Coast Highway. Clouds spewed in from the Pacific and I couldn't see rain, but I felt wetness on my face.

"Henry, you need to talk to someone. You can't keep going around trying to save the world because you feel guilty about some-one you didn't even know."

"It wasn't the first time. Something like this happened once before, Gus. There was a girl . . ."

"A suicide?"

"No . . . nope. But she's dead. We'd broken up."

He waited for more.

"I don't know what happened. We never fought. We were made for each other. Everything was great. Too great. I got scared and told her to get lost. Actually, I never told her, I just got lost myself."

"And she wouldn't let you back?"

"She would've let me back anytime. She didn't know why I was acting that way, but she was ready to forgive everything if I'd just come back. She loved me."

"But you didn't love her?"

"Yeah, I loved her. Fuck yeah, I loved her. That's the thing. I . . . I was young and I guess I couldn't believe that true love could come to me so soon. I met her in high school. It was serious. By college it was getting scary. I wasn't ready for it all right then. I just . . . couldn't go all the way with it."

I felt another surge in my chest and started feeling around for a Klonopin.

"She called and I wouldn't answer. She sent letters and I couldn't even read them. I shut her out. We were both young and I figured we'd pick it up later. I'd have a run, she'd do her thing, and then we'd get back together after college and everything would be okay. But then she died—a car accident, down South—and it was over. I didn't even know about it for two weeks because she lived out of state and I was the shithead who'd broken her heart. And even though I was ripped to shreds, I wouldn't cry. I didn't deserve to. And that's why it's twelve years later and I'm thirty-three and I can't walk down the street without a pocketful of downers."

The fog had dipped down to the tops of the palm trees and there was a sudden coolness.

"I miss her," I said. "I miss her so much, Gus."

Gus and I walked north along the bluff, beside the railing. We passed several groups of homeless people, some sitting on picnic benches, others settling into sleeping bags. When we stopped, we were in front of the suicide building, but Gus never looked at it, he just stared out to sea.

"We went out," he said.

"Huh?"

"Bonnie and I. We went out."

"What do you mean?"

"She was my girlfriend."

"Jesus, Gus . . . I didn't know you were . . ."

"I . . . I purposely didn't, you know, want you to feel . . . We were moving in . . . you know, just to see."

He tapped his front teeth together.

"How soon? When . . . when were you . . . ?"

"That day."

I put my hand to my mouth.

"We were going to try it out, so I went out and borrowed a van and packed her up. She brought up some boxes, then said she was running out for a couple sandwiches. I said I'd go with her, but she said no, she wanted to go alone. She asked me to meet her at Baskin-Robbins. She was tall—Bonnie—taller than average even, and I wanted her to be comfortable, so all that week I'd bought big stuff: chairs, a couch, a bed. California king-size the bed was, that's the biggest they make. I admit it, I was proud of having a tall girlfriend and then I got the bed home and, shit, I practically needed a pole vault to get up there.''

He made a pole vault motion and laughed unexpectedly. Gus looked surprised and a little embarrassed, as if he had forgotten that sound, and a sadness quickly enveloped him.

''The Santa Monica police called me that night and when I went to the building, I found the note in her car.''

Gus approached the fence at the edge of the bluff. He stood eye level with the top post, so he had to crouch to see the beach below.

''Jesus . . . that's fucking awful.''

He straightened up and turned to me.

''Want to hear something funny? In the letter she said she loved me as much as she loved herself.''

''Well . . . that's nice.''

''Henry, she committed suicide.''

A strained smile fell over Gus's face, causing dimples to appear above his cheeks, and I felt like hugging the poor bastard. I feared it was condescending, this impulse, like offering to buy him the ice cream cone, but I did it anyway, and it was probably the best moment I ever had in Southern California.

if my life were a Hollywood movie, the Mexican driver would've turned out to be the longtime gardener of Michael Eisner, and Eisner would have heard the story and admired my strength of conviction. He would have then offered me the next *Honey, I Maimed the Kids* installment, and it would've made a hundred and fifty million bucks, leading to many other jobs, and I probably would have been writing this story from an ocean view in the Malibu Colony.

But it was real life, and worse, it was Hollywood, so instead I packed up the dented Arrow and drove east on Route 10, past the monster windmills and the dinosaurs, past the Mafia town of Palm Springs, all the way to the other side of the continent, and then north, up the Eastern seaboard, to my home. It's a funny thing: When you drive east to west, New York seems a long way from Boston, but when you go the other way, the Manhattan skyline feels like home. I didn't give up on screenwriting, just Hollywood, and I never regretted that decision.

Ghost came out that year and was a smash hit, which put an end to any chances I had of selling *How I Won Her Back,* seeing as they were both about young people dealing with the death of a mate. Levine stuck by me, though, and after another year, I got a development deal with a producer at Universal who had made some of the most popular teen comedies of the eighties. I wrote the script in three and a half weeks with my brother and a friend and the day we turned it in we found out that the producer had had a falling out with the studio, "ankled" to Fox, and all his projects at Universal were dead. Even though nothing was getting made, I was grateful to be getting my at bats. I accepted the fact that the everyday struggle to succeed is what life is all about, and in fact it's the fun part.

Seinfeld ended up making *The Virgin,* but it was written by a staff guy and I didn't know about it until the day before it aired. When Levine called with the news, I was ecstatic and then pissed off when I realized they hadn't had the decency to let me watch it being filmed. I was to receive "story by" credit and the guy got the title "written by." They were kind enough to offer me another episode, though, which I wrote and was paid well for, but it never got made.

Ted Bowman never got *Ice Cream Man* made, either, to my knowledge, though I did stumble across a movie called *The Ice Cream Man* in a video store. It was a low-budget slasher movie starring Ron Howard's little brother Clint, but Bowman's name wasn't on it, nor was the "No More Mr. Softee" tag line. I continued to see Bowman's producer credit on action pictures, so I assumed he was doing fine financially, even though he had to settle his traffic case out of court.

For a long time I considered writing a magazine piece about successful Hollywood producers—I was going to call it *Success-pool*—but I couldn't muster the energy for such a negative undertaking, and the truth of the matter is that most of the producers I met were decent to me.

I never saw Colleen Driscoll again. It had taken me and Tiffany Pittman one afternoon to clean out my apartment and thankfully she never showed. I dropped the keys in the mail with an extra month's rent and a note for Mr. and Mrs. Beaupre and back in Boston I kept my number unlisted. As for Tiff, I always take her to dinner when I get back to L.A. for meetings, which is about three times a year. She brings me to the new hot spot and fills me in on the commercials she's shot, the pilots she's up for, and the famous people she's fucking.

Herb Silverman fell off the face of the earth. He moved from his apartment around the time I left town, and I never saw him on TV or in the movies. The only time I ever heard his name again was in a magazine article about up and coming L.A. club owners. I called to see if it was him, but he didn't call back, and that was that.

I used to talk about Colleen all the time, initially trying to make sense of it all, but eventually for the entertainment value. I'm not a psychiatrist, but I have learned that talking about crazy things is good therapy and I did come to enjoy the stories. Friends would approach me at bars and parties around Boston and ask me to tell other friends or even strangers about Doheny. This I was happy to do because after all she had become what I'd always hoped for: an annoying girl from my past who I told stories about. I'd recall the eating disorders and being clubbed by the two-iron and the plastic knife fight. I even told women about her, which was probably a mistake. Most were amused, some were alarmed by the violent turn the story took, a few even accused me of being in love with her. The truth was there was no way I could tell a woman about Doheny without sounding a little petty. In time Doheny gained a legendary status among a certain Boston crowd and a bartender at the Delux even named a drink after her, though it was called a Davy Crockett.

I couldn't get away from the girl. She was a big part of my history now, even inspiring me to write a children's story (see Appendix), which was published and got a nice mention in *Time* magazine. I dedicated it to her—out of guilt more than anything—seeing as she'd given me the idea (though I decided to go with a more uplifting version, as opposed to hers).

the red sox eked their way into the postseason in the fall of 1990, and I walked to all the home playoff games from my studio apartment in the Back Bay. They got squashed by the A's and even though the Celts and Bruins were having bad years, I enjoyed it when the weather turned cold again. I didn't like hot winters. I didn't like places where I had to stop and think about what month it was. I was glad to be around my parents, and my brothers and sisters, and friends. I liked living in a place where summer meant something. I'd missed the leaves and cranberry bogs. I'd missed meeting pretty girls who weren't automatically models. I'd missed Mike Barnicle. I wanted to meet someone and fall in love and treat her well for the rest of her life, but there was no rush. Odds are I'd never become a movie mogul living on the East Coast. I'd probably never see Amanda Parsons again, but I didn't feel too bad about that because Amanda didn't love me and Hollywood moguls come and go and someday I'd be lying on my deathbed, facing the void, and I was a blessed man because I knew the truth is there is a God, and that everything means something.

appendix

abigale

the happy whale

by Henry Halloran

once upon a time, a large family of Humpback Whales swam through the Santa Monica Bay toward the beaches of California. The sight of loud, happy Humpbacks was common in these waters—but these were not loud, happy Humpbacks. They were very quiet, and very, very sad. They paddled along, never looking back or singing or smiling. And strangest of all, these whales hardly even bothered to eat.

Except for Abigale the Happy Whale. She swam at the very back of the group, like the caboose of a train, which was about how big she was. As she floated past the chairs and refrigerators and broken glass that litterbugs had dumped on the ocean floor, Abigale ate about as much seaweed as a little whale can eat without throwing up all over the place. When she wasn't singing or laughing or eating, Abigale was playing with her friends, the smaller Sea People.

For a while the Golfin' Dolphin putted along beside her. Boy, was he ever teed off. One of the Land People had thrown a golf club into the sea and clobbered him on the snout. Abigale gave the fish a big kiss. This made him feel better.

"Do you have time to play nine holes?" the Golfin' Dolphin asked.

"Thanks for the offer, but I can't today," she said. "We're on our way to the beach."

"To the beach?" the confused dolphin repeated. "How can a whale go to the beach?"

He didn't get an answer, though, for Abigale was gone.

The whales continued to swim over junked cars and shipwrecks and lost Frisbees, and Abigale didn't stop until she ran into her old friend Clem the Clam. Clem was acting like a real dip because someone had dropped an old television set on his clam bed.

"What kind of chowderhead would do something like this?" the steamed clam snapped.

Abigale the Happy Whale couldn't answer, but because she dug this shellfish, she pushed the boob tube off his clam bed.

"I've got to go now," she said. "We're on our way to the beach."

Clem wanted to call out to the young whale, but he was so surprised he just clammed up.

The whales swam over rusty anchors and fishing poles covered with green gunk and even a mirror framed with barnacles. That's where Abigale saw the reflections of Blackie the Goldfish and Fred

Doofish the Red Bluefish. They were looking in the mirror and weren't exactly thrilled to the gills with what they saw.

"This is terrible!" Blackie the Goldfish cried. "I've got more oil on me than a can of sardines."

"Well, at least your problems are only scale-deep," Fred Doofish the Red Bluefish said. "I've got a liver the size of a beanbag chair and I'm turning red from the inside out."

This was because Fred had eaten seaweed that was polluted from a nearby factory.

"I don't care what you look like or how big your livers are," Abigale said. "I still love you both."

Fred and Blackie smiled and watched the Happy Whale splash away past an empty catfood can and a broken beach chair.

"Where you going, Abigale?" they called out.

"To the beach," she said, and their mouths dropped open like a couple surprised fish, which is what they were.

The Humpbacks were closing in on land when Abigale bumped into her old friend Wordsmith the Swordfish. Wordsmith was wearing a large black ring around his sword, which is where most people's noses are.

"Greetings, my dear," the well-spoken swordfish said in a nasally voice.

"How are you today, Wordsmith?" Abigale asked.

"I'm darn piqued," he said, which meant he was darn angry.

"You shouldn't be," she said. "I think your new ring looks great."

"For your edification," Wordsmith said, "this is not a ring. It's just a tire that some buffoon discarded into the sea and that somehow attached to my protrusive proboscis."

"Huh?" said the baffled whale.

"A tire got stuck on my nose!" he cried.

Luckily, Abigale was able to talk Dr. Gus the Octopus into making a house call. After the good doctor had jacked Wordsmith up and pulled the whitewall off the swordfish's snout, he asked Abigale where she was off to.

"We're going to the beach," she said and she started to drift away.

Well, let me tell you, Dr. Gus the Octopus was up in arms over this. Using his good seven arms (the doctor's eighth arm was in a sling because he'd hurt it on a pop-top from a soda can), he ran and caught Abigale.

"Whales can't go to the beach!" Dr. Gus the Octopus insisted. "You'll all get stuck in the sand."

This made Abigale stop and tread water for a while.

"Why would we be going to the beach if it would hurt us?" she wondered aloud.

"I have no idea," the doctor said, "but if you ask me, something smells terribly fishy."

Abigale the Happy Whale swam past all the sad, quiet whales until she got to the Head Whale, Henry Dale.

"Why are we going to the beach?" she asked him. "Dr. Gus the Octopus said it could be dangerous."

"We're not going to the beach," said Henry Dale the Head Whale, "we're beaching ourselves."

"But if we beach ourselves, then we'll get stuck in the sand," Abigale said.

A tear rolled out of one of her eyes.

"Look around you," the Head Whale wailed. "All you see is pollution. The Land People throw junk into the sea because they can't see us beneath the calm surface. We have to beach ourselves to get their attention." Then Henry Dale the Head Whale led the rest of the Humpbacks past Abigale until she was just another sad whale at the end of a very sad line.

The family of Humpbacks was only a few hundred yards from shore when Abigale passed under the broad shadow of Moby Duck. Moby was the biggest duck in the world because oil had spilled from a ship onto his feathers. At first he had looked like a licorice duck, but then things started sticking to him, and pretty soon he looked like a floating junkyard.

This is what was stuck to Moby Duck:

Two buoys with blinking lights.
A Wiffle ball bat.
Three Styrofoam cups.
Seven life preservers.
Four bottles with messages in them.
Two without.
A doll with one arm.
A sofa.
A Big Mac container.
Twenty-two corks.
A small rowboat.
A clogged-up snorkle.

A large rowboat.

And a pair of men's size 48 underwear that had the words BE MY VALENTINE written on them in red.

Needless to say, Moby Duck was feeling down.

"What are you doing so close to the shore?" Moby quacked.

"We're beaching ourselves," Abigale whispered in a choked-up voice.

"Oh, no!" the sad duck cried. "Why would you do something like that?"

"We have to let the Land People see us, so they'll stop polluting," the young whale replied.

"But that won't accomplish anything," Moby Duck said. "After all, they see me and they still pollute."

Abigale realized that this duck covered with yuck had a point. Beaching themselves wouldn't help anybody; it would only add to the litter. That's when she decided to take matters into her own fins.

Abigale skimmed across the ocean floor and in one big gulp ate a soup can, a tennis racquet, a compass, and a boot. Then she came to the surface and blew the stuff right out the spout on her back and onto the beach. The other Sea People had had it up to their gills with pollution, so they joined in to lend a helping fin.

The Golfin' Dolphin chipped in by whacking an old volleyball onto the beach with a nine-iron. Dr. Gus the Octopus tossed a six-pack of soda bottles and a rusty thermos at the same time. Wordsmith the Swordfish carved up an old ladder for Blackie the Goldfish and Fred Doofish the Red Bluefish to carry piece by piece to the shore. Clem the Clam was always willing to stick out his neck for friends, so he helped out, too. Before long, all of the Sea People were cleaning up the water. The Dogfish, Rin Fin Fin, was barking out orders to Sid the Squid and Neil the Eel. Tab the Crab was there in a pinch, and Bob the Lobster turned out to be an unselfish shellfish. Shucks, folks, even Rose Royster the Rich Oyster went to work for a while.

When Henry Dale the Head Whale saw what was happening, he too began gobbling up the garbage and blowing it back onto the shore through his great spout. Soon all the other whales started doing the same. In a little less than one afternoon, they swept the entire sea clean. And you want to know something else? They had a whale of a good time!

When the Land People saw all their junk coming back at them, they had no choice but to clean it up and properly dispose of it. After all, if they didn't, then there wouldn't be room to go to the beach. Big trucks came from far away and hauled the stuff off to real junkyards. The junk that went on the final truck was stuff they pulled off Moby Duck.

Then the school of whales swam back out to sea.

And for the first time in a long time, they were all as happy as Abigale the Happy Whale!

about the author

peter farrelly grew up in Rhode Island and graduated from Providence College and Columbia University. He cowrote and codirected *Dumb and Dumber* and *There's Something About Mary* and codirected *Kingpin*.